SWEENEY TODD

THE DEMON BARBER OF FLEET STREET

THE GRAPHIC NOVEL

ORIGINAL TEXT VERSION

Script Adaptation: Seán Michael Wilson
Linework: Declan Shalvey
Coloring: Jason Cardy & Kat Nicholson
Lettering: Jim Campbell
Design & Layout: Jo Wheeler, Carl Andrews
& Jenny Placentino
Associate Editor: Joe Sutliff Sanders
Editor in Chief: Clive Bryant

Sweeney Todd: The Graphic Novel
Original Text Version

First US edition published: 2012
Library bound edition published: 2012

Published by: Classical Comics Ltd

Acknowledgments: Every effort has been made to trace copyright holders of
material reproduced in this book. Any rights not acknowledged here will be
acknowledged in subsequent editions if notice is given to Classical Comics Ltd.

All enquiries should be addressed to:
Classical Comics Ltd.
PO Box 7280
Litchborough
Towcester
NN12 9AR
United Kingdom

info@classicalcomics.com
www.classicalcomics.com

Paperback ISBN: 978-1-907127-09-0
Library bound ISBN: 978-1-907127-82-3

Printed in the USA

This book is printed by CG Book Printers using environmentally safe inks, on paper from
responsible sources. This material can be disposed of by recycling, incineration for energy
recovery, composting and biodegradation.

MIX
Paper from
responsible sources
FSC® C008080

CONTENTS

~⌐

SWEENEY TODD

~⌐

DRAMATIS PERSONAE

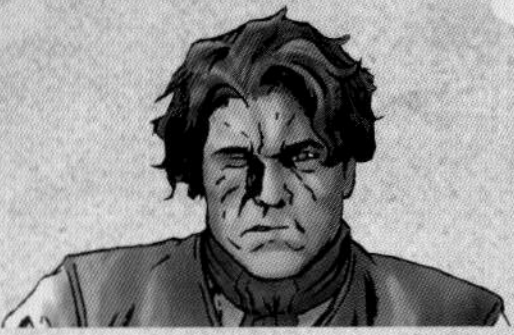

Sweeney Todd
The Demon Barber of Fleet Street

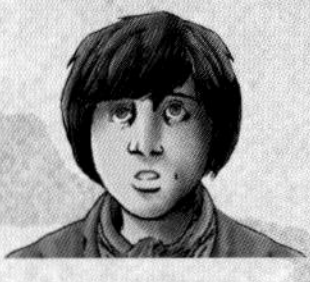

Tobias Ragg
Sweeney Todd's shop assistant

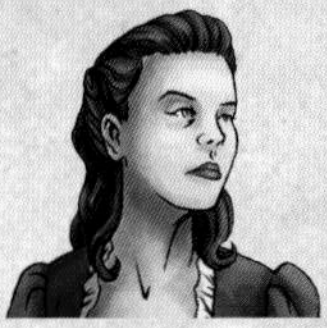

Margery Lovett
Pie shop owner

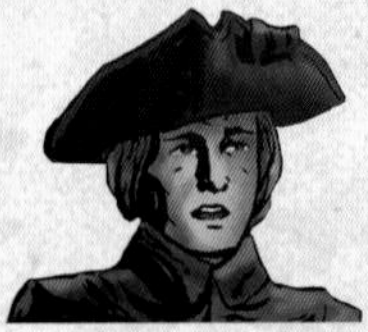

Colonel William Jeffery
Officer in the Indian Army

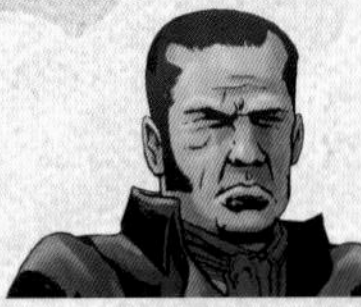

Captain Arthur Rose Ford
Captain of The Neptune

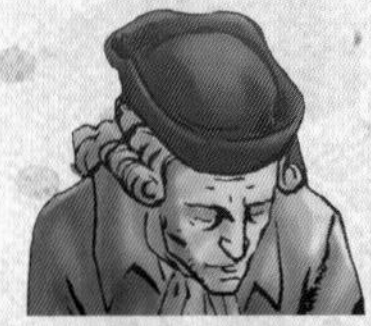

Lieutenant Francis Thornhill
Friend of Colonel Jeffery

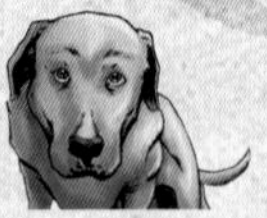

Hector
Thornhill's dog

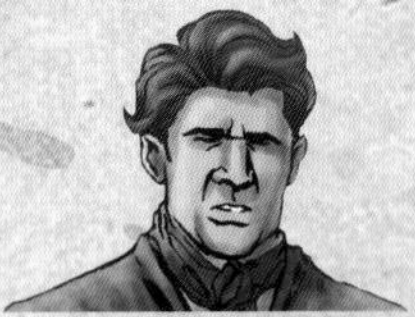

Captain Rathbone
Retired army captain and friend of Colonel Jeffery

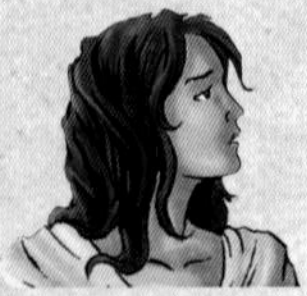

Johanna Oakley
Mark Ingestrie's fiancée

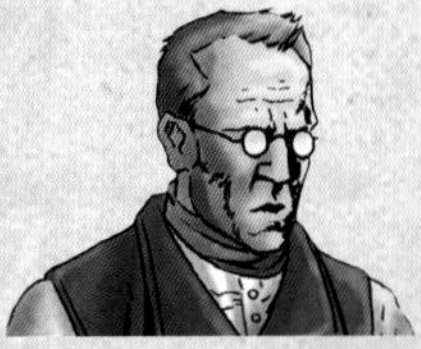

Mr. Oakley
Spectacle-maker and Johanna's father

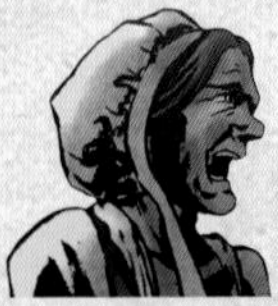

Mrs. Oakley
Mr. Oakley's wife and Johanna's mother

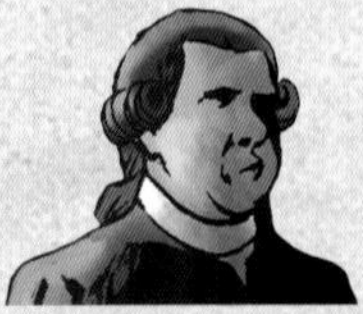

Mr. Lupin
Religious friend of Mrs. Oakley

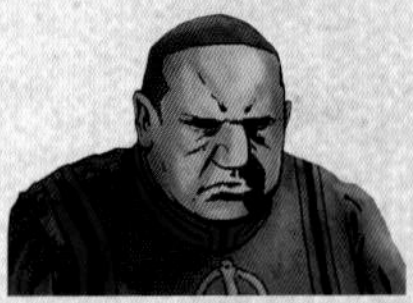

Big Ben the Beefeater
Cousin of Mr. Oakley

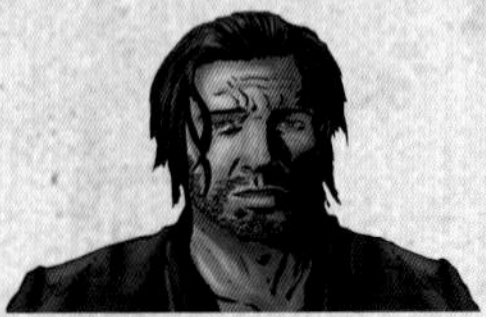

Jarvis Williams
A stranger, looking for work

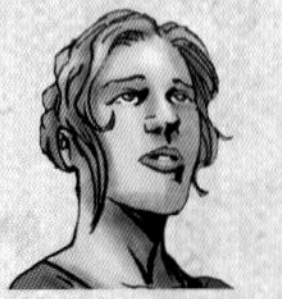

Arabella Wilmot
Johanna's friend

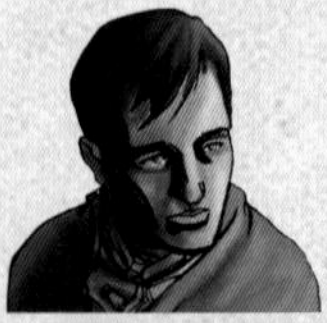

John Mundel
Provider of loans to wealthy individuals

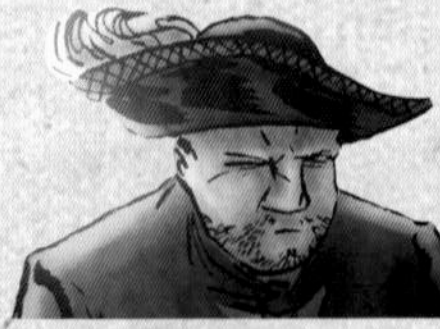

Mr. Wrankley
A local tobacconist

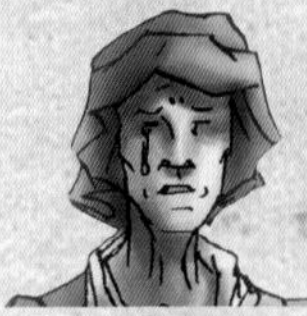

Mrs. Wrankley
Mr. Wrankley's wife, and cousin of John Mundel

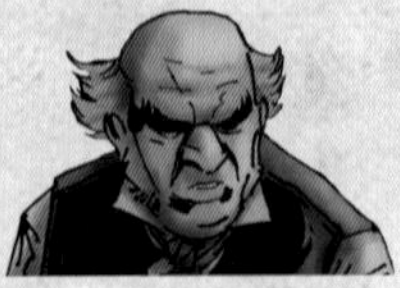

Mr. Fogg
Owner of a lunatic asylum

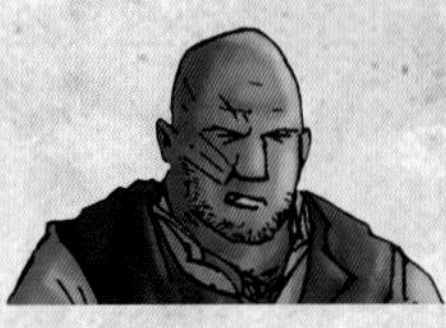

Watson
Mr. Fogg's assistant

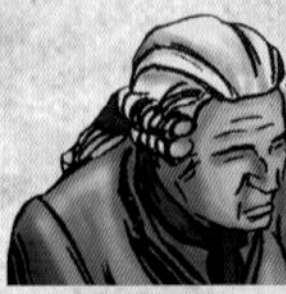

Dr. Popplejoy
Inspector of lunatic asylums

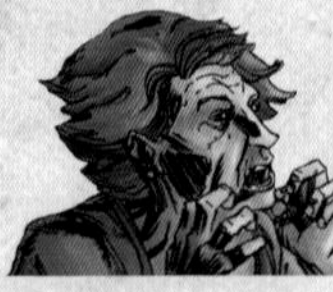

Mary
Inmate at Mr. Fogg's asylum

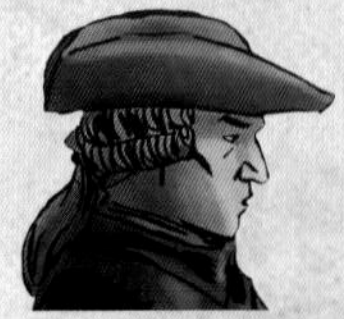

Sir Richard Blunt
A local magistrate

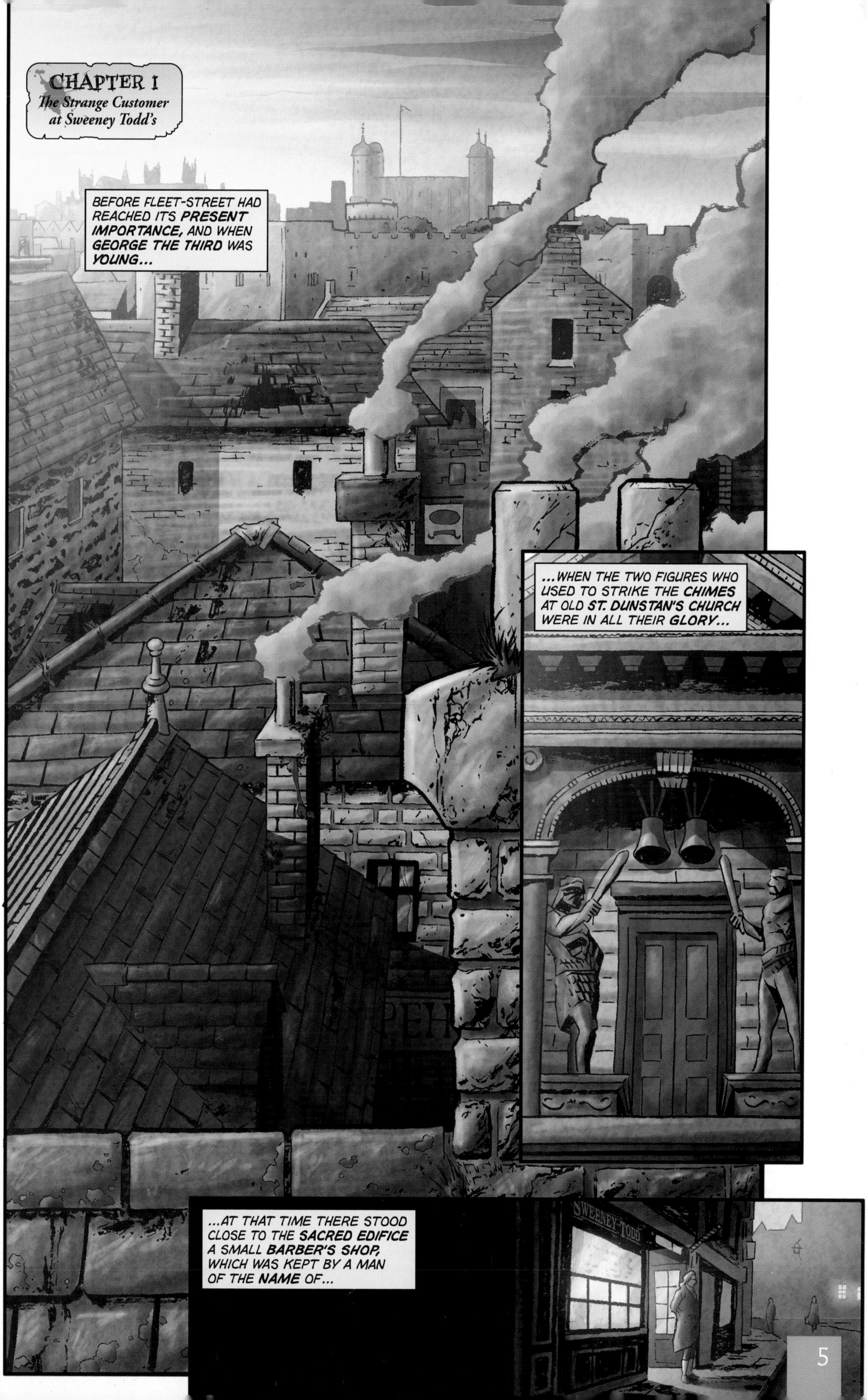
CHAPTER I
The Strange Customer at Sweeney Todd's
BEFORE FLEET-STREET HAD REACHED ITS PRESENT IMPORTANCE, AND WHEN GEORGE THE THIRD WAS YOUNG...
...WHEN THE TWO FIGURES WHO USED TO STRIKE THE CHIMES AT OLD ST. DUNSTAN'S CHURCH WERE IN ALL THEIR GLORY...
...AT THAT TIME THERE STOOD CLOSE TO THE SACRED EDIFICE A SMALL BARBER'S SHOP, WHICH WAS KEPT BY A MAN OF THE NAME OF...
SWEENEY TODD

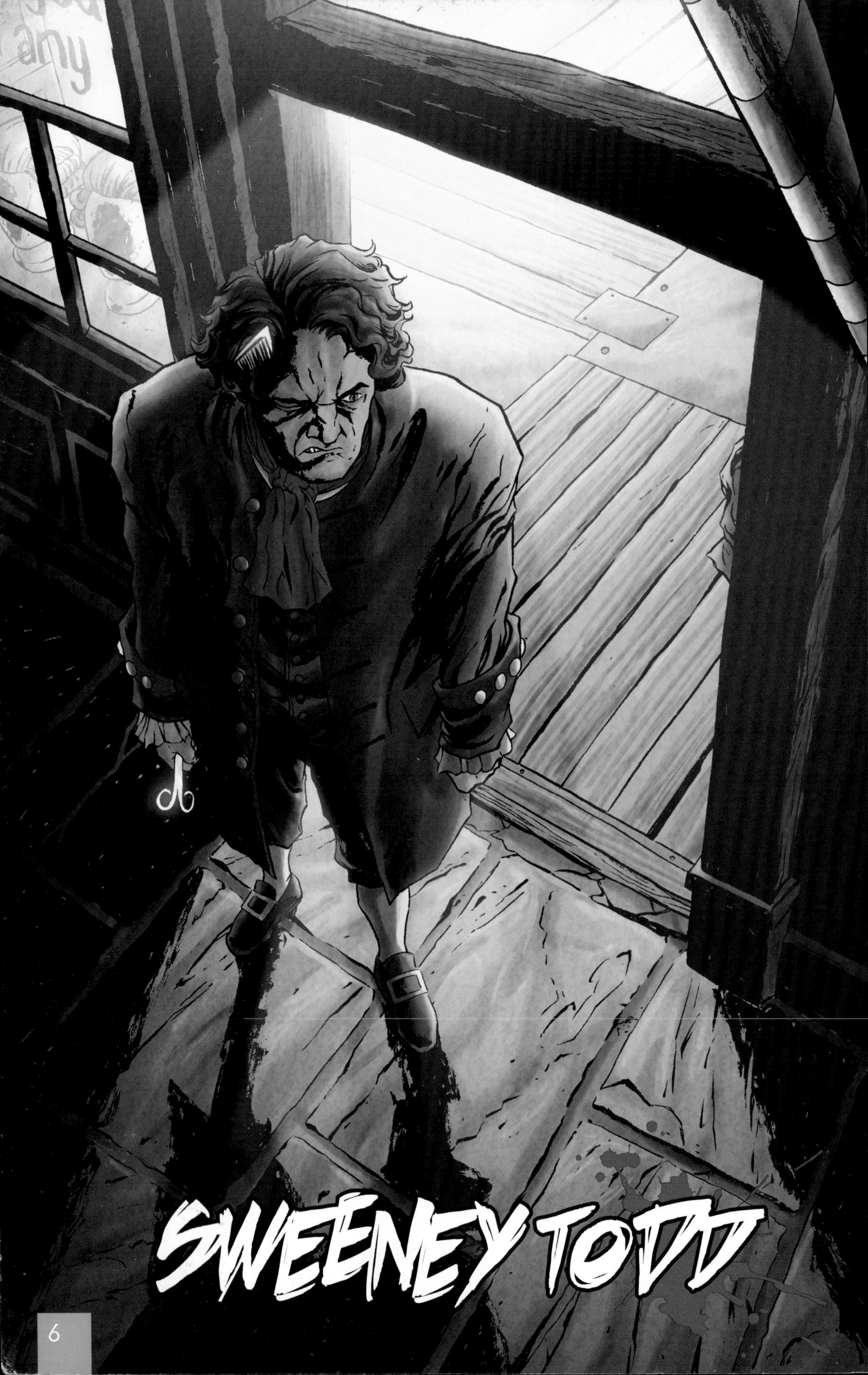
any
SWEENEY TODD

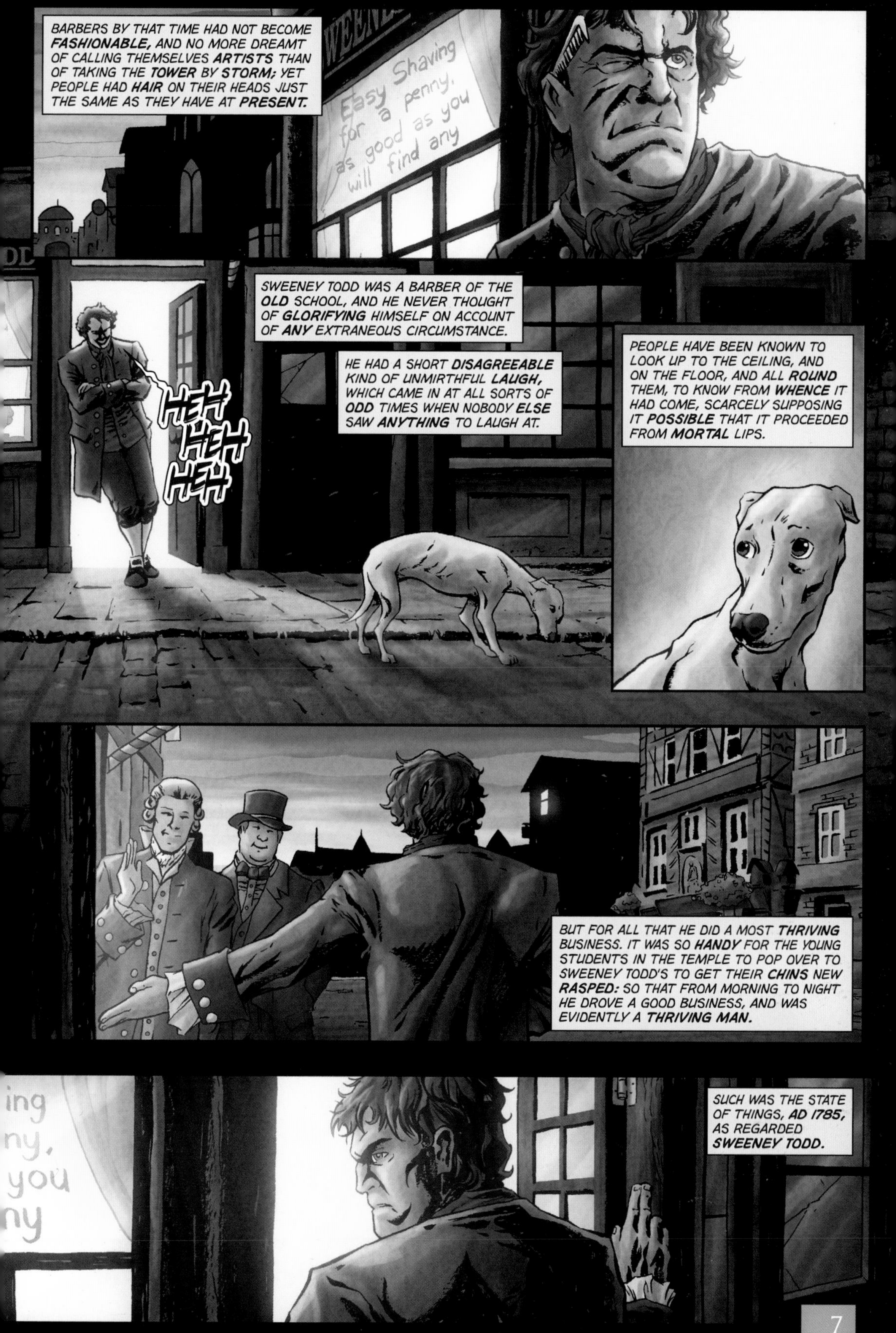
BARBERS BY THAT TIME HAD NOT BECOME FASHIONABLE, AND NO MORE DREAMT OF CALLING THEMSELVES ARTISTS THAN OF TAKING THE TOWER BY STORM; YET PEOPLE HAD HAIR ON THEIR HEADS JUST THE SAME AS THEY HAVE AT PRESENT.
Easy Shaving for a penny, as good as you will find any
SWEENEY TODD WAS A BARBER OF THE OLD SCHOOL, AND HE NEVER THOUGHT OF GLORIFYING HIMSELF ON ACCOUNT OF ANY EXTRANEOUS CIRCUMSTANCE.
HE HAD A SHORT DISAGREEABLE KIND OF UNMIRTHFUL LAUGH, WHICH CAME IN AT ALL SORTS OF ODD TIMES WHEN NOBODY ELSE SAW ANYTHING TO LAUGH AT.
HEH HEH HEH
PEOPLE HAVE BEEN KNOWN TO LOOK UP TO THE CEILING, AND ON THE FLOOR, AND ALL ROUND THEM, TO KNOW FROM WHENCE IT HAD COME, SCARCELY SUPPOSING IT POSSIBLE THAT IT PROCEEDED FROM MORTAL LIPS.
BUT FOR ALL THAT HE DID A MOST THRIVING BUSINESS. IT WAS SO HANDY FOR THE YOUNG STUDENTS IN THE TEMPLE TO POP OVER TO SWEENEY TODD'S TO GET THEIR CHINS NEW RASPED: SO THAT FROM MORNING TO NIGHT HE DROVE A GOOD BUSINESS, AND WAS EVIDENTLY A THRIVING MAN.
SUCH WAS THE STATE OF THINGS, AD 1785, AS REGARDED SWEENEY TODD.

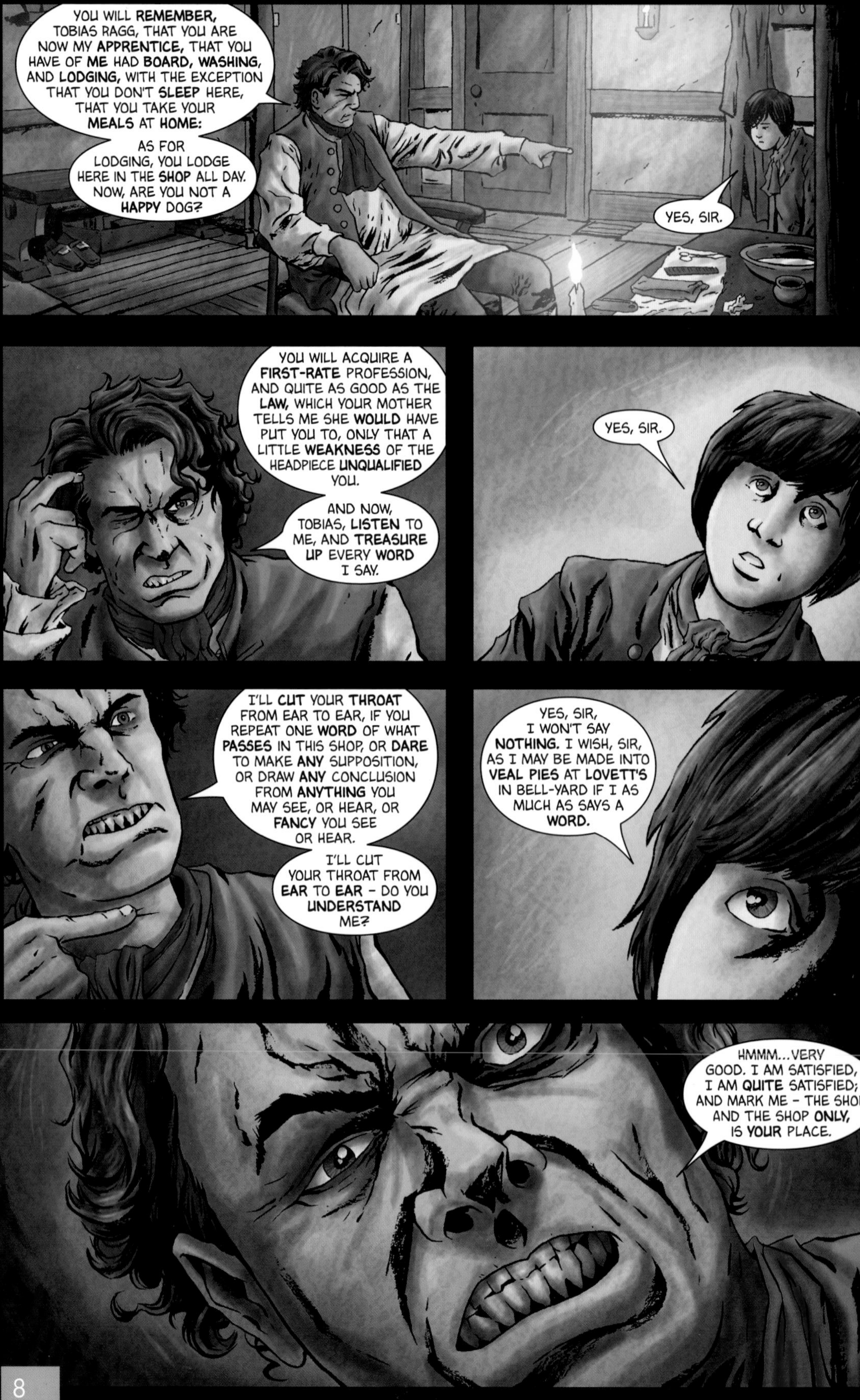
YOU WILL REMEMBER, TOBIAS RAGG, THAT YOU ARE NOW MY APPRENTICE, THAT YOU HAVE OF ME HAD BOARD, WASHING, AND LODGING, WITH THE EXCEPTION THAT YOU DON'T SLEEP HERE, THAT YOU TAKE YOUR MEALS AT HOME:
AS FOR LODGING, YOU LODGE HERE IN THE SHOP ALL DAY. NOW, ARE YOU NOT A HAPPY DOG?
YES, SIR.
YOU WILL ACQUIRE A FIRST-RATE PROFESSION, AND QUITE AS GOOD AS THE LAW, WHICH YOUR MOTHER TELLS ME SHE WOULD HAVE PUT YOU TO, ONLY THAT A LITTLE WEAKNESS OF THE HEADPIECE UNQUALIFIED YOU.
AND NOW, TOBIAS, LISTEN TO ME, AND TREASURE UP EVERY WORD I SAY.
YES, SIR.
I'LL CUT YOUR THROAT FROM EAR TO EAR, IF YOU REPEAT ONE WORD OF WHAT PASSES IN THIS SHOP, OR DARE TO MAKE ANY SUPPOSITION, OR DRAW ANY CONCLUSION FROM ANYTHING YOU MAY SEE, OR HEAR, OR FANCY YOU SEE OR HEAR.
I'LL CUT YOUR THROAT FROM EAR TO EAR - DO YOU UNDERSTAND ME?
YES, SIR, I WON'T SAY NOTHING. I WISH, SIR, AS I MAY BE MADE INTO VEAL PIES AT LOVETT'S IN BELL-YARD IF I AS MUCH AS SAYS A WORD.
HMMM...VERY GOOD. I AM SATISFIED, I AM QUITE SATISFIED; AND MARK ME - THE SHOP, AND THE SHOP ONLY, IS YOUR PLACE.

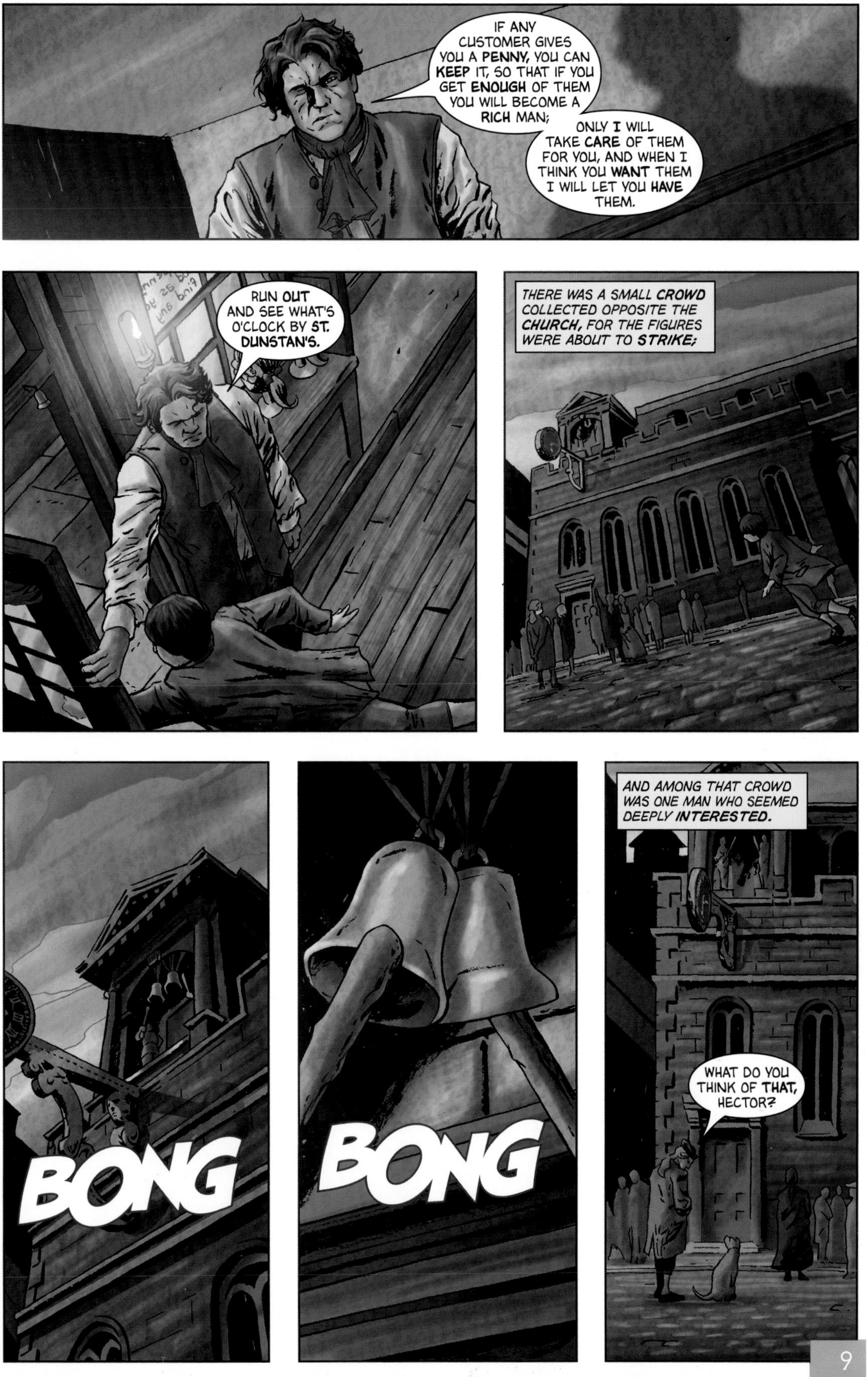
IF ANY CUSTOMER GIVES YOU A PENNY, YOU CAN KEEP IT, SO THAT IF YOU GET ENOUGH OF THEM YOU WILL BECOME A RICH MAN;
ONLY I WILL TAKE CARE OF THEM FOR YOU, AND WHEN I THINK YOU WANT THEM I WILL LET YOU HAVE THEM.
RUN OUT AND SEE WHAT'S O'CLOCK BY ST. DUNSTAN'S.
THERE WAS A SMALL CROWD COLLECTED OPPOSITE THE CHURCH, FOR THE FIGURES WERE ABOUT TO STRIKE;
BONG
BONG
AND AMONG THAT CROWD WAS ONE MAN WHO SEEMED DEEPLY INTERESTED.
WHAT DO YOU THINK OF THAT, HECTOR?

THERE IS A **BARBER'S** SHOP OPPOSITE, SO BEFORE I GO ANY FARTHER, AS I HAVE GOT TO SEE THE **LADIES**, ALTHOUGH IT'S ON A VERY **MELANCHOLY** ERRAND,

FOR I HAVE GOT TO TELL THEM THAT POOR **MARK INGESTRIE** IS NO MORE, AND HEAVEN **KNOWS** WHAT POOR SWEETHEART **JOHANNA** WILL SAY.

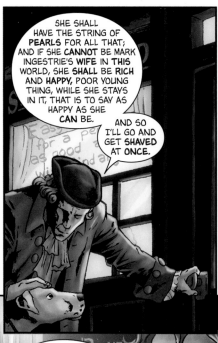

SHE SHALL HAVE THE STRING OF **PEARLS** FOR ALL THAT; AND IF SHE **CANNOT** BE MARK INGESTRIE'S **WIFE** IN **THIS** WORLD, SHE SHALL BE **RICH** AND **HAPPY**, POOR YOUNG THING, WHILE SHE STAYS IN IT, THAT IS TO SAY AS HAPPY AS SHE **CAN** BE.

AND SO I'LL GO AND GET **SHAVED** AT ONCE.

WHY, HECTOR, WHAT'S THE **MATTER?**

rrrrrrrrrrr

DOWN, SIR, **DOWN!**

I HAVE A **MORTAL FEAR** OF **DOGS**. WOULD YOU MIND HIM, SIR, SITTING **OUTSIDE** THE DOOR AND **WAITING** FOR YOU, IF IT'S ALL THE **SAME?** ONLY **LOOK** AT HIM, HE IS GOING TO **FLY** AT ME!

THEN YOU ARE THE **FIRST** PERSON HE **EVER** TOUCHED WITHOUT **PROVOCATION.**

I SUPPOSE HE DON'T LIKE YOUR **LOOKS**, AND I MUST CONFESS I AIN'T **MUCH** SURPRISED AT THAT. I HAVE SEEN A **FEW** RUM-LOOKING **GUYS** IN MY TIME, BUT HANG ME IF **EVER** I SAW SUCH A FIGURE-HEAD AS **YOURS.**

HEH HEH HEH HEH

WHAT THE DEVIL **NOISE** WAS **THAT?**

IT WAS ONLY **ME.** I LAUGHED.

TOBIAS, MY LAD, **GO** TO LEADENHALL-STREET, AND BRING A SMALL BAG OF THE THICK **BISCUITS** FROM MR. PETERSON'S.

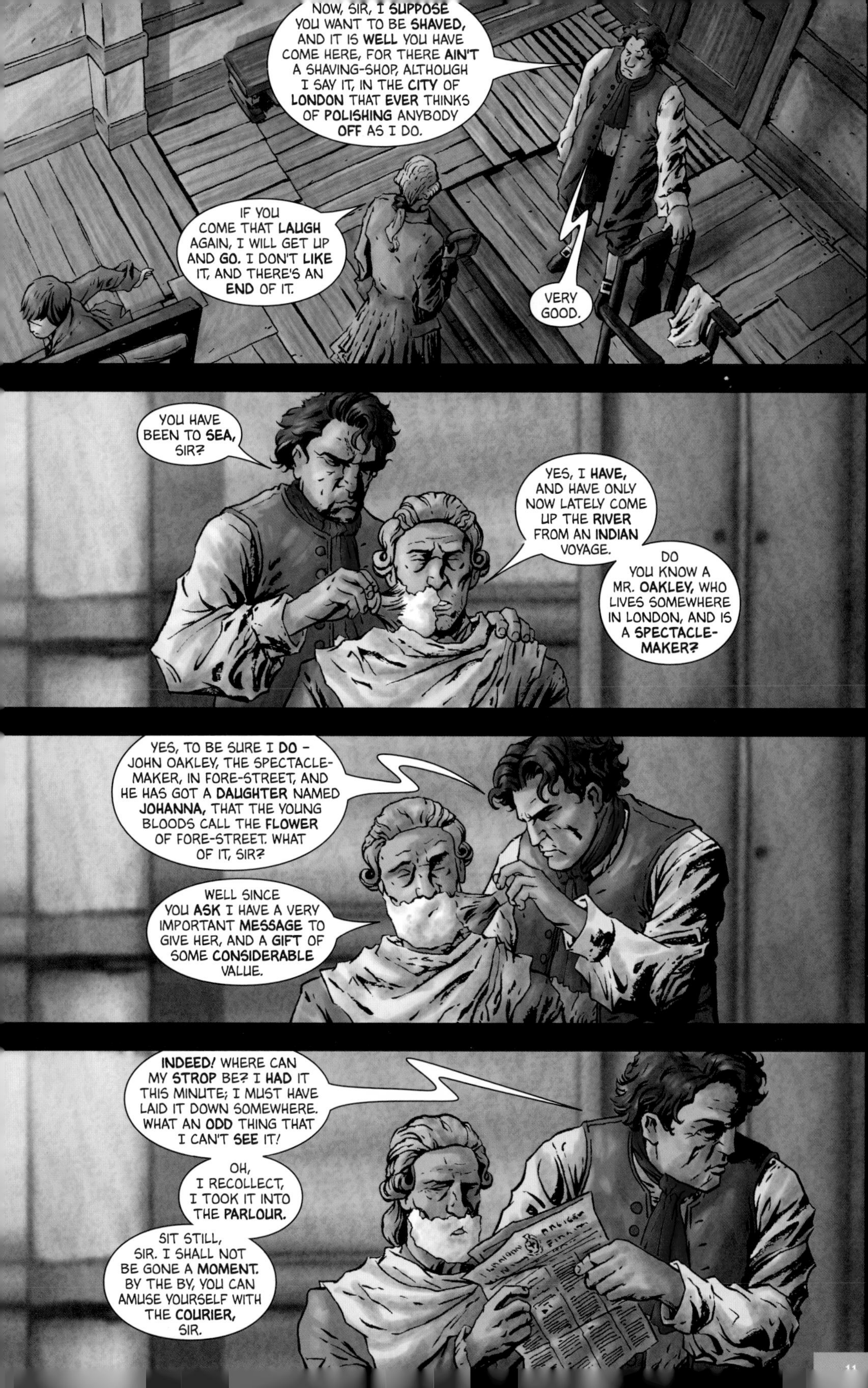
NOW, SIR, I SUPPOSE YOU WANT TO BE SHAVED, AND IT IS WELL YOU HAVE COME HERE, FOR THERE AIN'T A SHAVING-SHOP, ALTHOUGH I SAY IT, IN THE CITY OF LONDON THAT EVER THINKS OF POLISHING ANYBODY OFF AS I DO.
IF YOU COME THAT LAUGH AGAIN, I WILL GET UP AND GO. I DON'T LIKE IT, AND THERE'S AN END OF IT.
VERY GOOD.
YOU HAVE BEEN TO SEA, SIR?
YES, I HAVE, AND HAVE ONLY NOW LATELY COME UP THE RIVER FROM AN INDIAN VOYAGE.
DO YOU KNOW A MR. OAKLEY, WHO LIVES SOMEWHERE IN LONDON, AND IS A SPECTACLE-MAKER?
YES, TO BE SURE I DO - JOHN OAKLEY, THE SPECTACLE-MAKER, IN FORE-STREET, AND HE HAS GOT A DAUGHTER NAMED JOHANNA, THAT THE YOUNG BLOODS CALL THE FLOWER OF FORE-STREET. WHAT OF IT, SIR?
WELL SINCE YOU ASK I HAVE A VERY IMPORTANT MESSAGE TO GIVE HER, AND A GIFT OF SOME CONSIDERABLE VALUE.
INDEED! WHERE CAN MY STROP BE? I HAD IT THIS MINUTE; I MUST HAVE LAID IT DOWN SOMEWHERE. WHAT AN ODD THING THAT I CAN'T SEE IT!
OH, I RECOLLECT, I TOOK IT INTO THE PARLOUR.
SIT STILL, SIR. I SHALL NOT BE GONE A MOMENT. BY THE BY, YOU CAN AMUSE YOURSELF WITH THE COURIER, SIR.

creeeeak

fwoooosh

THUDDD

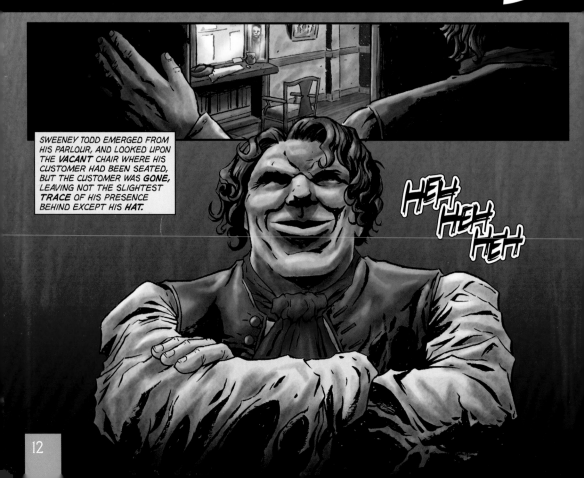

SWEENEY TODD EMERGED FROM HIS PARLOUR, AND LOOKED UPON THE *VACANT* CHAIR WHERE HIS CUSTOMER HAD BEEN SEATED, BUT THE CUSTOMER WAS *GONE*, LEAVING NOT THE SLIGHTEST *TRACE* OF HIS PRESENCE BEHIND EXCEPT HIS *HAT*.

HEH HEH HEH

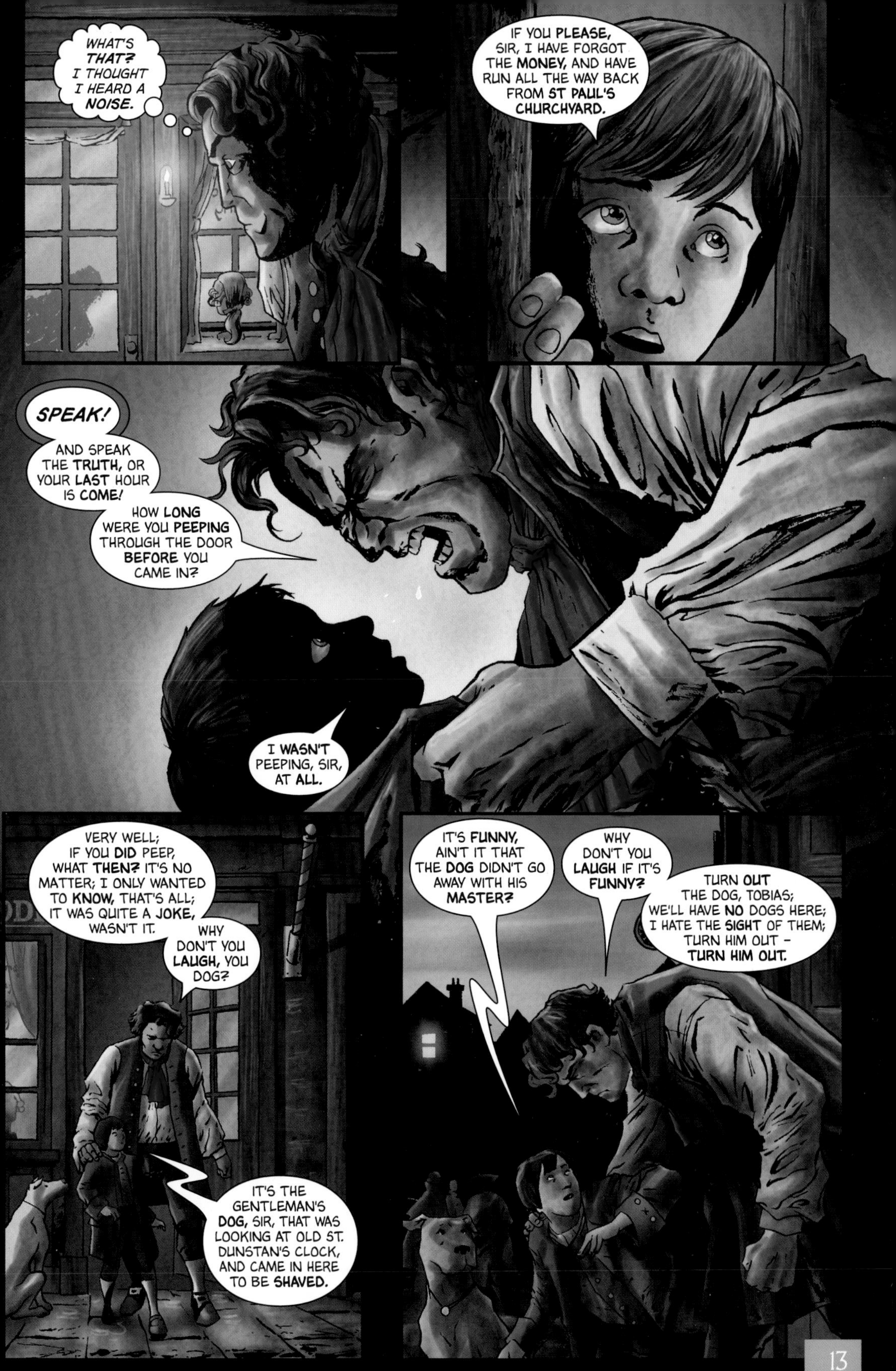
WHAT'S THAT? I THOUGHT I HEARD A NOISE.
IF YOU PLEASE, SIR, I HAVE FORGOT THE MONEY, AND HAVE RUN ALL THE WAY BACK FROM ST PAUL'S CHURCHYARD.
SPEAK!
AND SPEAK THE TRUTH, OR YOUR LAST HOUR IS COME!
HOW LONG WERE YOU PEEPING THROUGH THE DOOR BEFORE YOU CAME IN?
I WASN'T PEEPING, SIR, AT ALL.
VERY WELL; IF YOU DID PEEP, WHAT THEN? IT'S NO MATTER; I ONLY WANTED TO KNOW, THAT'S ALL; IT WAS QUITE A JOKE, WASN'T IT.
WHY DON'T YOU LAUGH, YOU DOG?
IT'S THE GENTLEMAN'S DOG, SIR, THAT WAS LOOKING AT OLD ST. DUNSTAN'S CLOCK, AND CAME IN HERE TO BE SHAVED.
IT'S FUNNY, AIN'T IT THAT THE DOG DIDN'T GO AWAY WITH HIS MASTER?
WHY DON'T YOU LAUGH IF IT'S FUNNY?
TURN OUT THE DOG, TOBIAS; WE'LL HAVE NO DOGS HERE; I HATE THE SIGHT OF THEM; TURN HIM OUT – TURN HIM OUT.

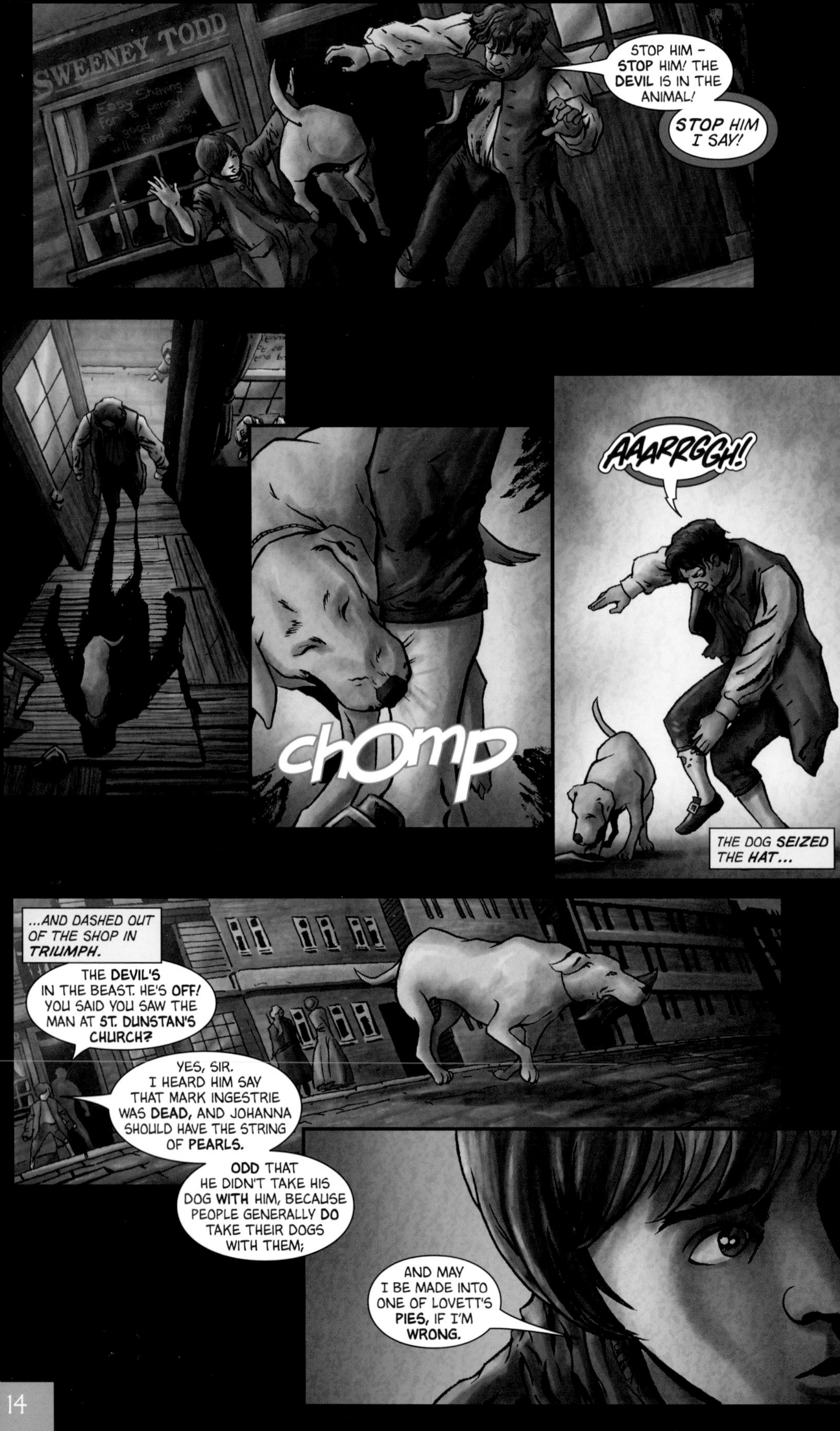
SWEENEY TODD
STOP HIM – STOP HIM! THE DEVIL IS IN THE ANIMAL!
STOP HIM I SAY!
chomp
AAARRGGH!
THE DOG SEIZED THE HAT...
...AND DASHED OUT OF THE SHOP IN TRIUMPH.
THE DEVIL'S IN THE BEAST. HE'S OFF! YOU SAID YOU SAW THE MAN AT ST. DUNSTAN'S CHURCH?
YES, SIR. I HEARD HIM SAY THAT MARK INGESTRIE WAS DEAD, AND JOHANNA SHOULD HAVE THE STRING OF PEARLS.
ODD THAT HE DIDN'T TAKE HIS DOG WITH HIM, BECAUSE PEOPLE GENERALLY DO TAKE THEIR DOGS WITH THEM;
AND MAY I BE MADE INTO ONE OF LOVETT'S PIES, IF I'M WRONG.

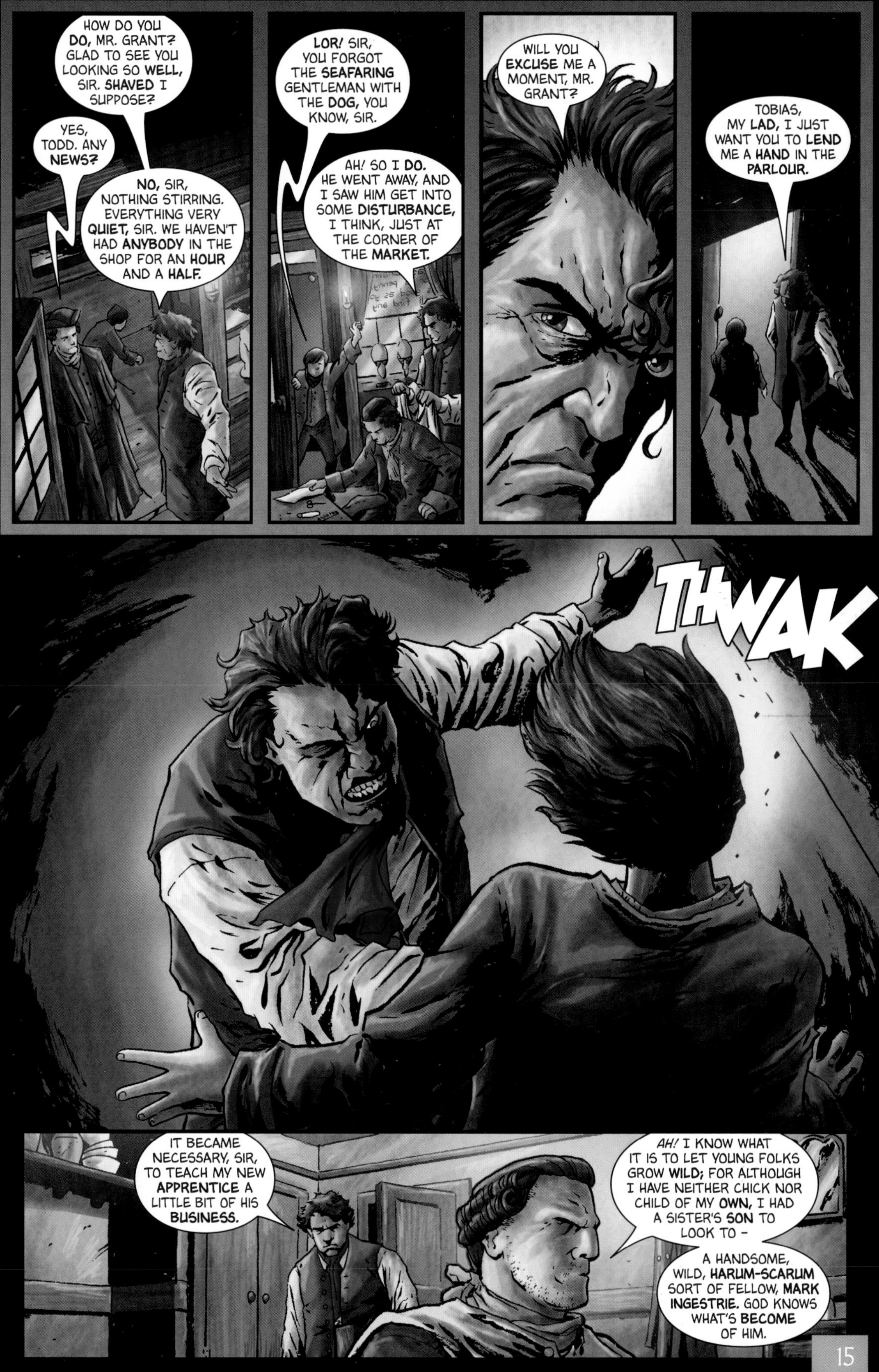
HOW DO YOU DO, MR. GRANT? GLAD TO SEE YOU LOOKING SO WELL, SIR. SHAVED I SUPPOSE?
YES, TODD. ANY NEWS?
NO, SIR, NOTHING STIRRING. EVERYTHING VERY QUIET, SIR. WE HAVEN'T HAD ANYBODY IN THE SHOP FOR AN HOUR AND A HALF.
LOR! SIR, YOU FORGOT THE SEAFARING GENTLEMAN WITH THE DOG, YOU KNOW, SIR.
AH! SO I DO. HE WENT AWAY, AND I SAW HIM GET INTO SOME DISTURBANCE, I THINK, JUST AT THE CORNER OF THE MARKET.
WILL YOU EXCUSE ME A MOMENT, MR. GRANT?
TOBIAS, MY LAD, I JUST WANT YOU TO LEND ME A HAND IN THE PARLOUR.
THWAK
IT BECAME NECESSARY, SIR, TO TEACH MY NEW APPRENTICE A LITTLE BIT OF HIS BUSINESS.
AH! I KNOW WHAT IT IS TO LET YOUNG FOLKS GROW WILD; FOR ALTHOUGH I HAVE NEITHER CHICK NOR CHILD OF MY OWN, I HAD A SISTER'S SON TO LOOK TO -
A HANDSOME, WILD, HARUM-SCARUM SORT OF FELLOW, MARK INGESTRIE. GOD KNOWS WHAT'S BECOME OF HIM.

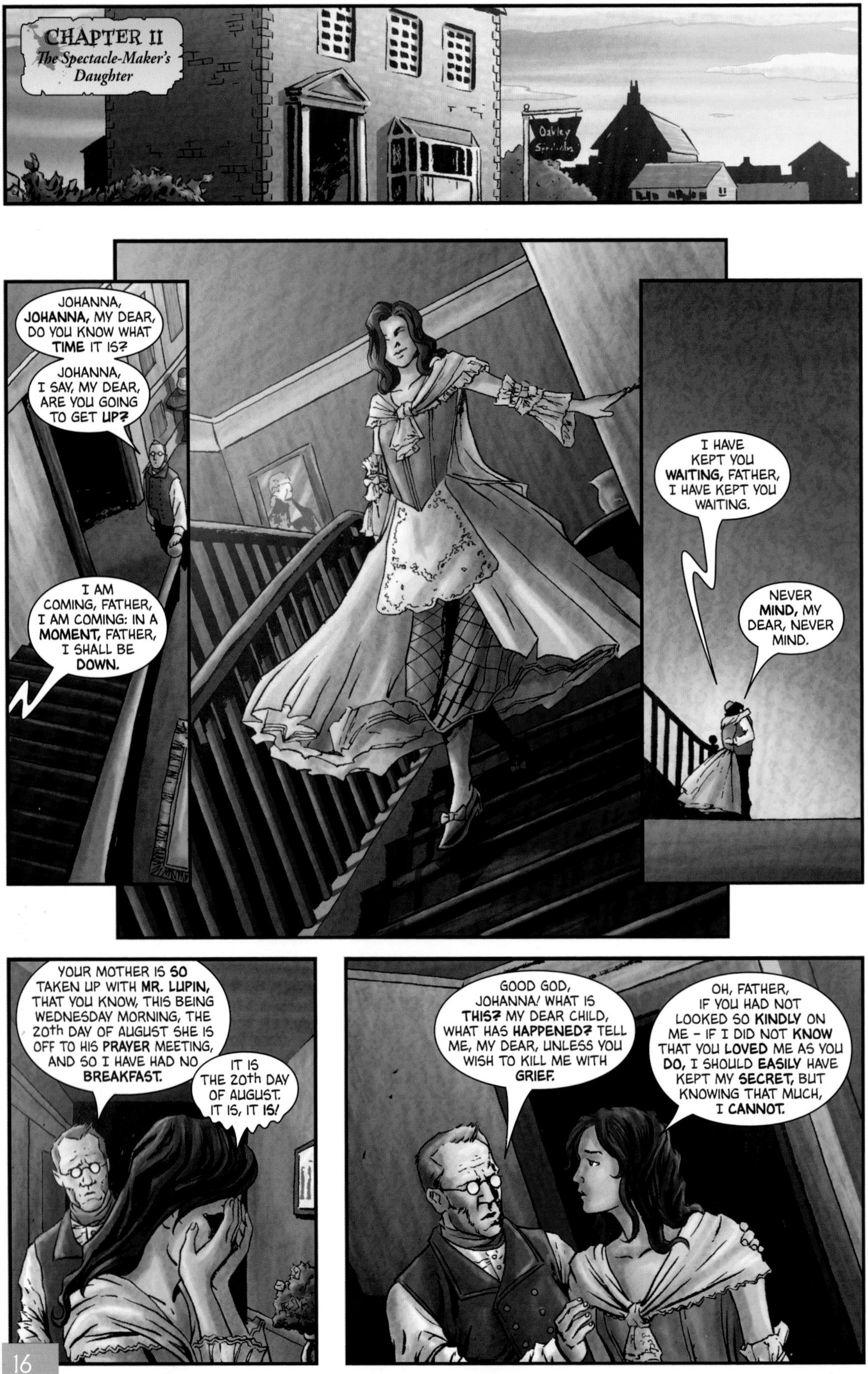

CHAPTER II
The Spectacle-Maker's Daughter
Oakley Spectacles
JOHANNA, JOHANNA, MY DEAR, DO YOU KNOW WHAT TIME IT IS?
JOHANNA, I SAY, MY DEAR, ARE YOU GOING TO GET UP?
I AM COMING, FATHER, I AM COMING: IN A MOMENT, FATHER, I SHALL BE DOWN.
I HAVE KEPT YOU WAITING, FATHER, I HAVE KEPT YOU WAITING.
NEVER MIND, MY DEAR, NEVER MIND.
YOUR MOTHER IS SO TAKEN UP WITH MR. LUPIN, THAT YOU KNOW, THIS BEING WEDNESDAY MORNING, THE 20th DAY OF AUGUST SHE IS OFF TO HIS PRAYER MEETING, AND SO I HAVE HAD NO BREAKFAST.
IT IS THE 20th DAY OF AUGUST. IT IS, IT IS!
GOOD GOD, JOHANNA! WHAT IS THIS? MY DEAR CHILD, WHAT HAS HAPPENED? TELL ME, MY DEAR, UNLESS YOU WISH TO KILL ME WITH GRIEF.
OH, FATHER, IF YOU HAD NOT LOOKED SO KINDLY ON ME – IF I DID NOT KNOW THAT YOU LOVED ME AS YOU DO, I SHOULD EASILY HAVE KEPT MY SECRET, BUT KNOWING THAT MUCH, I CANNOT.

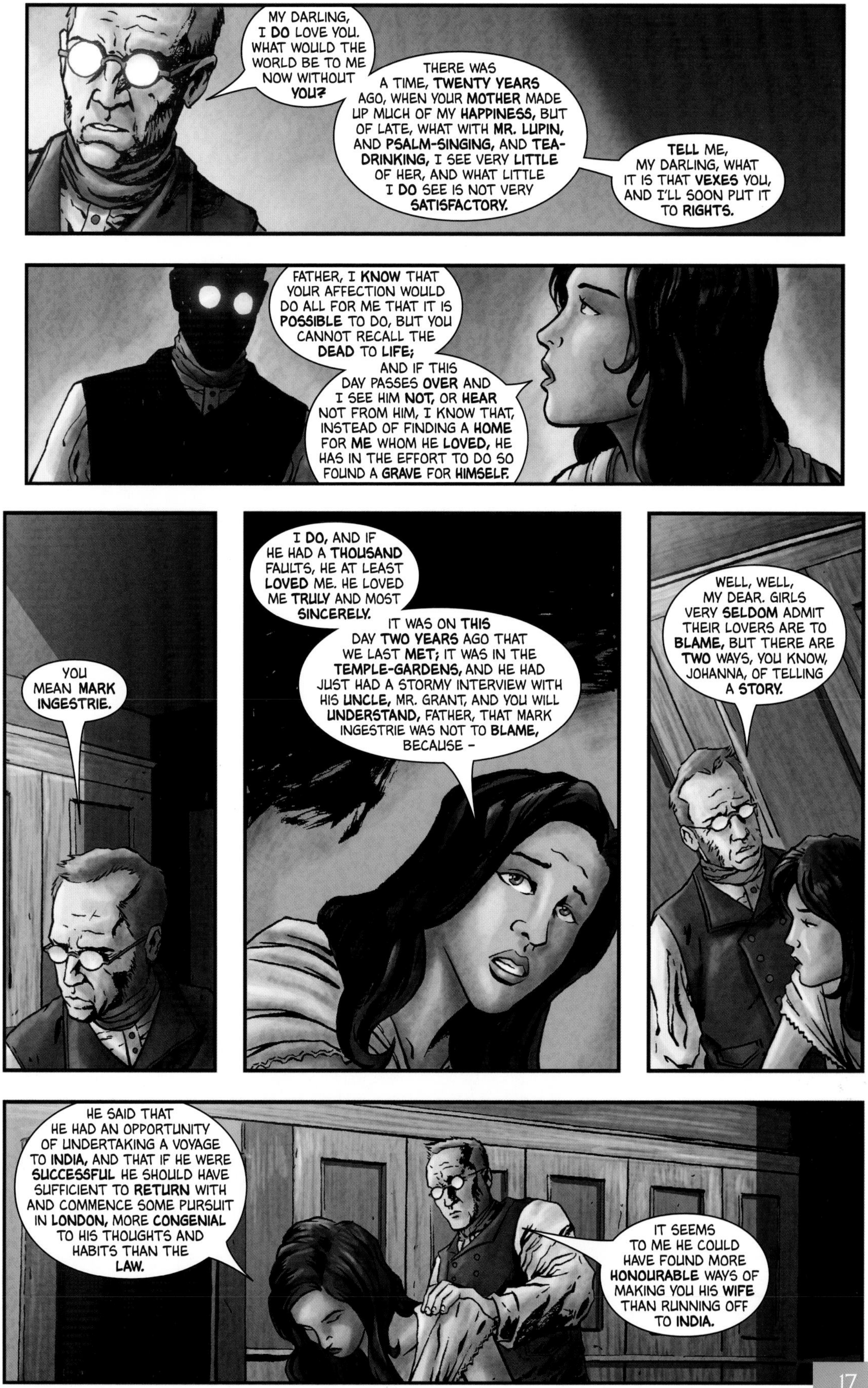

MY DARLING, I DO LOVE YOU. WHAT WOULD THE WORLD BE TO ME NOW WITHOUT YOU?
THERE WAS A TIME, TWENTY YEARS AGO, WHEN YOUR MOTHER MADE UP MUCH OF MY HAPPINESS, BUT OF LATE, WHAT WITH MR. LUPIN, AND PSALM-SINGING, AND TEA-DRINKING, I SEE VERY LITTLE OF HER, AND WHAT LITTLE I DO SEE IS NOT VERY SATISFACTORY.
TELL ME, MY DARLING, WHAT IT IS THAT VEXES YOU, AND I'LL SOON PUT IT TO RIGHTS.
FATHER, I KNOW THAT YOUR AFFECTION WOULD DO ALL FOR ME THAT IT IS POSSIBLE TO DO, BUT YOU CANNOT RECALL THE DEAD TO LIFE;
AND IF THIS DAY PASSES OVER AND I SEE HIM NOT, OR HEAR NOT FROM HIM, I KNOW THAT, INSTEAD OF FINDING A HOME FOR ME WHOM HE LOVED, HE HAS IN THE EFFORT TO DO SO FOUND A GRAVE FOR HIMSELF.
YOU MEAN MARK INGESTRIE.
I DO, AND IF HE HAD A THOUSAND FAULTS, HE AT LEAST LOVED ME. HE LOVED ME TRULY AND MOST SINCERELY.
IT WAS ON THIS DAY TWO YEARS AGO THAT WE LAST MET; IT WAS IN THE TEMPLE-GARDENS, AND HE HAD JUST HAD A STORMY INTERVIEW WITH HIS UNCLE, MR. GRANT, AND YOU WILL UNDERSTAND, FATHER, THAT MARK INGESTRIE WAS NOT TO BLAME, BECAUSE –
WELL, WELL, MY DEAR. GIRLS VERY SELDOM ADMIT THEIR LOVERS ARE TO BLAME, BUT THERE ARE TWO WAYS, YOU KNOW, JOHANNA, OF TELLING A STORY.
HE SAID THAT HE HAD AN OPPORTUNITY OF UNDERTAKING A VOYAGE TO INDIA, AND THAT IF HE WERE SUCCESSFUL HE SHOULD HAVE SUFFICIENT TO RETURN WITH AND COMMENCE SOME PURSUIT IN LONDON, MORE CONGENIAL TO HIS THOUGHTS AND HABITS THAN THE LAW.
IT SEEMS TO ME HE COULD HAVE FOUND MORE HONOURABLE WAYS OF MAKING YOU HIS WIFE THAN RUNNING OFF TO INDIA.

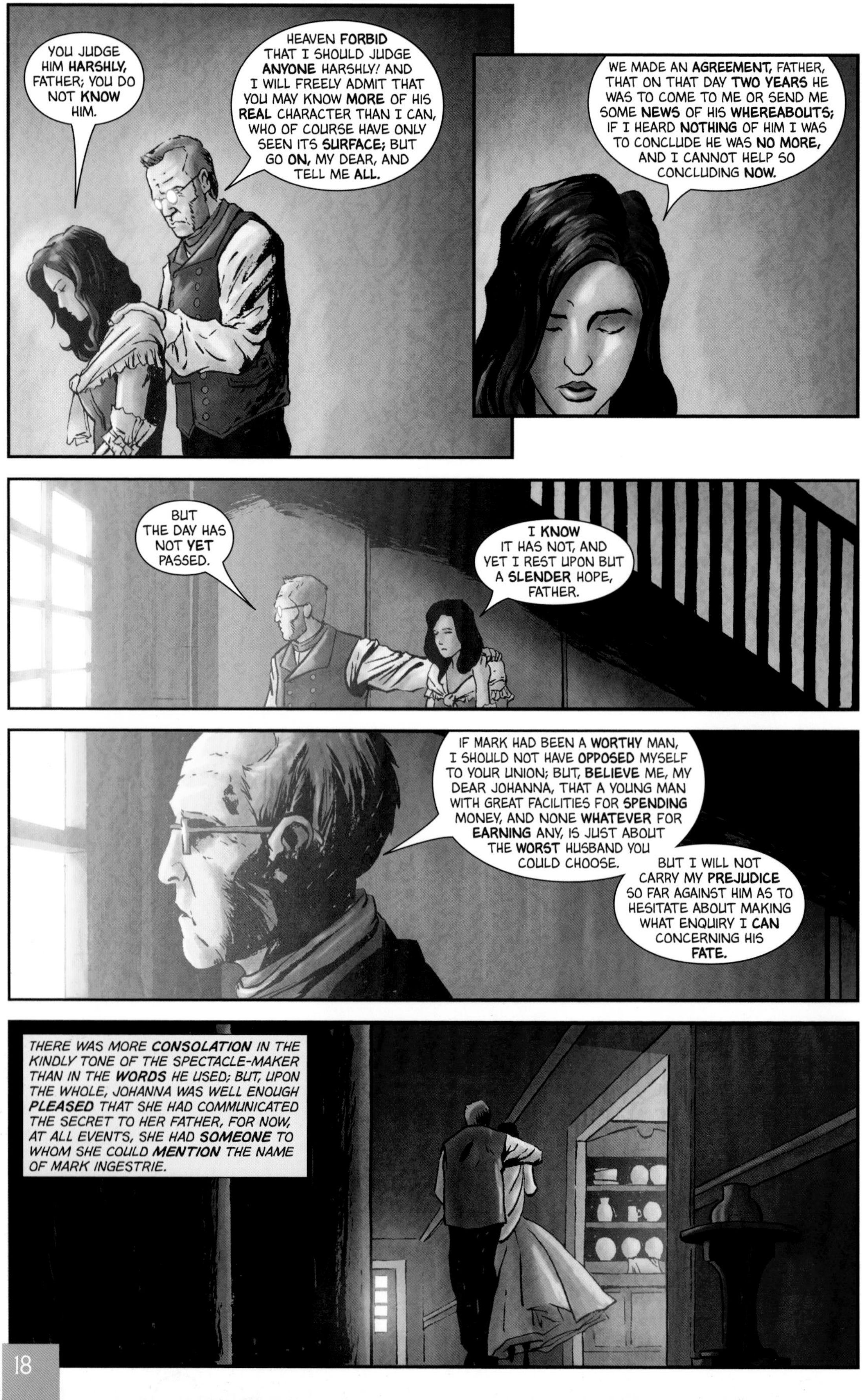
YOU JUDGE HIM **HARSHLY,** FATHER; YOU DO NOT **KNOW** HIM.
HEAVEN **FORBID** THAT I SHOULD JUDGE **ANYONE** HARSHLY! AND I WILL FREELY ADMIT THAT YOU MAY KNOW **MORE** OF HIS **REAL** CHARACTER THAN I CAN, WHO OF COURSE HAVE ONLY SEEN ITS **SURFACE;** BUT GO **ON,** MY DEAR, AND TELL ME **ALL.**
WE MADE AN **AGREEMENT,** FATHER, THAT ON THAT DAY **TWO YEARS** HE WAS TO COME TO ME OR SEND ME SOME **NEWS** OF HIS **WHEREABOUTS;** IF I HEARD **NOTHING** OF HIM I WAS TO CONCLUDE HE WAS **NO MORE,** AND I CANNOT HELP SO CONCLUDING **NOW.**
BUT THE DAY HAS NOT **YET** PASSED.
I **KNOW** IT HAS NOT, AND YET I REST UPON BUT A **SLENDER** HOPE, FATHER.
IF MARK HAD BEEN A **WORTHY** MAN, I SHOULD NOT HAVE **OPPOSED** MYSELF TO YOUR UNION; BUT, **BELIEVE** ME, MY DEAR JOHANNA, THAT A YOUNG MAN WITH GREAT FACILITIES FOR **SPENDING** MONEY, AND NONE **WHATEVER** FOR **EARNING** ANY, IS JUST ABOUT THE **WORST** HUSBAND YOU COULD CHOOSE.
BUT I WILL NOT CARRY MY **PREJUDICE** SO FAR AGAINST HIM AS TO HESITATE ABOUT MAKING WHAT ENQUIRY I **CAN** CONCERNING HIS **FATE.**
*THERE WAS MORE **CONSOLATION** IN THE KINDLY TONE OF THE SPECTACLE-MAKER THAN IN THE **WORDS** HE USED; BUT, UPON THE WHOLE, JOHANNA WAS WELL ENOUGH **PLEASED** THAT SHE HAD COMMUNICATED THE SECRET TO HER FATHER, FOR NOW, AT ALL EVENTS, SHE HAD **SOMEONE** TO WHOM SHE COULD **MENTION** THE NAME OF MARK INGESTRIE.*

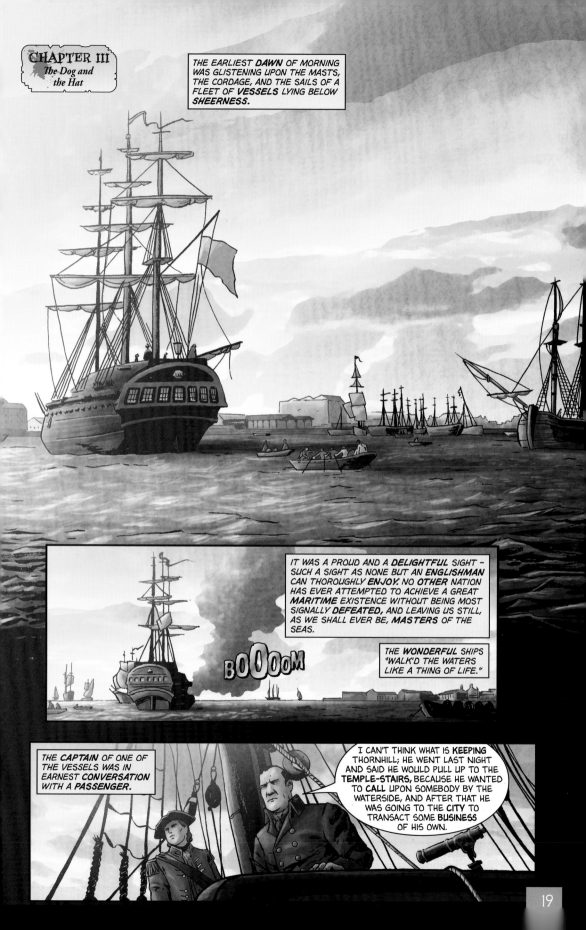

CHAPTER III
The Dog and the Hat

THE EARLIEST *DAWN* OF MORNING WAS GLISTENING UPON THE MASTS, THE CORDAGE, AND THE SAILS OF A FLEET OF *VESSELS* LYING BELOW *SHEERNESS.*

IT WAS A PROUD AND A *DELIGHTFUL* SIGHT – SUCH A SIGHT AS NONE BUT AN *ENGLISHMAN* CAN THOROUGHLY *ENJOY.* NO *OTHER* NATION HAS EVER ATTEMPTED TO ACHIEVE A GREAT *MARITIME* EXISTENCE WITHOUT BEING MOST SIGNALLY *DEFEATED,* AND LEAVING US STILL, AS WE SHALL EVER BE, *MASTERS* OF THE SEAS.

BOOOOM

THE *WONDERFUL* SHIPS "WALK'D THE WATERS LIKE A THING OF LIFE."

THE *CAPTAIN* OF ONE OF THE VESSELS WAS IN EARNEST *CONVERSATION* WITH A *PASSENGER.*

I CAN'T THINK WHAT IS *KEEPING* THORNHILL; HE WENT LAST NIGHT AND SAID HE WOULD PULL UP TO THE *TEMPLE-STAIRS,* BECAUSE HE WANTED TO *CALL* UPON SOMEBODY BY THE WATERSIDE, AND AFTER THAT HE WAS GOING TO THE *CITY* TO TRANSACT SOME *BUSINESS* OF HIS OWN.

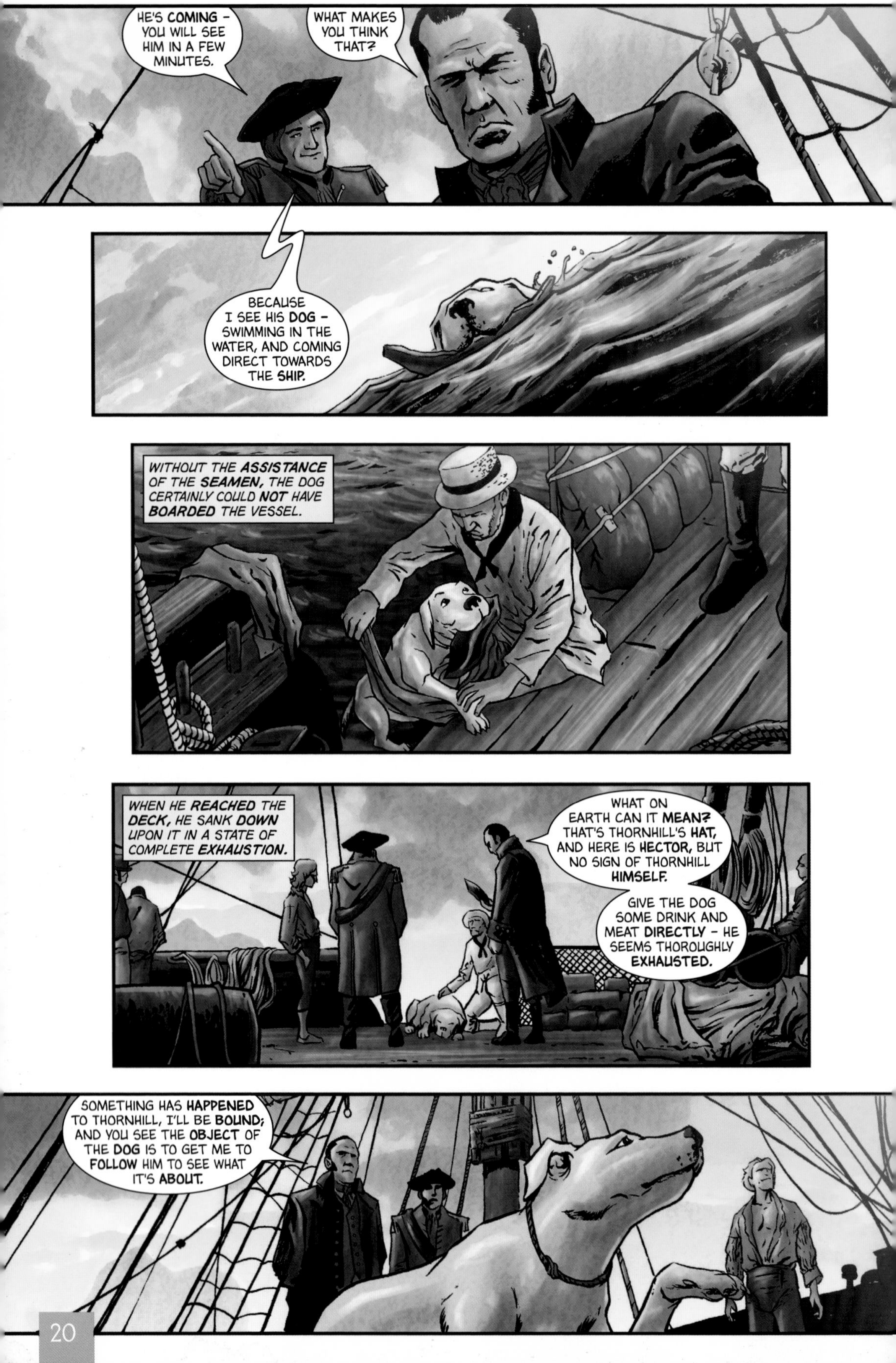

HE'S COMING – YOU WILL SEE HIM IN A FEW MINUTES.
WHAT MAKES YOU THINK THAT?
BECAUSE I SEE HIS DOG – SWIMMING IN THE WATER, AND COMING DIRECT TOWARDS THE SHIP.
WITHOUT THE ASSISTANCE OF THE SEAMEN, THE DOG CERTAINLY COULD NOT HAVE BOARDED THE VESSEL.
WHEN HE REACHED THE DECK, HE SANK DOWN UPON IT IN A STATE OF COMPLETE EXHAUSTION.
WHAT ON EARTH CAN IT MEAN? THAT'S THORNHILL'S HAT, AND HERE IS HECTOR, BUT NO SIGN OF THORNHILL HIMSELF.
GIVE THE DOG SOME DRINK AND MEAT DIRECTLY – HE SEEMS THOROUGHLY EXHAUSTED.
SOMETHING HAS HAPPENED TO THORNHILL, I'LL BE BOUND; AND YOU SEE THE OBJECT OF THE DOG IS TO GET ME TO FOLLOW HIM TO SEE WHAT IT'S ABOUT.

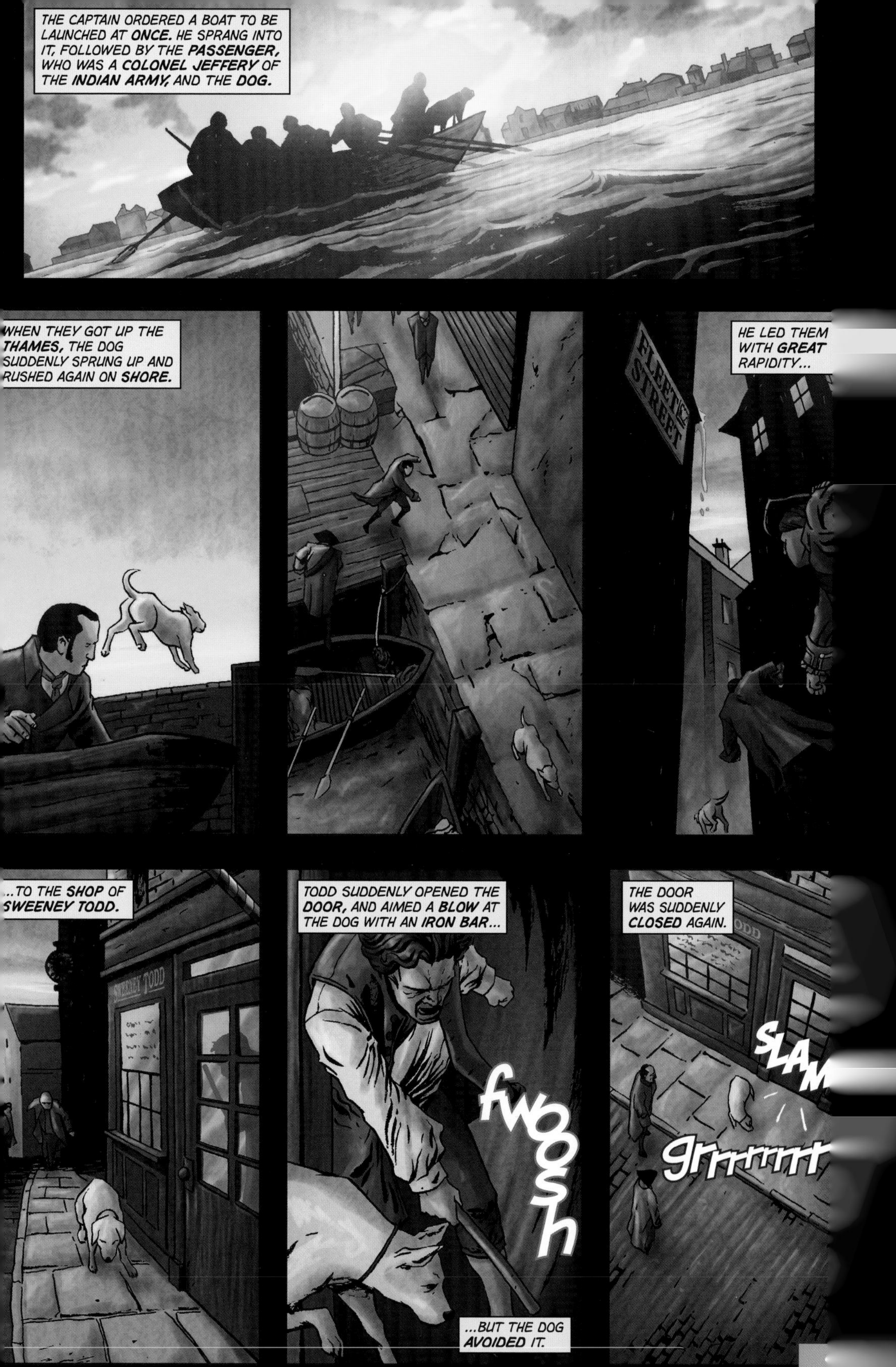

THE CAPTAIN ORDERED A BOAT TO BE LAUNCHED AT ONCE. HE SPRANG INTO IT, FOLLOWED BY THE PASSENGER, WHO WAS A COLONEL JEFFERY OF THE INDIAN ARMY, AND THE DOG.
WHEN THEY GOT UP THE THAMES, THE DOG SUDDENLY SPRUNG UP AND RUSHED AGAIN ON SHORE.
FLEET STREET
HE LED THEM WITH GREAT RAPIDITY...
...TO THE SHOP OF SWEENEY TODD.
SWEENEY TODD
TODD SUDDENLY OPENED THE DOOR, AND AIMED A BLOW AT THE DOG WITH AN IRON BAR...
fwoosh
...BUT THE DOG AVOIDED IT.
THE DOOR WAS SUDDENLY CLOSED AGAIN.
SLAM
grrrrrrr

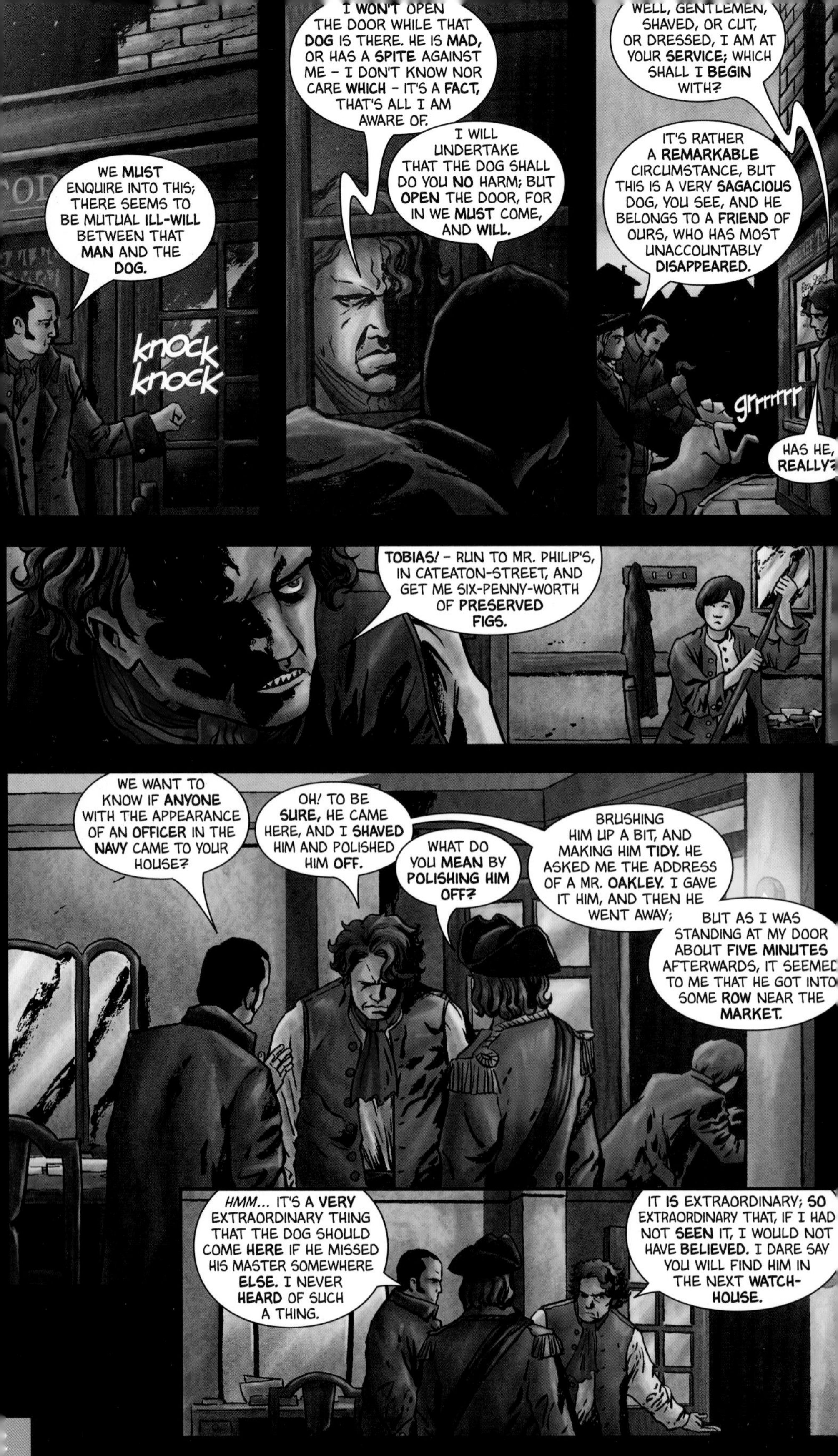
WE MUST ENQUIRE INTO THIS; THERE SEEMS TO BE MUTUAL ILL-WILL BETWEEN THAT MAN AND THE DOG.
knock knock
I WON'T OPEN THE DOOR WHILE THAT DOG IS THERE. HE IS MAD, OR HAS A SPITE AGAINST ME – I DON'T KNOW NOR CARE WHICH – IT'S A FACT, THAT'S ALL I AM AWARE OF.
I WILL UNDERTAKE THAT THE DOG SHALL DO YOU NO HARM; BUT OPEN THE DOOR, FOR IN WE MUST COME, AND WILL.
WELL, GENTLEMEN, SHAVED, OR CUT, OR DRESSED, I AM AT YOUR SERVICE; WHICH SHALL I BEGIN WITH?
IT'S RATHER A REMARKABLE CIRCUMSTANCE, BUT THIS IS A VERY SAGACIOUS DOG, YOU SEE, AND HE BELONGS TO A FRIEND OF OURS, WHO HAS MOST UNACCOUNTABLY DISAPPEARED.
grrrrrr
HAS HE, REALLY?
TOBIAS! – RUN TO MR. PHILIP'S, IN CATEATON-STREET, AND GET ME SIX-PENNY-WORTH OF PRESERVED FIGS.
WE WANT TO KNOW IF ANYONE WITH THE APPEARANCE OF AN OFFICER IN THE NAVY CAME TO YOUR HOUSE?
OH! TO BE SURE, HE CAME HERE, AND I SHAVED HIM AND POLISHED HIM OFF.
WHAT DO YOU MEAN BY POLISHING HIM OFF?
BRUSHING HIM UP A BIT, AND MAKING HIM TIDY. HE ASKED ME THE ADDRESS OF A MR. OAKLEY. I GAVE IT HIM, AND THEN HE WENT AWAY;
BUT AS I WAS STANDING AT MY DOOR ABOUT FIVE MINUTES AFTERWARDS, IT SEEMED TO ME THAT HE GOT INTO SOME ROW NEAR THE MARKET.
HMM... IT'S A VERY EXTRAORDINARY THING THAT THE DOG SHOULD COME HERE IF HE MISSED HIS MASTER SOMEWHERE ELSE. I NEVER HEARD OF SUCH A THING.
IT IS EXTRAORDINARY; SO EXTRAORDINARY THAT, IF I HAD NOT SEEN IT, I WOULD NOT HAVE BELIEVED. I DARE SAY YOU WILL FIND HIM IN THE NEXT WATCH-HOUSE.

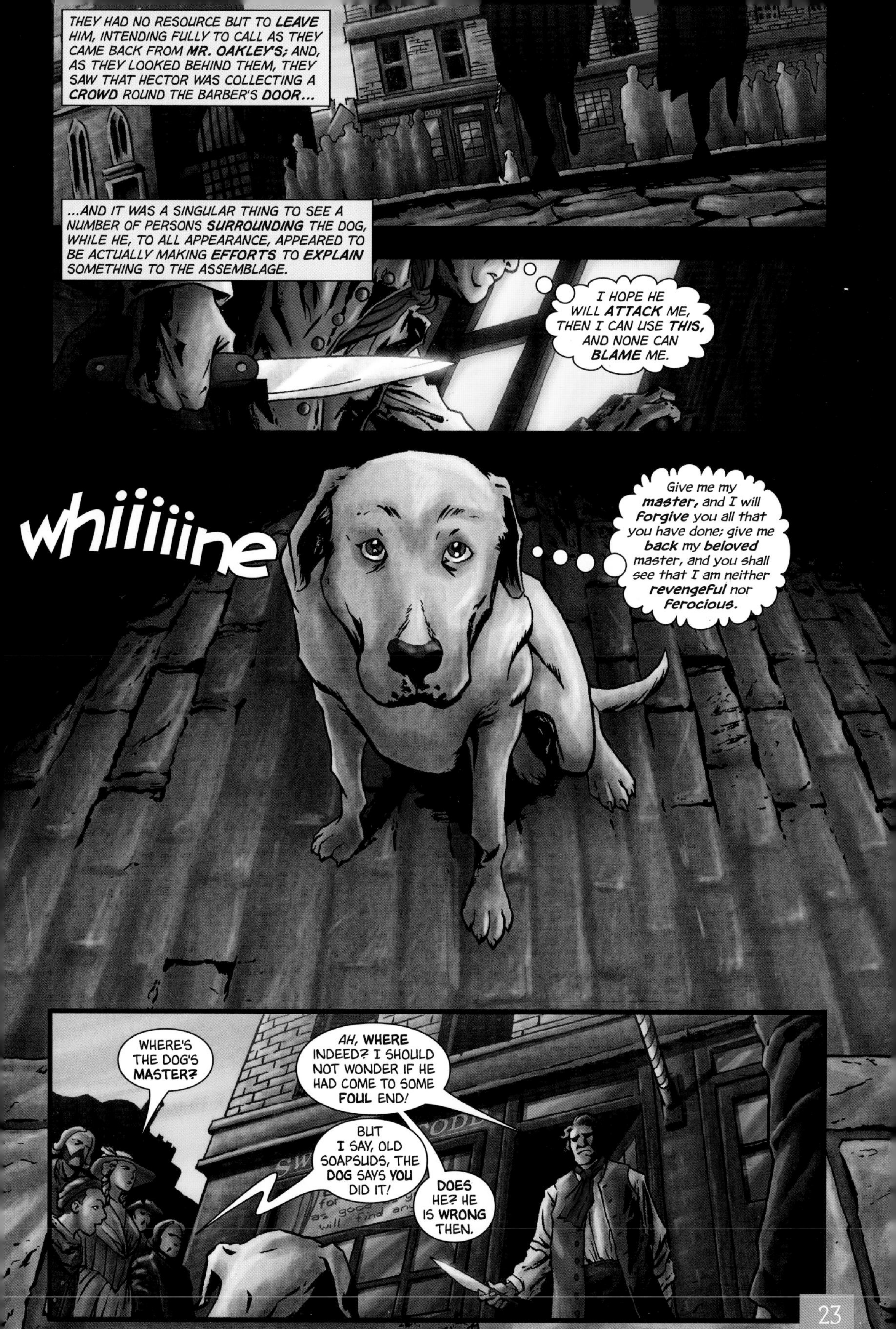
THEY HAD NO RESOURCE BUT TO LEAVE HIM, INTENDING FULLY TO CALL AS THEY CAME BACK FROM MR. OAKLEY'S; AND, AS THEY LOOKED BEHIND THEM, THEY SAW THAT HECTOR WAS COLLECTING A CROWD ROUND THE BARBER'S DOOR...
...AND IT WAS A SINGULAR THING TO SEE A NUMBER OF PERSONS SURROUNDING THE DOG, WHILE HE, TO ALL APPEARANCE, APPEARED TO BE ACTUALLY MAKING EFFORTS TO EXPLAIN SOMETHING TO THE ASSEMBLAGE.
I HOPE HE WILL ATTACK ME, THEN I CAN USE THIS, AND NONE CAN BLAME ME.
whiiiiine
Give me my master, and I will forgive you all that you have done; give me back my beloved master, and you shall see that I am neither revengeful nor ferocious.
WHERE'S THE DOG'S MASTER?
AH, WHERE INDEED? I SHOULD NOT WONDER IF HE HAD COME TO SOME FOUL END!
BUT I SAY, OLD SOAPSUDS, THE DOG SAYS YOU DID IT!
DOES HE? HE IS WRONG THEN.

ON THE LEFT-HAND SIDE OF BELL-YARD WAS *LOVETT'S PIE-SHOP* – ONE OF THE MOST *CELEBRATED* SHOPS FOR THE SALE OF *VEAL* AND *PORK PIES* THAT LONDON *EVER* PRODUCED.

HIGH AND LOW, RICH AND POOR, RESORTED TO IT; ITS *FAME* HAD SPREAD *FAR* AND *WIDE;* AND IT WAS BECAUSE THE *FIRST* BATCH OF THOSE PIES CAME UP AT *TWELVE O'CLOCK* THAT THERE WAS SUCH A *RUSH* OF THE LEGAL PROFESSION TO OBTAIN THEM.

AND WELL DID THEY *DESERVE* THEIR *REPUTATION,* THOSE *DELICIOUS* PIES. THERE WAS ABOUT THEM A *FLAVOUR* NEVER *SURPASSED,* THE PASTE WAS OF THE MOST *DELICATE* CONSTRUCTION, IMPREGNATED WITH THE AROMA OF A *DELICIOUS* GRAVY THAT *DEFIES* DESCRIPTION.

THEN THE SMALL PORTIONS OF *MEAT* WHICH THEY CONTAINED WERE SO *TENDER,* AND THE FAT AND THE LEAN SO *ARTISTICALLY* MIXED UP, THAT TO EAT *ONE* OF LOVETT'S PIES WAS SUCH A *PROVOCATIVE* TO EAT ANOTHER.

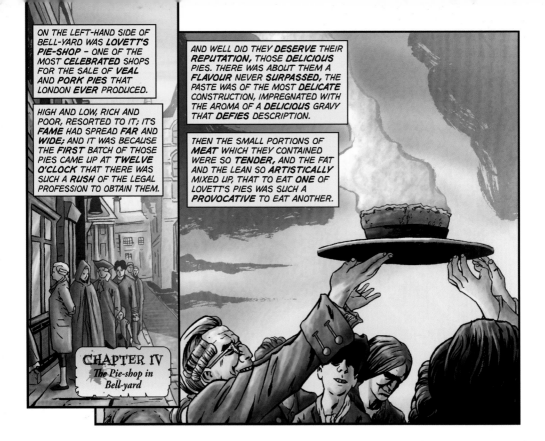

CHAPTER IV
The Pie-shop in Bell-yard

THE COUNTER IN LOVETT'S PIE-SHOP WAS IN THE SHAPE OF A *HORSESHOE,* AND IT WAS THE CUSTOM OF THE *YOUNG BLOODS* FROM THE TEMPLE AND LINCOLN'S-INN TO SIT IN A *ROW* UPON ITS EDGE WHILE THEY *PARTOOK* OF THE DELICIOUS PIES, AND *CHATTED* GAILY ABOUT ONE CONCERN AND ANOTHER.

MANY AN *APPOINTMENT* WAS MADE AT LOVETT'S PIE-SHOP, AND MANY A PIECE OF GOSSIPING *SCANDAL* WAS THERE *FIRST* CIRCULATED. THE DIN OF TONGUES WAS *PRODIGIOUS* – AND OH WITH WHAT *RAPIDITY* THE PIES *DISAPPEARED!*

chomp chomp

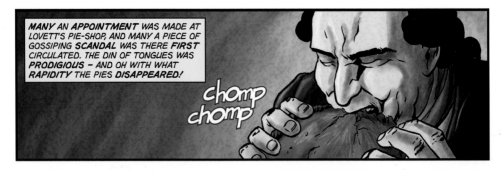

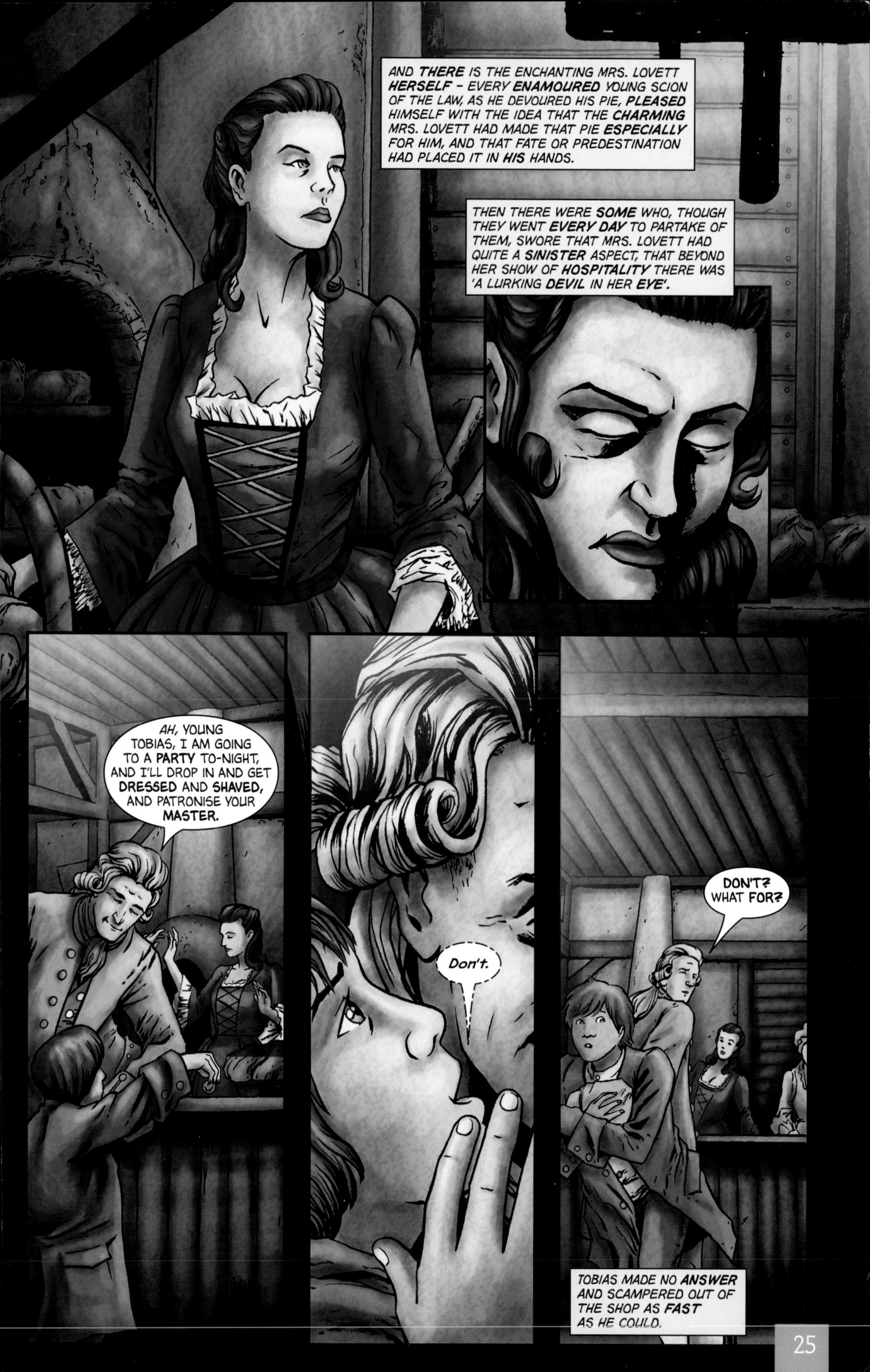
AND **THERE** IS THE ENCHANTING MRS. LOVETT **HERSELF** – EVERY **ENAMOURED** YOUNG SCION OF THE LAW, AS HE DEVOURED HIS PIE, **PLEASED** HIMSELF WITH THE IDEA THAT THE **CHARMING** MRS. LOVETT HAD MADE THAT PIE **ESPECIALLY** FOR HIM, AND THAT FATE OR PREDESTINATION HAD PLACED IT IN **HIS** HANDS.
THEN THERE WERE **SOME** WHO, THOUGH THEY WENT **EVERY DAY** TO PARTAKE OF THEM, SWORE THAT MRS. LOVETT HAD QUITE A **SINISTER** ASPECT, THAT BEYOND HER SHOW OF **HOSPITALITY** THERE WAS 'A LURKING **DEVIL** IN HER **EYE**'.
AH, YOUNG TOBIAS, I AM GOING TO A **PARTY** TO-NIGHT, AND I'LL DROP IN AND GET **DRESSED** AND **SHAVED**, AND PATRONISE YOUR **MASTER**.
Don't.
DON'T? WHAT FOR?
TOBIAS MADE NO **ANSWER** AND SCAMPERED OUT OF THE SHOP AS **FAST** AS HE COULD.

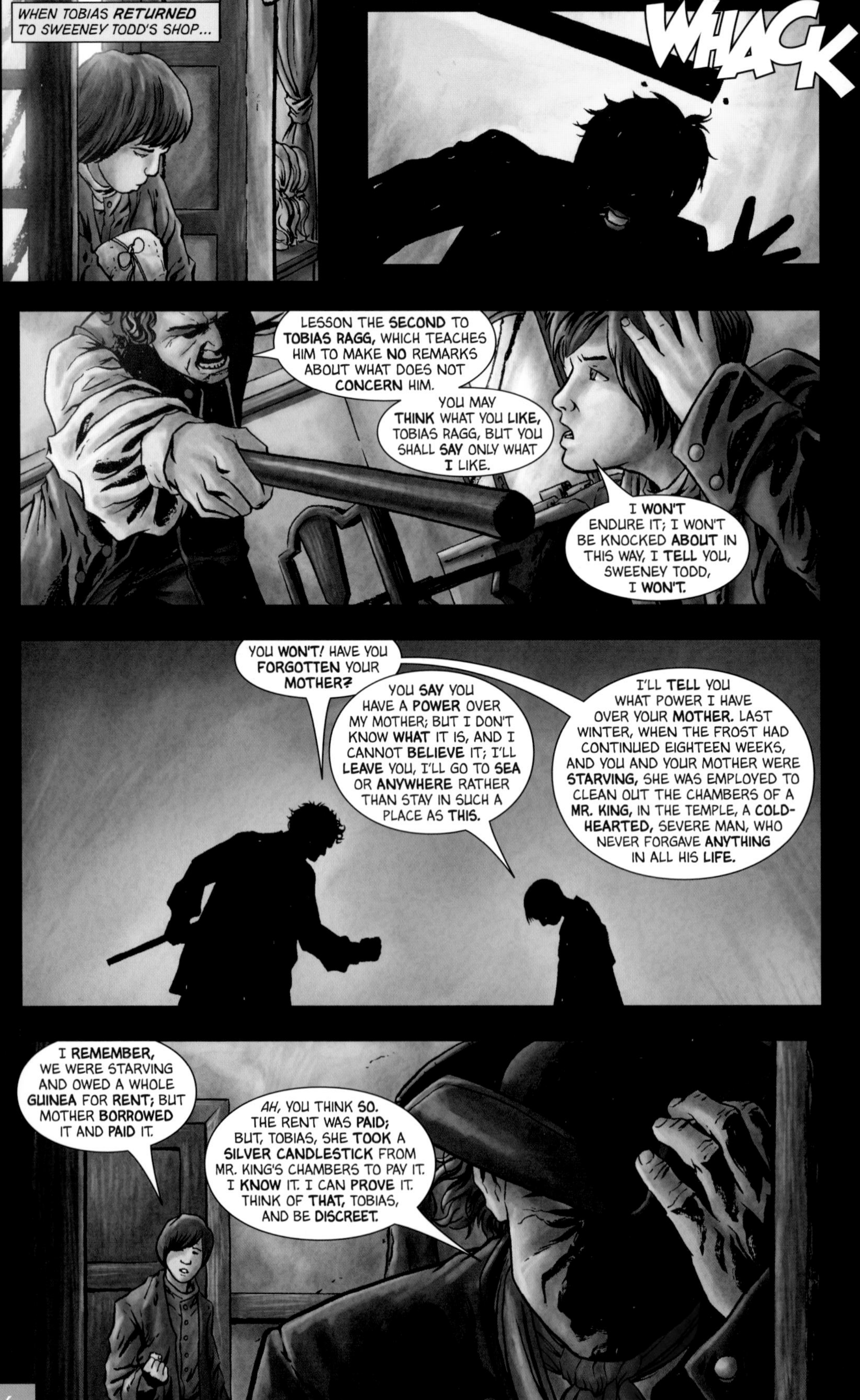
WHEN TOBIAS RETURNED TO SWEENEY TODD'S SHOP...
WHACK
LESSON THE SECOND TO TOBIAS RAGG, WHICH TEACHES HIM TO MAKE NO REMARKS ABOUT WHAT DOES NOT CONCERN HIM.
YOU MAY THINK WHAT YOU LIKE, TOBIAS RAGG, BUT YOU SHALL SAY ONLY WHAT I LIKE.
I WON'T ENDURE IT; I WON'T BE KNOCKED ABOUT IN THIS WAY, I TELL YOU, SWEENEY TODD, I WON'T.
YOU WON'T! HAVE YOU FORGOTTEN YOUR MOTHER?
YOU SAY YOU HAVE A POWER OVER MY MOTHER; BUT I DON'T KNOW WHAT IT IS, AND I CANNOT BELIEVE IT; I'LL LEAVE YOU, I'LL GO TO SEA OR ANYWHERE RATHER THAN STAY IN SUCH A PLACE AS THIS.
I'LL TELL YOU WHAT POWER I HAVE OVER YOUR MOTHER. LAST WINTER, WHEN THE FROST HAD CONTINUED EIGHTEEN WEEKS, AND YOU AND YOUR MOTHER WERE STARVING, SHE WAS EMPLOYED TO CLEAN OUT THE CHAMBERS OF A MR. KING, IN THE TEMPLE, A COLD-HEARTED, SEVERE MAN, WHO NEVER FORGAVE ANYTHING IN ALL HIS LIFE.
I REMEMBER, WE WERE STARVING AND OWED A WHOLE GUINEA FOR RENT; BUT MOTHER BORROWED IT AND PAID IT.
AH, YOU THINK SO. THE RENT WAS PAID; BUT, TOBIAS, SHE TOOK A SILVER CANDLESTICK FROM MR. KING'S CHAMBERS TO PAY IT. I KNOW IT. I CAN PROVE IT. THINK OF THAT, TOBIAS, AND BE DISCREET.

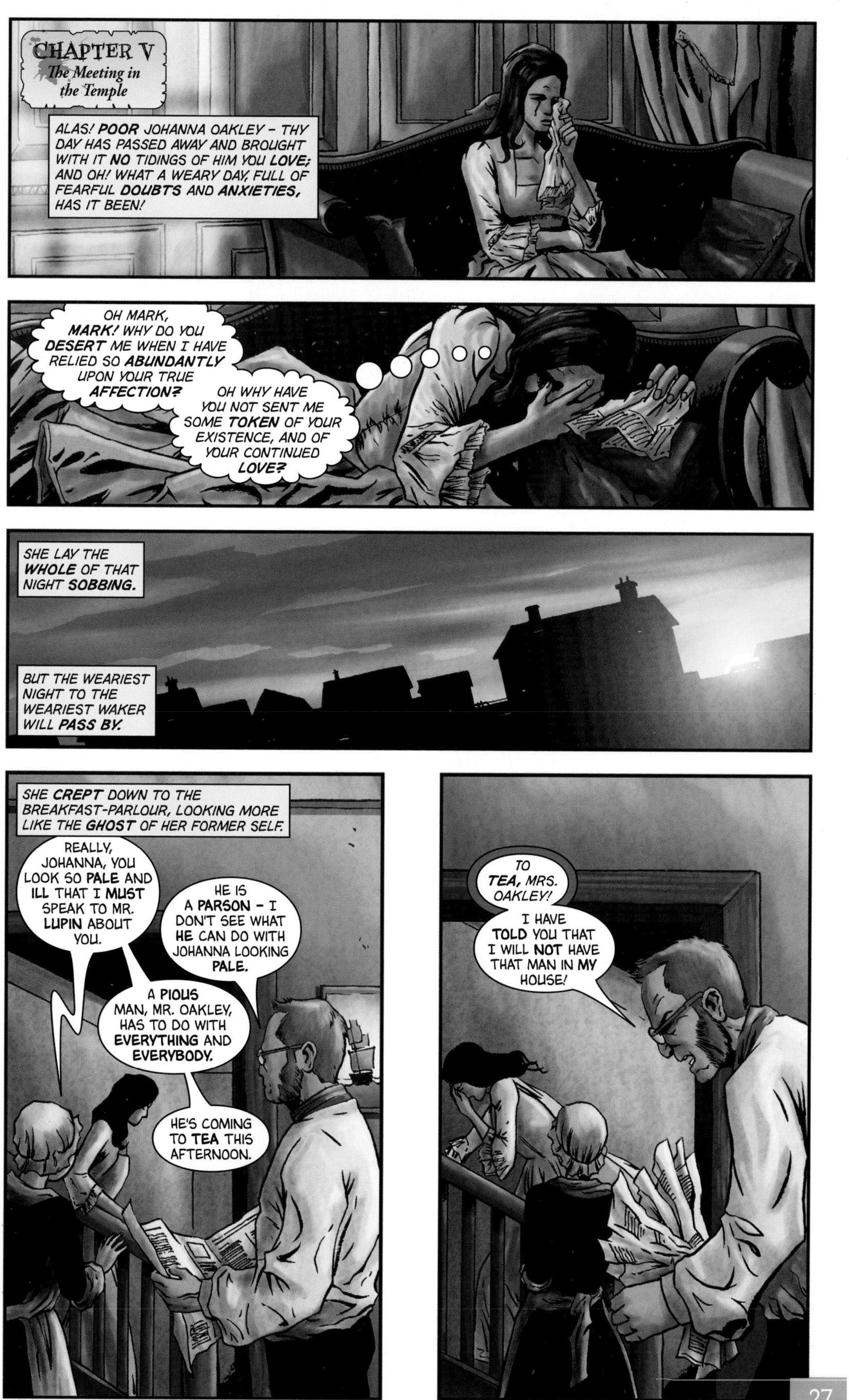
CHAPTER V
The Meeting in the Temple
ALAS! POOR JOHANNA OAKLEY – THY DAY HAS PASSED AWAY AND BROUGHT WITH IT NO TIDINGS OF HIM YOU LOVE; AND OH! WHAT A WEARY DAY, FULL OF FEARFUL DOUBTS AND ANXIETIES, HAS IT BEEN!
OH MARK, MARK! WHY DO YOU DESERT ME WHEN I HAVE RELIED SO ABUNDANTLY UPON YOUR TRUE AFFECTION?
OH WHY HAVE YOU NOT SENT ME SOME TOKEN OF YOUR EXISTENCE, AND OF YOUR CONTINUED LOVE?
SHE LAY THE WHOLE OF THAT NIGHT SOBBING.
BUT THE WEARIEST NIGHT TO THE WEARIEST WAKER WILL PASS BY.
SHE CREPT DOWN TO THE BREAKFAST-PARLOUR, LOOKING MORE LIKE THE GHOST OF HER FORMER SELF.
REALLY, JOHANNA, YOU LOOK SO PALE AND ILL THAT I MUST SPEAK TO MR. LUPIN ABOUT YOU.
HE IS A PARSON – I DON'T SEE WHAT HE CAN DO WITH JOHANNA LOOKING PALE.
A PIOUS MAN, MR. OAKLEY, HAS TO DO WITH EVERYTHING AND EVERYBODY.
HE'S COMING TO TEA THIS AFTERNOON.
TO TEA, MRS. OAKLEY!
I HAVE TOLD YOU THAT I WILL NOT HAVE THAT MAN IN MY HOUSE!

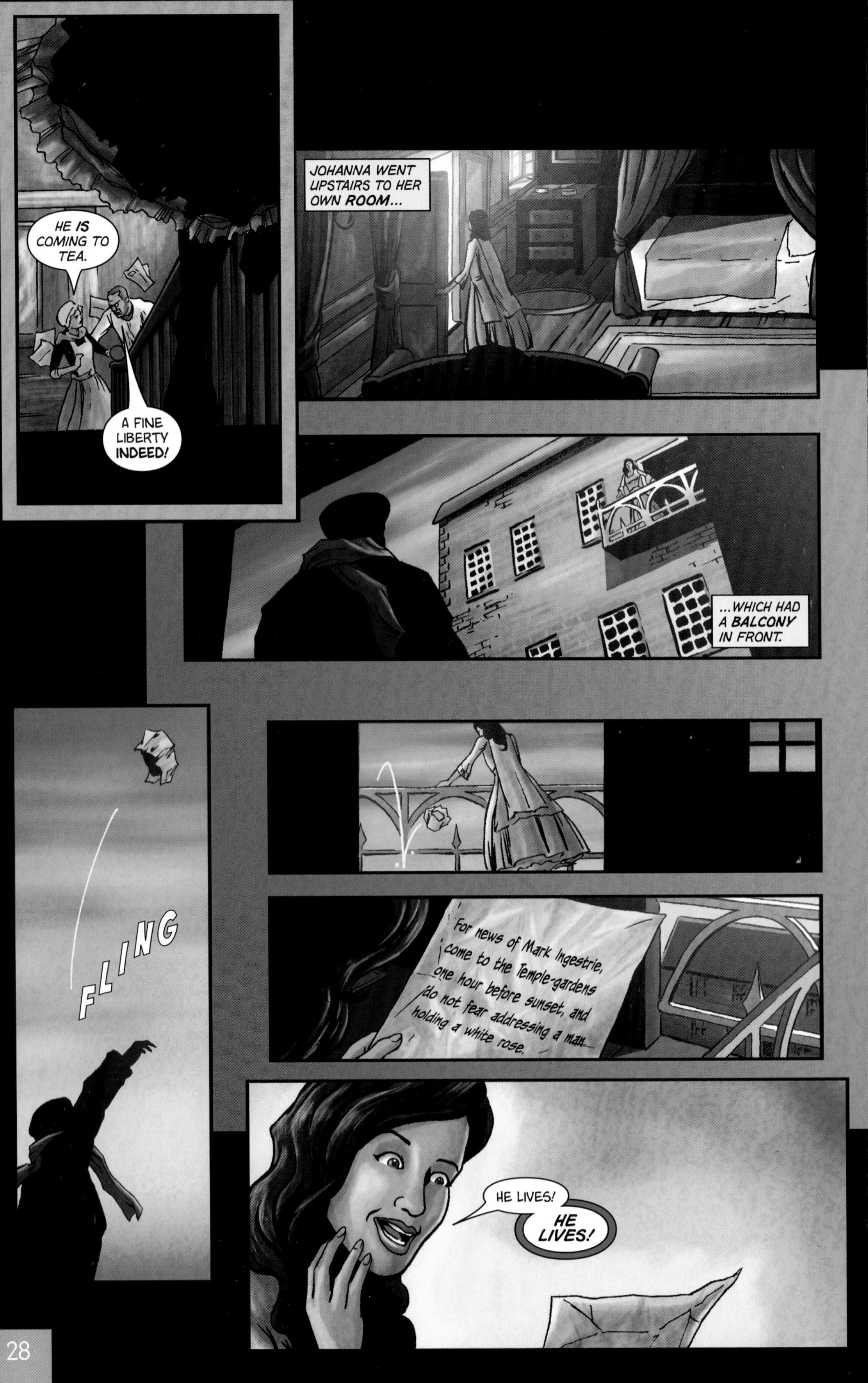
HE IS COMING TO TEA.
A FINE LIBERTY INDEED!
JOHANNA WENT UPSTAIRS TO HER OWN ROOM...
...WHICH HAD A BALCONY IN FRONT.
FLING
For news of Mark Ingestrie, come to the Temple-gardens one hour before sunset, and do not fear addressing a man holding a white rose.
HE LIVES!
HE LIVES!

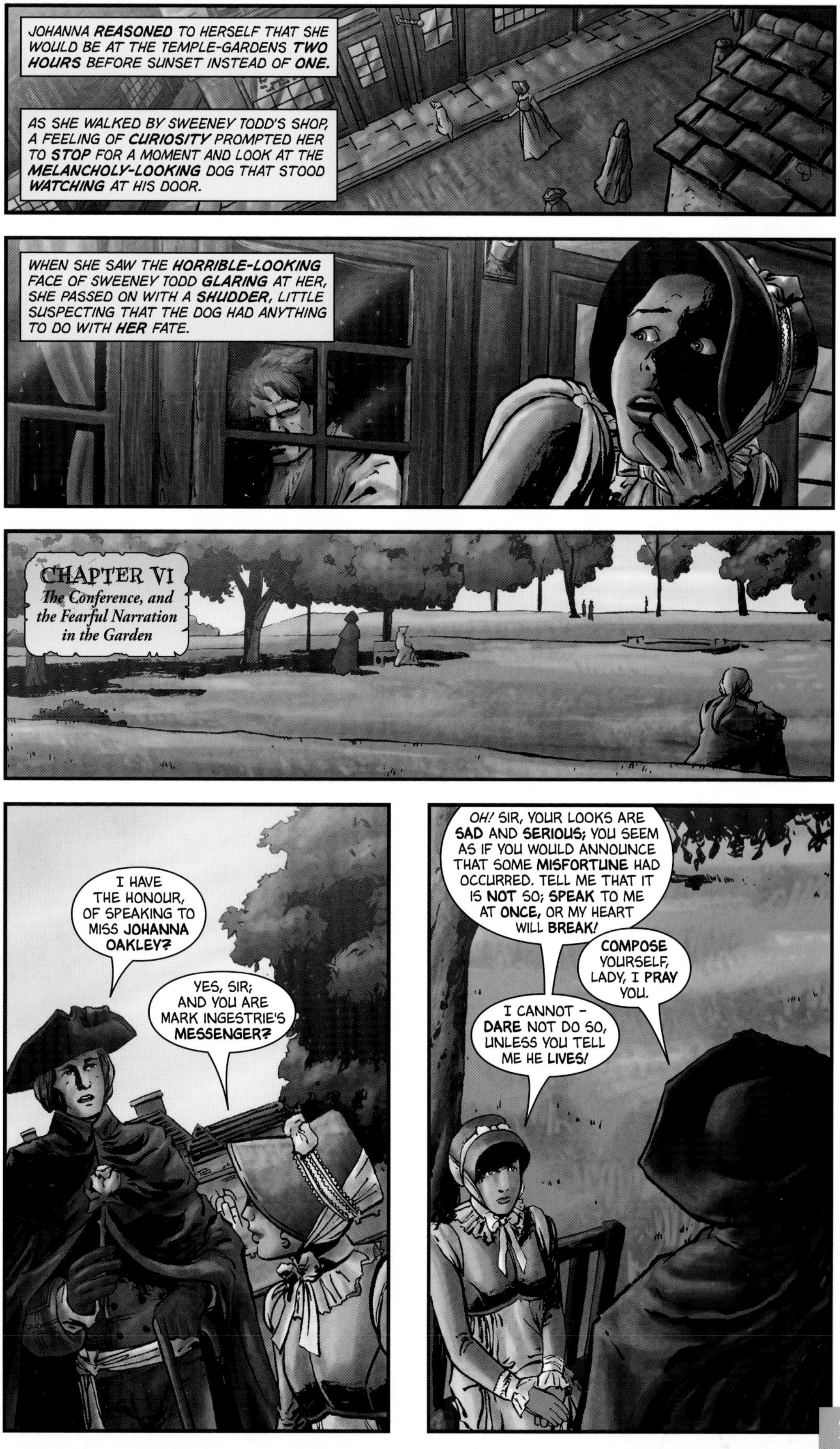
JOHANNA REASONED TO HERSELF THAT SHE WOULD BE AT THE TEMPLE-GARDENS TWO HOURS BEFORE SUNSET INSTEAD OF ONE.
AS SHE WALKED BY SWEENEY TODD'S SHOP, A FEELING OF CURIOSITY PROMPTED HER TO STOP FOR A MOMENT AND LOOK AT THE MELANCHOLY-LOOKING DOG THAT STOOD WATCHING AT HIS DOOR.
WHEN SHE SAW THE HORRIBLE-LOOKING FACE OF SWEENEY TODD GLARING AT HER, SHE PASSED ON WITH A SHUDDER, LITTLE SUSPECTING THAT THE DOG HAD ANYTHING TO DO WITH HER FATE.
CHAPTER VI
The Conference, and the Fearful Narration in the Garden
I HAVE THE HONOUR, OF SPEAKING TO MISS JOHANNA OAKLEY?
YES, SIR; AND YOU ARE MARK INGESTRIE'S MESSENGER?
OH! SIR, YOUR LOOKS ARE SAD AND SERIOUS; YOU SEEM AS IF YOU WOULD ANNOUNCE THAT SOME MISFORTUNE HAD OCCURRED. TELL ME THAT IT IS NOT SO; SPEAK TO ME AT ONCE, OR MY HEART WILL BREAK!
COMPOSE YOURSELF, LADY, I PRAY YOU.
I CANNOT - DARE NOT DO SO, UNLESS YOU TELL ME HE LIVES!

THERE IS MUCH TO **HEAR** AND MUCH TO **SPECULATE** UPON; AND IF, FROM ALL THAT I HAVE LEARNT, I CANNOT, **DARE** NOT TELL YOU THAT MARK INGESTRIE **LIVES**, I **LIKEWISE** SHRINK FROM TELLING YOU HE IS **NO MORE.**

THERE **IS** A HOPE, THEN – OH, THERE IS A HOPE!

THERE **IS** A HOPE, BUT PLEASE LISTEN TO MY **STORY.**

I SHALL **LISTEN** TO YOU WITH MY WHOLE **SOUL.**

"MY NAME IS **JEFFERY**, AND I AM A COLONEL IN THE **INDIAN ARMY.** I NEVER **MET** MARK INGESTRIE. ALL THAT I **SAY** CONCERNING HIM IS FROM THE **DESCRIPTION** OF **ANOTHER** WHO **DID** KNOW HIM **WELL**, AND WHO **SAILED** WITH HIM IN THE VESSEL, THE **STAR**, THAT LEFT THE PORT OF LONDON ON THE VAGUE AND **WILD** ADVENTURE I WILL NOW **RECOUNT.**

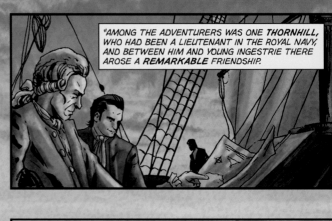

"AMONG THE ADVENTURERS WAS ONE **THORNHILL**, WHO HAD BEEN A LIEUTENANT IN THE ROYAL NAVY, AND BETWEEN HIM AND YOUNG INGESTRIE THERE AROSE A **REMARKABLE** FRIENDSHIP.

"IT APPEARS THAT WITHOUT ACCIDENT THE STAR **REACHED** THE **INDIAN OCEAN**, AND THE SUPPOSED IMMEDIATE LOCALITY OF THE SPOT WHERE THE **TREASURE** WAS TO BE FOUND, AND THERE SHE WAS SPOKEN WITH BY A VESSEL **HOMEWARD-BOUND** FROM INDIA, CALLED THE **NEPTUNE.** I WAS ON BOARD THE NEPTUNE.

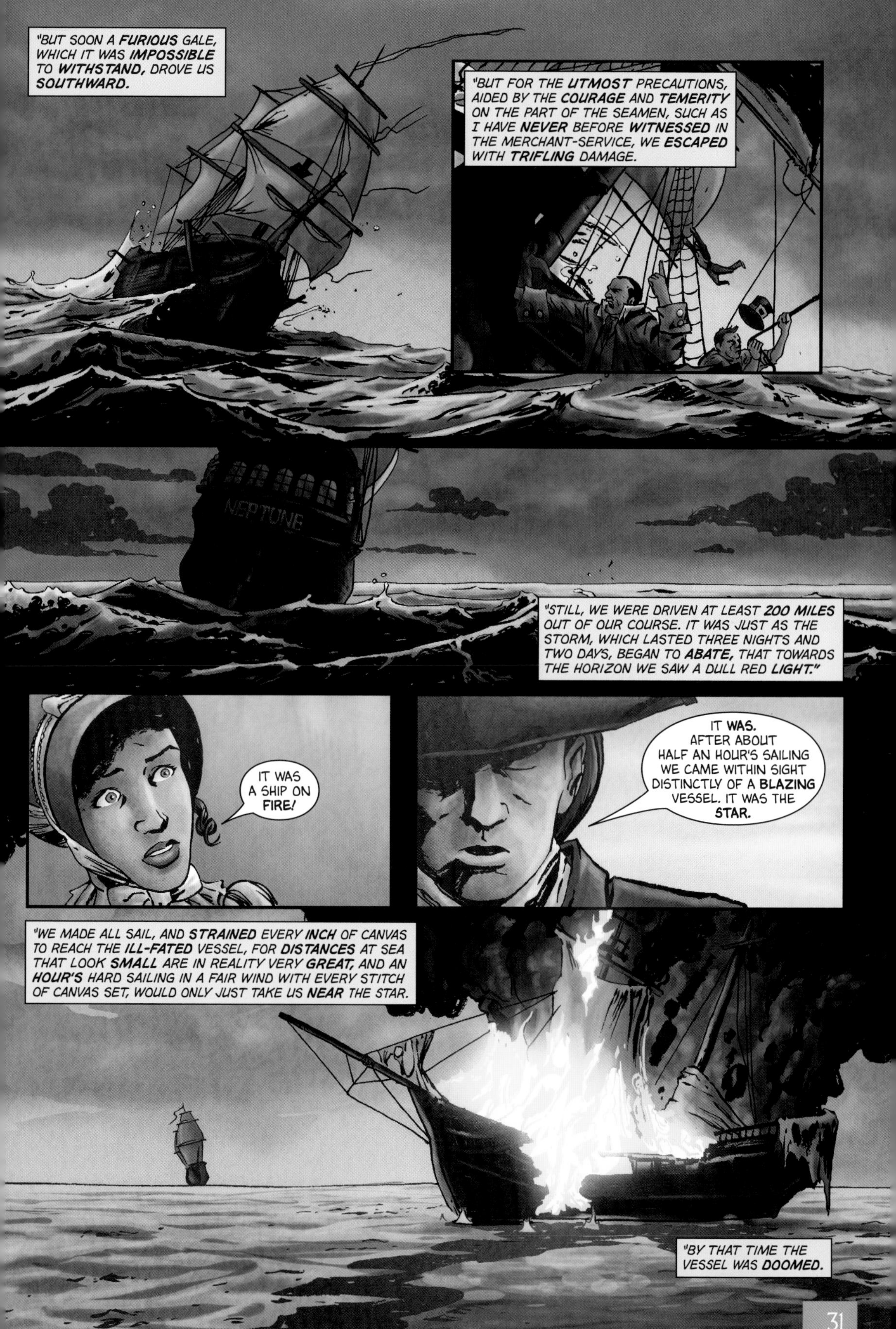
"BUT SOON A **FURIOUS** GALE, WHICH IT WAS **IMPOSSIBLE** TO **WITHSTAND,** DROVE US **SOUTHWARD.**
"BUT FOR THE **UTMOST** PRECAUTIONS, AIDED BY THE **COURAGE** AND **TEMERITY** ON THE PART OF THE SEAMEN, SUCH AS I HAVE **NEVER** BEFORE **WITNESSED** IN THE MERCHANT-SERVICE, WE **ESCAPED** WITH **TRIFLING** DAMAGE.
NEPTUNE
"STILL, WE WERE DRIVEN AT LEAST **200 MILES** OUT OF OUR COURSE. IT WAS JUST AS THE STORM, WHICH LASTED THREE NIGHTS AND TWO DAYS, BEGAN TO **ABATE,** THAT TOWARDS THE HORIZON WE SAW A DULL RED **LIGHT.**"
IT WAS A SHIP ON **FIRE!**
IT **WAS.** AFTER ABOUT HALF AN HOUR'S SAILING WE CAME WITHIN SIGHT DISTINCTLY OF A **BLAZING** VESSEL. IT WAS THE **STAR.**
"WE MADE ALL SAIL, AND **STRAINED** EVERY **INCH** OF CANVAS TO REACH THE **ILL-FATED** VESSEL, FOR **DISTANCES** AT SEA THAT LOOK **SMALL** ARE IN REALITY VERY **GREAT,** AND AN **HOUR'S** HARD SAILING IN A FAIR WIND WITH EVERY STITCH OF CANVAS SET, WOULD ONLY JUST TAKE US **NEAR** THE STAR.
"BY THAT TIME THE VESSEL WAS **DOOMED.**

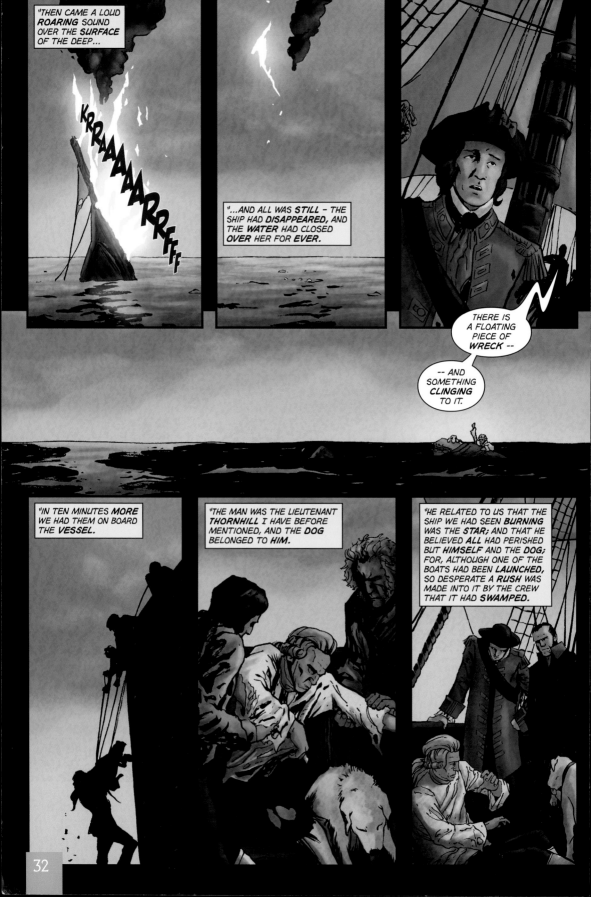

"THEN CAME A LOUD **ROARING** SOUND OVER THE **SURFACE** OF THE DEEP...

KRRAAAAARRFFF

"...AND ALL WAS **STILL** – THE SHIP HAD **DISAPPEARED**, AND THE **WATER** HAD CLOSED **OVER** HER FOR **EVER**.

THERE IS A FLOATING PIECE OF **WRECK** --

-- AND SOMETHING **CLINGING** TO IT.

"IN TEN MINUTES **MORE** WE HAD THEM ON BOARD THE **VESSEL**.

"THE MAN WAS THE LIEUTENANT **THORNHILL** I HAVE BEFORE MENTIONED, AND THE **DOG** BELONGED TO **HIM**.

"HE RELATED TO US THAT THE SHIP WE HAD SEEN **BURNING** WAS THE **STAR**; AND THAT HE BELIEVED **ALL** HAD PERISHED BUT **HIMSELF** AND THE **DOG**; FOR, ALTHOUGH ONE OF THE BOATS HAD BEEN **LAUNCHED**, SO DESPERATE A **RUSH** WAS MADE INTO IT BY THE CREW THAT IT HAD **SWAMPED**.

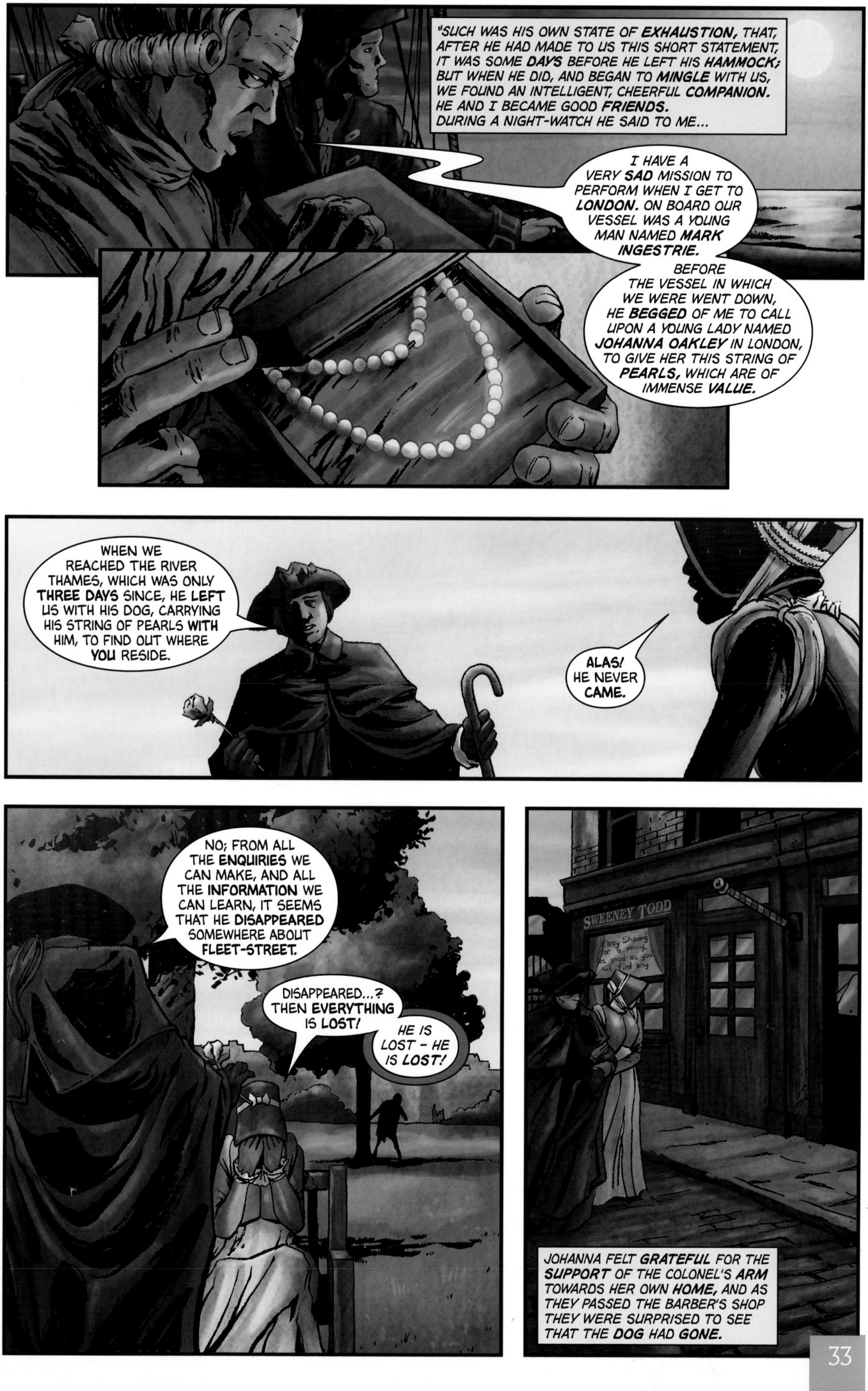
"SUCH WAS HIS OWN STATE OF EXHAUSTION, THAT, AFTER HE HAD MADE TO US THIS SHORT STATEMENT, IT WAS SOME DAYS BEFORE HE LEFT HIS HAMMOCK; BUT WHEN HE DID, AND BEGAN TO MINGLE WITH US, WE FOUND AN INTELLIGENT, CHEERFUL COMPANION. HE AND I BECAME GOOD FRIENDS. DURING A NIGHT-WATCH HE SAID TO ME...
I HAVE A VERY SAD MISSION TO PERFORM WHEN I GET TO LONDON. ON BOARD OUR VESSEL WAS A YOUNG MAN NAMED MARK INGESTRIE.
BEFORE THE VESSEL IN WHICH WE WERE WENT DOWN, HE BEGGED OF ME TO CALL UPON A YOUNG LADY NAMED JOHANNA OAKLEY IN LONDON, TO GIVE HER THIS STRING OF PEARLS, WHICH ARE OF IMMENSE VALUE.
WHEN WE REACHED THE RIVER THAMES, WHICH WAS ONLY THREE DAYS SINCE, HE LEFT US WITH HIS DOG, CARRYING HIS STRING OF PEARLS WITH HIM, TO FIND OUT WHERE YOU RESIDE.
ALAS! HE NEVER CAME.
NO; FROM ALL THE ENQUIRIES WE CAN MAKE, AND ALL THE INFORMATION WE CAN LEARN, IT SEEMS THAT HE DISAPPEARED SOMEWHERE ABOUT FLEET-STREET.
DISAPPEARED...? THEN EVERYTHING IS LOST!
HE IS LOST – HE IS LOST!
SWEENEY TODD
Easy Shaving for a penny, as good as you will find any
JOHANNA FELT GRATEFUL FOR THE SUPPORT OF THE COLONEL'S ARM TOWARDS HER OWN HOME, AND AS THEY PASSED THE BARBER'S SHOP THEY WERE SURPRISED TO SEE THAT THE DOG HAD GONE.

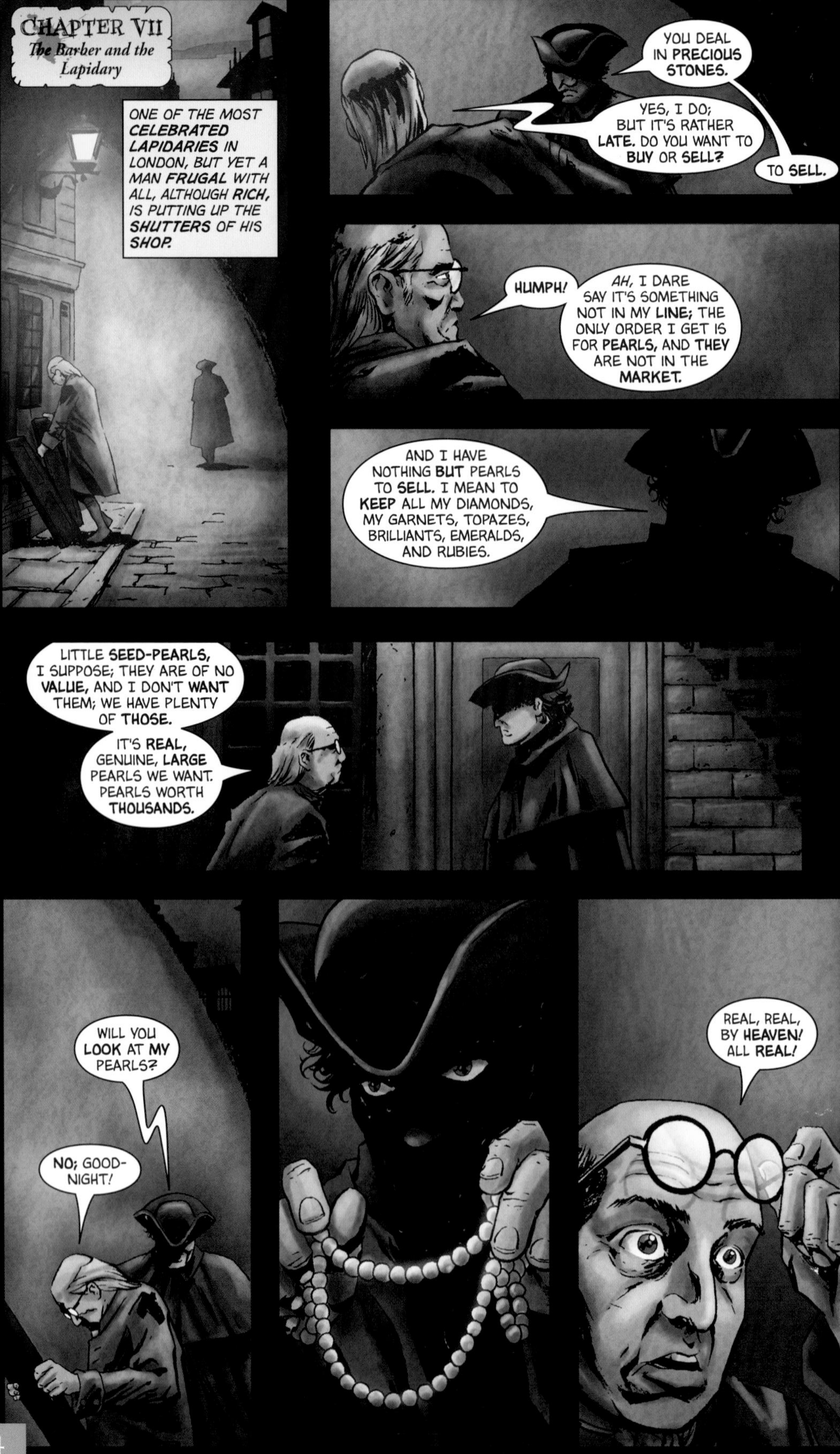
CHAPTER VII
The Barber and the Lapidary
ONE OF THE MOST CELEBRATED LAPIDARIES IN LONDON, BUT YET A MAN FRUGAL WITH ALL, ALTHOUGH RICH, IS PUTTING UP THE SHUTTERS OF HIS SHOP.
YOU DEAL IN PRECIOUS STONES.
YES, I DO; BUT IT'S RATHER LATE. DO YOU WANT TO BUY OR SELL?
TO SELL.
HUMPH!
AH, I DARE SAY IT'S SOMETHING NOT IN MY LINE; THE ONLY ORDER I GET IS FOR PEARLS, AND THEY ARE NOT IN THE MARKET.
AND I HAVE NOTHING BUT PEARLS TO SELL. I MEAN TO KEEP ALL MY DIAMONDS, MY GARNETS, TOPAZES, BRILLIANTS, EMERALDS, AND RUBIES.
LITTLE SEED-PEARLS, I SUPPOSE; THEY ARE OF NO VALUE, AND I DON'T WANT THEM; WE HAVE PLENTY OF THOSE.
IT'S REAL, GENUINE, LARGE PEARLS WE WANT. PEARLS WORTH THOUSANDS.
WILL YOU LOOK AT MY PEARLS?
NO; GOOD-NIGHT!
REAL, REAL, BY HEAVEN! ALL REAL!

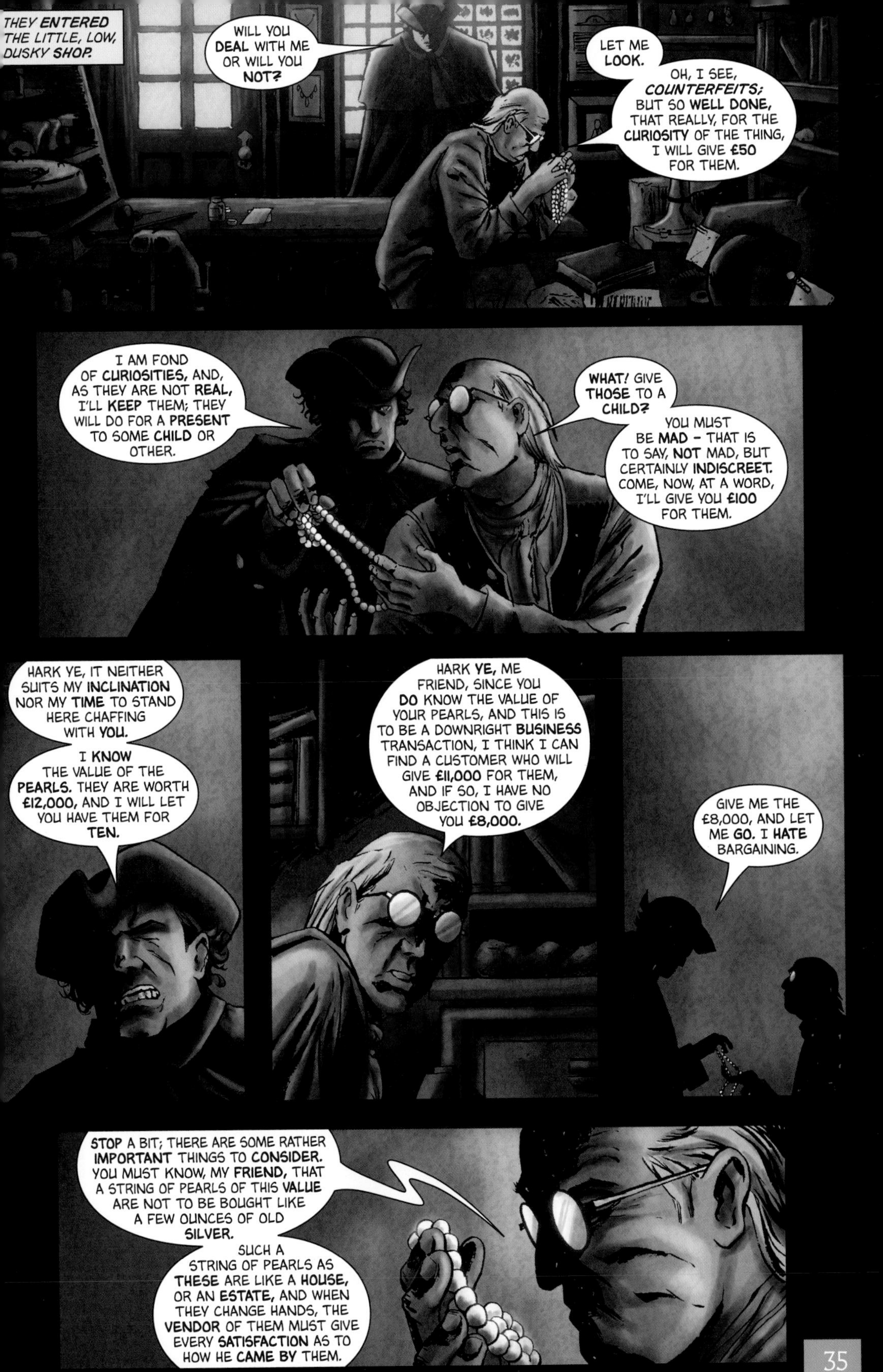
THEY ENTERED THE LITTLE, LOW, DUSKY SHOP.
WILL YOU DEAL WITH ME OR WILL YOU NOT?
LET ME LOOK.
OH, I SEE, COUNTERFEITS; BUT SO WELL DONE, THAT REALLY, FOR THE CURIOSITY OF THE THING, I WILL GIVE £50 FOR THEM.
I AM FOND OF CURIOSITIES, AND, AS THEY ARE NOT REAL, I'LL KEEP THEM; THEY WILL DO FOR A PRESENT TO SOME CHILD OR OTHER.
WHAT! GIVE THOSE TO A CHILD?
YOU MUST BE MAD – THAT IS TO SAY, NOT MAD, BUT CERTAINLY INDISCREET. COME, NOW, AT A WORD, I'LL GIVE YOU £100 FOR THEM.
HARK YE, IT NEITHER SUITS MY INCLINATION NOR MY TIME TO STAND HERE CHAFFING WITH YOU.
I KNOW THE VALUE OF THE PEARLS. THEY ARE WORTH £12,000, AND I WILL LET YOU HAVE THEM FOR TEN.
HARK YE, ME FRIEND, SINCE YOU DO KNOW THE VALUE OF YOUR PEARLS, AND THIS IS TO BE A DOWNRIGHT BUSINESS TRANSACTION, I THINK I CAN FIND A CUSTOMER WHO WILL GIVE £11,000 FOR THEM, AND IF SO, I HAVE NO OBJECTION TO GIVE YOU £8,000.
GIVE ME THE £8,000, AND LET ME GO. I HATE BARGAINING.
STOP A BIT; THERE ARE SOME RATHER IMPORTANT THINGS TO CONSIDER. YOU MUST KNOW, MY FRIEND, THAT A STRING OF PEARLS OF THIS VALUE ARE NOT TO BE BOUGHT LIKE A FEW OUNCES OF OLD SILVER.
SUCH A STRING OF PEARLS AS THESE ARE LIKE A HOUSE, OR AN ESTATE, AND WHEN THEY CHANGE HANDS, THE VENDOR OF THEM MUST GIVE EVERY SATISFACTION AS TO HOW HE CAME BY THEM.

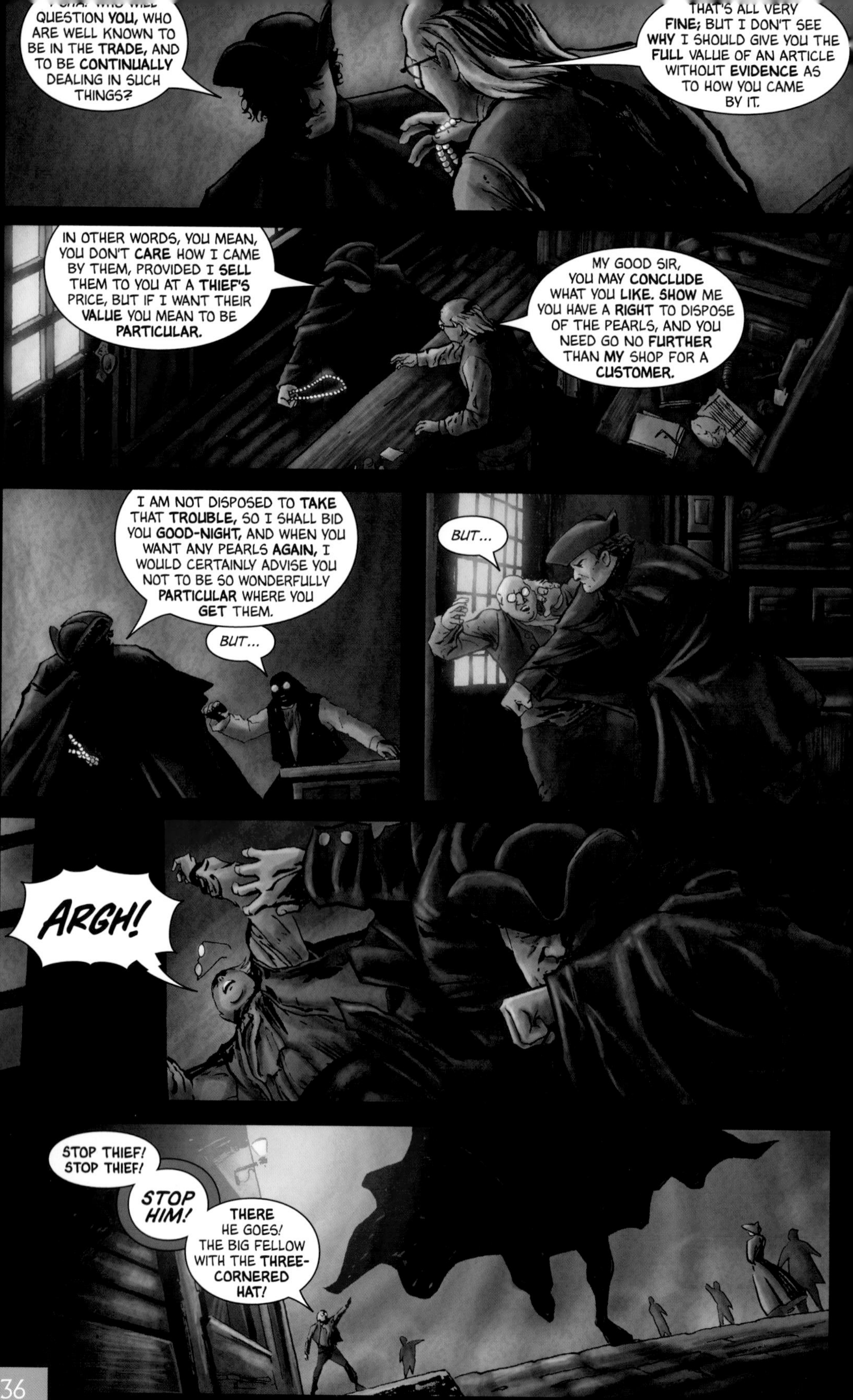
QUESTION YOU, WHO ARE WELL KNOWN TO BE IN THE TRADE, AND TO BE CONTINUALLY DEALING IN SUCH THINGS?
THAT'S ALL VERY FINE; BUT I DON'T SEE WHY I SHOULD GIVE YOU THE FULL VALUE OF AN ARTICLE WITHOUT EVIDENCE AS TO HOW YOU CAME BY IT.
IN OTHER WORDS, YOU MEAN, YOU DON'T CARE HOW I CAME BY THEM, PROVIDED I SELL THEM TO YOU AT A THIEF'S PRICE, BUT IF I WANT THEIR VALUE YOU MEAN TO BE PARTICULAR.
MY GOOD SIR, YOU MAY CONCLUDE WHAT YOU LIKE. SHOW ME YOU HAVE A RIGHT TO DISPOSE OF THE PEARLS, AND YOU NEED GO NO FURTHER THAN MY SHOP FOR A CUSTOMER.
I AM NOT DISPOSED TO TAKE THAT TROUBLE, SO I SHALL BID YOU GOOD-NIGHT, AND WHEN YOU WANT ANY PEARLS AGAIN, I WOULD CERTAINLY ADVISE YOU NOT TO BE SO WONDERFULLY PARTICULAR WHERE YOU GET THEM.
BUT...
BUT...
ARGH!
STOP THIEF! STOP THIEF!
STOP HIM!
THERE HE GOES! THE BIG FELLOW WITH THE THREE-CORNERED HAT!

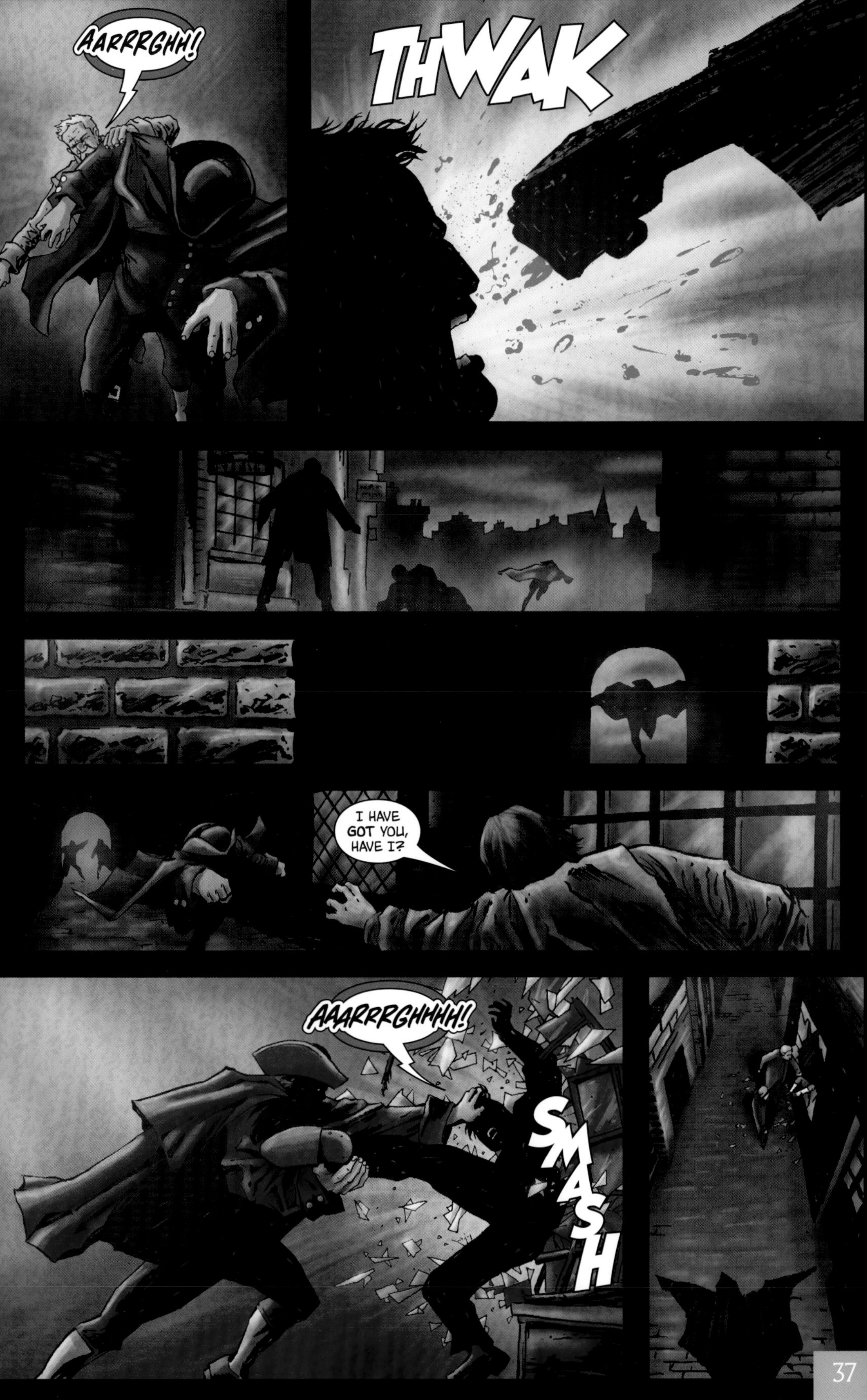
AARRRGHH!
THWAK
I HAVE GOT YOU, HAVE I?
AAARRRGHHHH!
SMASH

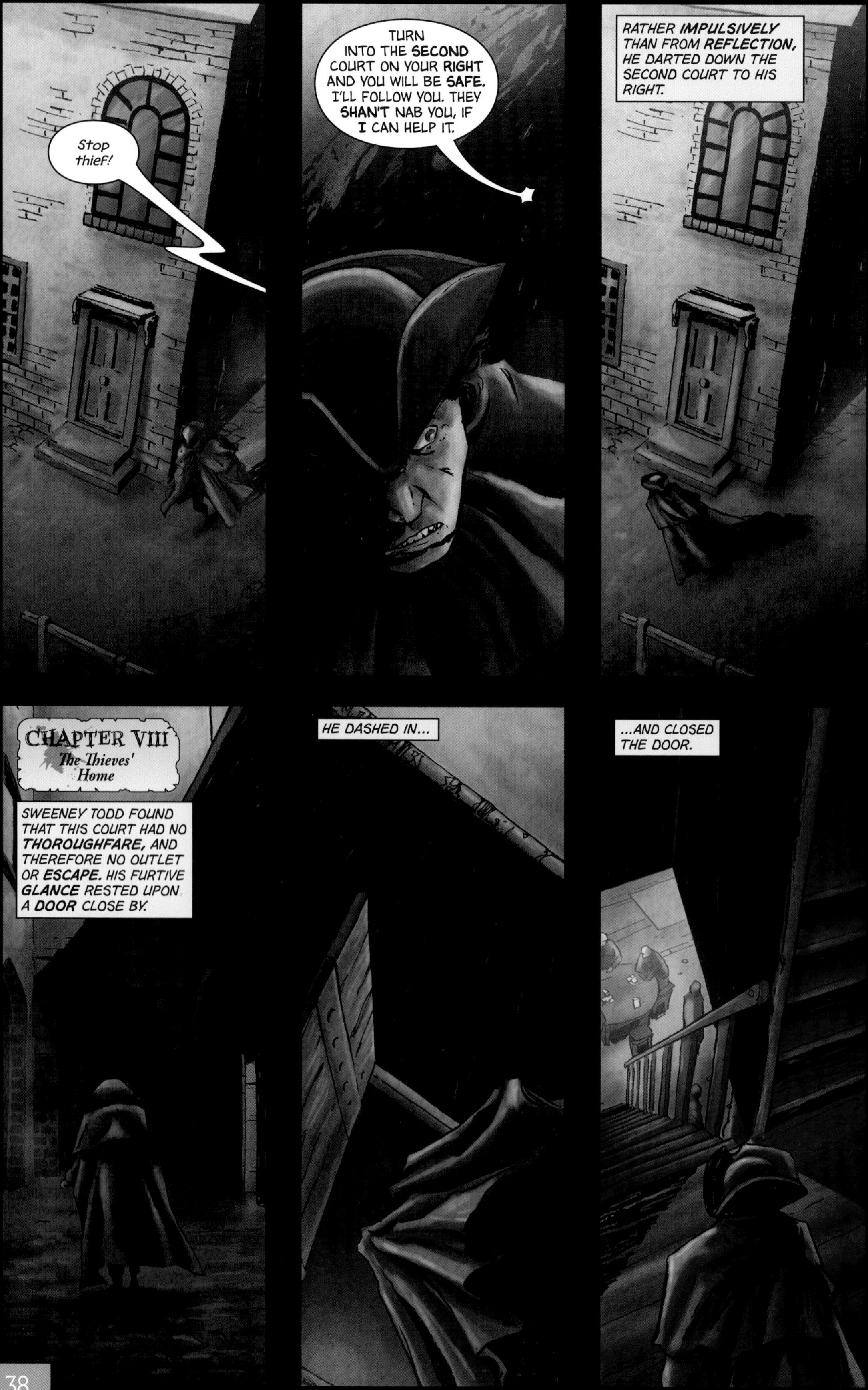
Stop thief!
TURN INTO THE SECOND COURT ON YOUR RIGHT AND YOU WILL BE SAFE. I'LL FOLLOW YOU. THEY SHAN'T NAB YOU, IF I CAN HELP IT.
RATHER IMPULSIVELY THAN FROM REFLECTION, HE DARTED DOWN THE SECOND COURT TO HIS RIGHT.
CHAPTER VIII
The Thieves' Home
SWEENEY TODD FOUND THAT THIS COURT HAD NO THOROUGHFARE, AND THEREFORE NO OUTLET OR ESCAPE. HIS FURTIVE GLANCE RESTED UPON A DOOR CLOSE BY.
HE DASHED IN...
...AND CLOSED THE DOOR.

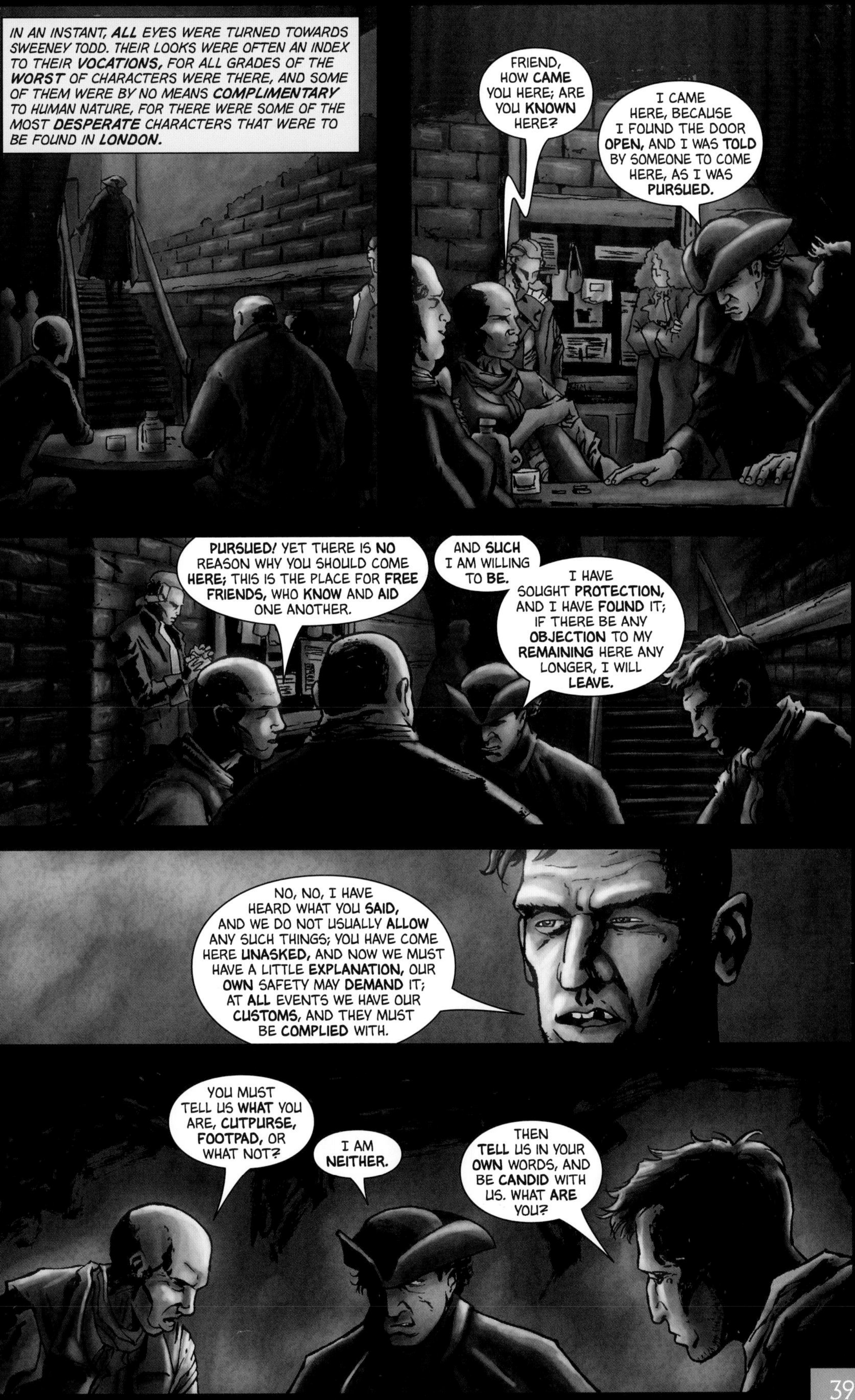
IN AN INSTANT, ALL EYES WERE TURNED TOWARDS SWEENEY TODD. THEIR LOOKS WERE OFTEN AN INDEX TO THEIR VOCATIONS, FOR ALL GRADES OF THE WORST OF CHARACTERS WERE THERE, AND SOME OF THEM WERE BY NO MEANS COMPLIMENTARY TO HUMAN NATURE, FOR THERE WERE SOME OF THE MOST DESPERATE CHARACTERS THAT WERE TO BE FOUND IN LONDON.
FRIEND, HOW CAME YOU HERE; ARE YOU KNOWN HERE?
I CAME HERE, BECAUSE I FOUND THE DOOR OPEN, AND I WAS TOLD BY SOMEONE TO COME HERE, AS I WAS PURSUED.
PURSUED! YET THERE IS NO REASON WHY YOU SHOULD COME HERE; THIS IS THE PLACE FOR FREE FRIENDS, WHO KNOW AND AID ONE ANOTHER.
AND SUCH I AM WILLING TO BE.
I HAVE SOUGHT PROTECTION, AND I HAVE FOUND IT; IF THERE BE ANY OBJECTION TO MY REMAINING HERE ANY LONGER, I WILL LEAVE.
NO, NO, I HAVE HEARD WHAT YOU SAID, AND WE DO NOT USUALLY ALLOW ANY SUCH THINGS; YOU HAVE COME HERE UNASKED, AND NOW WE MUST HAVE A LITTLE EXPLANATION, OUR OWN SAFETY MAY DEMAND IT; AT ALL EVENTS WE HAVE OUR CUSTOMS, AND THEY MUST BE COMPLIED WITH.
YOU MUST TELL US WHAT YOU ARE, CUTPURSE, FOOTPAD, OR WHAT NOT?
I AM NEITHER.
THEN TELL US IN YOUR OWN WORDS, AND BE CANDID WITH US. WHAT ARE YOU?

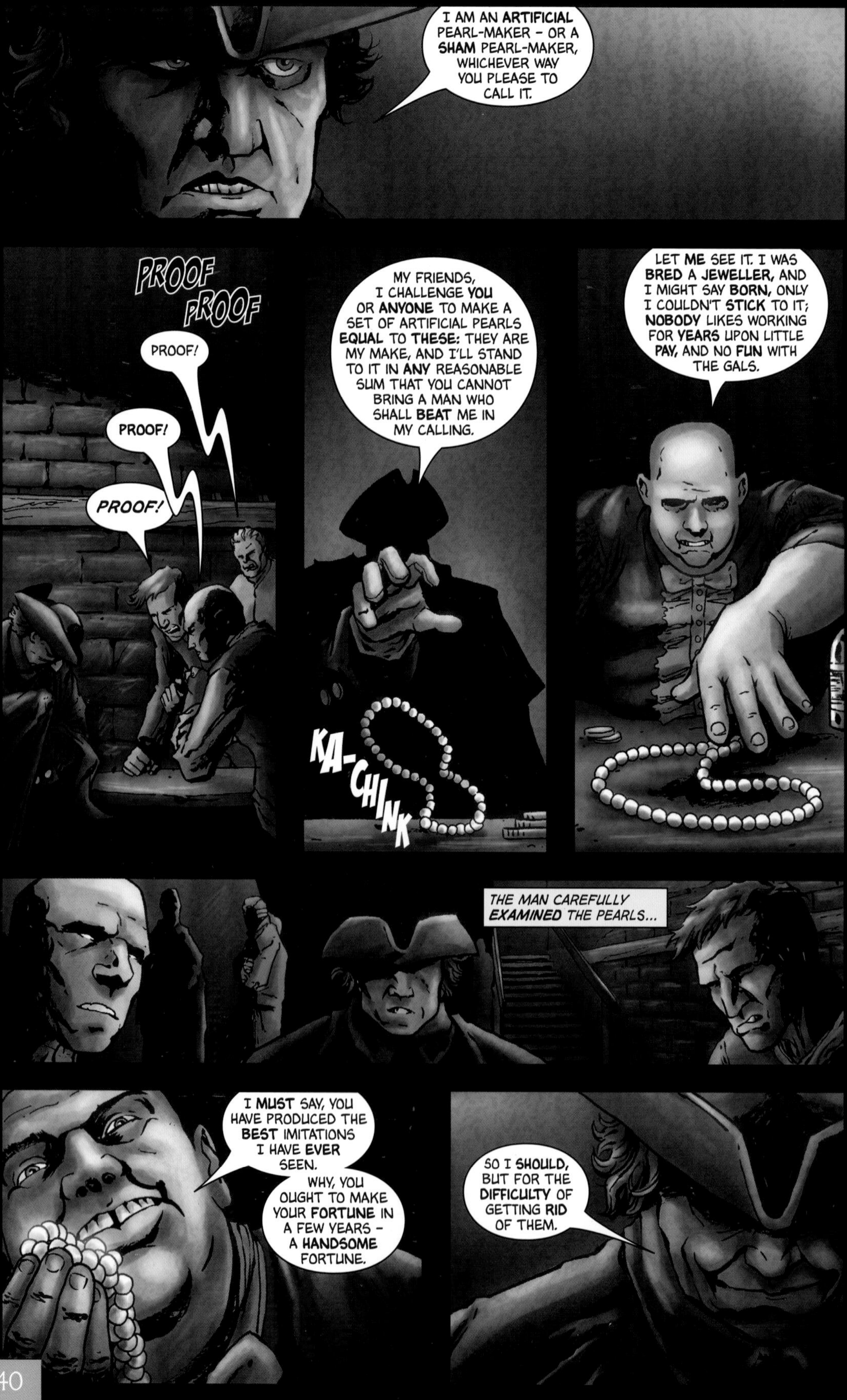
I AM AN ARTIFICIAL PEARL-MAKER – OR A SHAM PEARL-MAKER, WHICHEVER WAY YOU PLEASE TO CALL IT.
PROOF PROOF
PROOF!
PROOF!
PROOF!
MY FRIENDS, I CHALLENGE YOU OR ANYONE TO MAKE A SET OF ARTIFICIAL PEARLS EQUAL TO THESE: THEY ARE MY MAKE, AND I'LL STAND TO IT IN ANY REASONABLE SUM THAT YOU CANNOT BRING A MAN WHO SHALL BEAT ME IN MY CALLING.
KA-CHINK
LET ME SEE IT. I WAS BRED A JEWELLER, AND I MIGHT SAY BORN, ONLY I COULDN'T STICK TO IT; NOBODY LIKES WORKING FOR YEARS UPON LITTLE PAY, AND NO FUN WITH THE GALS.
THE MAN CAREFULLY EXAMINED THE PEARLS...
I MUST SAY, YOU HAVE PRODUCED THE BEST IMITATIONS I HAVE EVER SEEN.
WHY, YOU OUGHT TO MAKE YOUR FORTUNE IN A FEW YEARS – A HANDSOME FORTUNE.
SO I SHOULD, BUT FOR THE DIFFICULTY OF GETTING RID OF THEM.

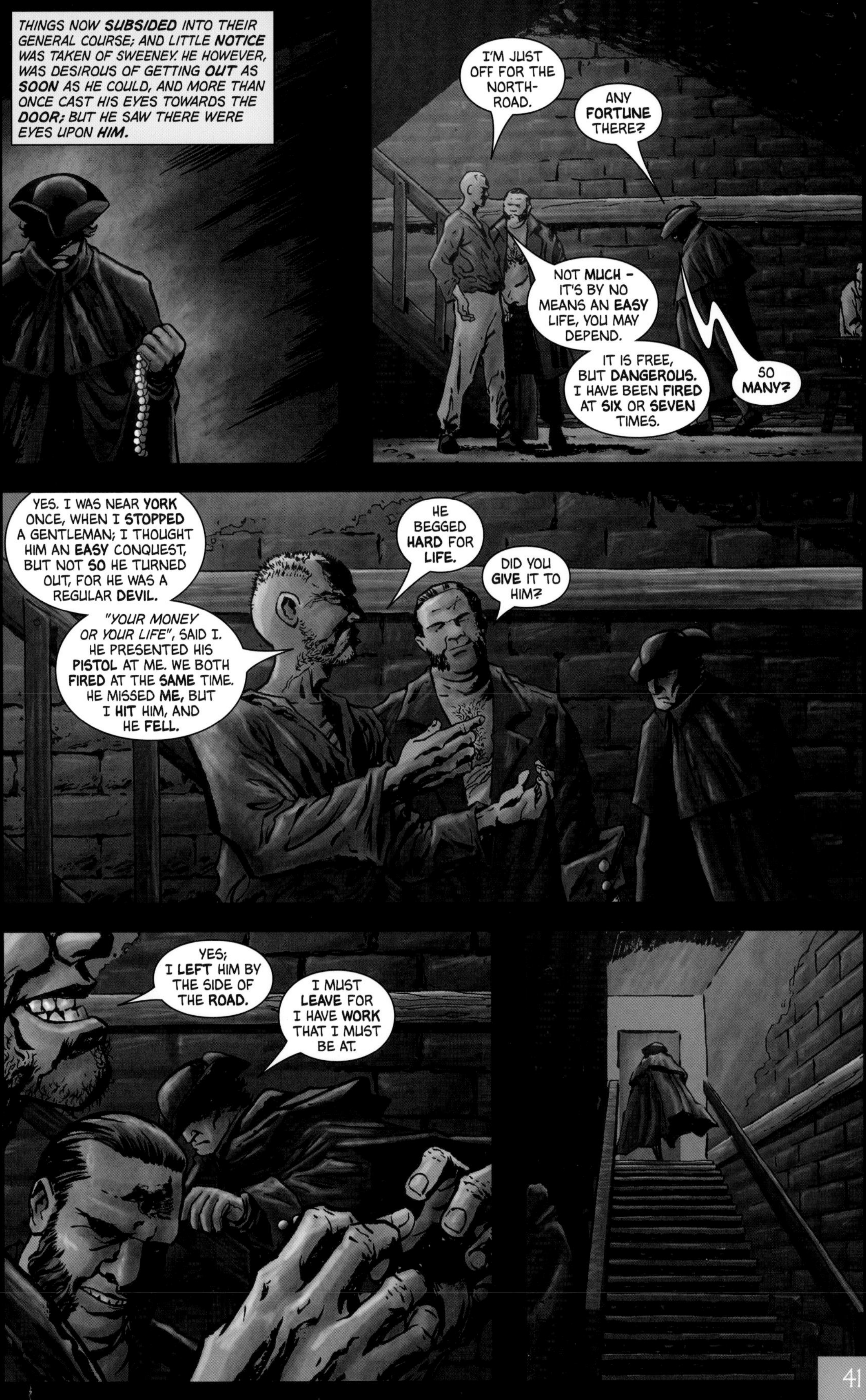
THINGS NOW SUBSIDED INTO THEIR GENERAL COURSE; AND LITTLE NOTICE WAS TAKEN OF SWEENEY. HE HOWEVER, WAS DESIROUS OF GETTING OUT AS SOON AS HE COULD, AND MORE THAN ONCE CAST HIS EYES TOWARDS THE DOOR; BUT HE SAW THERE WERE EYES UPON HIM.
I'M JUST OFF FOR THE NORTH-ROAD.
ANY FORTUNE THERE?
NOT MUCH - IT'S BY NO MEANS AN EASY LIFE, YOU MAY DEPEND.
IT IS FREE, BUT DANGEROUS. I HAVE BEEN FIRED AT SIX OR SEVEN TIMES.
SO MANY?
YES. I WAS NEAR YORK ONCE, WHEN I STOPPED A GENTLEMAN; I THOUGHT HIM AN EASY CONQUEST, BUT NOT SO HE TURNED OUT, FOR HE WAS A REGULAR DEVIL.
"YOUR MONEY OR YOUR LIFE", SAID I. HE PRESENTED HIS PISTOL AT ME. WE BOTH FIRED AT THE SAME TIME. HE MISSED ME, BUT I HIT HIM, AND HE FELL.
HE BEGGED HARD FOR LIFE.
DID YOU GIVE IT TO HIM?
YES; I LEFT HIM BY THE SIDE OF THE ROAD.
I MUST LEAVE FOR I HAVE WORK THAT I MUST BE AT.

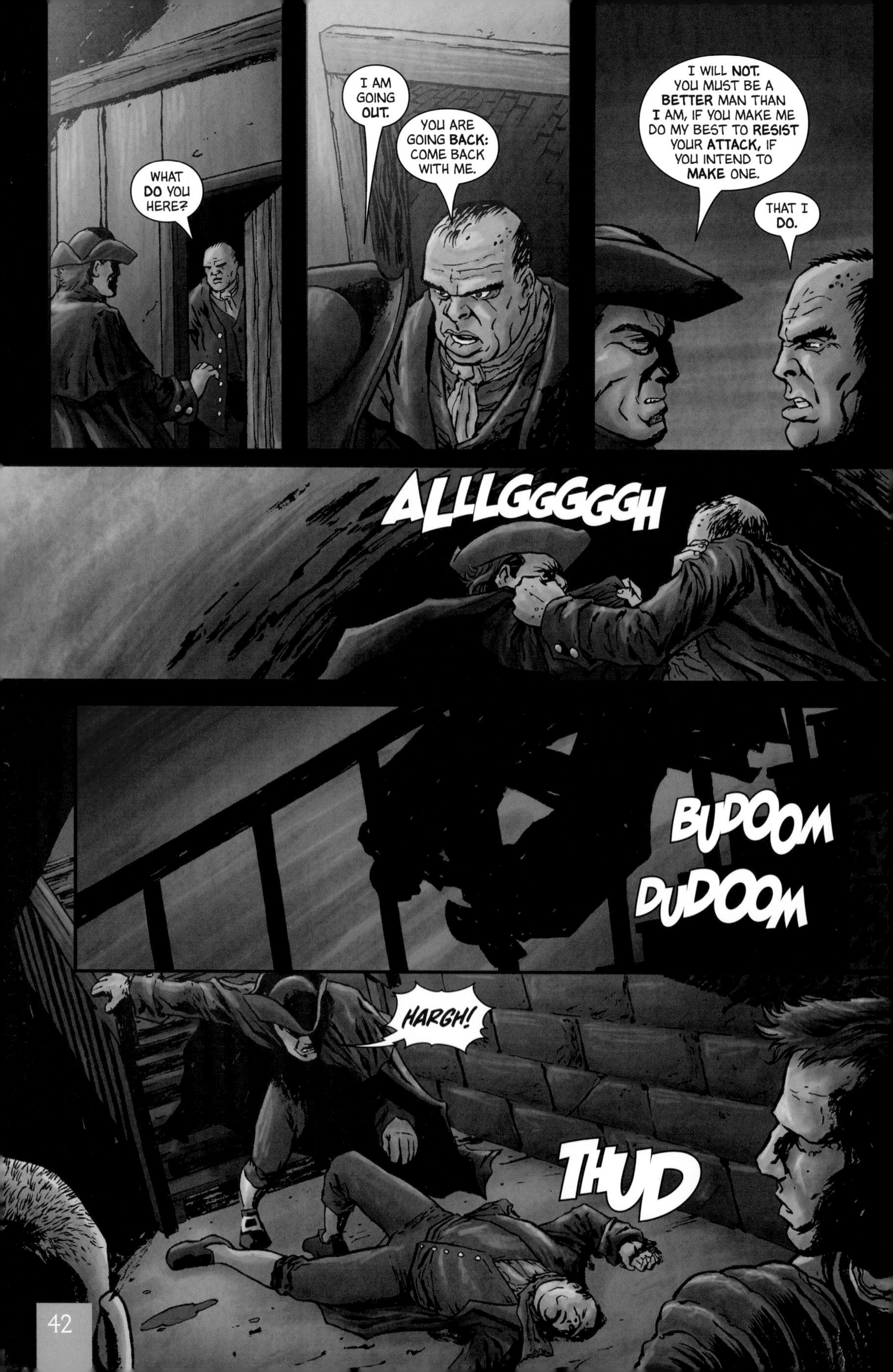
WHAT DO YOU HERE?
I AM GOING OUT.
YOU ARE GOING BACK: COME BACK WITH ME.
I WILL NOT. YOU MUST BE A BETTER MAN THAN I AM, IF YOU MAKE ME DO MY BEST TO RESIST YOUR ATTACK, IF YOU INTEND TO MAKE ONE.
THAT I DO.
ALLLGGGGGH
BUDOOM
DUDOOM
HARGH!
THUD

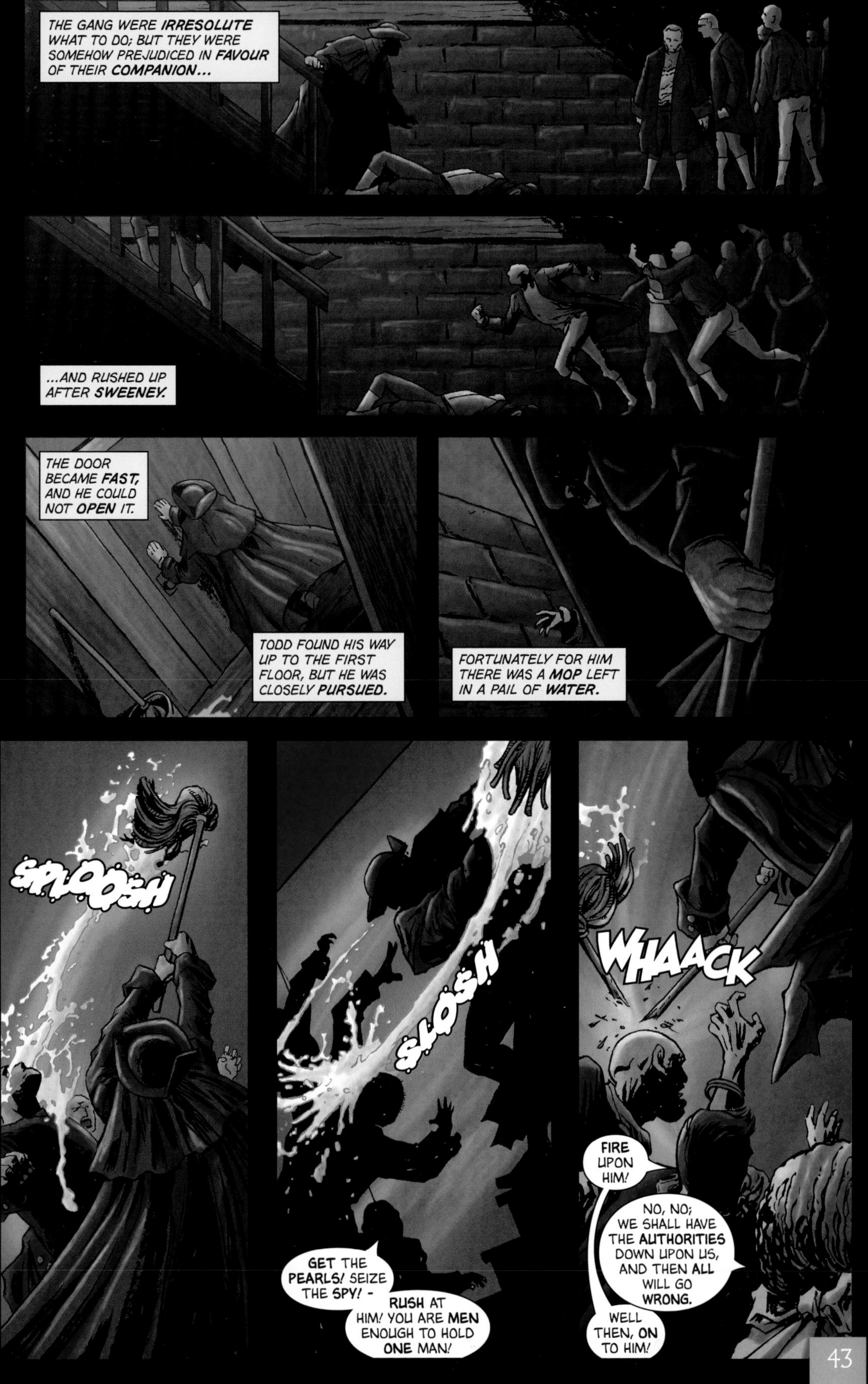
THE GANG WERE IRRESOLUTE WHAT TO DO; BUT THEY WERE SOMEHOW PREJUDICED IN FAVOUR OF THEIR COMPANION...
...AND RUSHED UP AFTER SWEENEY.
THE DOOR BECAME FAST, AND HE COULD NOT OPEN IT.
TODD FOUND HIS WAY UP TO THE FIRST FLOOR, BUT HE WAS CLOSELY PURSUED.
FORTUNATELY FOR HIM THERE WAS A MOP LEFT IN A PAIL OF WATER.
SPLOOSH
SLOSH
GET THE PEARLS! SEIZE THE SPY! -
RUSH AT HIM! YOU ARE MEN ENOUGH TO HOLD ONE MAN!
WHAACK
FIRE UPON HIM!
NO, NO; WE SHALL HAVE THE AUTHORITIES DOWN UPON US, AND THEN ALL WILL GO WRONG.
WELL THEN, ON TO HIM!

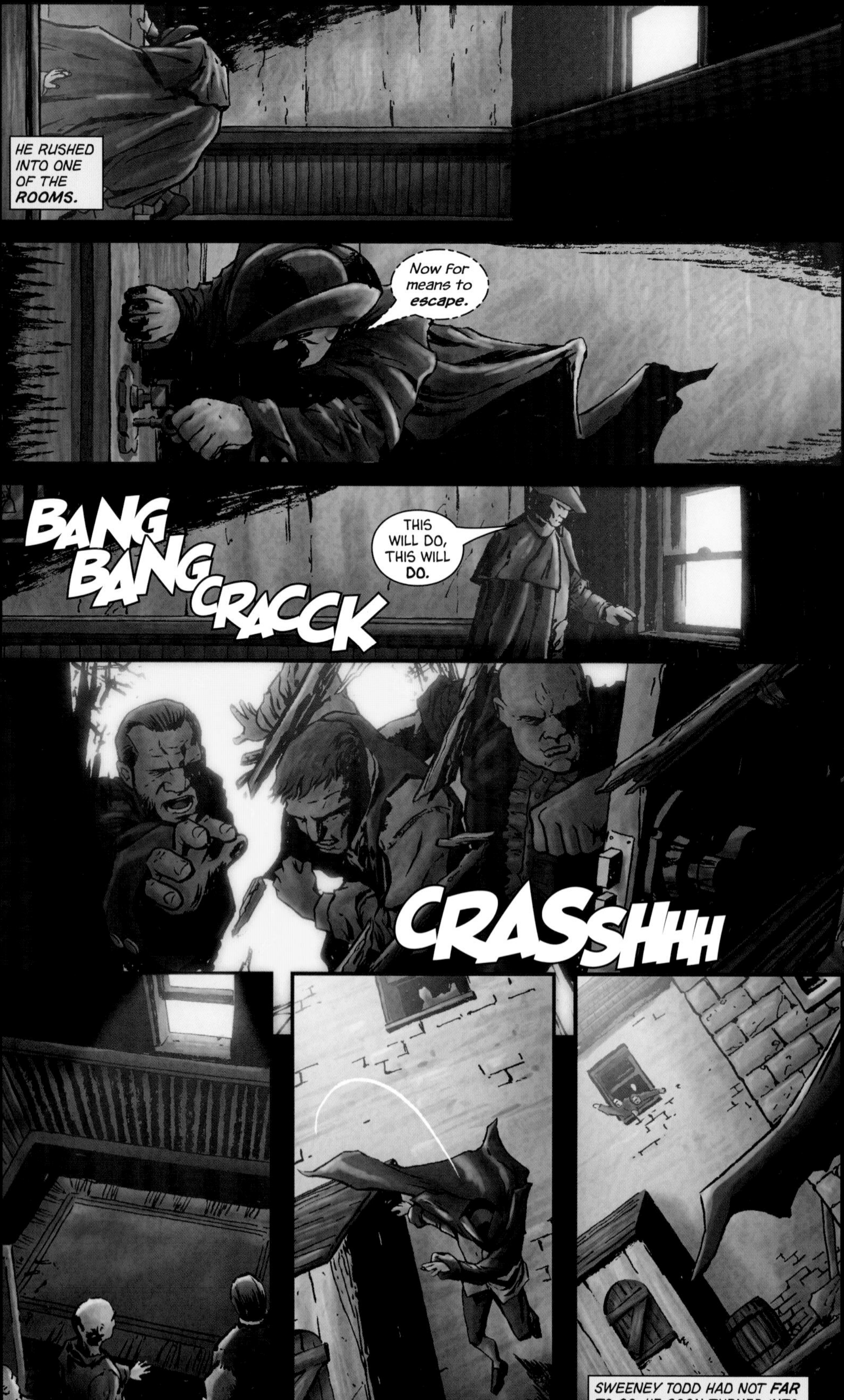
HE RUSHED INTO ONE OF THE ROOMS.
Now for means to escape.
BANG BANG CRACCK
THIS WILL DO, THIS WILL DO.
CRASSHHH
SWEENEY TODD HAD NOT FAR TO GO; HE SOON TURNED INTO FLEET-STREET AND MADE FOR HIS OWN HOUSE.

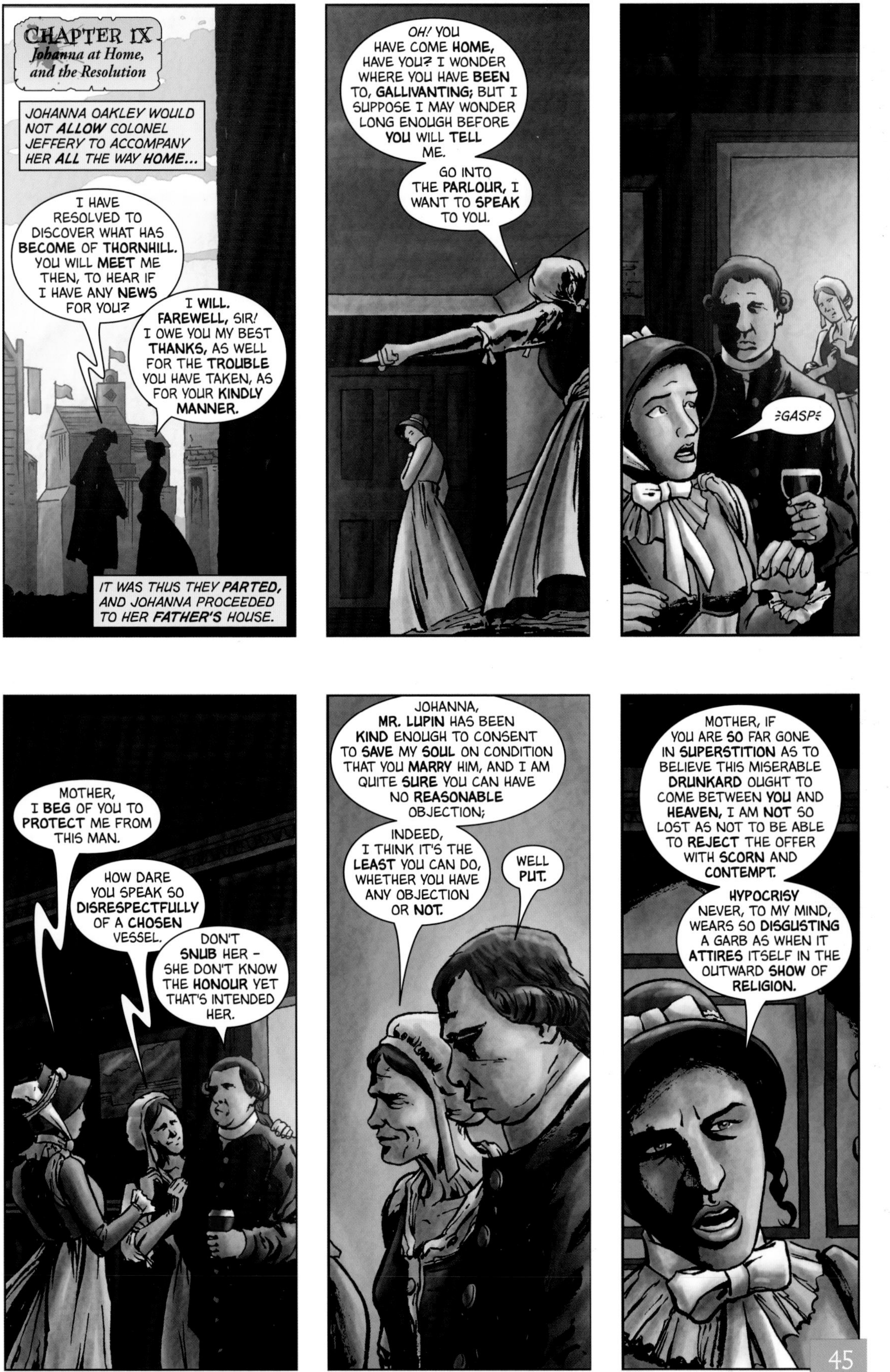
CHAPTER IX
Johanna at Home, and the Resolution
JOHANNA OAKLEY WOULD NOT ALLOW COLONEL JEFFERY TO ACCOMPANY HER ALL THE WAY HOME...
I HAVE RESOLVED TO DISCOVER WHAT HAS BECOME OF THORNHILL. YOU WILL MEET ME THEN, TO HEAR IF I HAVE ANY NEWS FOR YOU?
I WILL. FAREWELL, SIR! I OWE YOU MY BEST THANKS, AS WELL FOR THE TROUBLE YOU HAVE TAKEN, AS FOR YOUR KINDLY MANNER.
IT WAS THUS THEY PARTED, AND JOHANNA PROCEEDED TO HER FATHER'S HOUSE.
OH! YOU HAVE COME HOME, HAVE YOU? I WONDER WHERE YOU HAVE BEEN TO, GALLIVANTING; BUT I SUPPOSE I MAY WONDER LONG ENOUGH BEFORE YOU WILL TELL ME.
GO INTO THE PARLOUR, I WANT TO SPEAK TO YOU.
GASP
MOTHER, I BEG OF YOU TO PROTECT ME FROM THIS MAN.
HOW DARE YOU SPEAK SO DISRESPECTFULLY OF A CHOSEN VESSEL.
DON'T SNUB HER – SHE DON'T KNOW THE HONOUR YET THAT'S INTENDED HER.
JOHANNA, MR. LUPIN HAS BEEN KIND ENOUGH TO CONSENT TO SAVE MY SOUL ON CONDITION THAT YOU MARRY HIM, AND I AM QUITE SURE YOU CAN HAVE NO REASONABLE OBJECTION;
INDEED, I THINK IT'S THE LEAST YOU CAN DO, WHETHER YOU HAVE ANY OBJECTION OR NOT.
WELL PUT.
MOTHER, IF YOU ARE SO FAR GONE IN SUPERSTITION AS TO BELIEVE THIS MISERABLE DRUNKARD OUGHT TO COME BETWEEN YOU AND HEAVEN, I AM NOT SO LOST AS NOT TO BE ABLE TO REJECT THE OFFER WITH SCORN AND CONTEMPT.
HYPOCRISY NEVER, TO MY MIND, WEARS SO DISGUSTING A GARB AS WHEN IT ATTIRES ITSELF IN THE OUTWARD SHOW OF RELIGION.

THIS CONDUCT IS *UNBEARABLE*; AM I TO HAVE ONE OF THE LORD'S SAINTS *INSULTED* UNDER MY *OWN* ROOF?

IF HE WERE *TEN* TIMES A *SAINT*, MOTHER, INSTEAD OF BEING NOTHING BUT A MISERABLE DRUNKEN *PROFLIGATE*, IT WOULD BE BETTER THAT HE SHOULD BE *INSULTED* TEN TIMES OVER, THAN THAT *YOU* SHOULD *PERMIT* YOUR *OWN* CHILD TO *SUFFER* THIS INDIGNITY.

THAT'S *RIGHT*, MY DEAR; YOU NEVER SPOKE *TRUER* WORDS IN YOUR *LIFE*.

GET BEHIND ME, SATAN! MR. OAKLEY, YOU WILL BE *DAMNED* IF YOU SAY A *WORD* TO ME.

IT'S ALL THE *SAME*, THEN, FOR I'LL BE *DAMNED* IF I *DON'T*. COME IN, BEN!

I'M A-COMING, OAKLEY, MY BOY. PUT ON YOUR *BLESSED* SPECTACLES, AND TELL ME *WHICH* IS THE FELLOW.

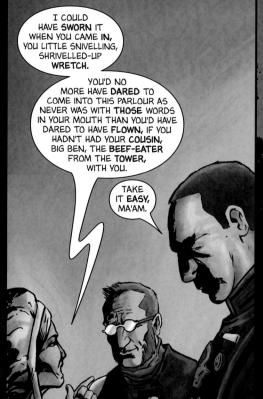

I COULD HAVE *SWORN* IT WHEN YOU CAME *IN*, YOU LITTLE SNIVELLING, SHRIVELLED-UP *WRETCH*.

YOU'D NO MORE HAVE *DARED* TO COME INTO THIS PARLOUR AS NEVER WAS WITH *THOSE* WORDS IN YOUR MOUTH THAN YOU'D HAVE DARED TO HAVE *FLOWN*, IF YOU HADN'T HAD YOUR *COUSIN*, BIG BEN, THE *BEEF-EATER* FROM THE *TOWER*, WITH YOU.

TAKE IT *EASY*, MA'AM.

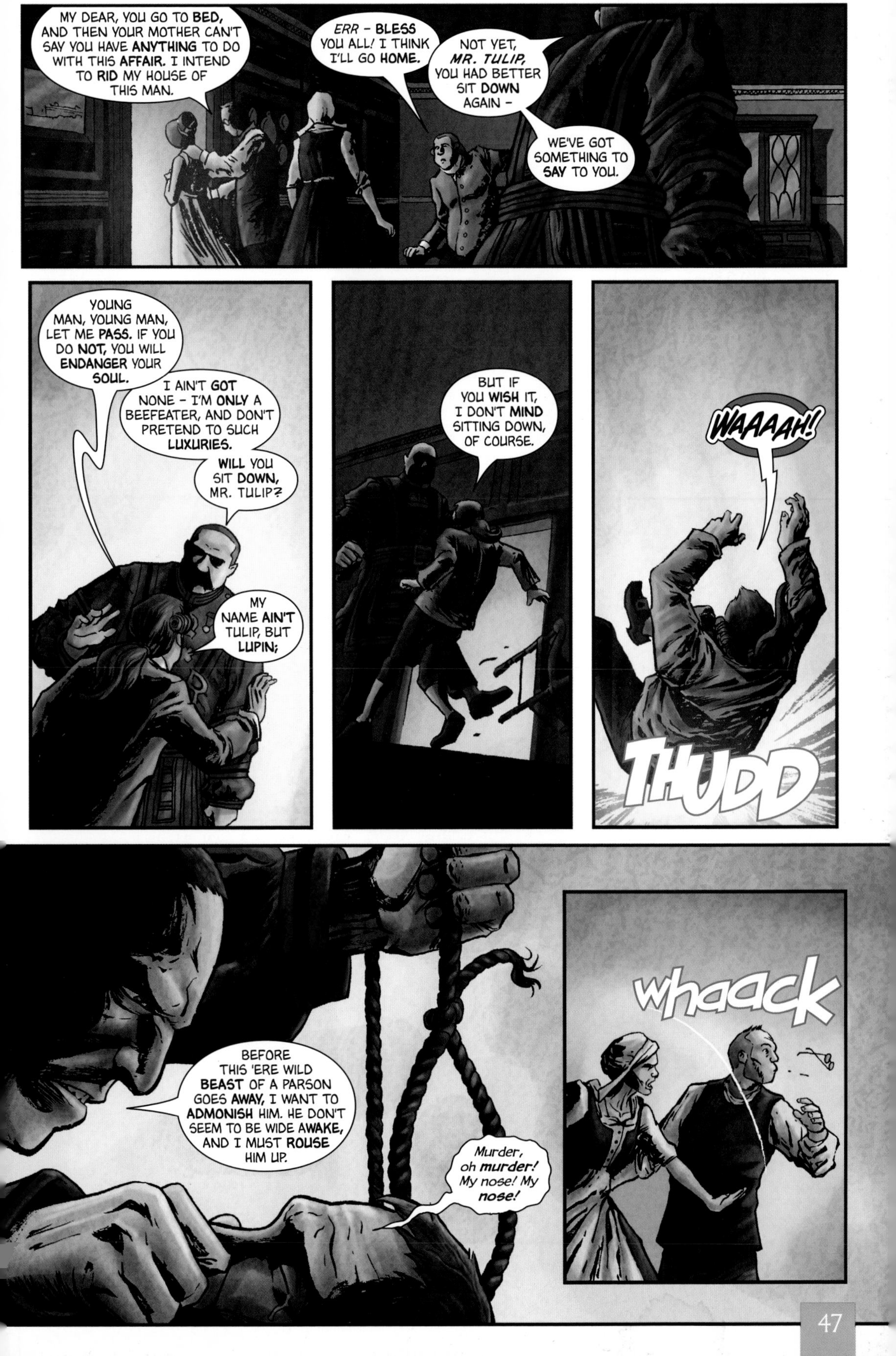
MY DEAR, YOU GO TO BED, AND THEN YOUR MOTHER CAN'T SAY YOU HAVE ANYTHING TO DO WITH THIS AFFAIR. I INTEND TO RID MY HOUSE OF THIS MAN.
ERR – BLESS YOU ALL! I THINK I'LL GO HOME.
NOT YET, MR. TULIP, YOU HAD BETTER SIT DOWN AGAIN –
WE'VE GOT SOMETHING TO SAY TO YOU.
YOUNG MAN, YOUNG MAN, LET ME PASS. IF YOU DO NOT, YOU WILL ENDANGER YOUR SOUL.
I AIN'T GOT NONE – I'M ONLY A BEEFEATER, AND DON'T PRETEND TO SUCH LUXURIES.
WILL YOU SIT DOWN, MR. TULIP?
MY NAME AIN'T TULIP, BUT LUPIN;
BUT IF YOU WISH IT, I DON'T MIND SITTING DOWN, OF COURSE.
WAAAAH!
THUDD
BEFORE THIS 'ERE WILD BEAST OF A PARSON GOES AWAY, I WANT TO ADMONISH HIM. HE DON'T SEEM TO BE WIDE AWAKE, AND I MUST ROUSE HIM UP.
Murder, oh murder! My nose! My nose!
whaack

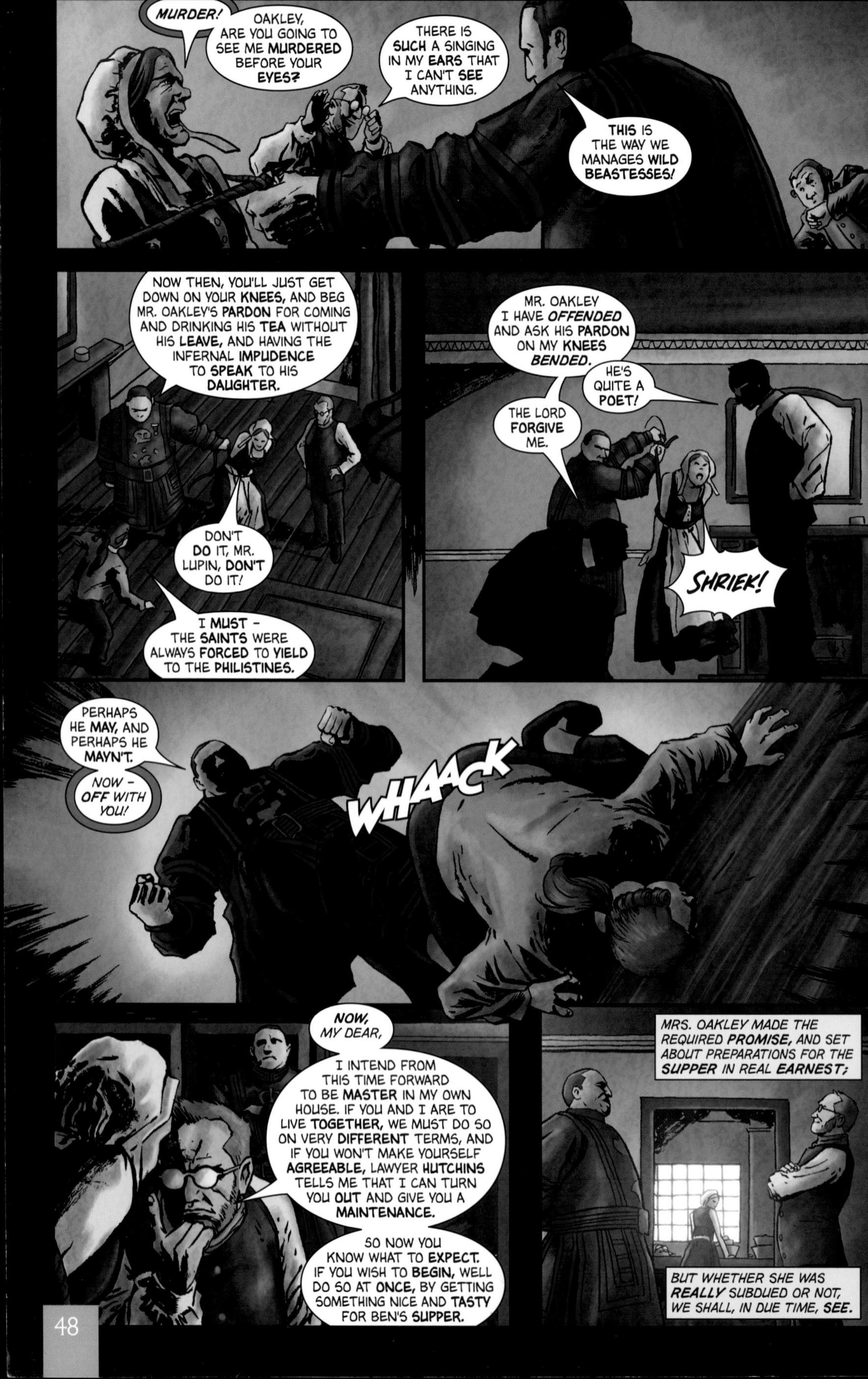
MURDER!
OAKLEY, ARE YOU GOING TO SEE ME MURDERED BEFORE YOUR EYES?
THERE IS SUCH A SINGING IN MY EARS THAT I CAN'T SEE ANYTHING.
THIS IS THE WAY WE MANAGES WILD BEASTESSES!
NOW THEN, YOU'LL JUST GET DOWN ON YOUR KNEES, AND BEG MR. OAKLEY'S PARDON FOR COMING AND DRINKING HIS TEA WITHOUT HIS LEAVE, AND HAVING THE INFERNAL IMPUDENCE TO SPEAK TO HIS DAUGHTER.
DON'T DO IT, MR. LUPIN, DON'T DO IT!
I MUST - THE SAINTS WERE ALWAYS FORCED TO YIELD TO THE PHILISTINES.
MR. OAKLEY I HAVE OFFENDED AND ASK HIS PARDON ON MY KNEES BENDED.
HE'S QUITE A POET!
THE LORD FORGIVE ME.
SHRIEK!
PERHAPS HE MAY, AND PERHAPS HE MAYN'T.
NOW - OFF WITH YOU!
WHAACK
NOW, MY DEAR,
I INTEND FROM THIS TIME FORWARD TO BE MASTER IN MY OWN HOUSE. IF YOU AND I ARE TO LIVE TOGETHER, WE MUST DO SO ON VERY DIFFERENT TERMS, AND IF YOU WON'T MAKE YOURSELF AGREEABLE, LAWYER HUTCHINS TELLS ME THAT I CAN TURN YOU OUT AND GIVE YOU A MAINTENANCE.
SO NOW YOU KNOW WHAT TO EXPECT. IF YOU WISH TO BEGIN, WELL DO SO AT ONCE, BY GETTING SOMETHING NICE AND TASTY FOR BEN'S SUPPER.
MRS. OAKLEY MADE THE REQUIRED PROMISE, AND SET ABOUT PREPARATIONS FOR THE SUPPER IN REAL EARNEST;
BUT WHETHER SHE WAS REALLY SUBDUED OR NOT, WE SHALL, IN DUE TIME, SEE.

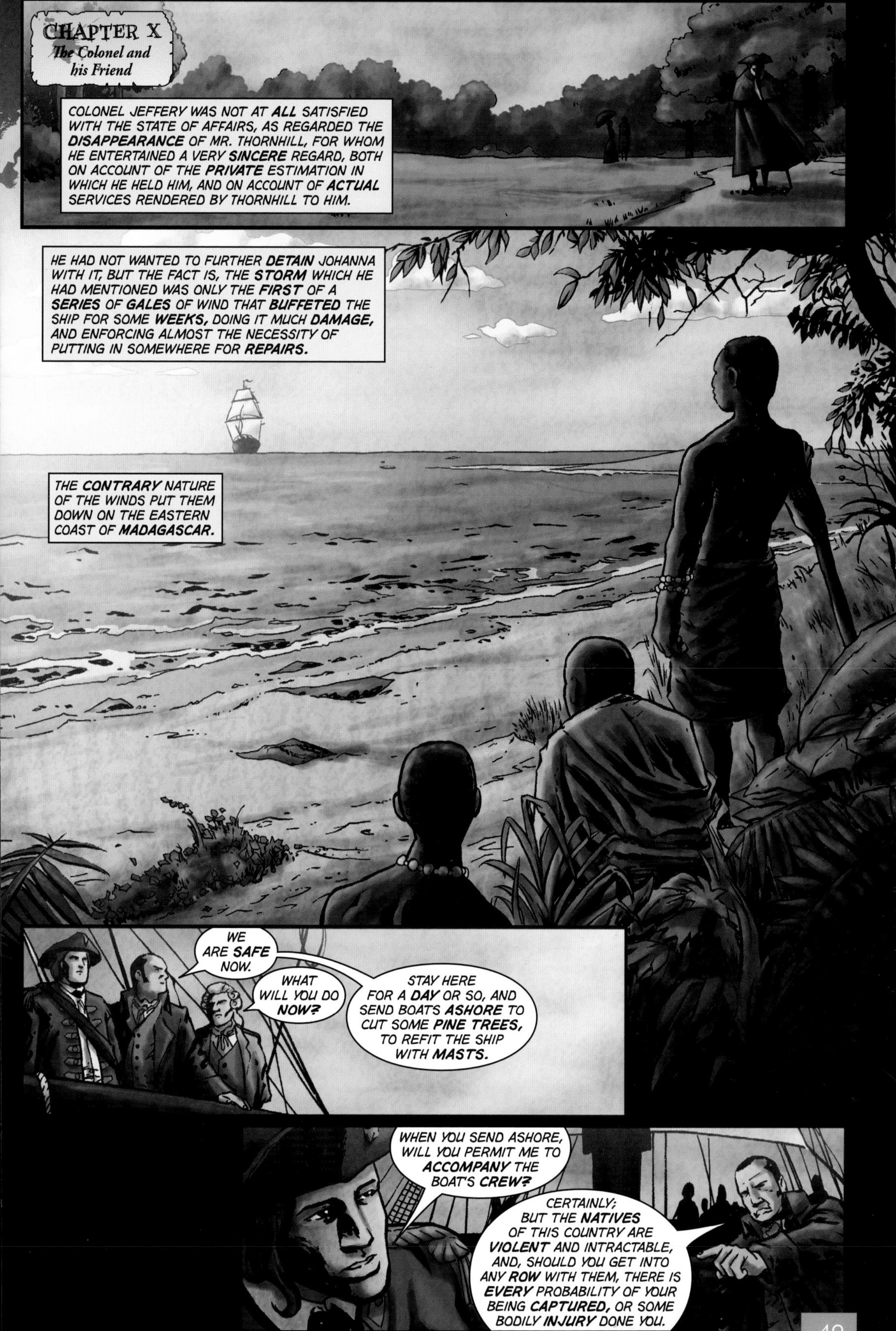
CHAPTER X
The Colonel and his Friend
COLONEL JEFFERY WAS NOT AT ALL SATISFIED WITH THE STATE OF AFFAIRS, AS REGARDED THE DISAPPEARANCE OF MR. THORNHILL, FOR WHOM HE ENTERTAINED A VERY SINCERE REGARD, BOTH ON ACCOUNT OF THE PRIVATE ESTIMATION IN WHICH HE HELD HIM, AND ON ACCOUNT OF ACTUAL SERVICES RENDERED BY THORNHILL TO HIM.
HE HAD NOT WANTED TO FURTHER DETAIN JOHANNA WITH IT, BUT THE FACT IS, THE STORM WHICH HE HAD MENTIONED WAS ONLY THE FIRST OF A SERIES OF GALES OF WIND THAT BUFFETED THE SHIP FOR SOME WEEKS, DOING IT MUCH DAMAGE, AND ENFORCING ALMOST THE NECESSITY OF PUTTING IN SOMEWHERE FOR REPAIRS.
THE CONTRARY NATURE OF THE WINDS PUT THEM DOWN ON THE EASTERN COAST OF MADAGASCAR.
WE ARE SAFE NOW.
WHAT WILL YOU DO NOW?
STAY HERE FOR A DAY OR SO, AND SEND BOATS ASHORE TO CUT SOME PINE TREES, TO REFIT THE SHIP WITH MASTS.
WHEN YOU SEND ASHORE, WILL YOU PERMIT ME TO ACCOMPANY THE BOAT'S CREW?
CERTAINLY; BUT THE NATIVES OF THIS COUNTRY ARE VIOLENT AND INTRACTABLE, AND, SHOULD YOU GET INTO ANY ROW WITH THEM, THERE IS EVERY PROBABILITY OF YOUR BEING CAPTURED, OR SOME BODILY INJURY DONE YOU.

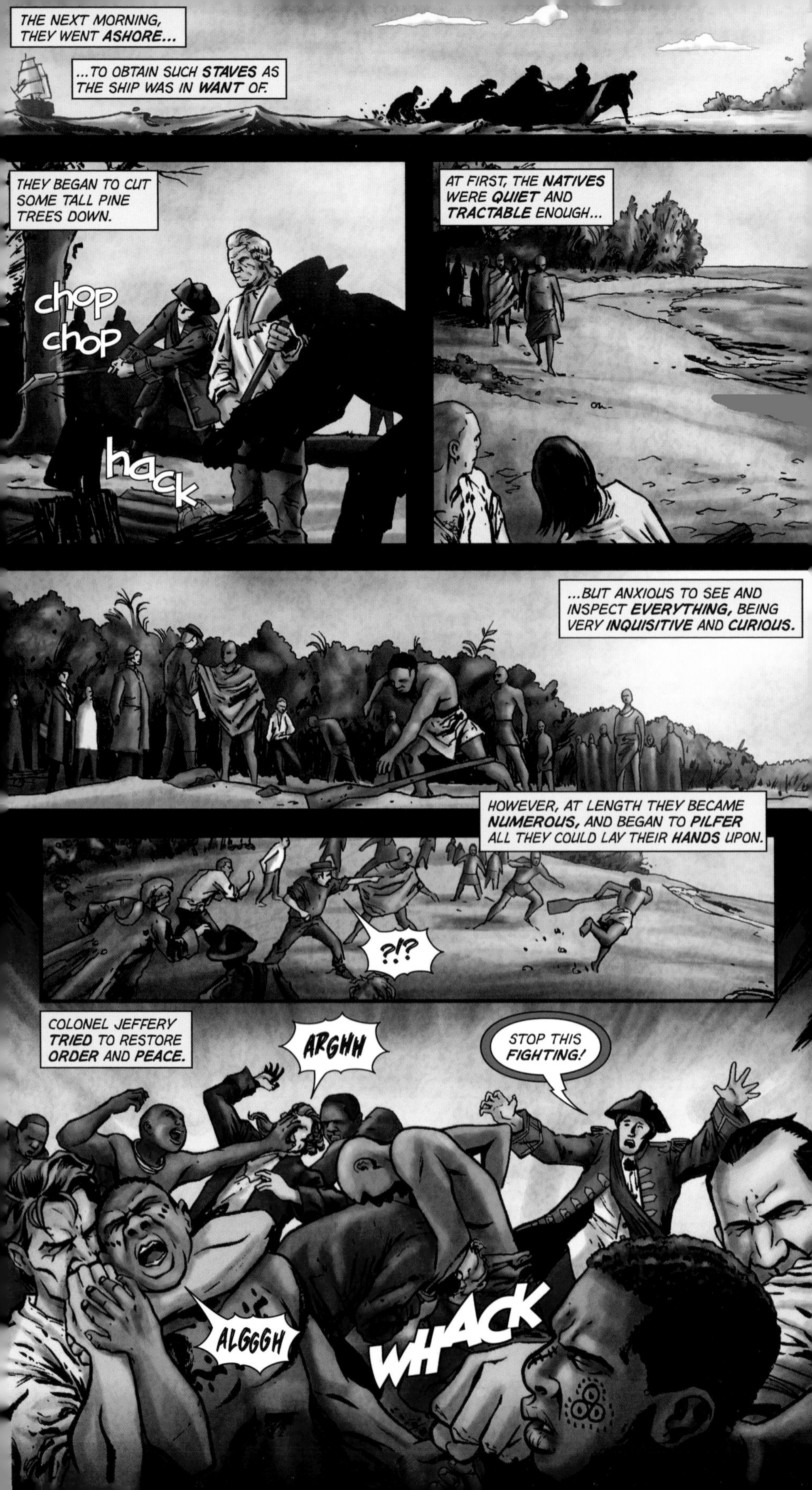
THE NEXT MORNING, THEY WENT ASHORE...
...TO OBTAIN SUCH STAVES AS THE SHIP WAS IN WANT OF.
THEY BEGAN TO CUT SOME TALL PINE TREES DOWN.
chop
chop
hack
AT FIRST, THE NATIVES WERE QUIET AND TRACTABLE ENOUGH...
...BUT ANXIOUS TO SEE AND INSPECT EVERYTHING, BEING VERY INQUISITIVE AND CURIOUS.
HOWEVER, AT LENGTH THEY BECAME NUMEROUS, AND BEGAN TO PILFER ALL THEY COULD LAY THEIR HANDS UPON.
?!?
COLONEL JEFFERY TRIED TO RESTORE ORDER AND PEACE.
ARGHH
STOP THIS FIGHTING!
ALGGGH
WHACK

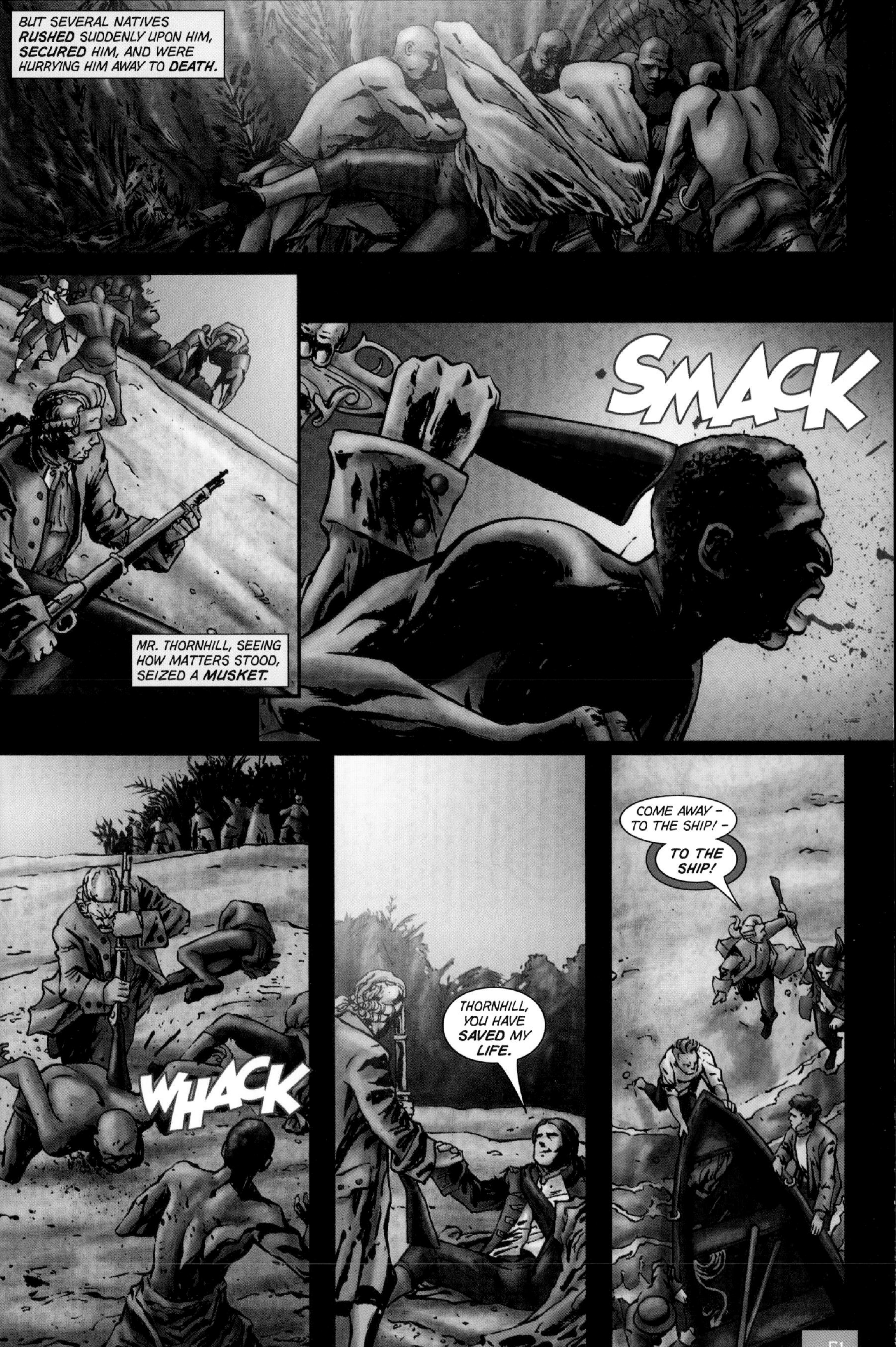
BUT SEVERAL NATIVES **RUSHED** SUDDENLY UPON HIM, **SECURED** HIM, AND WERE HURRYING HIM AWAY TO **DEATH.**
MR. THORNHILL, SEEING HOW MATTERS STOOD, SEIZED A **MUSKET.**
SMACK
WHACK
THORNHILL, YOU HAVE **SAVED** MY LIFE.
COME AWAY - TO THE SHIP! -
TO THE SHIP!

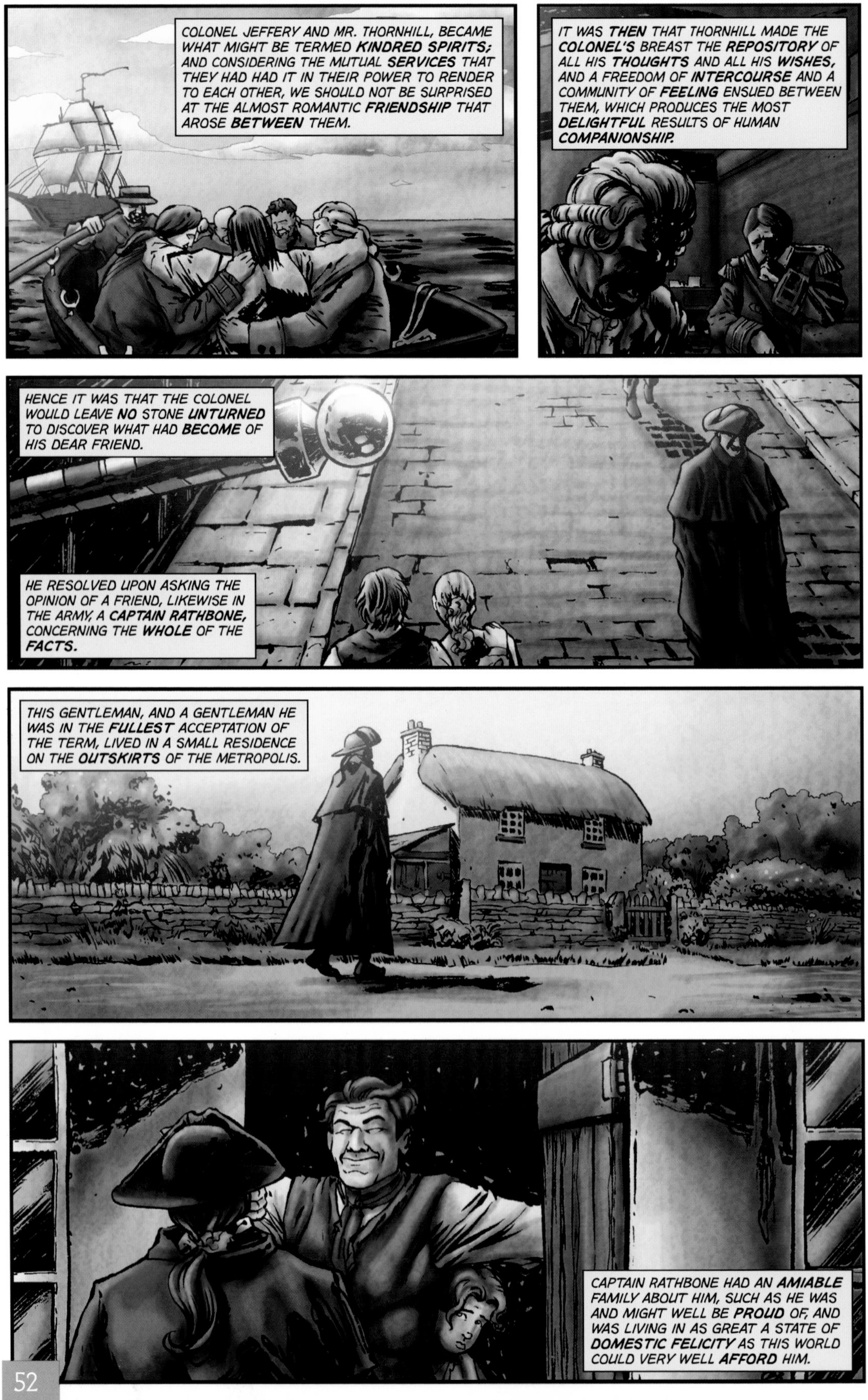
COLONEL JEFFERY AND MR. THORNHILL, BECAME WHAT MIGHT BE TERMED KINDRED SPIRITS; AND CONSIDERING THE MUTUAL SERVICES THAT THEY HAD HAD IT IN THEIR POWER TO RENDER TO EACH OTHER, WE SHOULD NOT BE SURPRISED AT THE ALMOST ROMANTIC FRIENDSHIP THAT AROSE BETWEEN THEM.
IT WAS THEN THAT THORNHILL MADE THE COLONEL'S BREAST THE REPOSITORY OF ALL HIS THOUGHTS AND ALL HIS WISHES, AND A FREEDOM OF INTERCOURSE AND A COMMUNITY OF FEELING ENSUED BETWEEN THEM, WHICH PRODUCES THE MOST DELIGHTFUL RESULTS OF HUMAN COMPANIONSHIP.
HENCE IT WAS THAT THE COLONEL WOULD LEAVE NO STONE UNTURNED TO DISCOVER WHAT HAD BECOME OF HIS DEAR FRIEND.
HE RESOLVED UPON ASKING THE OPINION OF A FRIEND, LIKEWISE IN THE ARMY, A CAPTAIN RATHBONE, CONCERNING THE WHOLE OF THE FACTS.
THIS GENTLEMAN, AND A GENTLEMAN HE WAS IN THE FULLEST ACCEPTATION OF THE TERM, LIVED IN A SMALL RESIDENCE ON THE OUTSKIRTS OF THE METROPOLIS.
CAPTAIN RATHBONE HAD AN AMIABLE FAMILY ABOUT HIM, SUCH AS HE WAS AND MIGHT WELL BE PROUD OF, AND WAS LIVING IN AS GREAT A STATE OF DOMESTIC FELICITY AS THIS WORLD COULD VERY WELL AFFORD HIM.

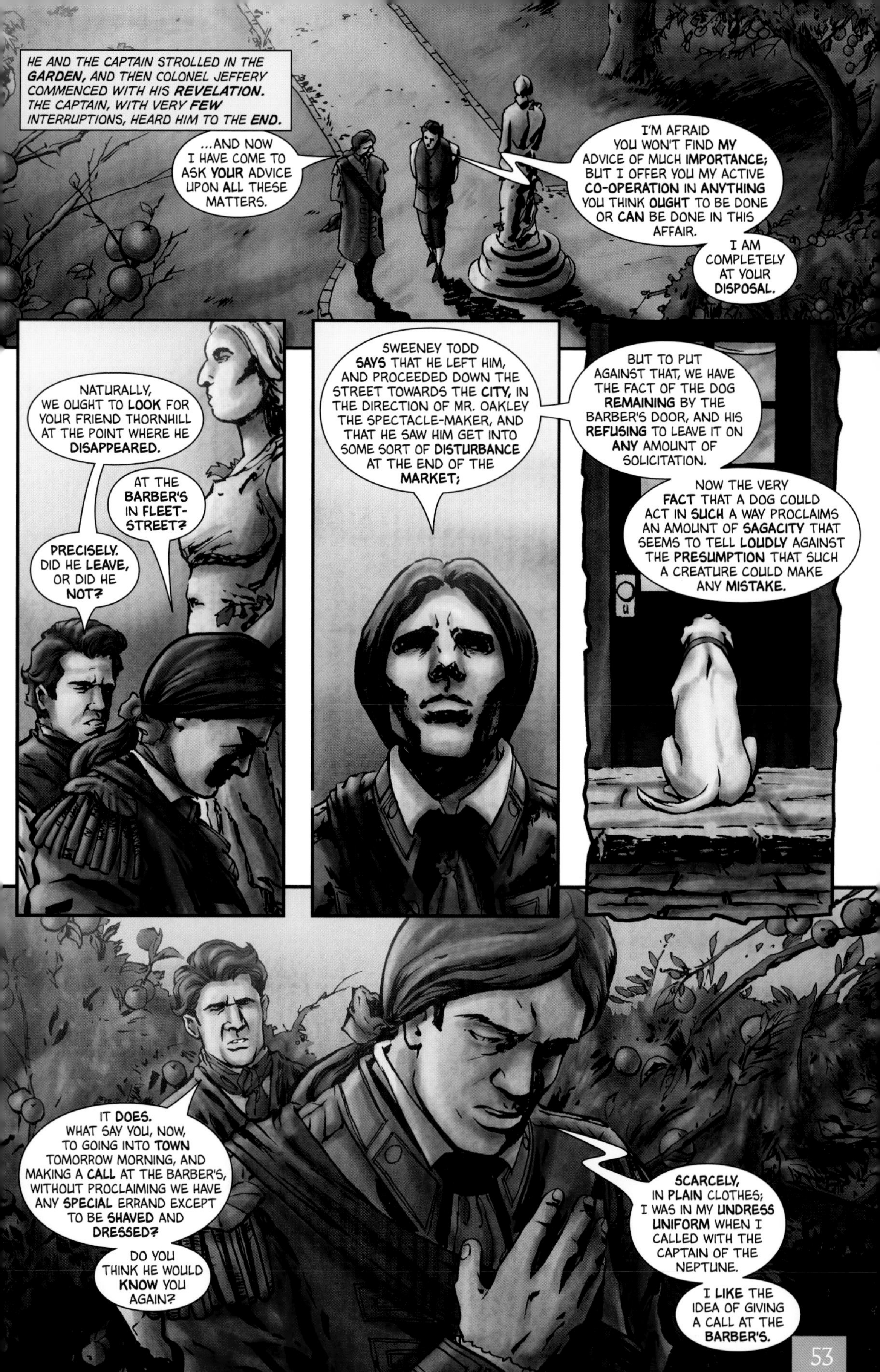

HE AND THE CAPTAIN STROLLED IN THE GARDEN, AND THEN COLONEL JEFFERY COMMENCED WITH HIS REVELATION. THE CAPTAIN, WITH VERY FEW INTERRUPTIONS, HEARD HIM TO THE END.
...AND NOW I HAVE COME TO ASK YOUR ADVICE UPON ALL THESE MATTERS.
I'M AFRAID YOU WON'T FIND MY ADVICE OF MUCH IMPORTANCE; BUT I OFFER YOU MY ACTIVE CO-OPERATION IN ANYTHING YOU THINK OUGHT TO BE DONE OR CAN BE DONE IN THIS AFFAIR.
I AM COMPLETELY AT YOUR DISPOSAL.
NATURALLY, WE OUGHT TO LOOK FOR YOUR FRIEND THORNHILL AT THE POINT WHERE HE DISAPPEARED.
AT THE BARBER'S IN FLEET-STREET?
PRECISELY. DID HE LEAVE, OR DID HE NOT?
SWEENEY TODD SAYS THAT HE LEFT HIM, AND PROCEEDED DOWN THE STREET TOWARDS THE CITY, IN THE DIRECTION OF MR. OAKLEY THE SPECTACLE-MAKER, AND THAT HE SAW HIM GET INTO SOME SORT OF DISTURBANCE AT THE END OF THE MARKET;
BUT TO PUT AGAINST THAT, WE HAVE THE FACT OF THE DOG REMAINING BY THE BARBER'S DOOR, AND HIS REFUSING TO LEAVE IT ON ANY AMOUNT OF SOLICITATION.
NOW THE VERY FACT THAT A DOG COULD ACT IN SUCH A WAY PROCLAIMS AN AMOUNT OF SAGACITY THAT SEEMS TO TELL LOUDLY AGAINST THE PRESUMPTION THAT SUCH A CREATURE COULD MAKE ANY MISTAKE.
IT DOES. WHAT SAY YOU, NOW, TO GOING INTO TOWN TOMORROW MORNING, AND MAKING A CALL AT THE BARBER'S, WITHOUT PROCLAIMING WE HAVE ANY SPECIAL ERRAND EXCEPT TO BE SHAVED AND DRESSED?
DO YOU THINK HE WOULD KNOW YOU AGAIN?
SCARCELY, IN PLAIN CLOTHES; I WAS IN MY UNDRESS UNIFORM WHEN I CALLED WITH THE CAPTAIN OF THE NEPTUNE.
I LIKE THE IDEA OF GIVING A CALL AT THE BARBER'S.

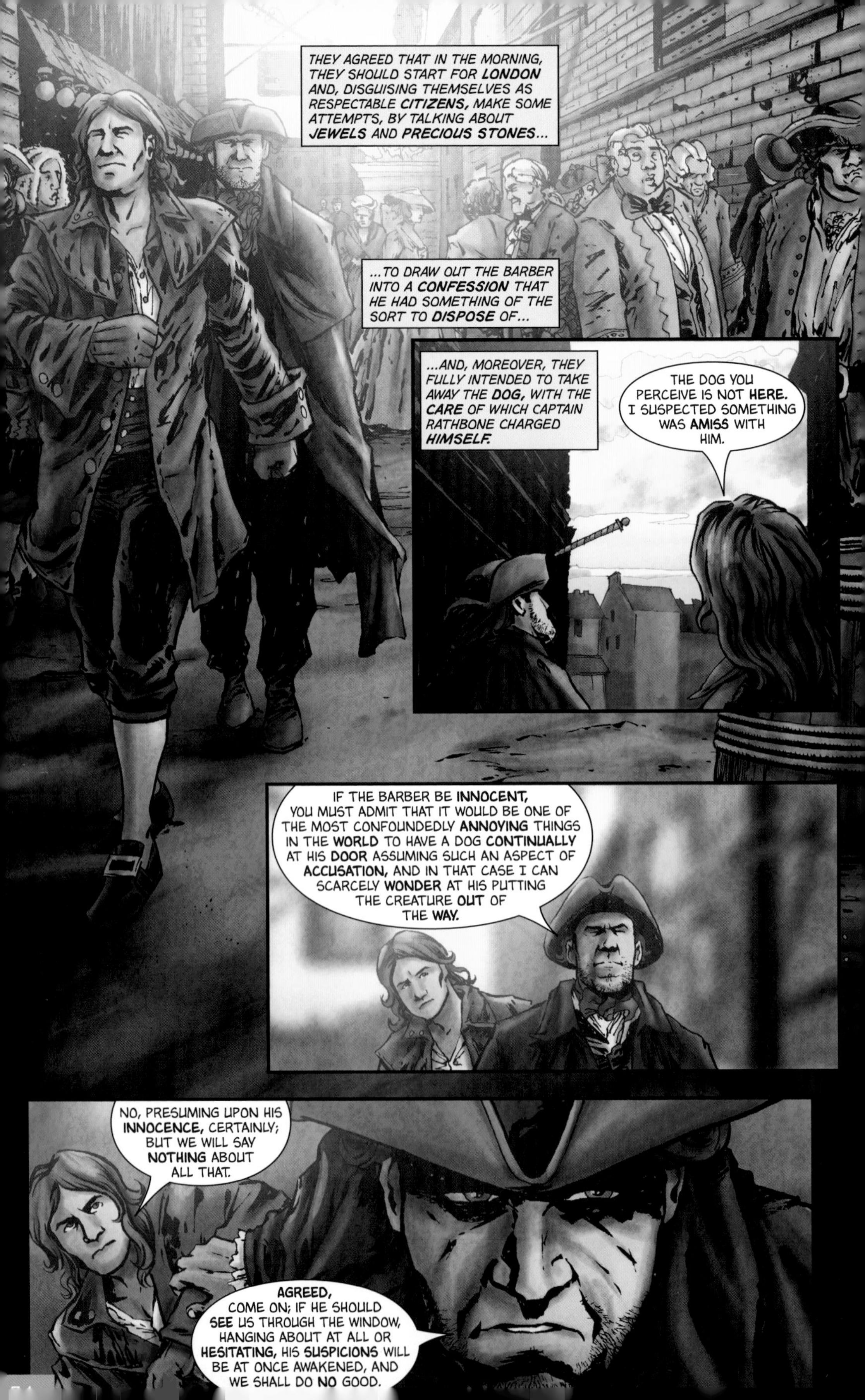
THEY AGREED THAT IN THE MORNING, THEY SHOULD START FOR LONDON AND, DISGUISING THEMSELVES AS RESPECTABLE CITIZENS, MAKE SOME ATTEMPTS, BY TALKING ABOUT JEWELS AND PRECIOUS STONES...
...TO DRAW OUT THE BARBER INTO A CONFESSION THAT HE HAD SOMETHING OF THE SORT TO DISPOSE OF...
...AND, MOREOVER, THEY FULLY INTENDED TO TAKE AWAY THE DOG, WITH THE CARE OF WHICH CAPTAIN RATHBONE CHARGED HIMSELF.
THE DOG YOU PERCEIVE IS NOT HERE. I SUSPECTED SOMETHING WAS AMISS WITH HIM.
IF THE BARBER BE INNOCENT, YOU MUST ADMIT THAT IT WOULD BE ONE OF THE MOST CONFOUNDEDLY ANNOYING THINGS IN THE WORLD TO HAVE A DOG CONTINUALLY AT HIS DOOR ASSUMING SUCH AN ASPECT OF ACCUSATION, AND IN THAT CASE I CAN SCARCELY WONDER AT HIS PUTTING THE CREATURE OUT OF THE WAY.
NO, PRESUMING UPON HIS INNOCENCE, CERTAINLY; BUT WE WILL SAY NOTHING ABOUT ALL THAT.
AGREED, COME ON; IF HE SHOULD SEE US THROUGH THE WINDOW, HANGING ABOUT AT ALL OR HESITATING, HIS SUSPICIONS WILL BE AT ONCE AWAKENED, AND WE SHALL DO NO GOOD.

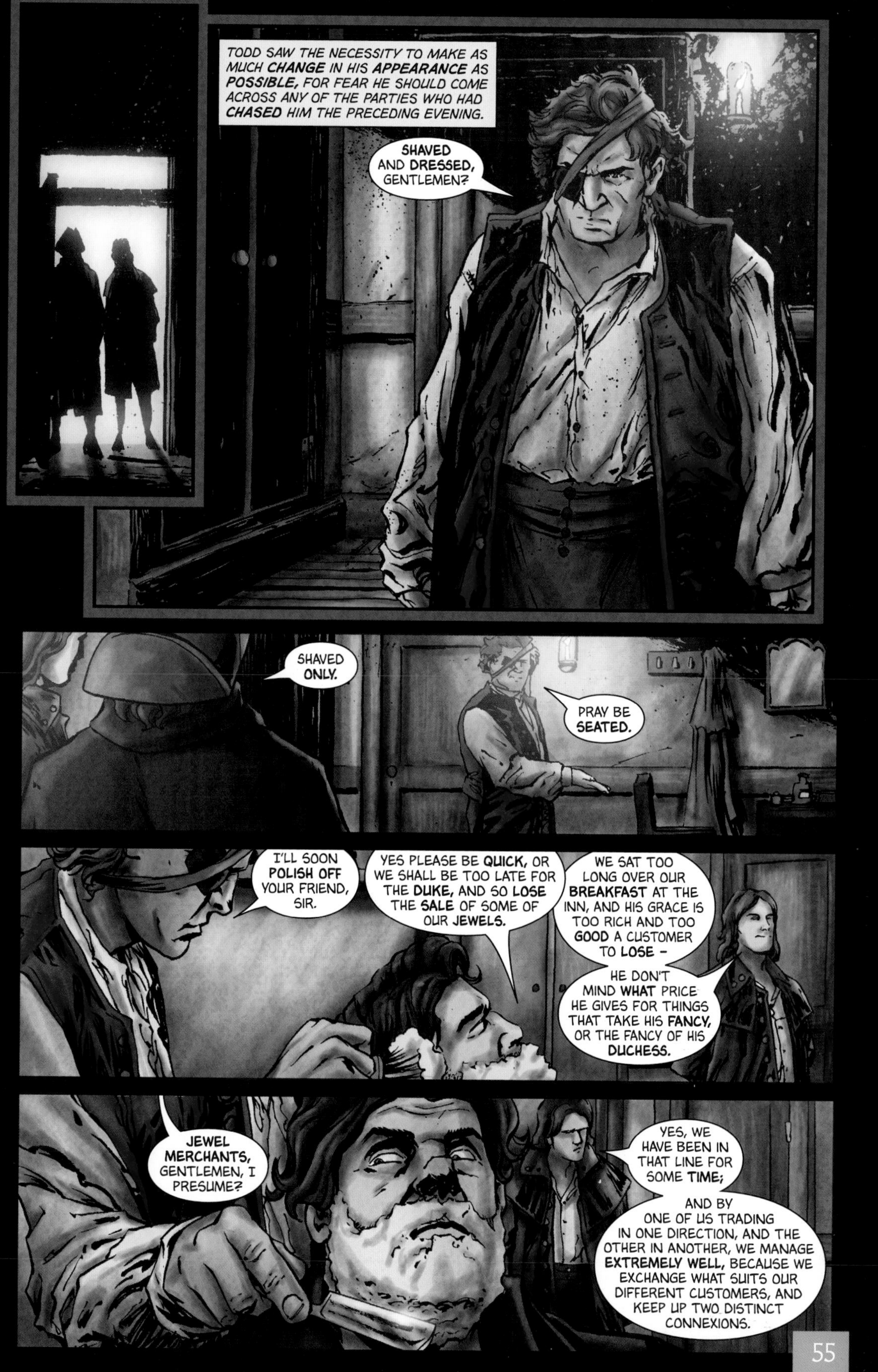
TODD SAW THE NECESSITY TO MAKE AS MUCH CHANGE IN HIS APPEARANCE AS POSSIBLE, FOR FEAR HE SHOULD COME ACROSS ANY OF THE PARTIES WHO HAD CHASED HIM THE PRECEDING EVENING.
SHAVED AND DRESSED, GENTLEMEN?
SHAVED ONLY.
PRAY BE SEATED.
I'LL SOON POLISH OFF YOUR FRIEND, SIR.
YES PLEASE BE QUICK, OR WE SHALL BE TOO LATE FOR THE DUKE, AND SO LOSE THE SALE OF SOME OF OUR JEWELS.
WE SAT TOO LONG OVER OUR BREAKFAST AT THE INN, AND HIS GRACE IS TOO RICH AND TOO GOOD A CUSTOMER TO LOSE –
HE DON'T MIND WHAT PRICE HE GIVES FOR THINGS THAT TAKE HIS FANCY, OR THE FANCY OF HIS DUCHESS.
JEWEL MERCHANTS, GENTLEMEN, I PRESUME?
YES, WE HAVE BEEN IN THAT LINE FOR SOME TIME;
AND BY ONE OF US TRADING IN ONE DIRECTION, AND THE OTHER IN ANOTHER, WE MANAGE EXTREMELY WELL, BECAUSE WE EXCHANGE WHAT SUITS OUR DIFFERENT CUSTOMERS, AND KEEP UP TWO DISTINCT CONNEXIONS.

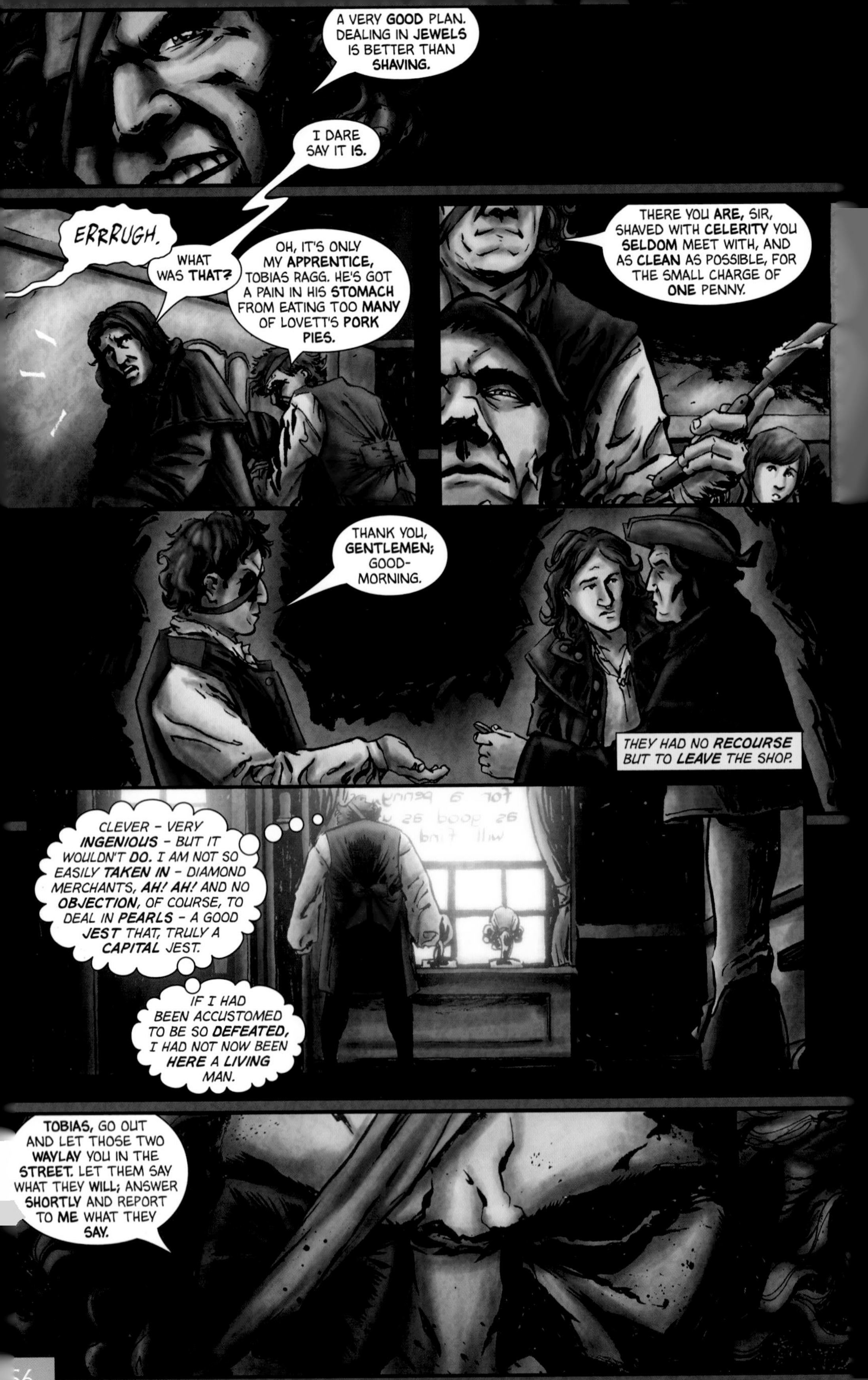
A VERY GOOD PLAN. DEALING IN JEWELS IS BETTER THAN SHAVING.
I DARE SAY IT IS.
ERRRUGH.
WHAT WAS THAT?
OH, IT'S ONLY MY APPRENTICE, TOBIAS RAGG. HE'S GOT A PAIN IN HIS STOMACH FROM EATING TOO MANY OF LOVETT'S PORK PIES.
THERE YOU ARE, SIR, SHAVED WITH CELERITY YOU SELDOM MEET WITH, AND AS CLEAN AS POSSIBLE, FOR THE SMALL CHARGE OF ONE PENNY.
THANK YOU, GENTLEMEN; GOOD-MORNING.
THEY HAD NO RECOURSE BUT TO LEAVE THE SHOP.
CLEVER - VERY INGENIOUS - BUT IT WOULDN'T DO. I AM NOT SO EASILY TAKEN IN - DIAMOND MERCHANTS, AH! AH! AND NO OBJECTION, OF COURSE, TO DEAL IN PEARLS - A GOOD JEST THAT, TRULY A CAPITAL JEST.
IF I HAD BEEN ACCUSTOMED TO BE SO DEFEATED, I HAD NOT NOW BEEN HERE A LIVING MAN.
TOBIAS, GO OUT AND LET THOSE TWO WAYLAY YOU IN THE STREET. LET THEM SAY WHAT THEY WILL; ANSWER SHORTLY AND REPORT TO ME WHAT THEY SAY.

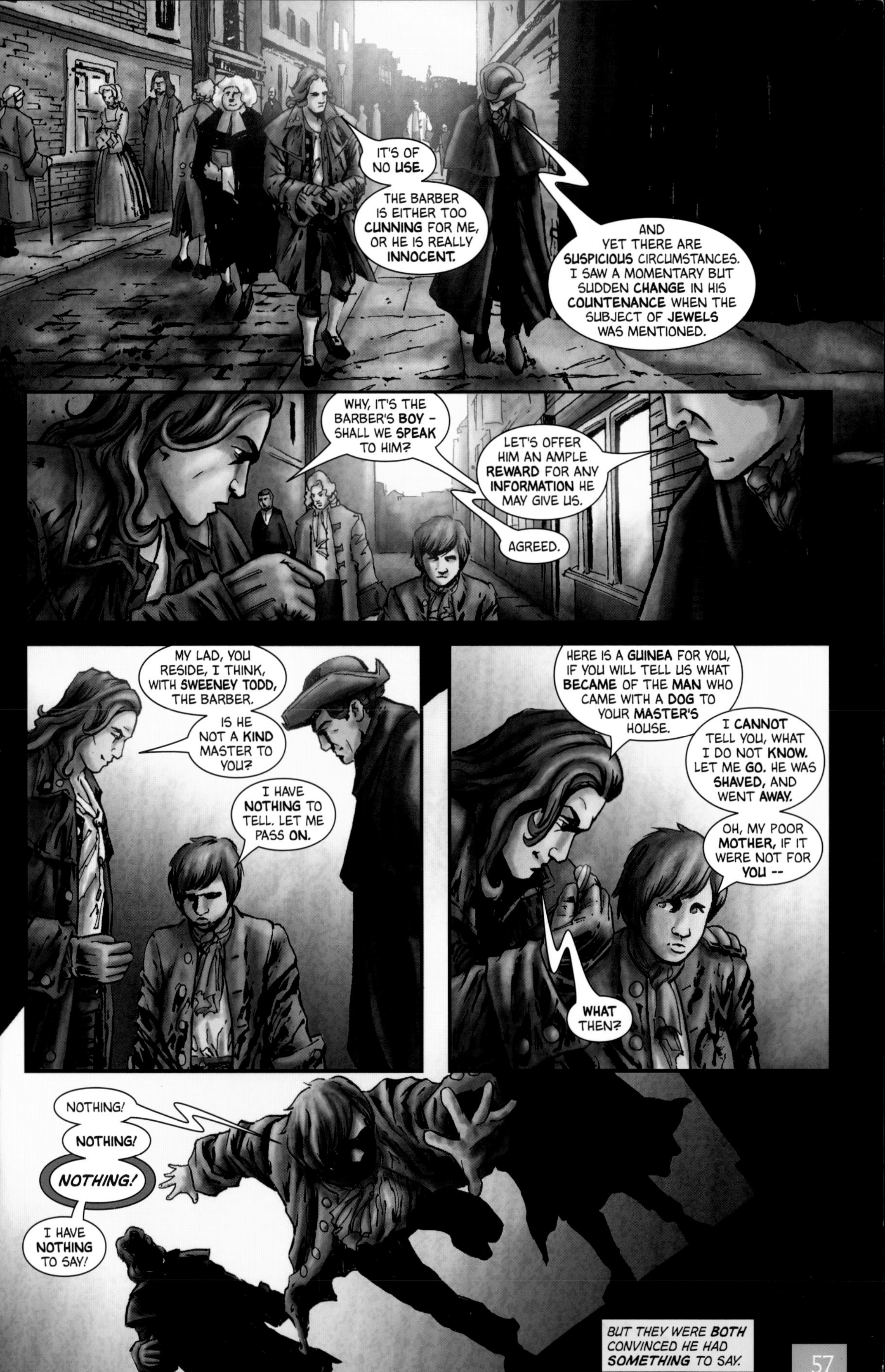

IT'S OF NO USE.
THE BARBER IS EITHER TOO CUNNING FOR ME, OR HE IS REALLY INNOCENT.
AND YET THERE ARE SUSPICIOUS CIRCUMSTANCES. I SAW A MOMENTARY BUT SUDDEN CHANGE IN HIS COUNTENANCE WHEN THE SUBJECT OF JEWELS WAS MENTIONED.
WHY, IT'S THE BARBER'S BOY - SHALL WE SPEAK TO HIM?
LET'S OFFER HIM AN AMPLE REWARD FOR ANY INFORMATION HE MAY GIVE US.
AGREED.
MY LAD, YOU RESIDE, I THINK, WITH SWEENEY TODD, THE BARBER.
IS HE NOT A KIND MASTER TO YOU?
I HAVE NOTHING TO TELL. LET ME PASS ON.
HERE IS A GUINEA FOR YOU, IF YOU WILL TELL US WHAT BECAME OF THE MAN WHO CAME WITH A DOG TO YOUR MASTER'S HOUSE.
I CANNOT TELL YOU, WHAT I DO NOT KNOW. LET ME GO. HE WAS SHAVED, AND WENT AWAY.
OH, MY POOR MOTHER, IF IT WERE NOT FOR YOU --
WHAT THEN?
NOTHING!
NOTHING!
NOTHING!
I HAVE NOTHING TO SAY!
BUT THEY WERE BOTH CONVINCED HE HAD SOMETHING TO SAY.

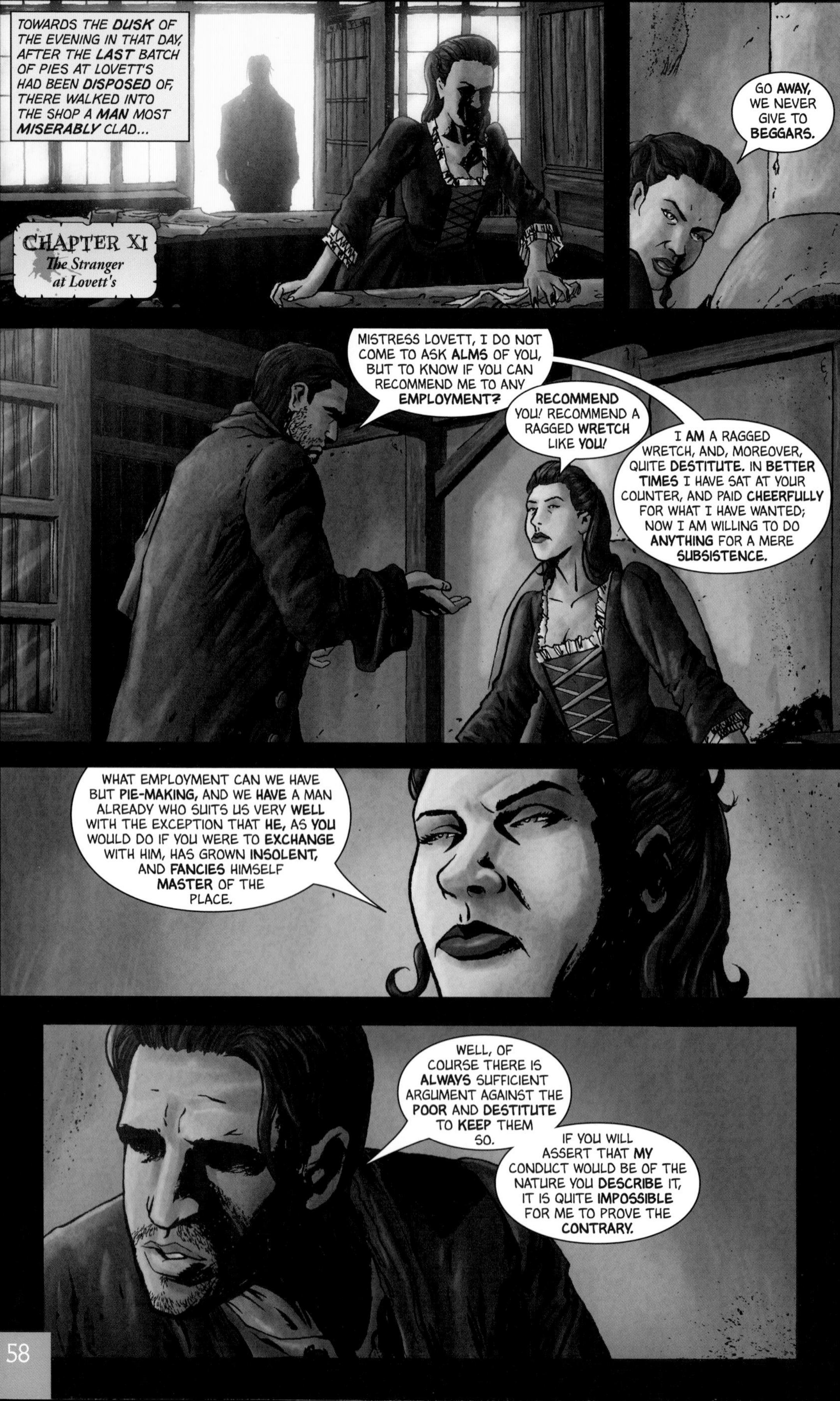

TOWARDS THE DUSK OF THE EVENING IN THAT DAY, AFTER THE LAST BATCH OF PIES AT LOVETT'S HAD BEEN DISPOSED OF, THERE WALKED INTO THE SHOP A MAN MOST MISERABLY CLAD...
CHAPTER XI
The Stranger at Lovett's
GO AWAY, WE NEVER GIVE TO BEGGARS.
MISTRESS LOVETT, I DO NOT COME TO ASK ALMS OF YOU, BUT TO KNOW IF YOU CAN RECOMMEND ME TO ANY EMPLOYMENT?
RECOMMEND YOU! RECOMMEND A RAGGED WRETCH LIKE YOU!
I AM A RAGGED WRETCH, AND, MOREOVER, QUITE DESTITUTE. IN BETTER TIMES I HAVE SAT AT YOUR COUNTER, AND PAID CHEERFULLY FOR WHAT I HAVE WANTED; NOW I AM WILLING TO DO ANYTHING FOR A MERE SUBSISTENCE.
WHAT EMPLOYMENT CAN WE HAVE BUT PIE-MAKING, AND WE HAVE A MAN ALREADY WHO SUITS US VERY WELL WITH THE EXCEPTION THAT HE, AS YOU WOULD DO IF YOU WERE TO EXCHANGE WITH HIM, HAS GROWN INSOLENT, AND FANCIES HIMSELF MASTER OF THE PLACE.
WELL, OF COURSE THERE IS ALWAYS SUFFICIENT ARGUMENT AGAINST THE POOR AND DESTITUTE TO KEEP THEM SO.
IF YOU WILL ASSERT THAT MY CONDUCT WOULD BE OF THE NATURE YOU DESCRIBE IT, IT IS QUITE IMPOSSIBLE FOR ME TO PROVE THE CONTRARY.

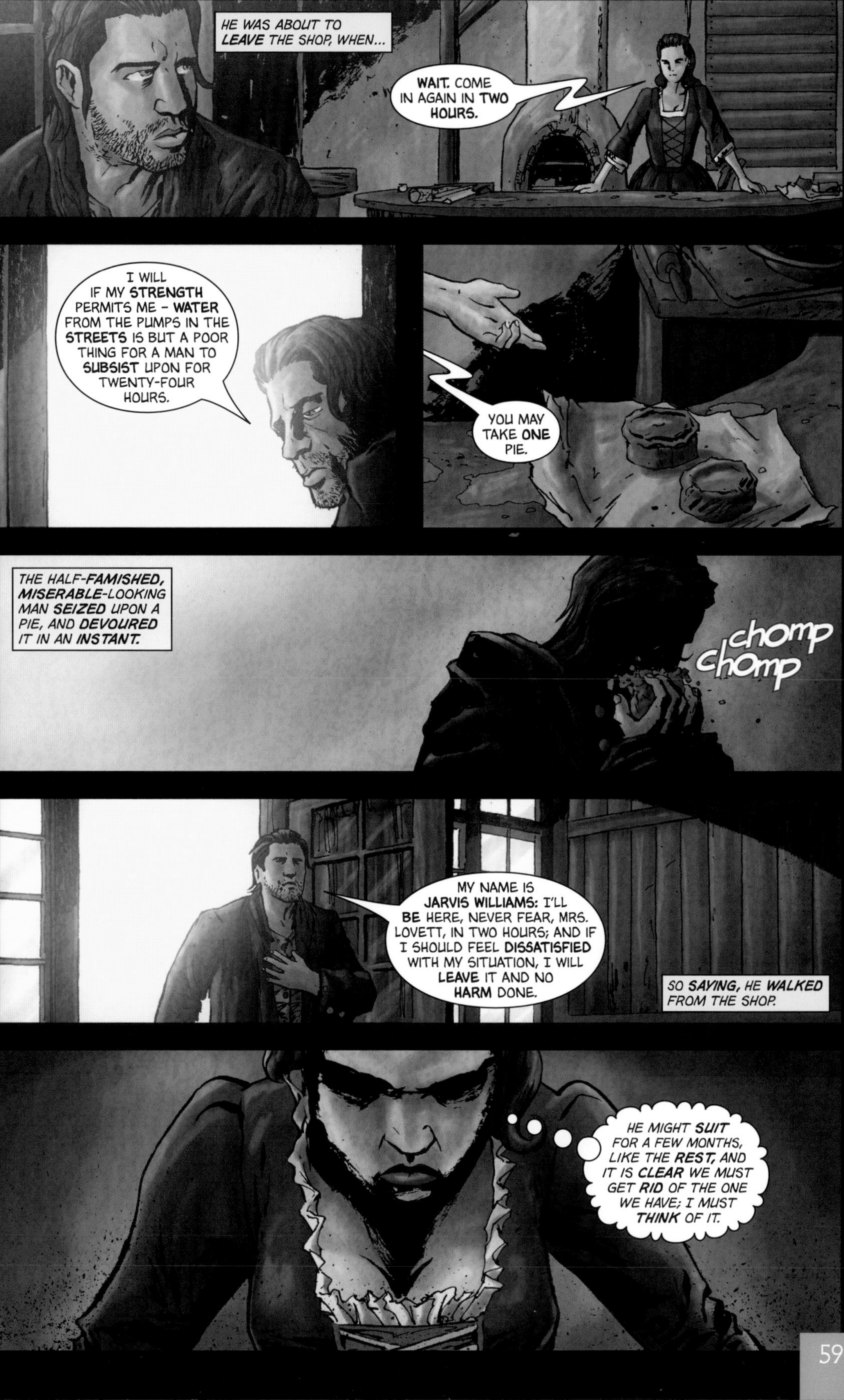
HE WAS ABOUT TO LEAVE THE SHOP, WHEN...
WAIT. COME IN AGAIN IN TWO HOURS.
I WILL IF MY STRENGTH PERMITS ME – WATER FROM THE PUMPS IN THE STREETS IS BUT A POOR THING FOR A MAN TO SUBSIST UPON FOR TWENTY-FOUR HOURS.
YOU MAY TAKE ONE PIE.
THE HALF-FAMISHED, MISERABLE-LOOKING MAN SEIZED UPON A PIE, AND DEVOURED IT IN AN INSTANT.
chomp chomp
MY NAME IS JARVIS WILLIAMS: I'LL BE HERE, NEVER FEAR, MRS. LOVETT, IN TWO HOURS; AND IF I SHOULD FEEL DISSATISFIED WITH MY SITUATION, I WILL LEAVE IT AND NO HARM DONE.
SO SAYING, HE WALKED FROM THE SHOP.
HE MIGHT SUIT FOR A FEW MONTHS, LIKE THE REST, AND IT IS CLEAR WE MUST GET RID OF THE ONE WE HAVE; I MUST THINK OF IT.

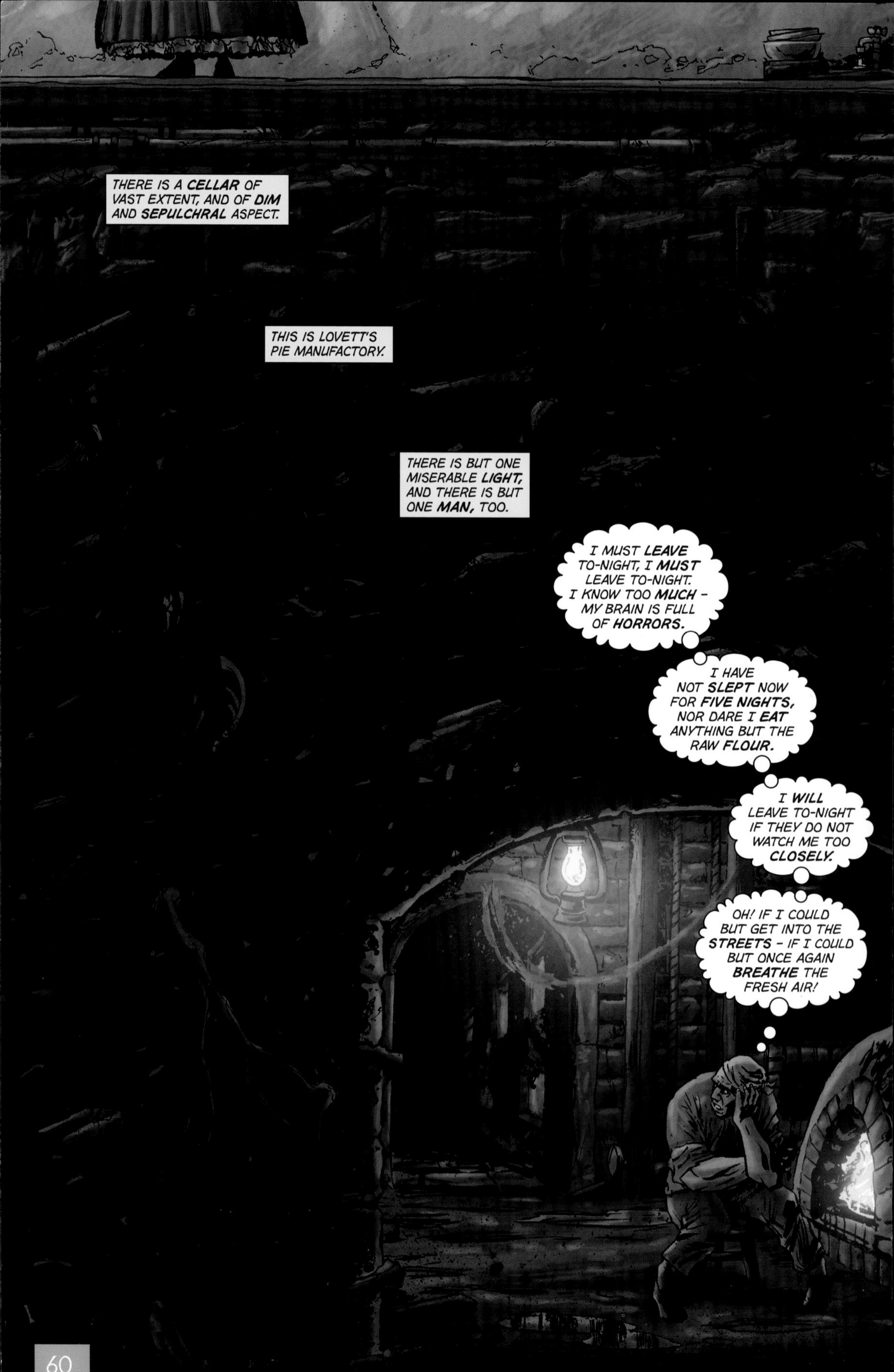
THERE IS A CELLAR OF VAST EXTENT, AND OF DIM AND SEPULCHRAL ASPECT.
THIS IS LOVETT'S PIE MANUFACTORY.
THERE IS BUT ONE MISERABLE LIGHT, AND THERE IS BUT ONE MAN, TOO.
I MUST LEAVE TO-NIGHT, I MUST LEAVE TO-NIGHT. I KNOW TOO MUCH - MY BRAIN IS FULL OF HORRORS.
I HAVE NOT SLEPT NOW FOR FIVE NIGHTS, NOR DARE I EAT ANYTHING BUT THE RAW FLOUR.
I WILL LEAVE TO-NIGHT IF THEY DO NOT WATCH ME TOO CLOSELY.
OH! IF I COULD BUT GET INTO THE STREETS - IF I COULD BUT ONCE AGAIN BREATHE THE FRESH AIR!

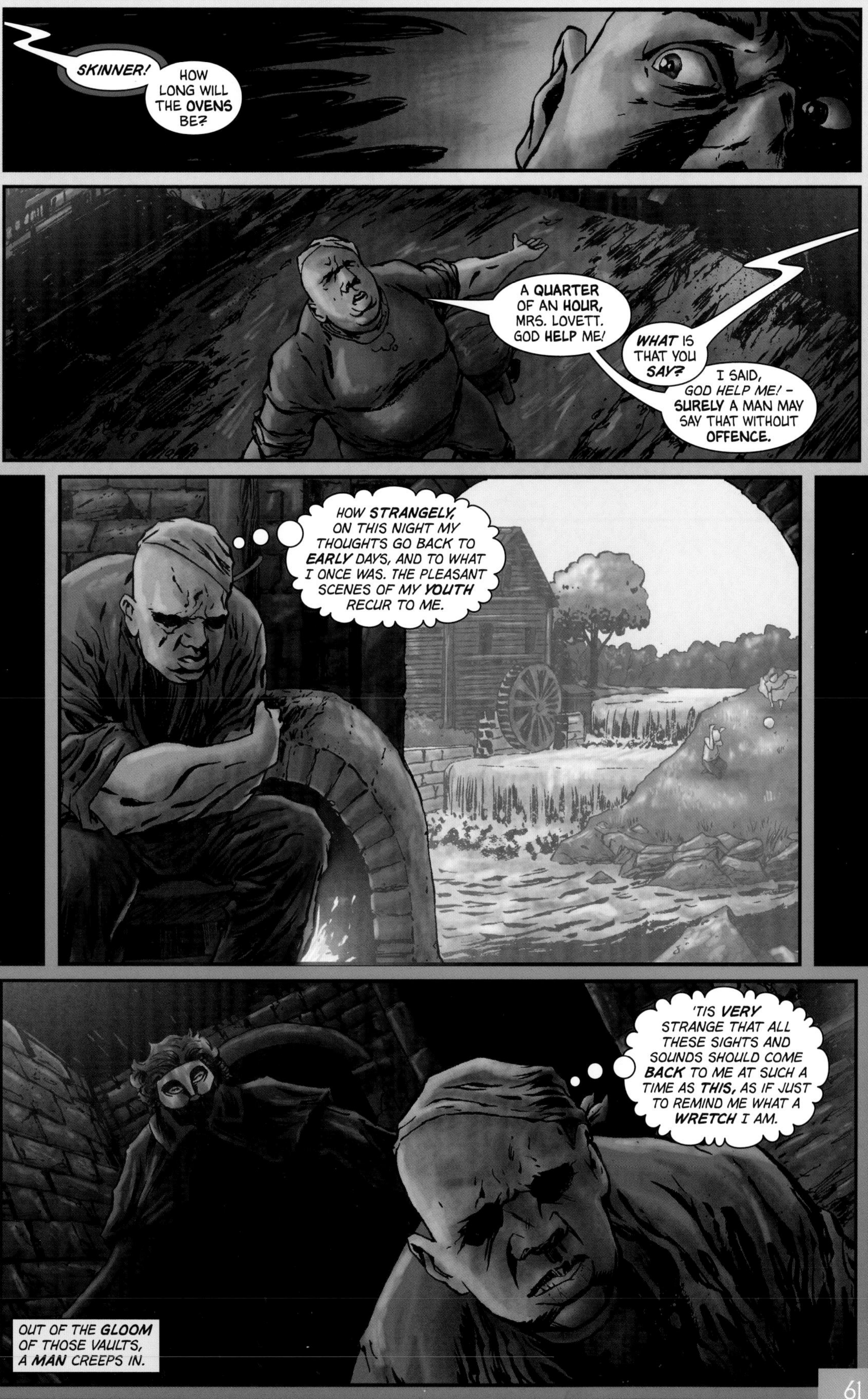
SKINNER!
HOW LONG WILL THE OVENS BE?
A QUARTER OF AN HOUR, MRS. LOVETT. GOD HELP ME!
WHAT IS THAT YOU SAY?
I SAID, GOD HELP ME! – SURELY A MAN MAY SAY THAT WITHOUT OFFENCE.
HOW STRANGELY, ON THIS NIGHT MY THOUGHTS GO BACK TO EARLY DAYS, AND TO WHAT I ONCE WAS. THE PLEASANT SCENES OF MY YOUTH RECUR TO ME.
'TIS VERY STRANGE THAT ALL THESE SIGHTS AND SOUNDS SHOULD COME BACK TO ME AT SUCH A TIME AS THIS, AS IF JUST TO REMIND ME WHAT A WRETCH I AM.
OUT OF THE GLOOM OF THOSE VAULTS, A MAN CREEPS IN.

IN ONE HAND HE CARRIES A DOUBLE-HEADED *HAMMER*, WITH A *POWERFUL* HANDLE.

IT IS EVIDENT THAT GREAT *SECRECY* IS HIS OBJECT, FOR HE IS WALKING ON HIS *STOCKING SOLES* ONLY.

HE *ADVANCES*, STEADILY AND *CAUTIOUSLY*.

GRASPING THE HAMMER *TIGHTLY* IN BOTH HANDS, HE *RAISES* IT ABOVE HIS *HEAD*...

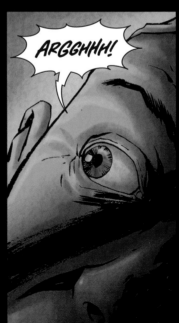

ARGGHHH!

KRAK

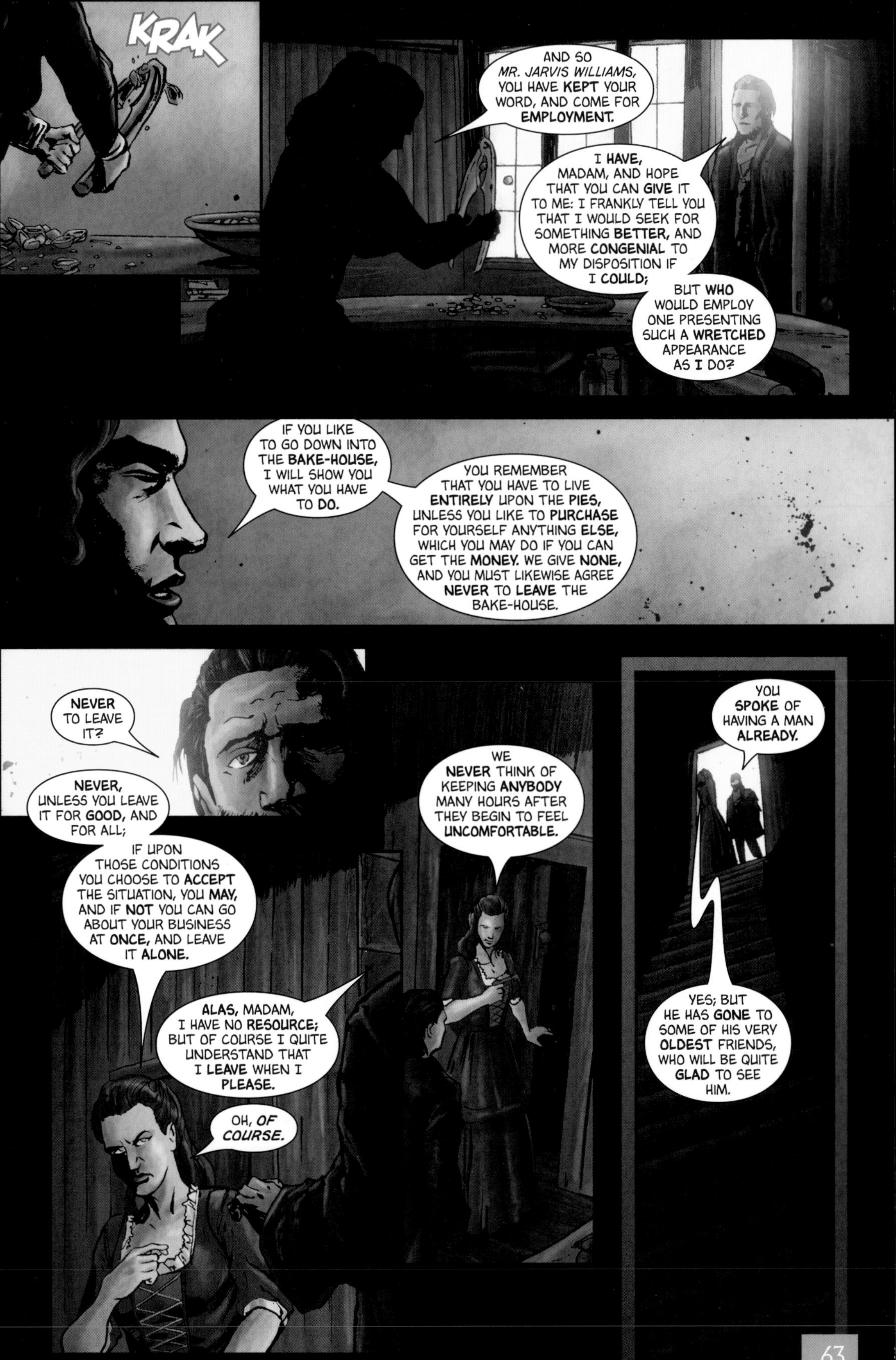
KRAK
AND SO MR. JARVIS WILLIAMS, YOU HAVE KEPT YOUR WORD, AND COME FOR EMPLOYMENT.
I HAVE, MADAM, AND HOPE THAT YOU CAN GIVE IT TO ME: I FRANKLY TELL YOU THAT I WOULD SEEK FOR SOMETHING BETTER, AND MORE CONGENIAL TO MY DISPOSITION IF I COULD;
BUT WHO WOULD EMPLOY ONE PRESENTING SUCH A WRETCHED APPEARANCE AS I DO?
IF YOU LIKE TO GO DOWN INTO THE BAKE-HOUSE, I WILL SHOW YOU WHAT YOU HAVE TO DO.
YOU REMEMBER THAT YOU HAVE TO LIVE ENTIRELY UPON THE PIES, UNLESS YOU LIKE TO PURCHASE FOR YOURSELF ANYTHING ELSE, WHICH YOU MAY DO IF YOU CAN GET THE MONEY. WE GIVE NONE, AND YOU MUST LIKEWISE AGREE NEVER TO LEAVE THE BAKE-HOUSE.
NEVER TO LEAVE IT?
NEVER, UNLESS YOU LEAVE IT FOR GOOD, AND FOR ALL;
IF UPON THOSE CONDITIONS YOU CHOOSE TO ACCEPT THE SITUATION, YOU MAY, AND IF NOT YOU CAN GO ABOUT YOUR BUSINESS AT ONCE, AND LEAVE IT ALONE.
ALAS, MADAM, I HAVE NO RESOURCE; BUT OF COURSE I QUITE UNDERSTAND THAT I LEAVE WHEN I PLEASE.
OH, OF COURSE.
WE NEVER THINK OF KEEPING ANYBODY MANY HOURS AFTER THEY BEGIN TO FEEL UNCOMFORTABLE.
YOU SPOKE OF HAVING A MAN ALREADY.
YES; BUT HE HAS GONE TO SOME OF HIS VERY OLDEST FRIENDS, WHO WILL BE QUITE GLAD TO SEE HIM.

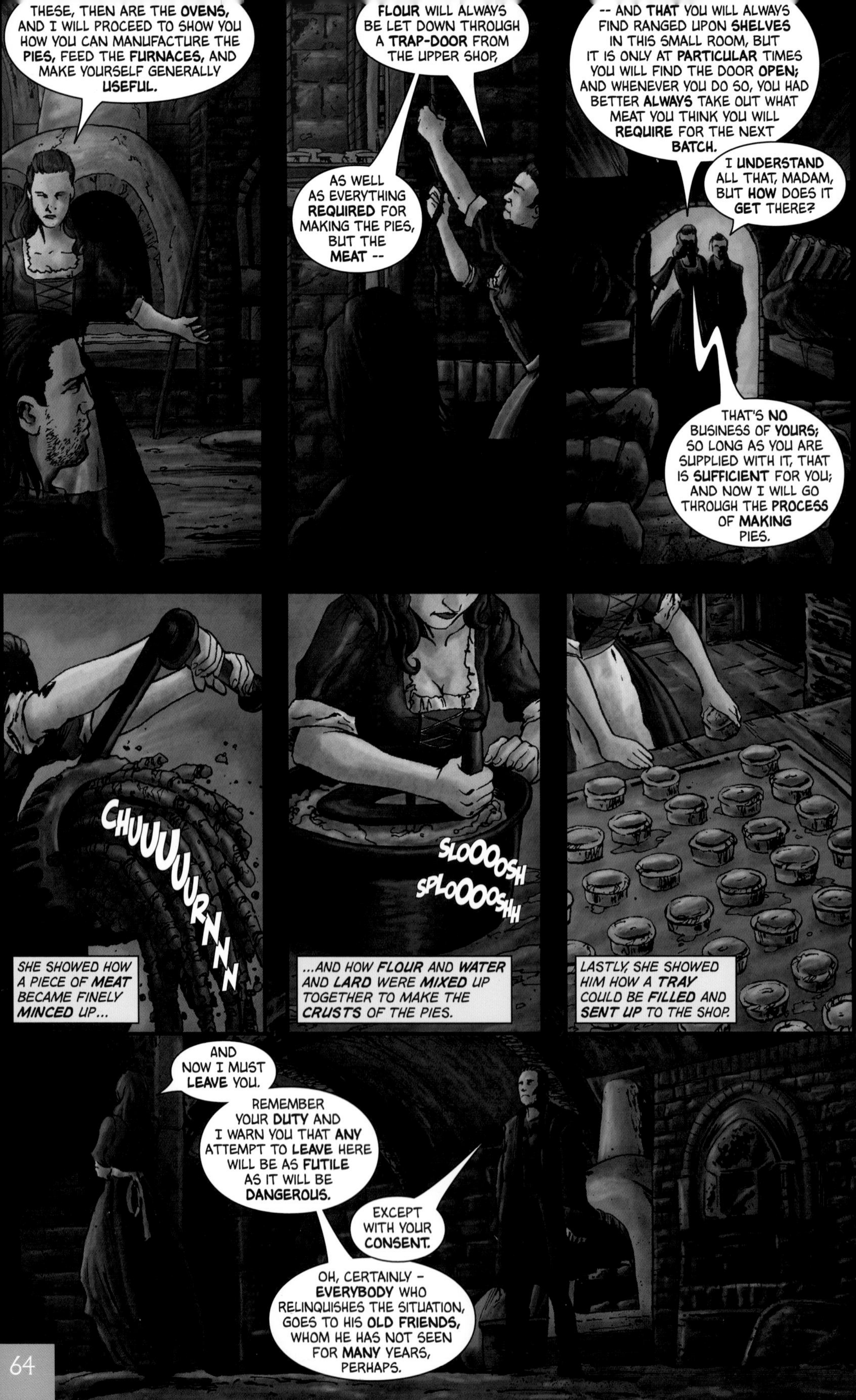
THESE, THEN ARE THE OVENS, AND I WILL PROCEED TO SHOW YOU HOW YOU CAN MANUFACTURE THE PIES, FEED THE FURNACES, AND MAKE YOURSELF GENERALLY USEFUL.
FLOUR WILL ALWAYS BE LET DOWN THROUGH A TRAP-DOOR FROM THE UPPER SHOP,
AS WELL AS EVERYTHING REQUIRED FOR MAKING THE PIES, BUT THE MEAT --
-- AND THAT YOU WILL ALWAYS FIND RANGED UPON SHELVES IN THIS SMALL ROOM, BUT IT IS ONLY AT PARTICULAR TIMES YOU WILL FIND THE DOOR OPEN; AND WHENEVER YOU DO SO, YOU HAD BETTER ALWAYS TAKE OUT WHAT MEAT YOU THINK YOU WILL REQUIRE FOR THE NEXT BATCH.
I UNDERSTAND ALL THAT, MADAM, BUT HOW DOES IT GET THERE?
THAT'S NO BUSINESS OF YOURS; SO LONG AS YOU ARE SUPPLIED WITH IT, THAT IS SUFFICIENT FOR YOU; AND NOW I WILL GO THROUGH THE PROCESS OF MAKING PIES.
CHUUUUURNNN
SHE SHOWED HOW A PIECE OF MEAT BECAME FINELY MINCED UP...
SLOOOOSH
SPLOOOOSHH
...AND HOW FLOUR AND WATER AND LARD WERE MIXED UP TOGETHER TO MAKE THE CRUSTS OF THE PIES.
LASTLY, SHE SHOWED HIM HOW A TRAY COULD BE FILLED AND SENT UP TO THE SHOP.
AND NOW I MUST LEAVE YOU.
REMEMBER YOUR DUTY AND I WARN YOU THAT ANY ATTEMPT TO LEAVE HERE WILL BE AS FUTILE AS IT WILL BE DANGEROUS.
EXCEPT WITH YOUR CONSENT.
OH, CERTAINLY – EVERYBODY WHO RELINQUISHES THE SITUATION, GOES TO HIS OLD FRIENDS, WHOM HE HAS NOT SEEN FOR MANY YEARS, PERHAPS.

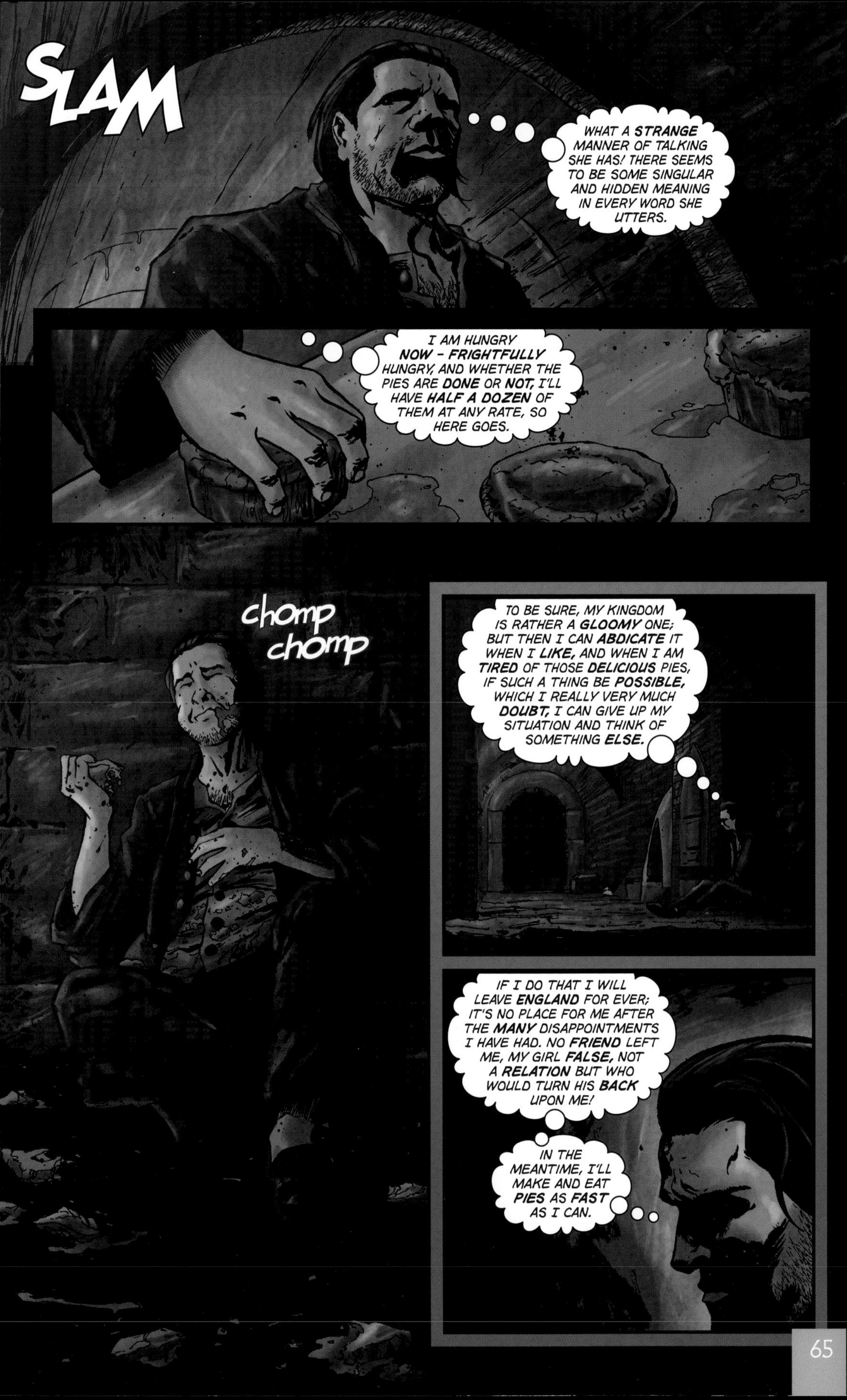
SLAM
WHAT A STRANGE MANNER OF TALKING SHE HAS! THERE SEEMS TO BE SOME SINGULAR AND HIDDEN MEANING IN EVERY WORD SHE UTTERS.
I AM HUNGRY NOW – FRIGHTFULLY HUNGRY, AND WHETHER THE PIES ARE DONE OR NOT, I'LL HAVE HALF A DOZEN OF THEM AT ANY RATE, SO HERE GOES.
chomp chomp
TO BE SURE, MY KINGDOM IS RATHER A GLOOMY ONE; BUT THEN I CAN ABDICATE IT WHEN I LIKE, AND WHEN I AM TIRED OF THOSE DELICIOUS PIES, IF SUCH A THING BE POSSIBLE, WHICH I REALLY VERY MUCH DOUBT, I CAN GIVE UP MY SITUATION AND THINK OF SOMETHING ELSE.
IF I DO THAT I WILL LEAVE ENGLAND FOR EVER; IT'S NO PLACE FOR ME AFTER THE MANY DISAPPOINTMENTS I HAVE HAD. NO FRIEND LEFT ME, MY GIRL FALSE, NOT A RELATION BUT WHO WOULD TURN HIS BACK UPON ME!
IN THE MEANTIME, I'LL MAKE AND EAT PIES AS FAST AS I CAN.

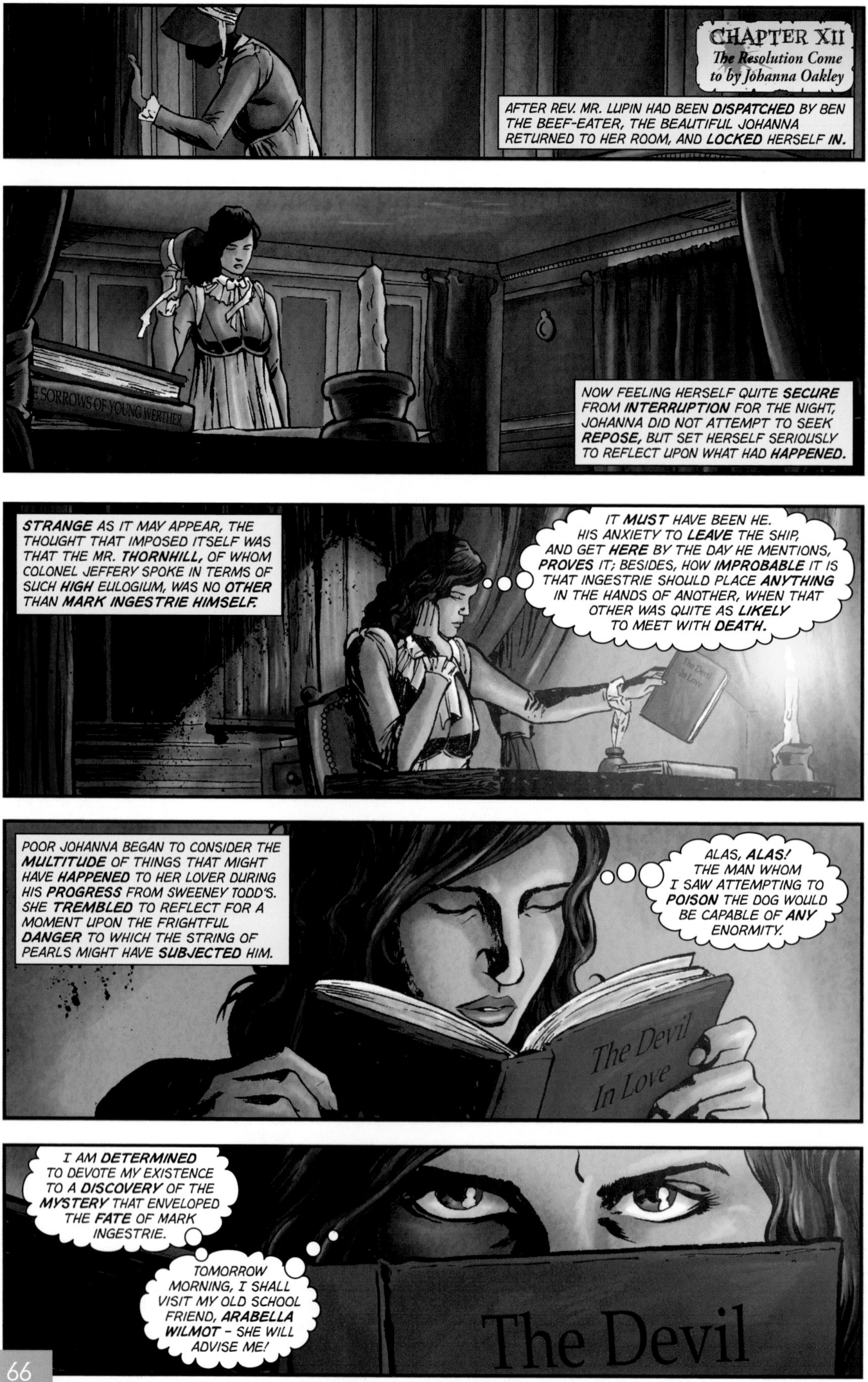
CHAPTER XII
The Resolution Come to by Johanna Oakley
AFTER REV. MR. LUPIN HAD BEEN DISPATCHED BY BEN THE BEEF-EATER, THE BEAUTIFUL JOHANNA RETURNED TO HER ROOM, AND LOCKED HERSELF IN.
THE SORROWS OF YOUNG WERTHER
NOW FEELING HERSELF QUITE SECURE FROM INTERRUPTION FOR THE NIGHT, JOHANNA DID NOT ATTEMPT TO SEEK REPOSE, BUT SET HERSELF SERIOUSLY TO REFLECT UPON WHAT HAD HAPPENED.
STRANGE AS IT MAY APPEAR, THE THOUGHT THAT IMPOSED ITSELF WAS THAT THE MR. THORNHILL, OF WHOM COLONEL JEFFERY SPOKE IN TERMS OF SUCH HIGH EULOGIUM, WAS NO OTHER THAN MARK INGESTRIE HIMSELF.
IT MUST HAVE BEEN HE. HIS ANXIETY TO LEAVE THE SHIP, AND GET HERE BY THE DAY HE MENTIONS, PROVES IT; BESIDES, HOW IMPROBABLE IT IS THAT INGESTRIE SHOULD PLACE ANYTHING IN THE HANDS OF ANOTHER, WHEN THAT OTHER WAS QUITE AS LIKELY TO MEET WITH DEATH.
The Devil In Love
POOR JOHANNA BEGAN TO CONSIDER THE MULTITUDE OF THINGS THAT MIGHT HAVE HAPPENED TO HER LOVER DURING HIS PROGRESS FROM SWEENEY TODD'S. SHE TREMBLED TO REFLECT FOR A MOMENT UPON THE FRIGHTFUL DANGER TO WHICH THE STRING OF PEARLS MIGHT HAVE SUBJECTED HIM.
ALAS, ALAS! THE MAN WHOM I SAW ATTEMPTING TO POISON THE DOG WOULD BE CAPABLE OF ANY ENORMITY.
The Devil In Love
I AM DETERMINED TO DEVOTE MY EXISTENCE TO A DISCOVERY OF THE MYSTERY THAT ENVELOPED THE FATE OF MARK INGESTRIE.
TOMORROW MORNING, I SHALL VISIT MY OLD SCHOOL FRIEND, ARABELLA WILMOT – SHE WILL ADVISE ME!
The Devil

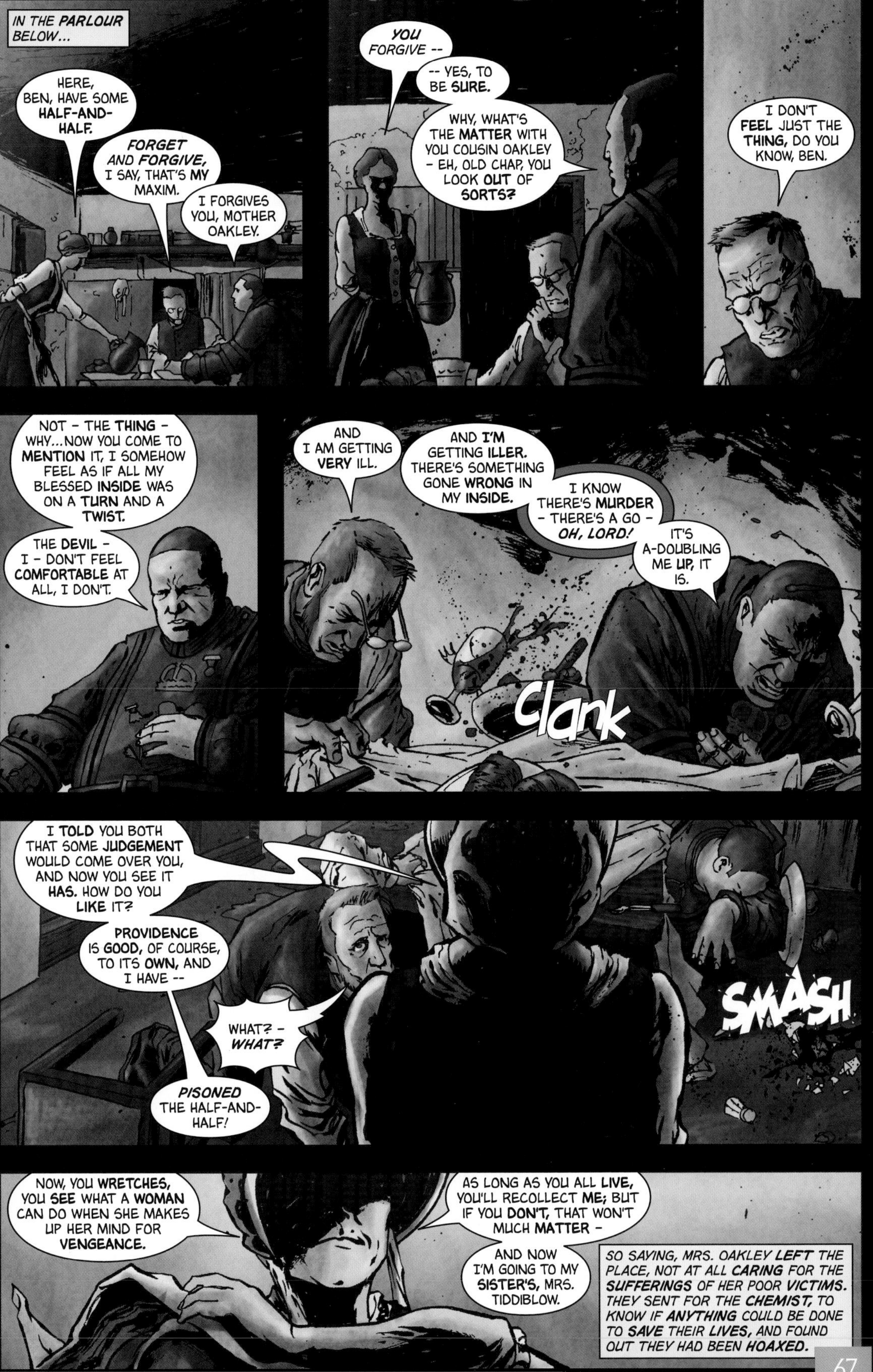
IN THE PARLOUR BELOW...
HERE, BEN, HAVE SOME HALF-AND-HALF.
FORGET AND FORGIVE, I SAY, THAT'S MY MAXIM.
I FORGIVES YOU, MOTHER OAKLEY.
YOU FORGIVE --
-- YES, TO BE SURE.
WHY, WHAT'S THE MATTER WITH YOU COUSIN OAKLEY - EH, OLD CHAP, YOU LOOK OUT OF SORTS?
I DON'T FEEL JUST THE THING, DO YOU KNOW, BEN.
NOT - THE THING - WHY...NOW YOU COME TO MENTION IT, I SOMEHOW FEEL AS IF ALL MY BLESSED INSIDE WAS ON A TURN AND A TWIST.
THE DEVIL - I - DON'T FEEL COMFORTABLE AT ALL, I DON'T.
AND I AM GETTING VERY ILL.
AND I'M GETTING ILLER. THERE'S SOMETHING GONE WRONG IN MY INSIDE.
I KNOW THERE'S MURDER - THERE'S A GO - OH, LORD!
IT'S A-DOUBLING ME UP, IT IS.
Clank
I TOLD YOU BOTH THAT SOME JUDGEMENT WOULD COME OVER YOU, AND NOW YOU SEE IT HAS. HOW DO YOU LIKE IT?
PROVIDENCE IS GOOD, OF COURSE, TO ITS OWN, AND I HAVE --
WHAT? - WHAT?
PISONED THE HALF-AND-HALF!
SMASH
NOW, YOU WRETCHES, YOU SEE WHAT A WOMAN CAN DO WHEN SHE MAKES UP HER MIND FOR VENGEANCE.
AS LONG AS YOU ALL LIVE, YOU'LL RECOLLECT ME; BUT IF YOU DON'T, THAT WON'T MUCH MATTER -
AND NOW I'M GOING TO MY SISTER'S, MRS. TIDDIBLOW.
SO SAYING, MRS. OAKLEY LEFT THE PLACE, NOT AT ALL CARING FOR THE SUFFERINGS OF HER POOR VICTIMS. THEY SENT FOR THE CHEMIST, TO KNOW IF ANYTHING COULD BE DONE TO SAVE THEIR LIVES, AND FOUND OUT THEY HAD BEEN HOAXED.

ALAS, *POOR* JOHANNA OAKLEY! *BETTER* HAD YOU LOVED SOMEONE OF LESS *ASPIRING* FEELINGS, AND OF LESS ARDENT *IMAGINATION*, THAN HIM TO WHOM YOU HAVE GIVEN YOUR HEART'S YOUNG *AFFECTIONS*.

IT IS *TRUE* THAT MARK INGESTRIE POSSESSED *GENIUS,* AND PERHAPS IT WAS THE GLORIOUS *LIGHT* THAT HOVERS AROUND THAT *FATAL* GIFT WHICH PROMPTED YOU TO *LOVE* HIM.

BUT GENIUS BRINGS *WITH* IT THAT UNHAPPY *RESTLESSNESS* OF INTELLECT WHICH IS *EVER* STRAINING AFTER THE *UNATTAINABLE*.

CHAPTER XIII
Johanna's interview with Arabella Wilmot, and the Advice

NOW, A *VISIT* FROM JOHANNA OAKLEY TO THE WILMOTS WAS NOT SO *RARE* A THING, THAT IT SHOULD EXCITE ANY UNUSUAL *SURPRISE*, BUT IN THIS CASE IT *DID* EXCITE UNUSUAL *PLEASURE* BECAUSE SHE HAD NOT BEEN *THERE* FOR SOME TIME.

WHY, JOHANNA, YOU SO *SELDOM* CALL UPON ME NOW, THAT I SUPPOSE I MUST ESTEEM IT AS A VERY *SPECIAL* ACT OF *GRACE* AND *FAVOUR* TO SEE YOU.

ARABELLA, I DO NOT KNOW *WHAT* YOU WILL SAY TO ME WHEN I TELL YOU THAT MY PRESENT VISIT TO YOU IS BECAUSE I AM IN A *DIFFICULTY*, AND WANT YOUR *ADVICE*.

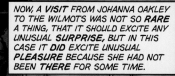

THEN YOU COULD *NOT* HAVE COME TO A *BETTER* PERSON,

FOR I HAVE READ ALL THE *NOVELS* IN *LONDON*, AND KNOW ALL THE *DIFFICULTIES* THAT ANYBODY CAN POSSIBLY GET INTO, AND, WHAT IS *MORE* IMPORTANT, I KNOW ALL THE *MEANS* OF GETTING *OUT* OF THEM, LET THEM BE WHAT THEY *MAY*.

JOHANNA THEN, WITH *GREAT* EARNESTNESS, RELATED TO HER FRIEND THE WHOLE OF THE *PARTICULARS* CONNECTED WITH HER DEEP AND SINCERE *ATTACHMENT* TO MARK INGESTRIE AND OF HER *SUSPICIONS* AGAINST *SWEENEY TODD.*

THE HILARITY OF *SPIRITS* WHICH HAD CHARACTERISED ARABELLA, IN THE *EARLIER* PART OF THEIR INTERVIEW, ENTIRELY *LEFT* HER, AS JOHANNA PROCEEDED IN HER *MOURNFUL* NARRATION, AND BY THE TIME SHE HAD CONCLUDED, TEARS OF THE MOST GENUINE *SYMPATHY* STOOD IN HER EYES.

I WILL OWN I DID *HESITATE* TO INFLICT UPON YOU MY *MISERIES,* FOR MISERIES THEY HAVE BEEN AND ALAS! MISERIES THEY SEEM DESTINED TO *REMAIN.*

AND DID YOU THINK SO *LIGHTLY* OF MY *FRIENDSHIP* THAT IT WAS TO BE ENTRUSTED WITH NOTHING BUT WHAT WORE A *PLEASANT* ASPECT?

TRUE FRIENDSHIP IS SURELY *BEST* SHOWN IN THE ENCOUNTER OF *DIFFICULTY* AND *DISTRESS.*

WHY, MY *DEAR* JOHANNA, YOU *MUST* PERCEIVE THAT ALL THE EVIDENCE YOU HAVE REGARDING THIS THORNHILL FOLLOWS HIM UP TO THAT *BARBER'S SHOP* IN FLEET-STREET, AND NO *FARTHER.*

THERE LIES THE MYSTERY OF HIS *FATE.*

FROM WHAT YOU HAVE *SEEN* OF THAT MAN, *TODD,* DO YOU THINK HE IS ONE WHO WOULD *HESITATE* EVEN AT A *MURDER?*

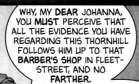

OH, HORROR! MY *OWN* THOUGHTS, BUT I DREADED TO *PRONOUNCE* THE WORD.

IT WOULD APPEAR THERE IS SOME *FEARFUL* MYSTERY; BUT DO NOT, JOHANNA, CONCLUDE *HASTILY,* THAT THAT MYSTERY IS ONE OF *DEATH.*

BE IT SO OR *NOT,* I *MUST* SOLVE IT, OR GO DISTRACTED. HEAVEN HAVE *MERCY* UPON ME; FOR EVEN NOW I FEEL A *FEVER* IN MY BRAIN, THAT PRECLUDES ALMOST THE *POSSIBILITY* OF RATIONAL THOUGHT.

BE *CALM,* BE *CALM,* WE WILL *THINK* THE MATTER OVER, CALMLY AND *SERIOUSLY;* AND WHO KNOWS, WE MAY THINK OF SOME *ADVENTITIOUS* MODE OF ARRIVING AT A KNOWLEDGE OF THE *TRUTH.*

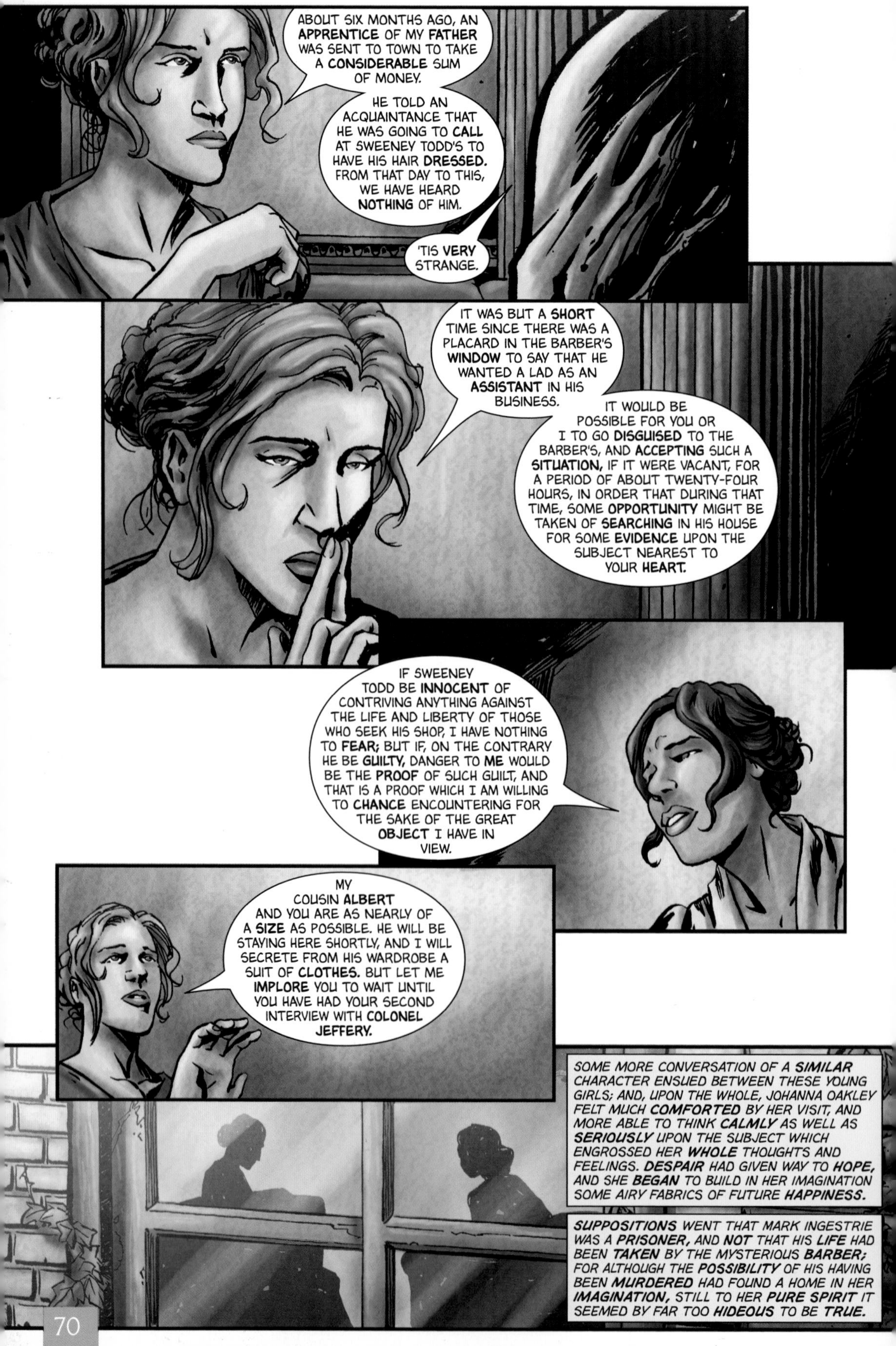
ABOUT SIX MONTHS AGO, AN APPRENTICE OF MY FATHER WAS SENT TO TOWN TO TAKE A CONSIDERABLE SUM OF MONEY.
HE TOLD AN ACQUAINTANCE THAT HE WAS GOING TO CALL AT SWEENEY TODD'S TO HAVE HIS HAIR DRESSED. FROM THAT DAY TO THIS, WE HAVE HEARD NOTHING OF HIM.
'TIS VERY STRANGE.
IT WAS BUT A SHORT TIME SINCE THERE WAS A PLACARD IN THE BARBER'S WINDOW TO SAY THAT HE WANTED A LAD AS AN ASSISTANT IN HIS BUSINESS.
IT WOULD BE POSSIBLE FOR YOU OR I TO GO DISGUISED TO THE BARBER'S, AND ACCEPTING SUCH A SITUATION, IF IT WERE VACANT, FOR A PERIOD OF ABOUT TWENTY-FOUR HOURS, IN ORDER THAT DURING THAT TIME, SOME OPPORTUNITY MIGHT BE TAKEN OF SEARCHING IN HIS HOUSE FOR SOME EVIDENCE UPON THE SUBJECT NEAREST TO YOUR HEART.
IF SWEENEY TODD BE INNOCENT OF CONTRIVING ANYTHING AGAINST THE LIFE AND LIBERTY OF THOSE WHO SEEK HIS SHOP, I HAVE NOTHING TO FEAR; BUT IF, ON THE CONTRARY HE BE GUILTY, DANGER TO ME WOULD BE THE PROOF OF SUCH GUILT, AND THAT IS A PROOF WHICH I AM WILLING TO CHANCE ENCOUNTERING FOR THE SAKE OF THE GREAT OBJECT I HAVE IN VIEW.
MY COUSIN ALBERT AND YOU ARE AS NEARLY OF A SIZE AS POSSIBLE. HE WILL BE STAYING HERE SHORTLY, AND I WILL SECRETE FROM HIS WARDROBE A SUIT OF CLOTHES. BUT LET ME IMPLORE YOU TO WAIT UNTIL YOU HAVE HAD YOUR SECOND INTERVIEW WITH COLONEL JEFFERY.
SOME MORE CONVERSATION OF A SIMILAR CHARACTER ENSUED BETWEEN THESE YOUNG GIRLS; AND, UPON THE WHOLE, JOHANNA OAKLEY FELT MUCH COMFORTED BY HER VISIT, AND MORE ABLE TO THINK CALMLY AS WELL AS SERIOUSLY UPON THE SUBJECT WHICH ENGROSSED HER WHOLE THOUGHTS AND FEELINGS. DESPAIR HAD GIVEN WAY TO HOPE, AND SHE BEGAN TO BUILD IN HER IMAGINATION SOME AIRY FABRICS OF FUTURE HAPPINESS.
SUPPOSITIONS WENT THAT MARK INGESTRIE WAS A PRISONER, AND NOT THAT HIS LIFE HAD BEEN TAKEN BY THE MYSTERIOUS BARBER; FOR ALTHOUGH THE POSSIBILITY OF HIS HAVING BEEN MURDERED HAD FOUND A HOME IN HER IMAGINATION, STILL TO HER PURE SPIRIT IT SEEMED BY FAR TOO HIDEOUS TO BE TRUE.

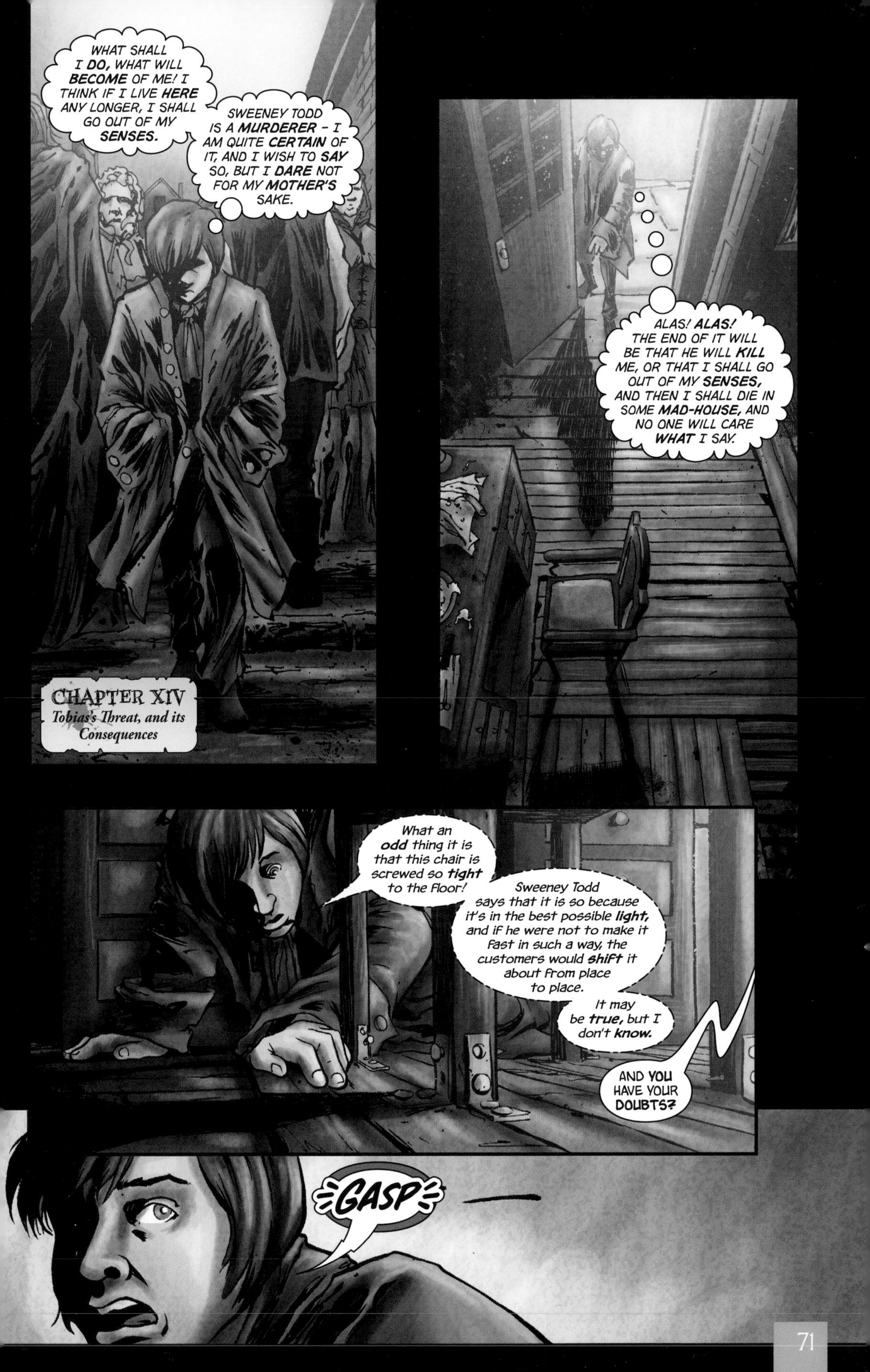
WHAT SHALL I DO, WHAT WILL BECOME OF ME! I THINK IF I LIVE HERE ANY LONGER, I SHALL GO OUT OF MY SENSES.
SWEENEY TODD IS A MURDERER – I AM QUITE CERTAIN OF IT, AND I WISH TO SAY SO, BUT I DARE NOT FOR MY MOTHER'S SAKE.
CHAPTER XIV
Tobias's Threat, and its Consequences
ALAS! ALAS! THE END OF IT WILL BE THAT HE WILL KILL ME, OR THAT I SHALL GO OUT OF MY SENSES, AND THEN I SHALL DIE IN SOME MAD-HOUSE, AND NO ONE WILL CARE WHAT I SAY.
What an odd thing it is that this chair is screwed so tight to the floor!
Sweeney Todd says that it is so because it's in the best possible light, and if he were not to make it fast in such a way, the customers would shift it about from place to place.
It may be true, but I don't know.
AND YOU HAVE YOUR DOUBTS?
GASP

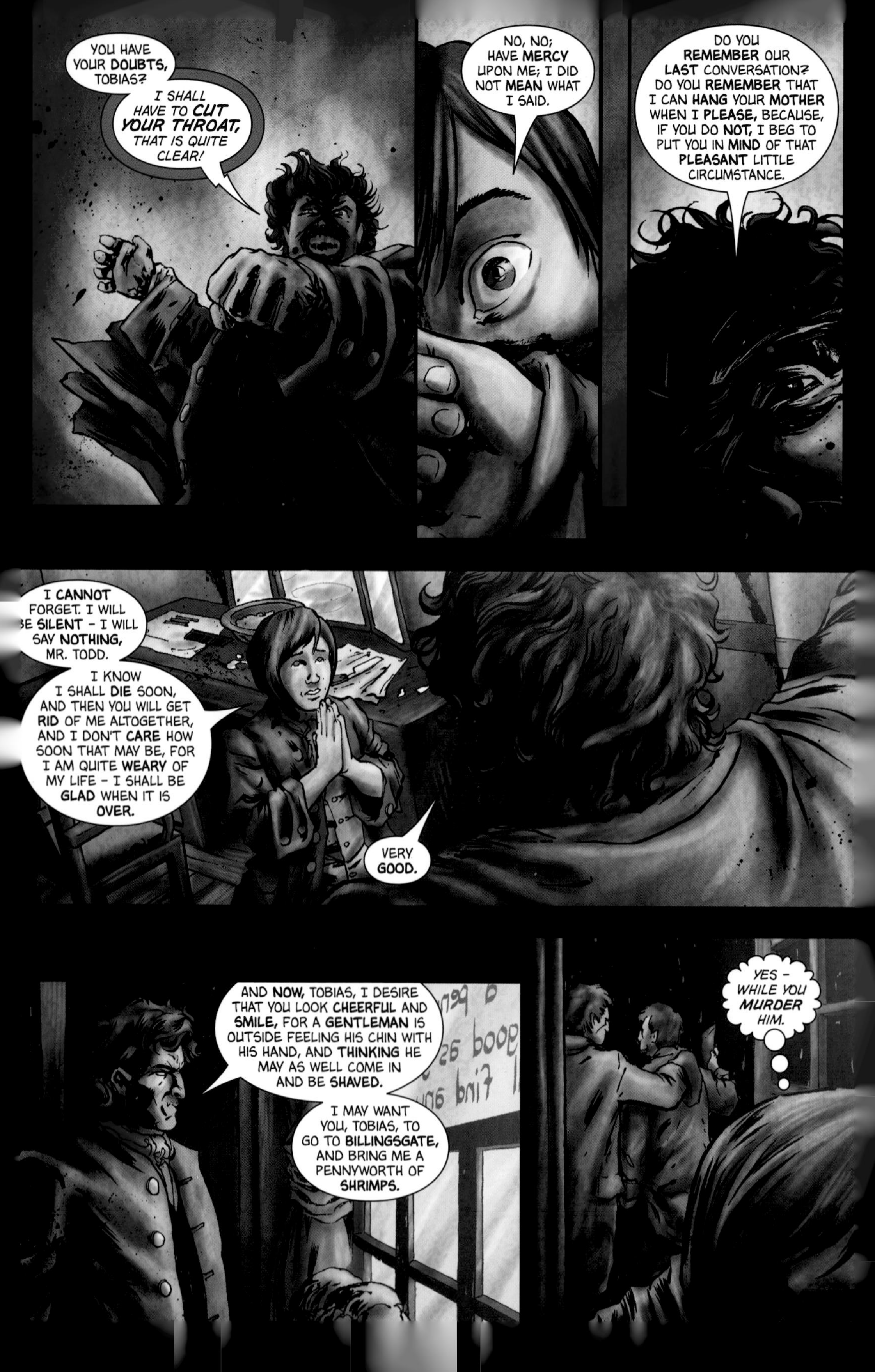
YOU HAVE YOUR DOUBTS, TOBIAS?
I SHALL HAVE TO CUT YOUR THROAT, THAT IS QUITE CLEAR!
NO, NO; HAVE MERCY UPON ME; I DID NOT MEAN WHAT I SAID.
DO YOU REMEMBER OUR LAST CONVERSATION? DO YOU REMEMBER THAT I CAN HANG YOUR MOTHER WHEN I PLEASE, BECAUSE, IF YOU DO NOT, I BEG TO PUT YOU IN MIND OF THAT PLEASANT LITTLE CIRCUMSTANCE.
I CANNOT FORGET. I WILL BE SILENT - I WILL SAY NOTHING, MR. TODD.
I KNOW I SHALL DIE SOON, AND THEN YOU WILL GET RID OF ME ALTOGETHER, AND I DON'T CARE HOW SOON THAT MAY BE, FOR I AM QUITE WEARY OF MY LIFE - I SHALL BE GLAD WHEN IT IS OVER.
VERY GOOD.
AND NOW, TOBIAS, I DESIRE THAT YOU LOOK CHEERFUL AND SMILE, FOR A GENTLEMAN IS OUTSIDE FEELING HIS CHIN WITH HIS HAND, AND THINKING HE MAY AS WELL COME IN AND BE SHAVED.
I MAY WANT YOU, TOBIAS, TO GO TO BILLINGSGATE, AND BRING ME A PENNYWORTH OF SHRIMPS.
YES - WHILE YOU MURDER HIM.

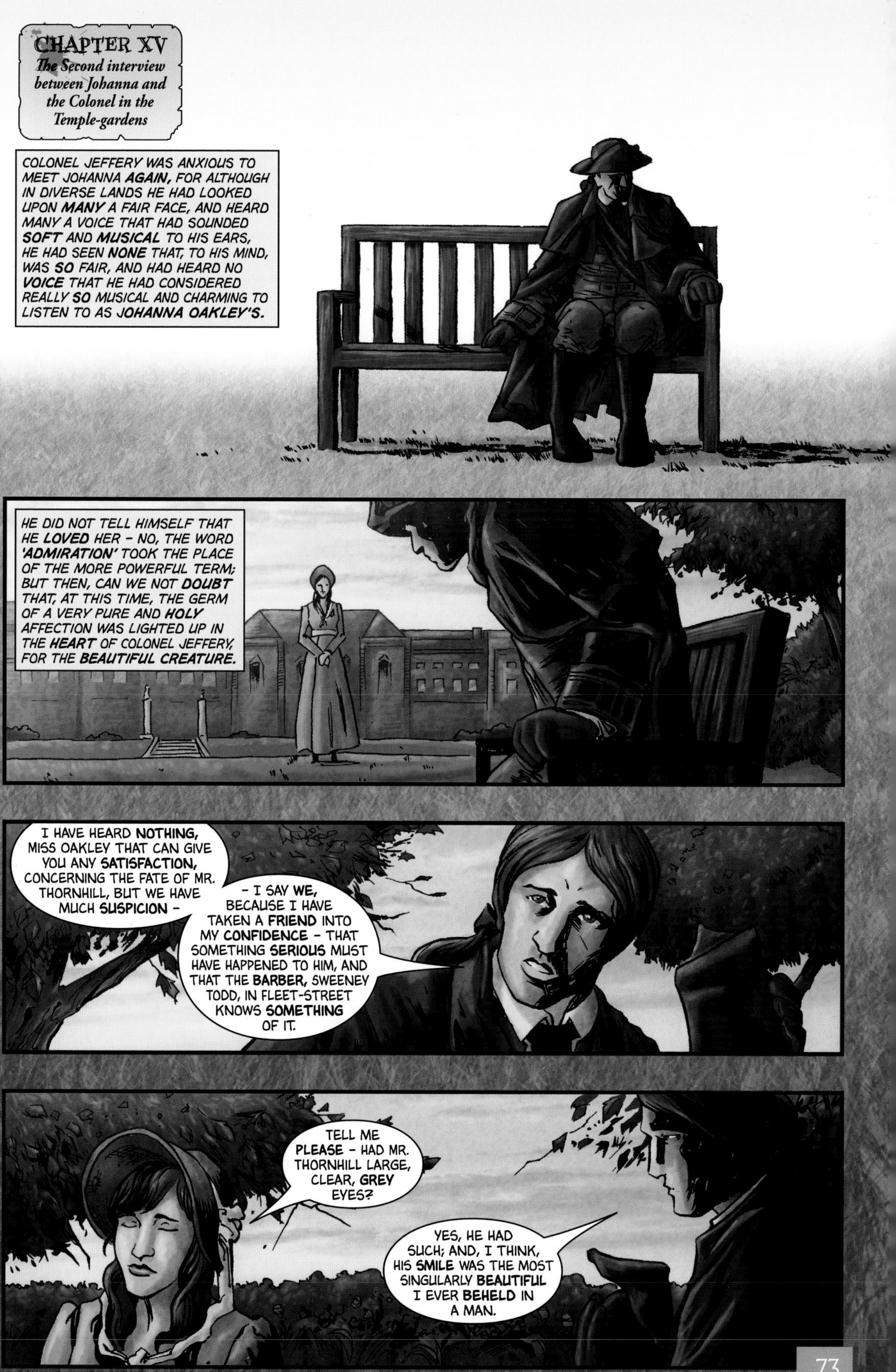
CHAPTER XV
The Second interview between Johanna and the Colonel in the Temple-gardens
COLONEL JEFFERY WAS ANXIOUS TO MEET JOHANNA AGAIN, FOR ALTHOUGH IN DIVERSE LANDS HE HAD LOOKED UPON MANY A FAIR FACE, AND HEARD MANY A VOICE THAT HAD SOUNDED SOFT AND MUSICAL TO HIS EARS, HE HAD SEEN NONE THAT, TO HIS MIND, WAS SO FAIR, AND HAD HEARD NO VOICE THAT HE HAD CONSIDERED REALLY SO MUSICAL AND CHARMING TO LISTEN TO AS JOHANNA OAKLEY'S.
HE DID NOT TELL HIMSELF THAT HE LOVED HER – NO, THE WORD 'ADMIRATION' TOOK THE PLACE OF THE MORE POWERFUL TERM; BUT THEN, CAN WE NOT DOUBT THAT, AT THIS TIME, THE GERM OF A VERY PURE AND HOLY AFFECTION WAS LIGHTED UP IN THE HEART OF COLONEL JEFFERY, FOR THE BEAUTIFUL CREATURE.
I HAVE HEARD NOTHING, MISS OAKLEY THAT CAN GIVE YOU ANY SATISFACTION, CONCERNING THE FATE OF MR. THORNHILL, BUT WE HAVE MUCH SUSPICION –
– I SAY WE, BECAUSE I HAVE TAKEN A FRIEND INTO MY CONFIDENCE – THAT SOMETHING SERIOUS MUST HAVE HAPPENED TO HIM, AND THAT THE BARBER, SWEENEY TODD, IN FLEET-STREET KNOWS SOMETHING OF IT.
TELL ME PLEASE – HAD MR. THORNHILL LARGE, CLEAR, GREY EYES?
YES, HE HAD SUCH; AND, I THINK, HIS SMILE WAS THE MOST SINGULARLY BEAUTIFUL I EVER BEHELD IN A MAN.

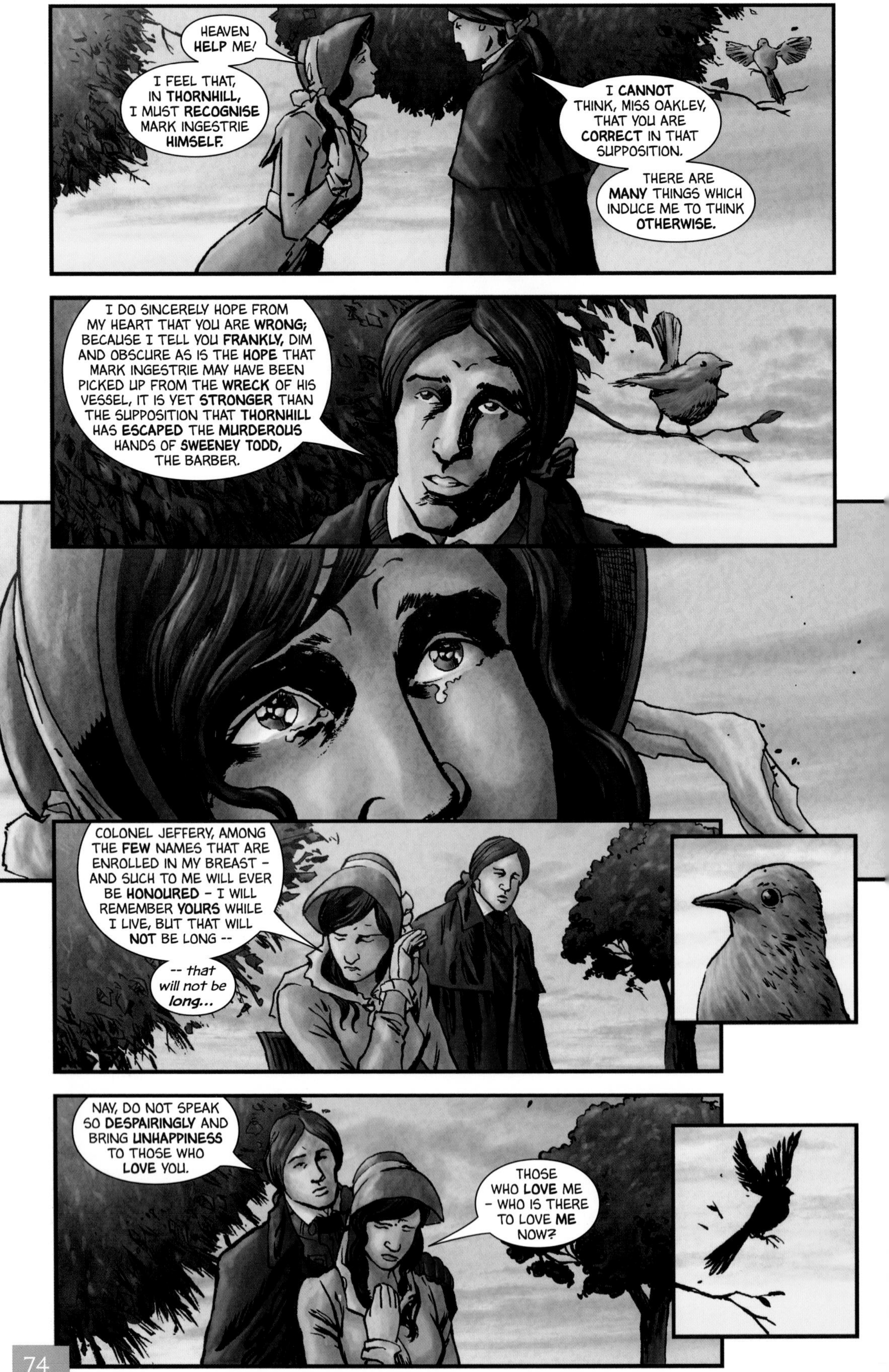
HEAVEN HELP ME!
I FEEL THAT, IN THORNHILL, I MUST RECOGNISE MARK INGESTRIE HIMSELF.
I CANNOT THINK, MISS OAKLEY, THAT YOU ARE CORRECT IN THAT SUPPOSITION.
THERE ARE MANY THINGS WHICH INDUCE ME TO THINK OTHERWISE.
I DO SINCERELY HOPE FROM MY HEART THAT YOU ARE WRONG; BECAUSE I TELL YOU FRANKLY, DIM AND OBSCURE AS IS THE HOPE THAT MARK INGESTRIE MAY HAVE BEEN PICKED UP FROM THE WRECK OF HIS VESSEL, IT IS YET STRONGER THAN THE SUPPOSITION THAT THORNHILL HAS ESCAPED THE MURDEROUS HANDS OF SWEENEY TODD, THE BARBER.
COLONEL JEFFERY, AMONG THE FEW NAMES THAT ARE ENROLLED IN MY BREAST – AND SUCH TO ME WILL EVER BE HONOURED – I WILL REMEMBER YOURS WHILE I LIVE, BUT THAT WILL NOT BE LONG --
-- that will not be long...
NAY, DO NOT SPEAK SO DESPAIRINGLY AND BRING UNHAPPINESS TO THOSE WHO LOVE YOU.
THOSE WHO LOVE ME – WHO IS THERE TO LOVE ME NOW?

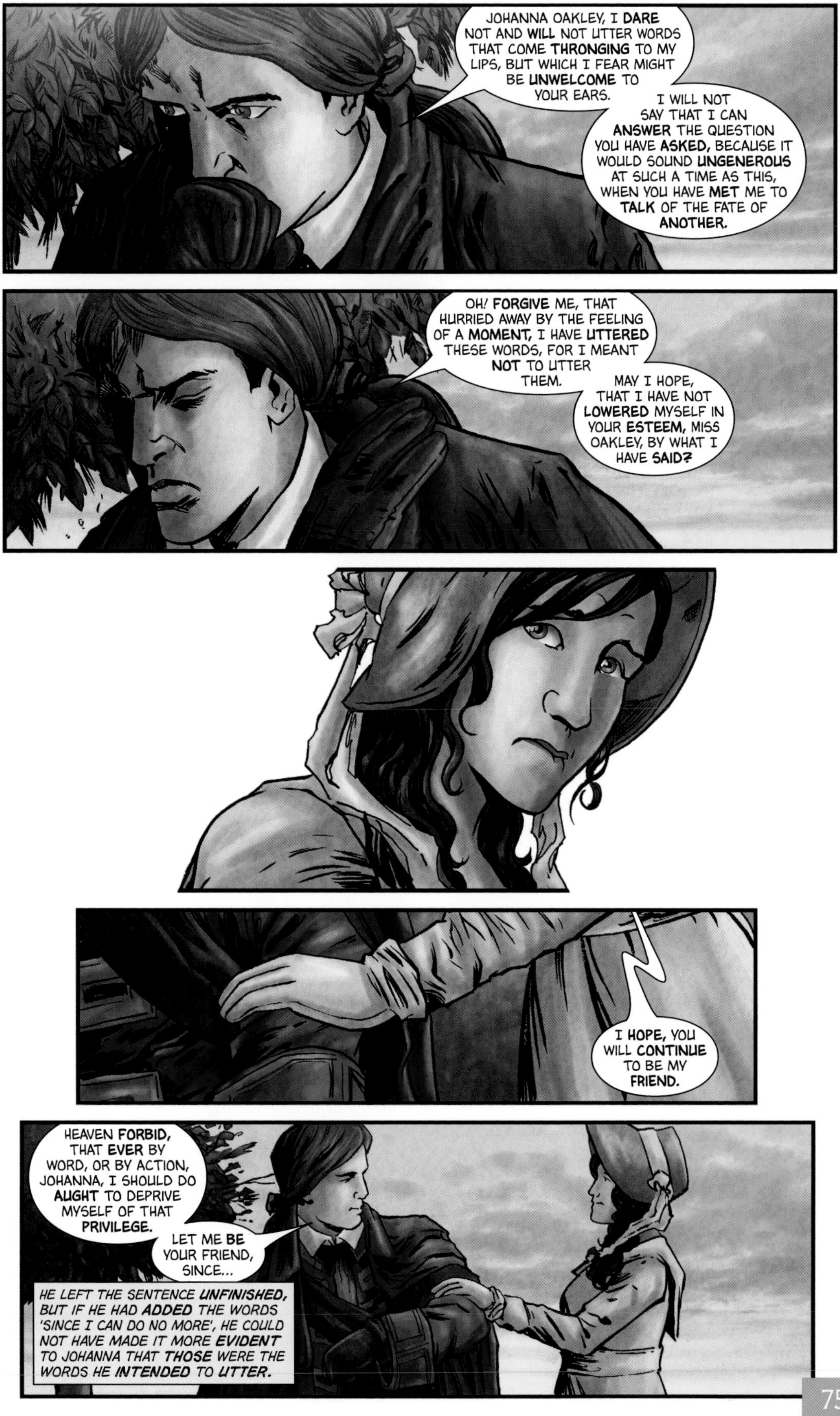
JOHANNA OAKLEY, I DARE NOT AND WILL NOT UTTER WORDS THAT COME THRONGING TO MY LIPS, BUT WHICH I FEAR MIGHT BE UNWELCOME TO YOUR EARS.
I WILL NOT SAY THAT I CAN ANSWER THE QUESTION YOU HAVE ASKED, BECAUSE IT WOULD SOUND UNGENEROUS AT SUCH A TIME AS THIS, WHEN YOU HAVE MET ME TO TALK OF THE FATE OF ANOTHER.
OH! FORGIVE ME, THAT HURRIED AWAY BY THE FEELING OF A MOMENT, I HAVE UTTERED THESE WORDS, FOR I MEANT NOT TO UTTER THEM.
MAY I HOPE, THAT I HAVE NOT LOWERED MYSELF IN YOUR ESTEEM, MISS OAKLEY, BY WHAT I HAVE SAID?
I HOPE, YOU WILL CONTINUE TO BE MY FRIEND.
HEAVEN FORBID, THAT EVER BY WORD, OR BY ACTION, JOHANNA, I SHOULD DO AUGHT TO DEPRIVE MYSELF OF THAT PRIVILEGE.
LET ME BE YOUR FRIEND, SINCE...
HE LEFT THE SENTENCE UNFINISHED, BUT IF HE HAD ADDED THE WORDS 'SINCE I CAN DO NO MORE', HE COULD NOT HAVE MADE IT MORE EVIDENT TO JOHANNA THAT THOSE WERE THE WORDS HE INTENDED TO UTTER.

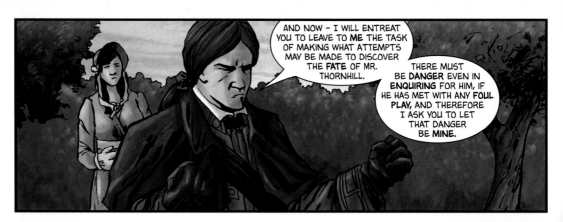

AND NOW – I WILL ENTREAT YOU TO LEAVE TO **ME** THE TASK OF MAKING WHAT ATTEMPTS MAY BE MADE TO DISCOVER THE **FATE** OF MR. THORNHILL.

THERE MUST BE **DANGER** EVEN IN **ENQUIRING** FOR HIM, IF HE HAS MET WITH ANY **FOUL PLAY**, AND THEREFORE I ASK YOU TO LET THAT DANGER BE **MINE**.

I WONDER IF I SHOULD **TELL** HIM ABOUT THE **SCHEME** OF OPERATIONS THAT HAD BEEN SUGGESTED BY ARABELLA WILMOT.

BUT, SOMEHOW OR ANOTHER, SHE **SHRANK** MOST WONDERFULLY FROM SO DOING, BOTH ON ACCOUNT OF THE **CENSURE** WHICH SHE CONCLUDED HE WOULD BE LIKELY TO CAST UPON IT, AND THE ROMANTIC, **STRANGE** NATURE OF THE PLAN **ITSELF**.

MAY I HOPE THAT THIS DAY WEEK I MAY SEE YOU **AGAIN**, IN ORDER THAT I MAY TELL YOU IF I HAVE MADE ANY **DISCOVERY**, AND THAT YOU MAY TELL ME THE **SAME?**

I WILL **COME**, IF I **CAN** COME.

HE **PARTED** WITH JOHANNA, AND HE WALKED SLOWLY AWAY WITH HIS **MIND** FULLY IMPRESSED WITH THE **EXCELLENCE** AND **BEAUTY** OF THE SPECTACLE-MAKER'S DAUGHTER.

I LOVE HER. I **LOVE** HER, BUT SHE SEEMS IN **NO** RESPECT WILLING TO ENCHAIN **HER** AFFECTIONS.

ALAS! HOW SAD IT IS FOR ME THAT THE **BEING** WHOM, ABOVE ALL **OTHERS**, I COULD **WISH** TO CALL MY **OWN**, INSTEAD OF BEING A **JOY** TO ME, I HAVE ONLY ENCOUNTERED THAT SHE MIGHT IMPART A **PANG** TO MY **HEART**.

WHACK

BEAUTIFUL AND **EXCELLENT** JOHANNA, I **LOVE YOU**, BUT I CAN SEE THAT YOUR **OWN** AFFECTIONS ARE WITHERED FOR **EVER**.

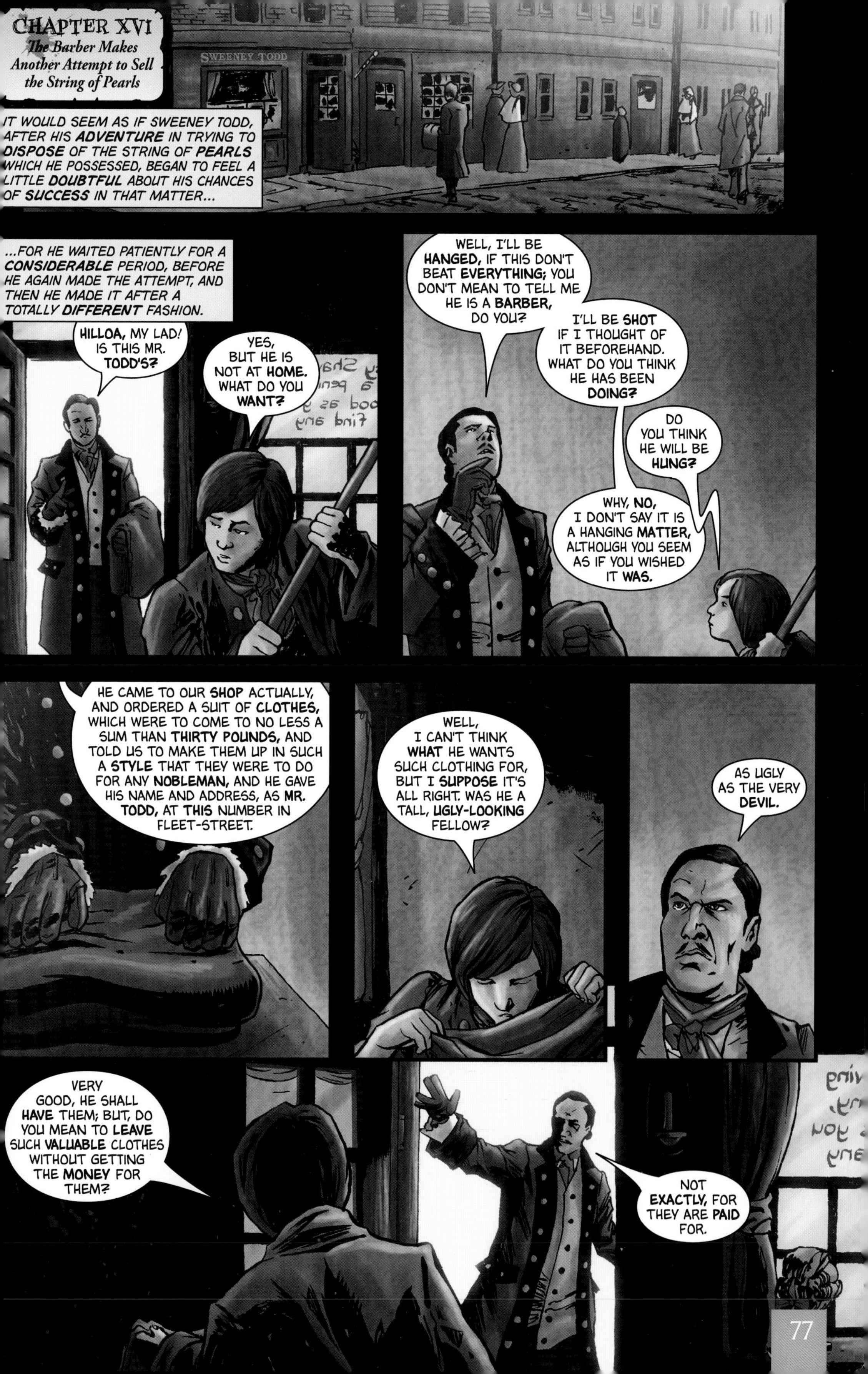
CHAPTER XVI
The Barber Makes Another Attempt to Sell the String of Pearls
SWEENEY TODD
IT WOULD SEEM AS IF SWEENEY TODD, AFTER HIS ADVENTURE IN TRYING TO DISPOSE OF THE STRING OF PEARLS WHICH HE POSSESSED, BEGAN TO FEEL A LITTLE DOUBTFUL ABOUT HIS CHANCES OF SUCCESS IN THAT MATTER...
...FOR HE WAITED PATIENTLY FOR A CONSIDERABLE PERIOD, BEFORE HE AGAIN MADE THE ATTEMPT, AND THEN HE MADE IT AFTER A TOTALLY DIFFERENT FASHION.
HILLOA, MY LAD! IS THIS MR. TODD'S?
YES, BUT HE IS NOT AT HOME. WHAT DO YOU WANT?
WELL, I'LL BE HANGED, IF THIS DON'T BEAT EVERYTHING; YOU DON'T MEAN TO TELL ME HE IS A BARBER, DO YOU?
I'LL BE SHOT IF I THOUGHT OF IT BEFOREHAND. WHAT DO YOU THINK HE HAS BEEN DOING?
DO YOU THINK HE WILL BE HUNG?
WHY, NO, I DON'T SAY IT IS A HANGING MATTER, ALTHOUGH YOU SEEM AS IF YOU WISHED IT WAS.
HE CAME TO OUR SHOP ACTUALLY, AND ORDERED A SUIT OF CLOTHES, WHICH WERE TO COME TO NO LESS A SUM THAN THIRTY POUNDS, AND TOLD US TO MAKE THEM UP IN SUCH A STYLE THAT THEY WERE TO DO FOR ANY NOBLEMAN, AND HE GAVE HIS NAME AND ADDRESS, AS MR. TODD, AT THIS NUMBER IN FLEET-STREET.
WELL, I CAN'T THINK WHAT HE WANTS SUCH CLOTHING FOR, BUT I SUPPOSE IT'S ALL RIGHT. WAS HE A TALL, UGLY-LOOKING FELLOW?
AS UGLY AS THE VERY DEVIL.
VERY GOOD, HE SHALL HAVE THEM; BUT, DO YOU MEAN TO LEAVE SUCH VALUABLE CLOTHES WITHOUT GETTING THE MONEY FOR THEM?
NOT EXACTLY, FOR THEY ARE PAID FOR.

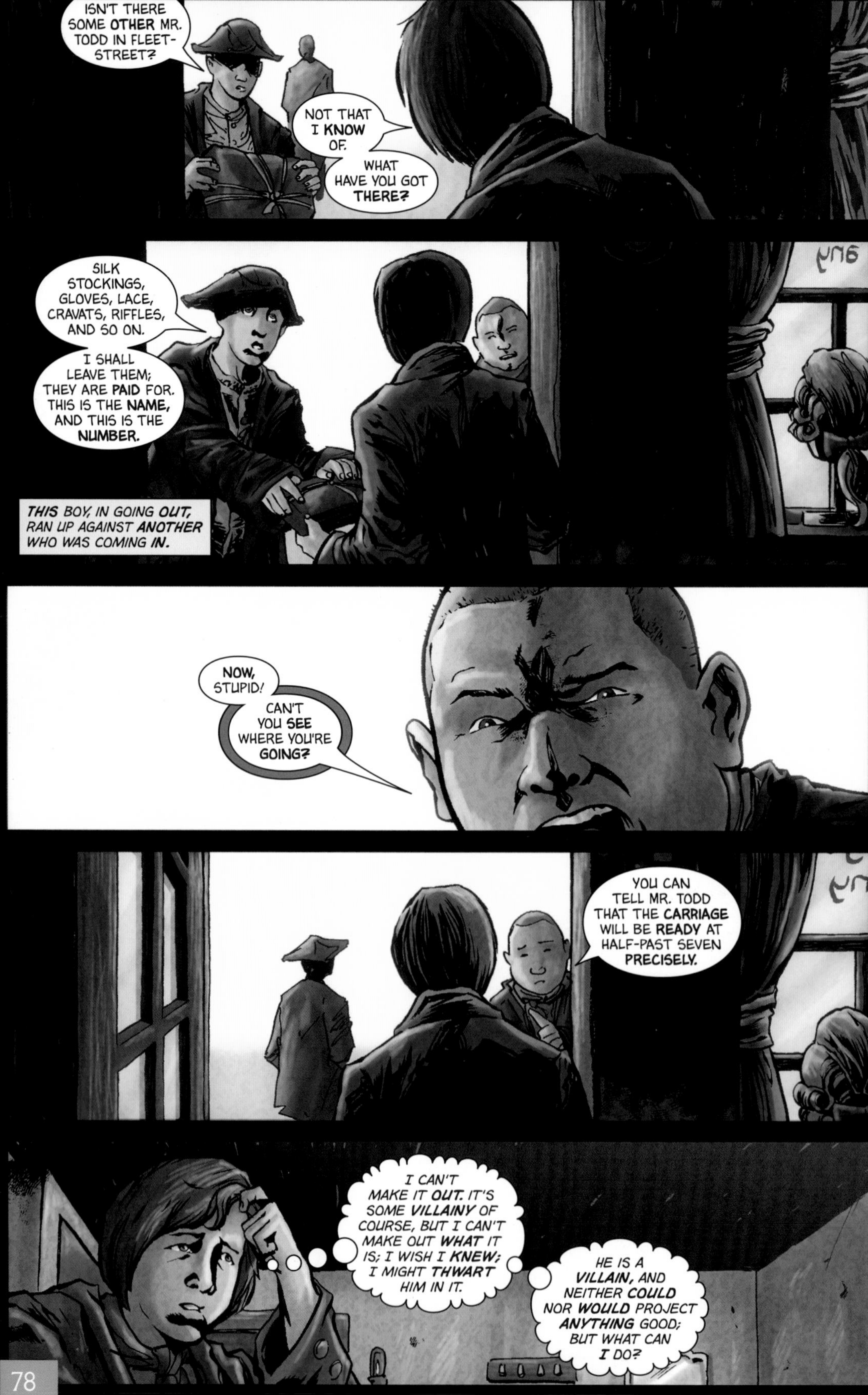
ISN'T THERE SOME OTHER MR. TODD IN FLEET-STREET?
NOT THAT I KNOW OF.
WHAT HAVE YOU GOT THERE?
SILK STOCKINGS, GLOVES, LACE, CRAVATS, RIFFLES, AND SO ON.
I SHALL LEAVE THEM; THEY ARE PAID FOR. THIS IS THE NAME, AND THIS IS THE NUMBER.
THIS BOY, IN GOING OUT, RAN UP AGAINST ANOTHER WHO WAS COMING IN.
NOW, STUPID!
CAN'T YOU SEE WHERE YOU'RE GOING?
YOU CAN TELL MR. TODD THAT THE CARRIAGE WILL BE READY AT HALF-PAST SEVEN PRECISELY.
I CAN'T MAKE IT OUT. IT'S SOME VILLAINY OF COURSE, BUT I CAN'T MAKE OUT WHAT IT IS; I WISH I KNEW; I MIGHT THWART HIM IN IT.
HE IS A VILLAIN, AND NEITHER COULD NOR WOULD PROJECT ANYTHING GOOD; BUT WHAT CAN I DO?

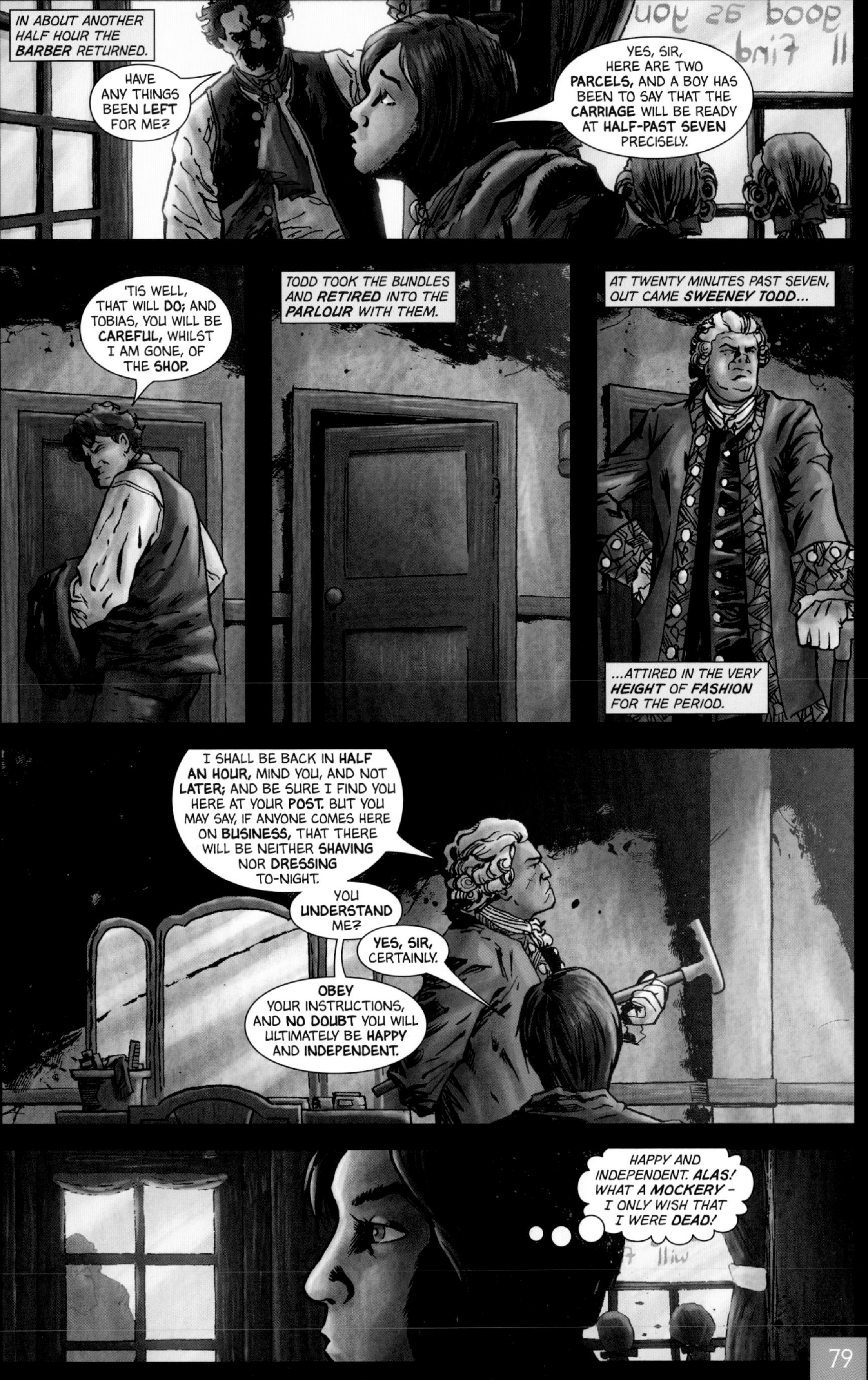
IN ABOUT ANOTHER HALF HOUR THE BARBER RETURNED.
HAVE ANY THINGS BEEN LEFT FOR ME?
YES, SIR, HERE ARE TWO PARCELS, AND A BOY HAS BEEN TO SAY THAT THE CARRIAGE WILL BE READY AT HALF-PAST SEVEN PRECISELY.
'TIS WELL, THAT WILL DO; AND TOBIAS, YOU WILL BE CAREFUL, WHILST I AM GONE, OF THE SHOP.
TODD TOOK THE BUNDLES AND RETIRED INTO THE PARLOUR WITH THEM.
AT TWENTY MINUTES PAST SEVEN, OUT CAME SWEENEY TODD...
...ATTIRED IN THE VERY HEIGHT OF FASHION FOR THE PERIOD.
I SHALL BE BACK IN HALF AN HOUR, MIND YOU, AND NOT LATER; AND BE SURE I FIND YOU HERE AT YOUR POST. BUT YOU MAY SAY, IF ANYONE COMES HERE ON BUSINESS, THAT THERE WILL BE NEITHER SHAVING NOR DRESSING TO-NIGHT.
YOU UNDERSTAND ME?
YES, SIR, CERTAINLY.
OBEY YOUR INSTRUCTIONS, AND NO DOUBT YOU WILL ULTIMATELY BE HAPPY AND INDEPENDENT.
HAPPY AND INDEPENDENT. ALAS! WHAT A MOCKERY - I ONLY WISH THAT I WERE DEAD!

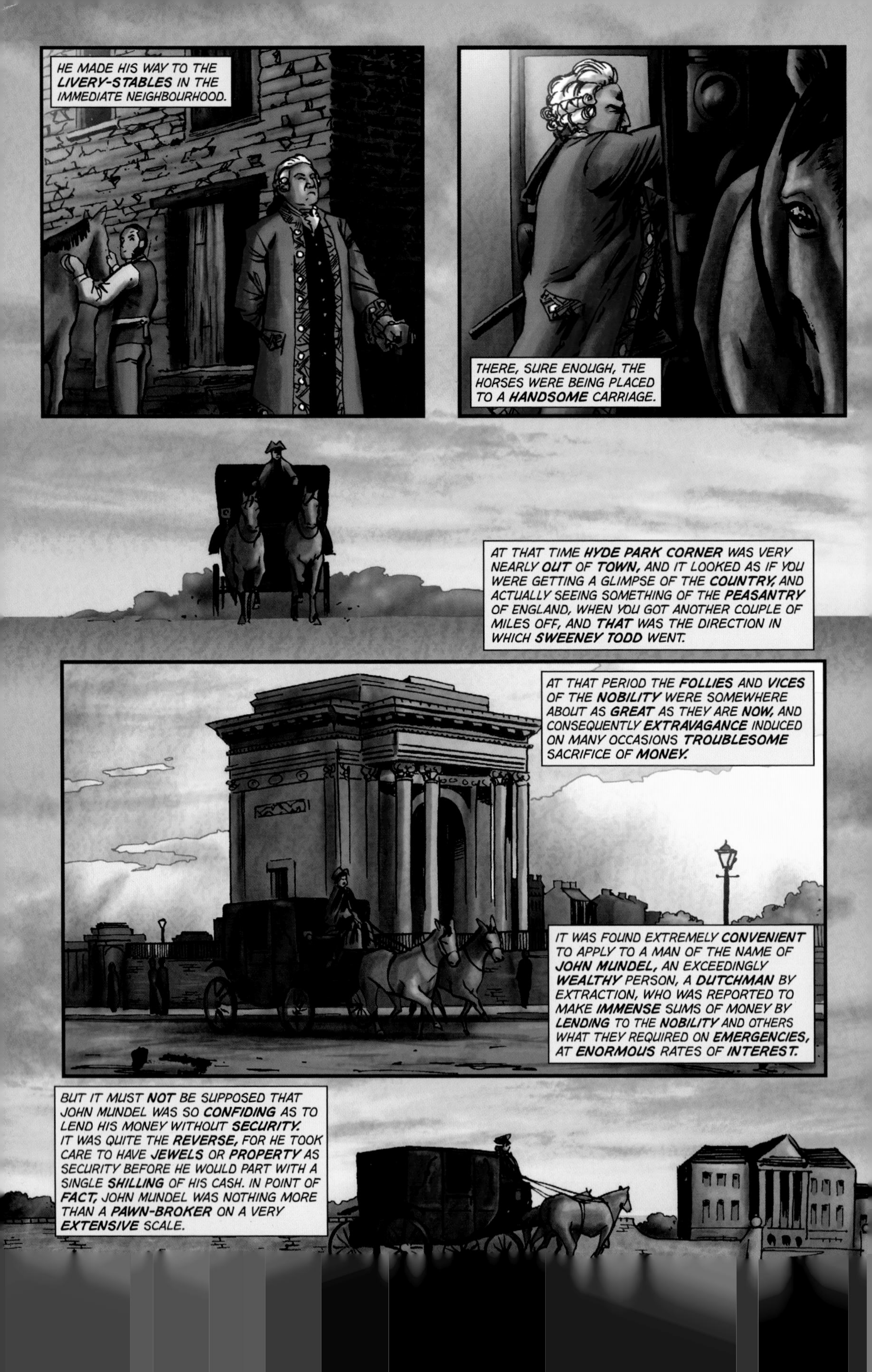
HE MADE HIS WAY TO THE LIVERY-STABLES IN THE IMMEDIATE NEIGHBOURHOOD.
THERE, SURE ENOUGH, THE HORSES WERE BEING PLACED TO A HANDSOME CARRIAGE.
AT THAT TIME HYDE PARK CORNER WAS VERY NEARLY OUT OF TOWN, AND IT LOOKED AS IF YOU WERE GETTING A GLIMPSE OF THE COUNTRY, AND ACTUALLY SEEING SOMETHING OF THE PEASANTRY OF ENGLAND, WHEN YOU GOT ANOTHER COUPLE OF MILES OFF, AND THAT WAS THE DIRECTION IN WHICH SWEENEY TODD WENT.
AT THAT PERIOD THE FOLLIES AND VICES OF THE NOBILITY WERE SOMEWHERE ABOUT AS GREAT AS THEY ARE NOW, AND CONSEQUENTLY EXTRAVAGANCE INDUCED ON MANY OCCASIONS TROUBLESOME SACRIFICE OF MONEY.
IT WAS FOUND EXTREMELY CONVENIENT TO APPLY TO A MAN OF THE NAME OF JOHN MUNDEL, AN EXCEEDINGLY WEALTHY PERSON, A DUTCHMAN BY EXTRACTION, WHO WAS REPORTED TO MAKE IMMENSE SUMS OF MONEY BY LENDING TO THE NOBILITY AND OTHERS WHAT THEY REQUIRED ON EMERGENCIES, AT ENORMOUS RATES OF INTEREST.
BUT IT MUST NOT BE SUPPOSED THAT JOHN MUNDEL WAS SO CONFIDING AS TO LEND HIS MONEY WITHOUT SECURITY. IT WAS QUITE THE REVERSE, FOR HE TOOK CARE TO HAVE JEWELS OR PROPERTY AS SECURITY BEFORE HE WOULD PART WITH A SINGLE SHILLING OF HIS CASH. IN POINT OF FACT, JOHN MUNDEL WAS NOTHING MORE THAN A PAWN-BROKER ON A VERY EXTENSIVE SCALE.

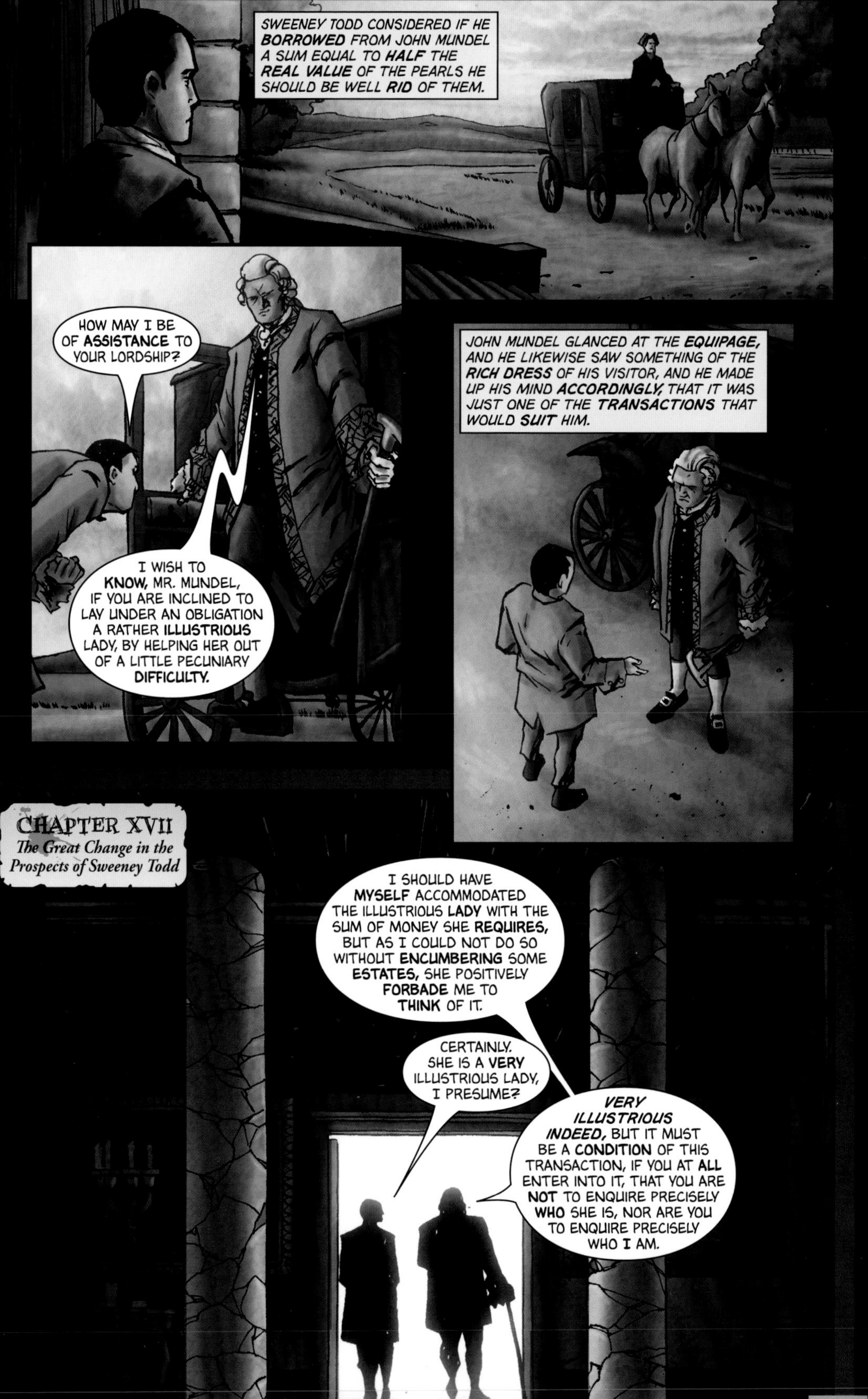
SWEENEY TODD CONSIDERED IF HE BORROWED FROM JOHN MUNDEL A SUM EQUAL TO HALF THE REAL VALUE OF THE PEARLS HE SHOULD BE WELL RID OF THEM.
HOW MAY I BE OF ASSISTANCE TO YOUR LORDSHIP?
I WISH TO KNOW, MR. MUNDEL, IF YOU ARE INCLINED TO LAY UNDER AN OBLIGATION A RATHER ILLUSTRIOUS LADY, BY HELPING HER OUT OF A LITTLE PECUNIARY DIFFICULTY.
JOHN MUNDEL GLANCED AT THE EQUIPAGE, AND HE LIKEWISE SAW SOMETHING OF THE RICH DRESS OF HIS VISITOR, AND HE MADE UP HIS MIND ACCORDINGLY, THAT IT WAS JUST ONE OF THE TRANSACTIONS THAT WOULD SUIT HIM.
CHAPTER XVII
The Great Change in the Prospects of Sweeney Todd
I SHOULD HAVE MYSELF ACCOMMODATED THE ILLUSTRIOUS LADY WITH THE SUM OF MONEY SHE REQUIRES, BUT AS I COULD NOT DO SO WITHOUT ENCUMBERING SOME ESTATES, SHE POSITIVELY FORBADE ME TO THINK OF IT.
CERTAINLY. SHE IS A VERY ILLUSTRIOUS LADY, I PRESUME?
VERY ILLUSTRIOUS INDEED, BUT IT MUST BE A CONDITION OF THIS TRANSACTION, IF YOU AT ALL ENTER INTO IT, THAT YOU ARE NOT TO ENQUIRE PRECISELY WHO SHE IS, NOR ARE YOU TO ENQUIRE PRECISELY WHO I AM.

IT'S NOT MY **USUAL** WAY OF CONDUCTING BUSINESS, BUT IF EVERYTHING **ELSE** BE SATISFACTORY, I SHALL NOT CAVIL AT **THAT.**

VERY GOOD.

I INFORMED THE ILLUSTRIOUS LADY THAT AS THE AFFAIR WAS TO BE WRAPPED UP IN SOMETHING OF A **MYSTERY,** THE SECURITY MUST BE EXTREMELY **AMPLE.**

TH... VERY VIEW T... THE ... MY...

*I WONDER IF HE IS A **DUKE;** I'LL CALL HIM **YOUR GRACE** NEXT TIME AND SEE IF HE OBJECTS TO IT.*

THEREFORE, THE ILLUSTRIOUS LADY PLACED IN **MY** HANDS **SECURITY** TO A THIRD **GREATER** AMOUNT THAN SHE REQUIRED.

CERTAINLY, CERTAINLY, A VERY **PROPER** ARRANGEMENT, **YOUR GRACE;** MAY I ASK THE **NATURE** OF THE PROFFERED **SECURITY?**

JEWELS.

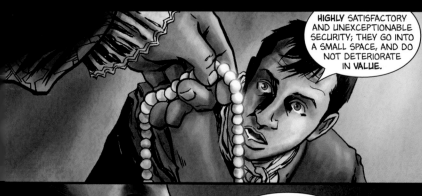

HIGHLY SATISFACTORY AND UNEXCEPTIONABLE SECURITY; THEY GO INTO A SMALL SPACE, AND DO NOT DETERIORATE IN **VALUE.**

AND IF THEY **DO,** IT WOULD MAKE NO DIFFERENCE TO **YOU,** FOR THE ILLUSTRIOUS PERSON'S **HONOUR** WILL BE COMMITTED TO THEIR REDEMPTION.

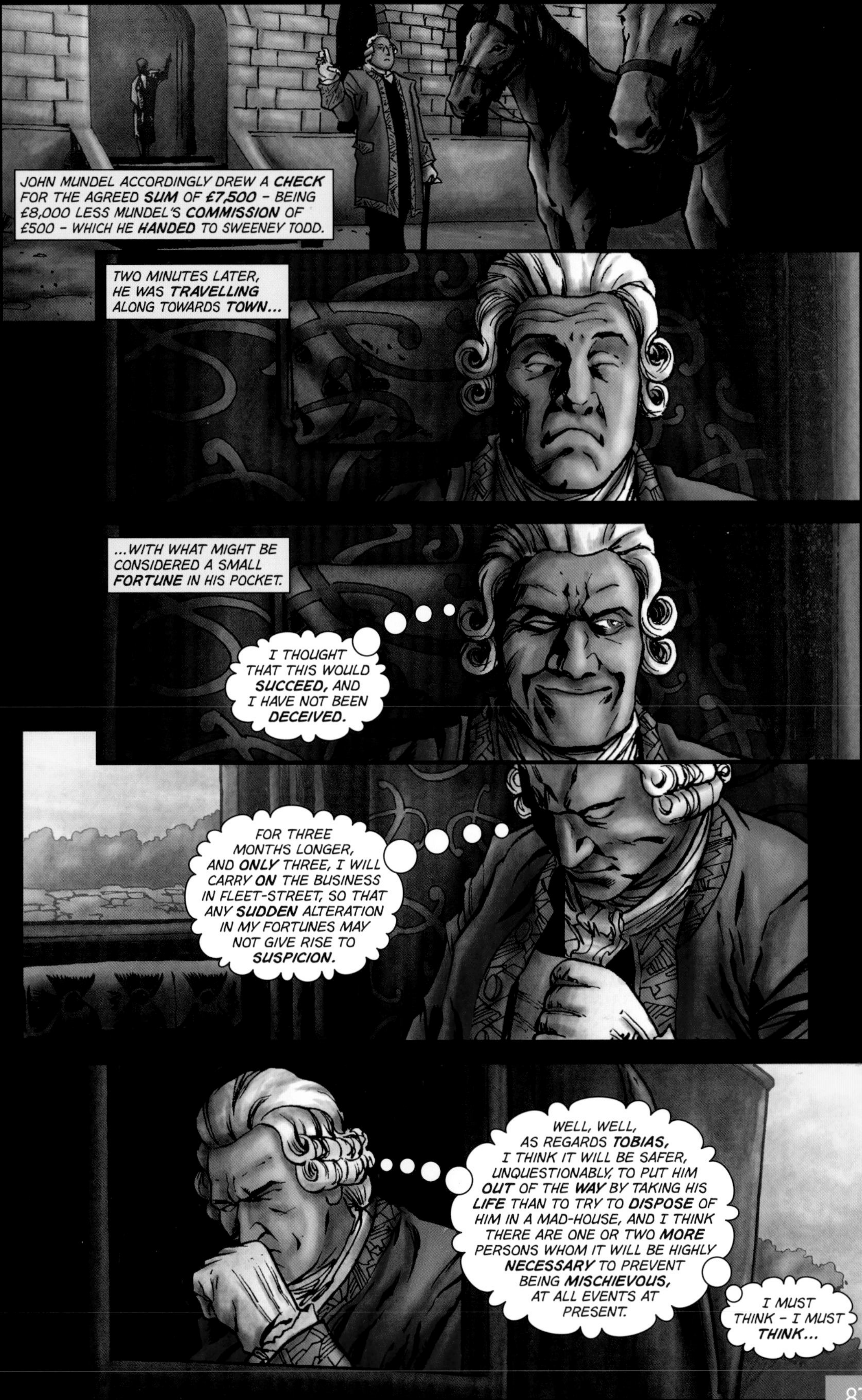

JOHN MUNDEL ACCORDINGLY DREW A **CHECK** FOR THE AGREED **SUM** OF **£7,500** – BEING £8,000 LESS MUNDEL'S **COMMISSION** OF £500 – WHICH HE **HANDED** TO SWEENEY TODD.
TWO MINUTES LATER, HE WAS **TRAVELLING** ALONG TOWARDS **TOWN...**
...WITH WHAT MIGHT BE CONSIDERED A SMALL **FORTUNE** IN HIS POCKET.
I THOUGHT THAT THIS WOULD **SUCCEED,** AND I HAVE NOT BEEN **DECEIVED.**
FOR THREE MONTHS LONGER, AND **ONLY** THREE, I WILL CARRY **ON** THE BUSINESS IN FLEET-STREET, SO THAT ANY **SUDDEN** ALTERATION IN MY FORTUNES MAY NOT GIVE RISE TO **SUSPICION.**
WELL, WELL, AS REGARDS **TOBIAS,** I THINK IT WILL BE SAFER, UNQUESTIONABLY, TO PUT HIM **OUT** OF THE **WAY** BY TAKING HIS **LIFE** THAN TO TRY TO **DISPOSE** OF HIM IN A MAD-HOUSE, AND I THINK THERE ARE ONE OR TWO **MORE** PERSONS WHOM IT WILL BE HIGHLY **NECESSARY** TO PREVENT BEING **MISCHIEVOUS,** AT ALL EVENTS AT PRESENT.
I MUST THINK – I MUST **THINK...**

BUT HE WAS NOT A MAN TO SHRINK FROM *ANYTHING,* AND, ON THE *CONTRARY,* THE MORE A SET OF CIRCUMSTANCES PRESENTED THEMSELVES IN A *GLOOMY* AND A *TERRIFIC* ASPECT, THE *BETTER* THEY SEEMED TO *SUIT* HIM, AND THE *PECULIAR* CONSTITUTION OF HIS MIND.

C-CLATTTEr

THERE CAN BE *NO* DOUBT BUT THAT THE *LOVE* OF *MONEY* WAS THE *PREDOMINANT* FEELING IN SWEENEY TODD'S INTELLECTUAL ORGANISATION AND THAT, BY THE *AMOUNT* IT WOULD *BRING* HIM, OR THE *AMOUNT* IT WOULD *DEPRIVE* HIM OF, HE MEASURED *EVERYTHING.*

THEY SHALL DIE – *DEAD* MEN TELL NO *TALES,* NOR WOMEN NOR BOYS EITHER, AND THEY SHALL *ALL* DIE, AFTER WHICH THERE WILL, I THINK, BE A SERIOUS *FIRE* IN FLEET-STREET.

HA! HA!

IT MAY SPREAD TO WHAT *MISCHIEF* IT *LIKES,* ALWAYS PROVIDED IT STOPS NOT SHORT OF THE ENTIRE DESTRUCTION OF MY *HOUSE* AND *PREMISES.*

BY A *STRANGE* STYLE OF *REASONING,* SUCH MEN AS SWEENEY TODD RECONCILE THEMSELVES TO THE MOST *HEINOUS* CRIMES UPON THE GROUND OF WHAT *THEY* CALL *POLICY.*

THAT IS TO SAY, THAT HAVING COMMITTED SOME SERIOUS *OFFENCE,* THEY ARE COMPELLED TO COMMIT A GREAT NUMBER *MORE* FOR THE PURPOSE OF ENDEAVOURING TO AVOID THE *CONSEQUENCES* OF THE *FIRST* LOT;

AND HENCE THE *CONTINUANCE* OF CRIMINALITY BECOMES A MATTER *NECESSARY* TO SELF-DEFENCE, AND AN ESSENTIAL INGREDIENT IN THEIR CONSIDERATION OF *SELF-PRESERVATION.*

THIS SEEMED A *PLEASANT* TRAIN OF REFLECTIONS TO SWEENEY TODD, AND AS THE COACH ENTERED FLEET-STREET, THERE SAT SUCH A GRIM *SMILE* UPON HIS COUNTENANCE THAT HE LOOKED LIKE SOME *FIEND* IN HUMAN SHAPE, WHO HAD JUST COMPLETED THE *DESTRUCTION* OF A HUMAN SOUL.

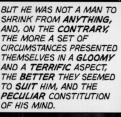

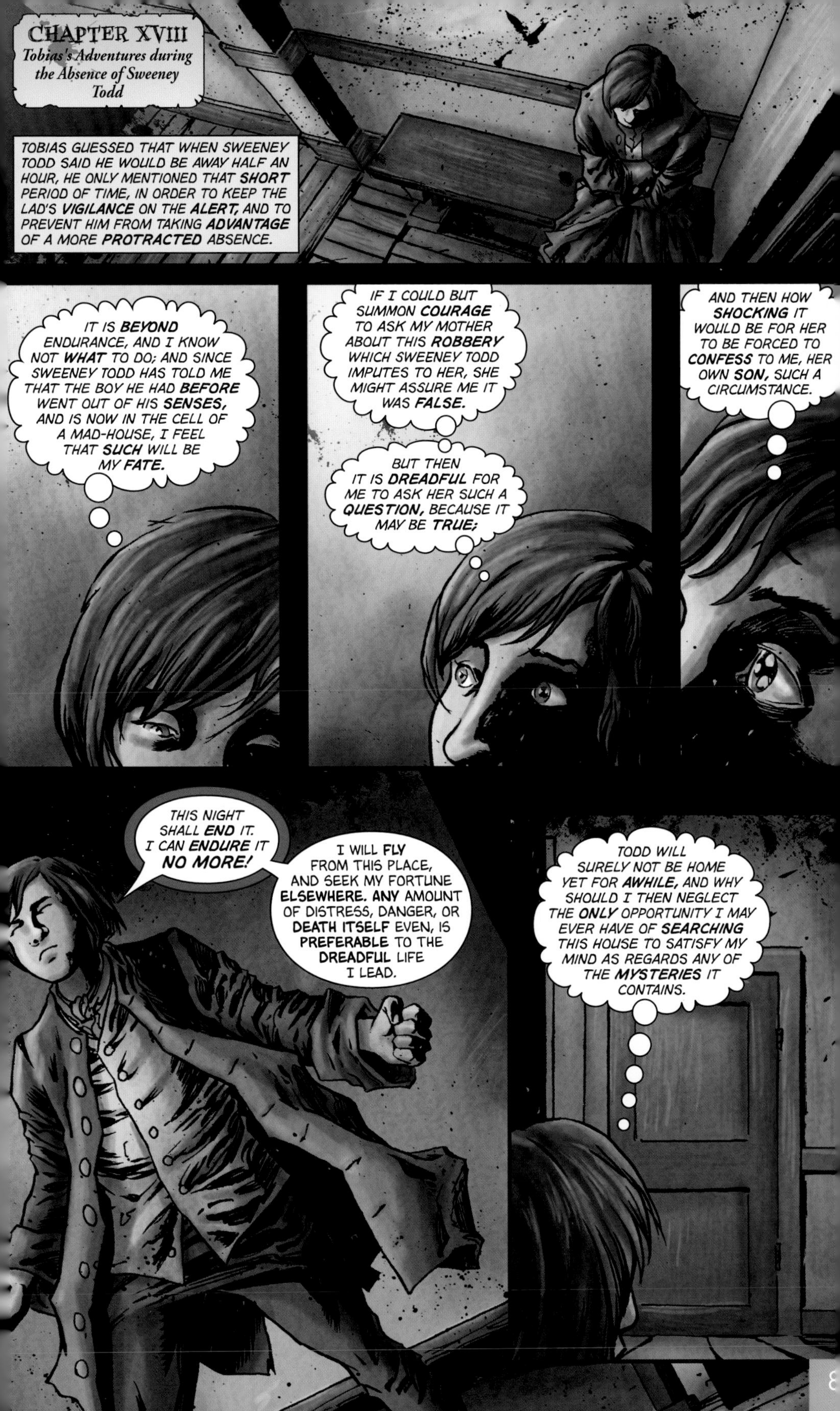
CHAPTER XVIII
Tobias's Adventures during the Absence of Sweeney Todd
TOBIAS GUESSED THAT WHEN SWEENEY TODD SAID HE WOULD BE AWAY HALF AN HOUR, HE ONLY MENTIONED THAT SHORT PERIOD OF TIME, IN ORDER TO KEEP THE LAD'S VIGILANCE ON THE ALERT, AND TO PREVENT HIM FROM TAKING ADVANTAGE OF A MORE PROTRACTED ABSENCE.
IT IS BEYOND ENDURANCE, AND I KNOW NOT WHAT TO DO; AND SINCE SWEENEY TODD HAS TOLD ME THAT THE BOY HE HAD BEFORE WENT OUT OF HIS SENSES, AND IS NOW IN THE CELL OF A MAD-HOUSE, I FEEL THAT SUCH WILL BE MY FATE.
IF I COULD BUT SUMMON COURAGE TO ASK MY MOTHER ABOUT THIS ROBBERY WHICH SWEENEY TODD IMPUTES TO HER, SHE MIGHT ASSURE ME IT WAS FALSE.
BUT THEN IT IS DREADFUL FOR ME TO ASK HER SUCH A QUESTION, BECAUSE IT MAY BE TRUE;
AND THEN HOW SHOCKING IT WOULD BE FOR HER TO BE FORCED TO CONFESS TO ME, HER OWN SON, SUCH A CIRCUMSTANCE.
THIS NIGHT SHALL END IT. I CAN ENDURE IT NO MORE!
I WILL FLY FROM THIS PLACE, AND SEEK MY FORTUNE ELSEWHERE. ANY AMOUNT OF DISTRESS, DANGER, OR DEATH ITSELF EVEN, IS PREFERABLE TO THE DREADFUL LIFE I LEAD.
TODD WILL SURELY NOT BE HOME YET FOR AWHILE, AND WHY SHOULD I THEN NEGLECT THE ONLY OPPORTUNITY I MAY EVER HAVE OF SEARCHING THIS HOUSE TO SATISFY MY MIND AS REGARDS ANY OF THE MYSTERIES IT CONTAINS.

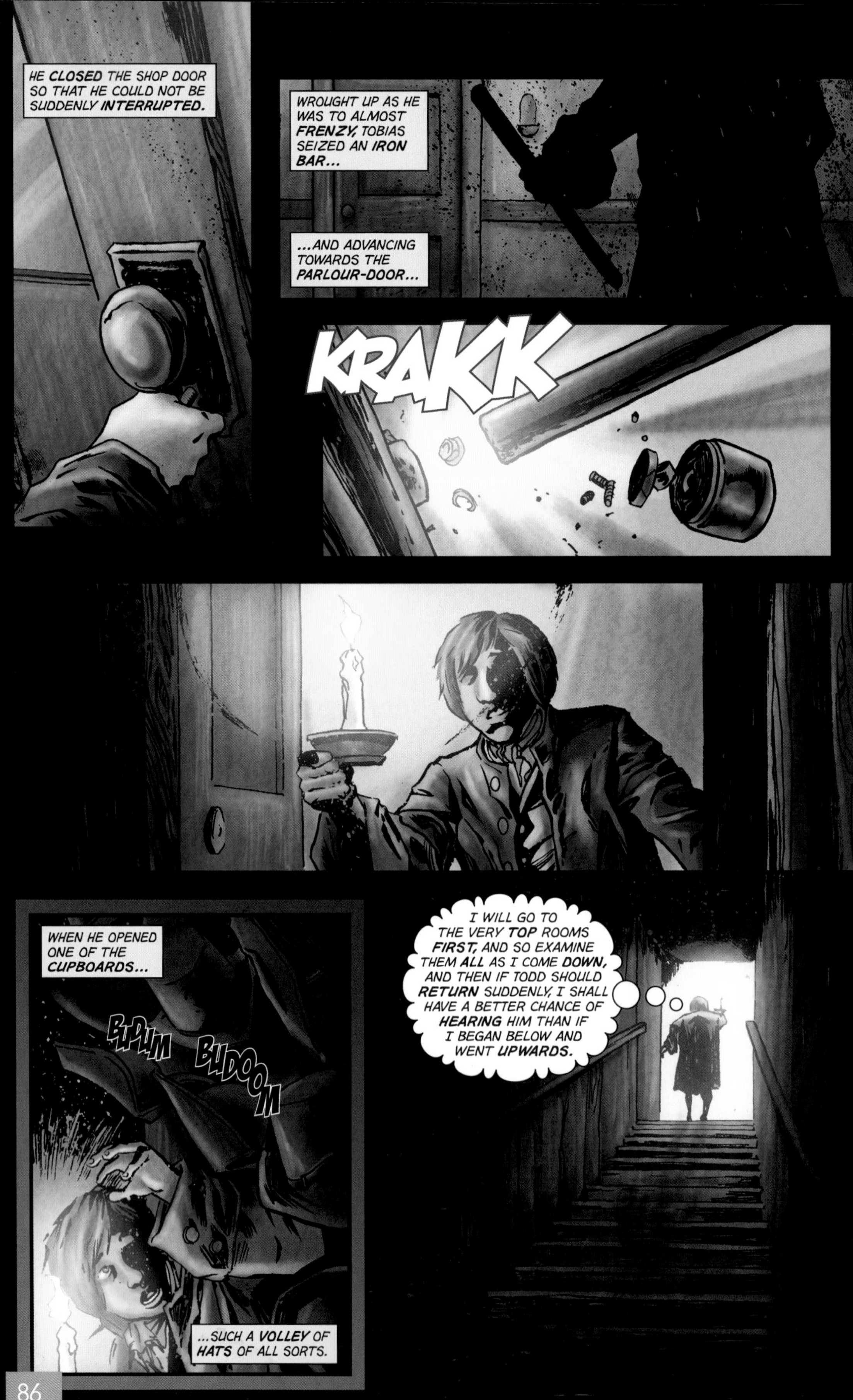
HE **CLOSED** THE SHOP DOOR SO THAT HE COULD NOT BE SUDDENLY **INTERRUPTED.**
WROUGHT UP AS HE WAS TO ALMOST **FRENZY,** TOBIAS SEIZED AN **IRON BAR...**
...AND ADVANCING TOWARDS THE **PARLOUR-DOOR...**
KRAKK
WHEN HE OPENED ONE OF THE **CUPBOARDS...**
BUDUM
BUDOOM
...SUCH A **VOLLEY** OF **HATS** OF ALL SORTS.
I WILL GO TO THE VERY **TOP** ROOMS **FIRST,** AND SO EXAMINE THEM **ALL** AS I COME **DOWN,** AND THEN IF TODD SHOULD **RETURN** SUDDENLY, I SHALL HAVE A BETTER CHANCE OF **HEARING** HIM THAN IF I BEGAN BELOW AND WENT **UPWARDS.**

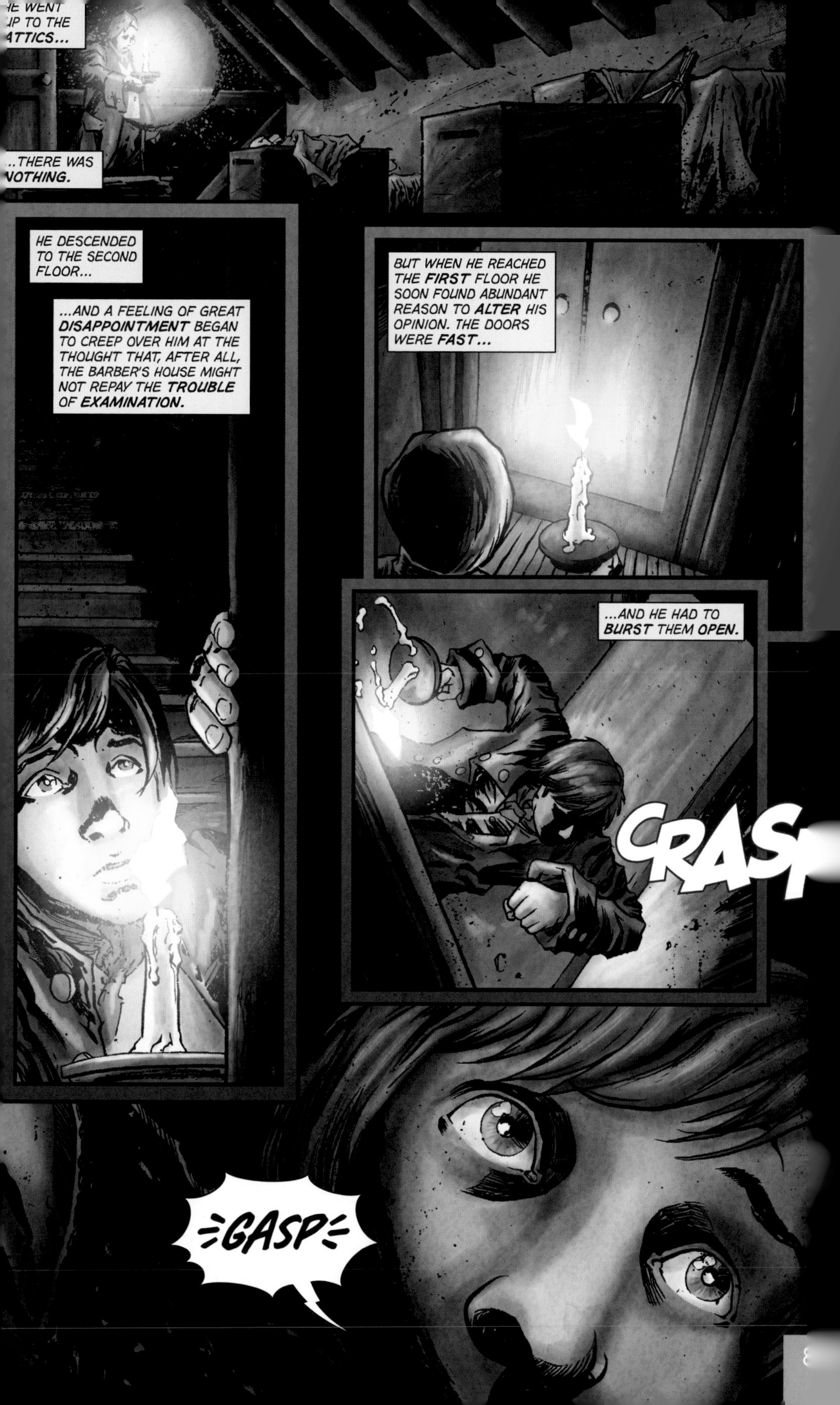

HE WENT UP TO THE ATTICS...
...THERE WAS NOTHING.
HE DESCENDED TO THE SECOND FLOOR...
...AND A FEELING OF GREAT **DISAPPOINTMENT** BEGAN TO CREEP OVER HIM AT THE THOUGHT THAT, AFTER ALL, THE BARBER'S HOUSE MIGHT NOT REPAY THE **TROUBLE** OF **EXAMINATION.**
BUT WHEN HE REACHED THE **FIRST** FLOOR HE SOON FOUND ABUNDANT REASON TO **ALTER** HIS OPINION. THE DOORS WERE **FAST...**
...AND HE HAD TO **BURST** THEM **OPEN.**
CRASH
GASP

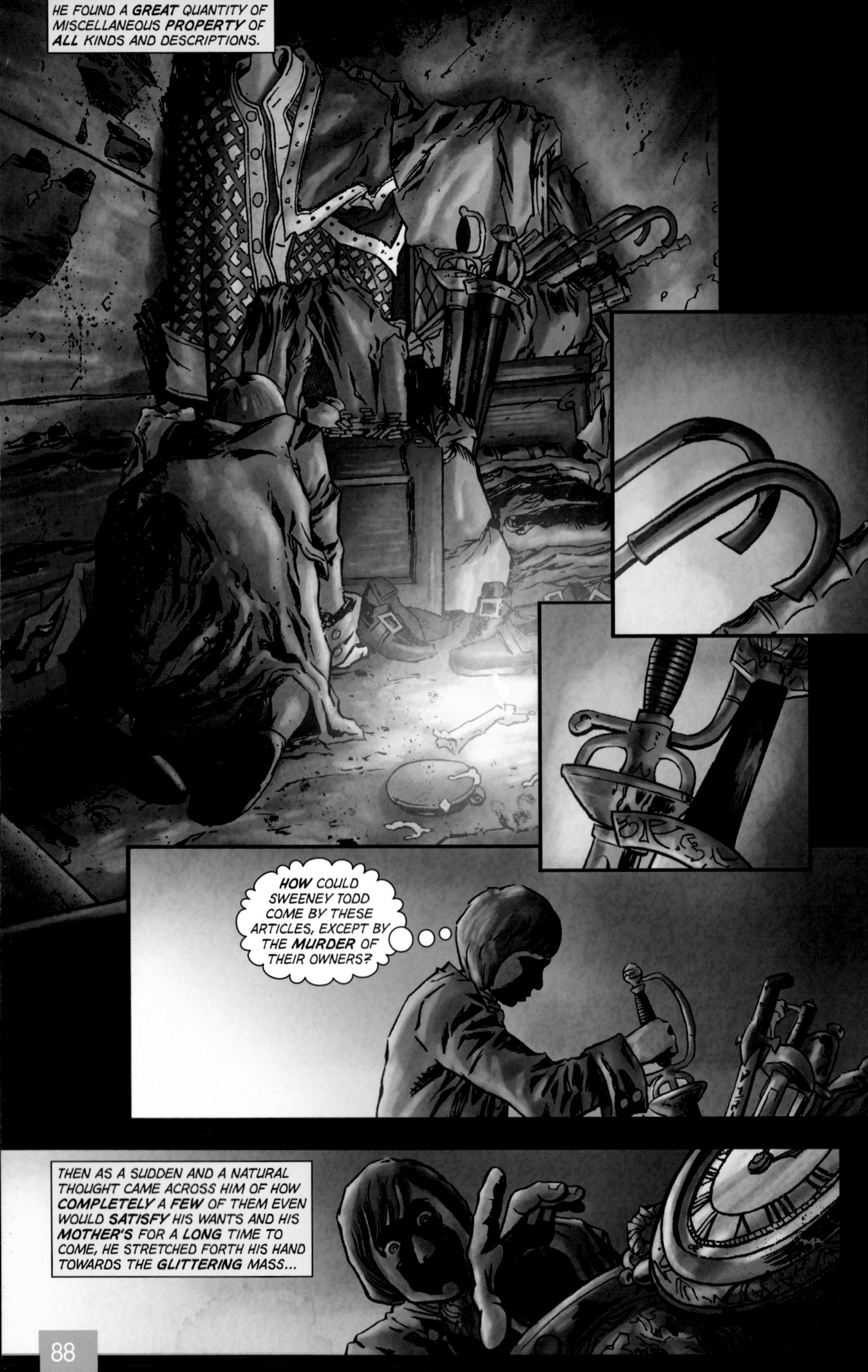
HE FOUND A **GREAT** QUANTITY OF MISCELLANEOUS **PROPERTY** OF **ALL** KINDS AND DESCRIPTIONS.
HOW COULD SWEENEY TODD COME BY THESE ARTICLES, EXCEPT BY THE **MURDER** OF THEIR OWNERS?
THEN AS A SUDDEN AND A NATURAL THOUGHT CAME ACROSS HIM OF HOW **COMPLETELY** A **FEW** OF THEM EVEN WOULD **SATISFY** HIS WANTS AND HIS **MOTHER'S** FOR A **LONG** TIME TO COME, HE STRETCHED FORTH HIS HAND TOWARDS THE **GLITTERING** MASS...

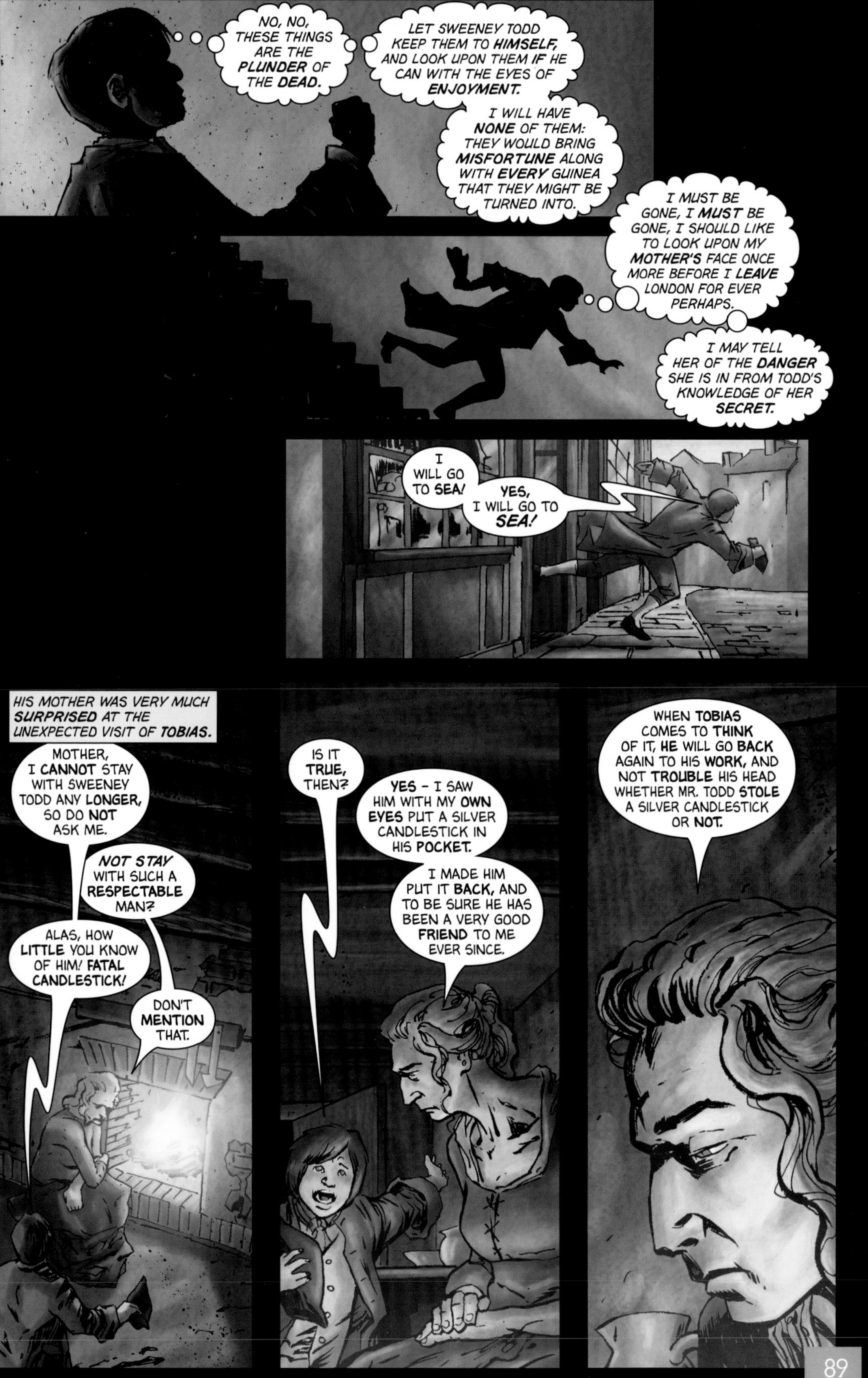
NO, NO, THESE THINGS ARE THE PLUNDER OF THE DEAD.
LET SWEENEY TODD KEEP THEM TO HIMSELF, AND LOOK UPON THEM IF HE CAN WITH THE EYES OF ENJOYMENT.
I WILL HAVE NONE OF THEM: THEY WOULD BRING MISFORTUNE ALONG WITH EVERY GUINEA THAT THEY MIGHT BE TURNED INTO.
I MUST BE GONE, I MUST BE GONE, I SHOULD LIKE TO LOOK UPON MY MOTHER'S FACE ONCE MORE BEFORE I LEAVE LONDON FOR EVER PERHAPS.
I MAY TELL HER OF THE DANGER SHE IS IN FROM TODD'S KNOWLEDGE OF HER SECRET.
I WILL GO TO SEA!
YES, I WILL GO TO SEA!
HIS MOTHER WAS VERY MUCH SURPRISED AT THE UNEXPECTED VISIT OF TOBIAS.
MOTHER, I CANNOT STAY WITH SWEENEY TODD ANY LONGER, SO DO NOT ASK ME.
NOT STAY WITH SUCH A RESPECTABLE MAN?
ALAS, HOW LITTLE YOU KNOW OF HIM! FATAL CANDLESTICK!
DON'T MENTION THAT.
IS IT TRUE, THEN?
YES – I SAW HIM WITH MY OWN EYES PUT A SILVER CANDLESTICK IN HIS POCKET.
I MADE HIM PUT IT BACK, AND TO BE SURE HE HAS BEEN A VERY GOOD FRIEND TO ME EVER SINCE.
WHEN TOBIAS COMES TO THINK OF IT, HE WILL GO BACK AGAIN TO HIS WORK, AND NOT TROUBLE HIS HEAD WHETHER MR. TODD STOLE A SILVER CANDLESTICK OR NOT.

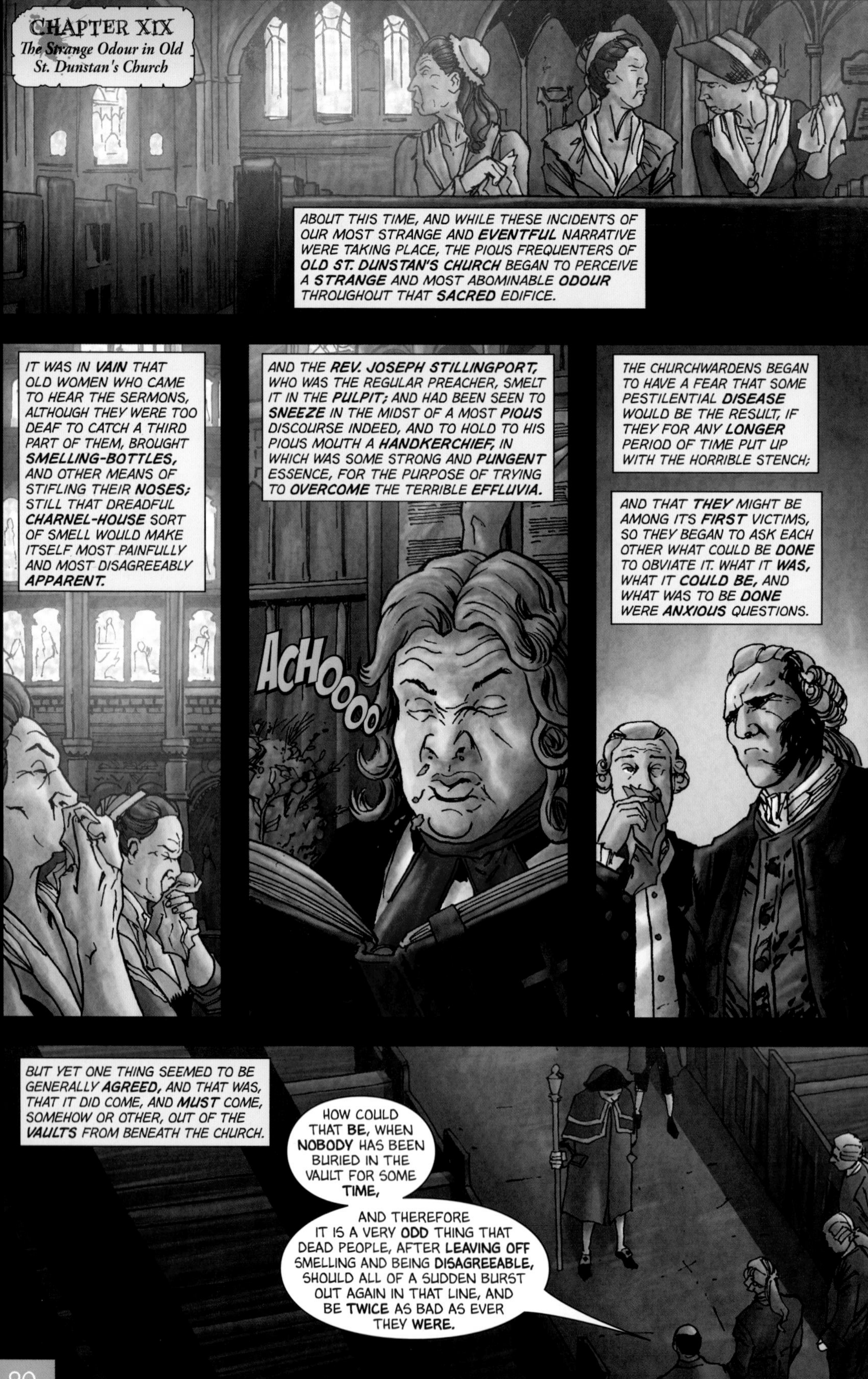
CHAPTER XIX
The Strange Odour in Old St. Dunstan's Church
ABOUT THIS TIME, AND WHILE THESE INCIDENTS OF OUR MOST STRANGE AND EVENTFUL NARRATIVE WERE TAKING PLACE, THE PIOUS FREQUENTERS OF OLD ST. DUNSTAN'S CHURCH BEGAN TO PERCEIVE A STRANGE AND MOST ABOMINABLE ODOUR THROUGHOUT THAT SACRED EDIFICE.
IT WAS IN VAIN THAT OLD WOMEN WHO CAME TO HEAR THE SERMONS, ALTHOUGH THEY WERE TOO DEAF TO CATCH A THIRD PART OF THEM, BROUGHT SMELLING-BOTTLES, AND OTHER MEANS OF STIFLING THEIR NOSES; STILL THAT DREADFUL CHARNEL-HOUSE SORT OF SMELL WOULD MAKE ITSELF MOST PAINFULLY AND MOST DISAGREEABLY APPARENT.
AND THE REV. JOSEPH STILLINGPORT, WHO WAS THE REGULAR PREACHER, SMELT IT IN THE PULPIT; AND HAD BEEN SEEN TO SNEEZE IN THE MIDST OF A MOST PIOUS DISCOURSE INDEED, AND TO HOLD TO HIS PIOUS MOUTH A HANDKERCHIEF, IN WHICH WAS SOME STRONG AND PUNGENT ESSENCE, FOR THE PURPOSE OF TRYING TO OVERCOME THE TERRIBLE EFFLUVIA.
ACHOOOOO
THE CHURCHWARDENS BEGAN TO HAVE A FEAR THAT SOME PESTILENTIAL DISEASE WOULD BE THE RESULT, IF THEY FOR ANY LONGER PERIOD OF TIME PUT UP WITH THE HORRIBLE STENCH;
AND THAT THEY MIGHT BE AMONG ITS FIRST VICTIMS, SO THEY BEGAN TO ASK EACH OTHER WHAT COULD BE DONE TO OBVIATE IT. WHAT IT WAS, WHAT IT COULD BE, AND WHAT WAS TO BE DONE WERE ANXIOUS QUESTIONS.
BUT YET ONE THING SEEMED TO BE GENERALLY AGREED, AND THAT WAS, THAT IT DID COME, AND MUST COME, SOMEHOW OR OTHER, OUT OF THE VAULTS FROM BENEATH THE CHURCH.
HOW COULD THAT BE, WHEN NOBODY HAS BEEN BURIED IN THE VAULT FOR SOME TIME,
AND THEREFORE IT IS A VERY ODD THING THAT DEAD PEOPLE, AFTER LEAVING OFF SMELLING AND BEING DISAGREEABLE, SHOULD ALL OF A SUDDEN BURST OUT AGAIN IN THAT LINE, AND BE TWICE AS BAD AS EVER THEY WERE.

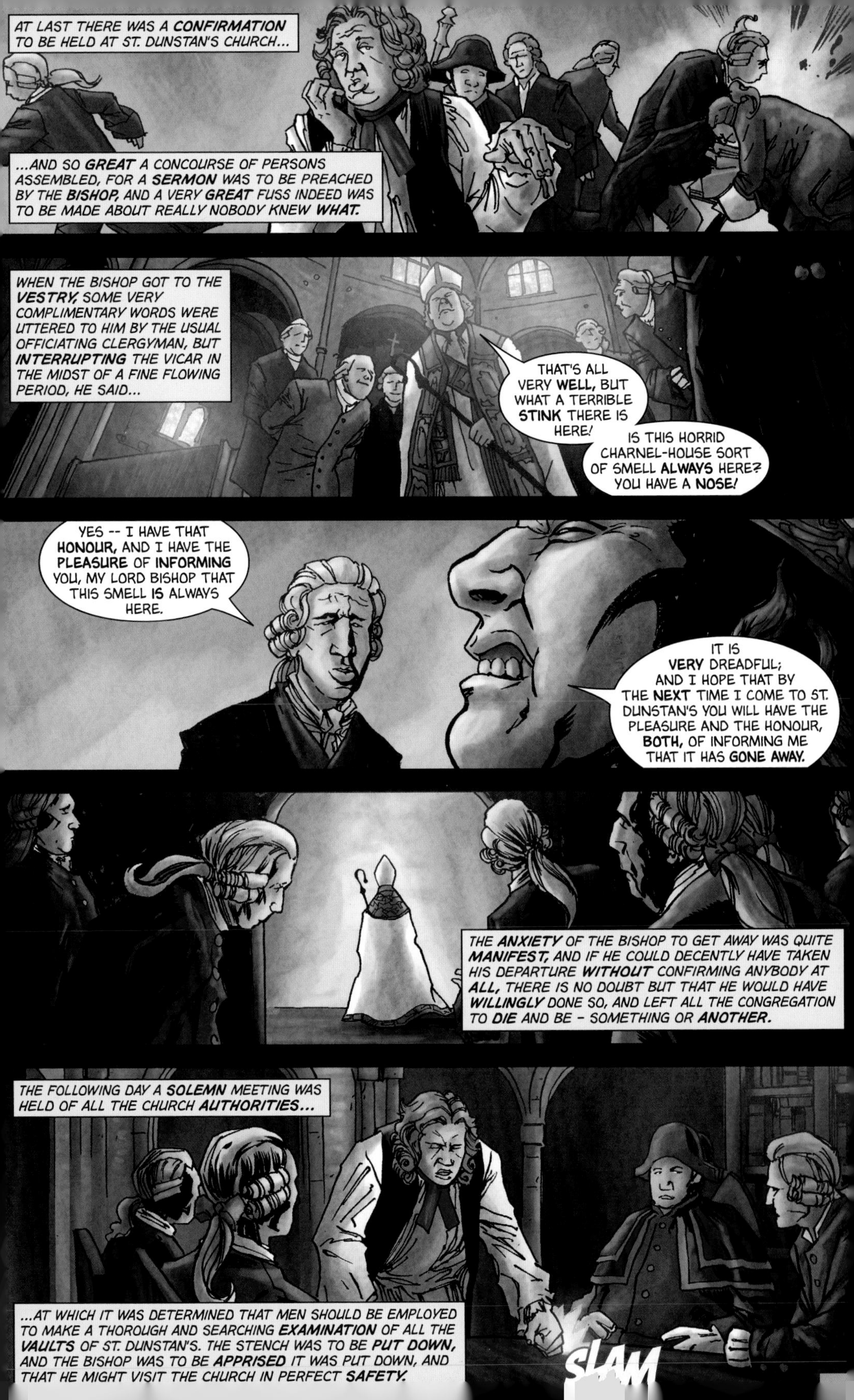
AT LAST THERE WAS A CONFIRMATION TO BE HELD AT ST. DUNSTAN'S CHURCH...
...AND SO GREAT A CONCOURSE OF PERSONS ASSEMBLED, FOR A SERMON WAS TO BE PREACHED BY THE BISHOP, AND A VERY GREAT FUSS INDEED WAS TO BE MADE ABOUT REALLY NOBODY KNEW WHAT.
WHEN THE BISHOP GOT TO THE VESTRY, SOME VERY COMPLIMENTARY WORDS WERE UTTERED TO HIM BY THE USUAL OFFICIATING CLERGYMAN, BUT INTERRUPTING THE VICAR IN THE MIDST OF A FINE FLOWING PERIOD, HE SAID...
THAT'S ALL VERY WELL, BUT WHAT A TERRIBLE STINK THERE IS HERE!
IS THIS HORRID CHARNEL-HOUSE SORT OF SMELL ALWAYS HERE? YOU HAVE A NOSE!
YES -- I HAVE THAT HONOUR, AND I HAVE THE PLEASURE OF INFORMING YOU, MY LORD BISHOP THAT THIS SMELL IS ALWAYS HERE.
IT IS VERY DREADFUL; AND I HOPE THAT BY THE NEXT TIME I COME TO ST. DUNSTAN'S YOU WILL HAVE THE PLEASURE AND THE HONOUR, BOTH, OF INFORMING ME THAT IT HAS GONE AWAY.
THE ANXIETY OF THE BISHOP TO GET AWAY WAS QUITE MANIFEST, AND IF HE COULD DECENTLY HAVE TAKEN HIS DEPARTURE WITHOUT CONFIRMING ANYBODY AT ALL, THERE IS NO DOUBT BUT THAT HE WOULD HAVE WILLINGLY DONE SO, AND LEFT ALL THE CONGREGATION TO DIE AND BE - SOMETHING OR ANOTHER.
THE FOLLOWING DAY A SOLEMN MEETING WAS HELD OF ALL THE CHURCH AUTHORITIES...
...AT WHICH IT WAS DETERMINED THAT MEN SHOULD BE EMPLOYED TO MAKE A THOROUGH AND SEARCHING EXAMINATION OF ALL THE VAULTS OF ST. DUNSTAN'S. THE STENCH WAS TO BE PUT DOWN, AND THE BISHOP WAS TO BE APPRISED IT WAS PUT DOWN, AND THAT HE MIGHT VISIT THE CHURCH IN PERFECT SAFETY.
SLAM

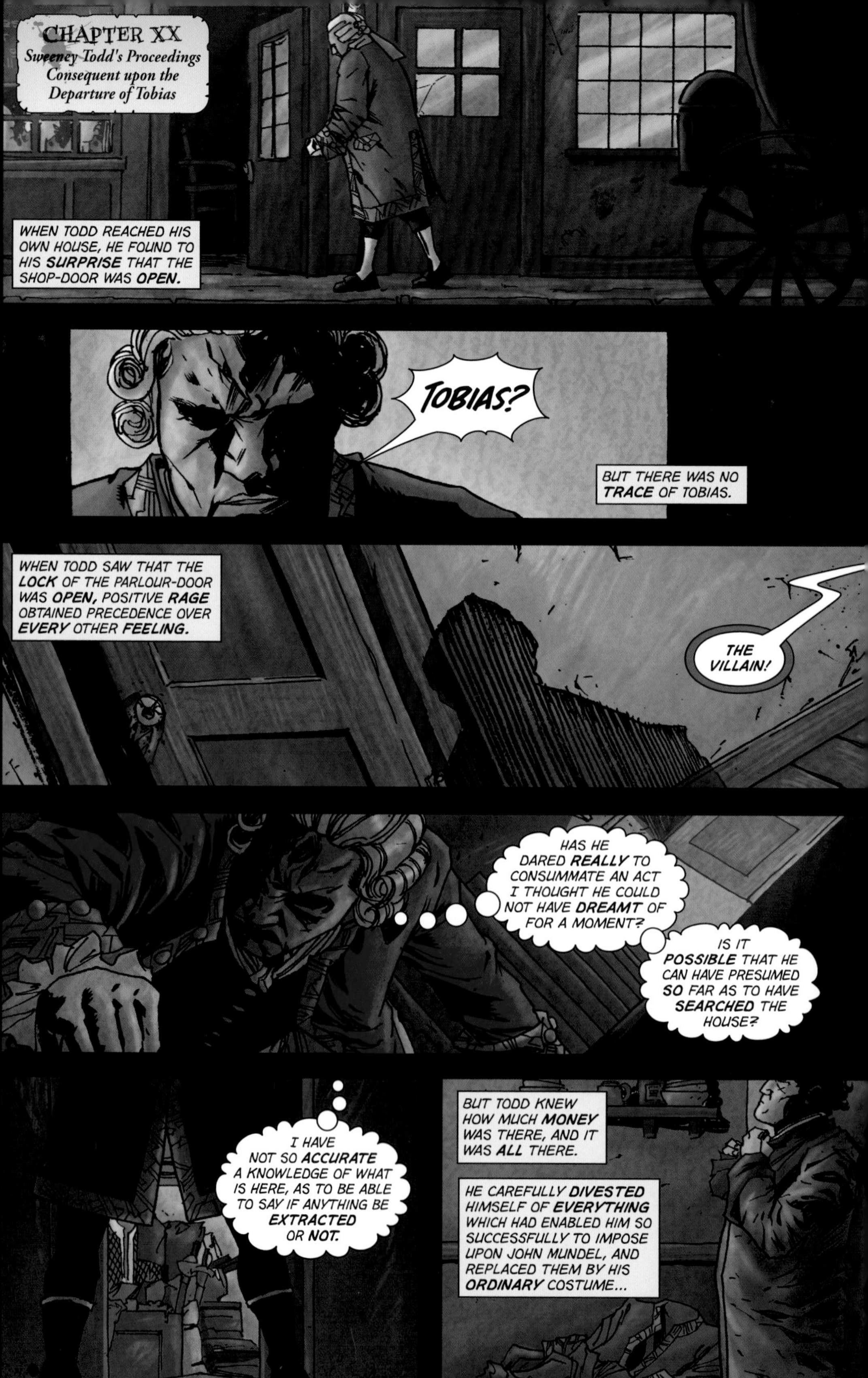
CHAPTER XX
Sweeney Todd's Proceedings Consequent upon the Departure of Tobias
WHEN TODD REACHED HIS OWN HOUSE, HE FOUND TO HIS SURPRISE THAT THE SHOP-DOOR WAS OPEN.
TOBIAS?
BUT THERE WAS NO TRACE OF TOBIAS.
WHEN TODD SAW THAT THE LOCK OF THE PARLOUR-DOOR WAS OPEN, POSITIVE RAGE OBTAINED PRECEDENCE OVER EVERY OTHER FEELING.
THE VILLAIN!
HAS HE DARED REALLY TO CONSUMMATE AN ACT I THOUGHT HE COULD NOT HAVE DREAMT OF FOR A MOMENT?
IS IT POSSIBLE THAT HE CAN HAVE PRESUMED SO FAR AS TO HAVE SEARCHED THE HOUSE?
I HAVE NOT SO ACCURATE A KNOWLEDGE OF WHAT IS HERE, AS TO BE ABLE TO SAY IF ANYTHING BE EXTRACTED OR NOT.
BUT TODD KNEW HOW MUCH MONEY WAS THERE, AND IT WAS ALL THERE.
HE CAREFULLY DIVESTED HIMSELF OF EVERYTHING WHICH HAD ENABLED HIM SO SUCCESSFULLY TO IMPOSE UPON JOHN MUNDEL, AND REPLACED THEM BY HIS ORDINARY COSTUME...

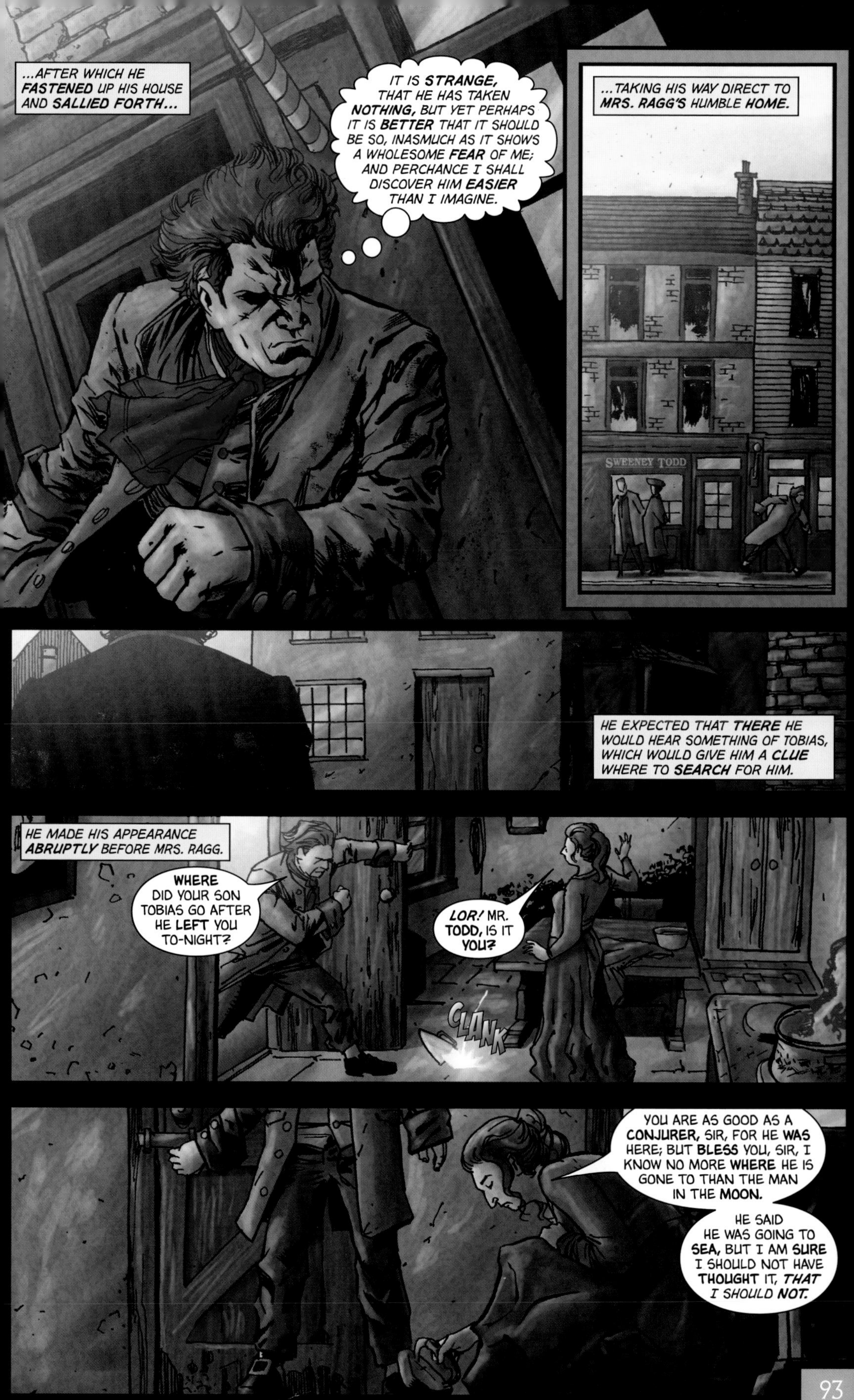
...AFTER WHICH HE FASTENED UP HIS HOUSE AND SALLIED FORTH...
IT IS STRANGE, THAT HE HAS TAKEN NOTHING, BUT YET PERHAPS IT IS BETTER THAT IT SHOULD BE SO, INASMUCH AS IT SHOWS A WHOLESOME FEAR OF ME; AND PERCHANCE I SHALL DISCOVER HIM EASIER THAN I IMAGINE.
...TAKING HIS WAY DIRECT TO MRS. RAGG'S HUMBLE HOME.
SWEENEY TODD
HE EXPECTED THAT THERE HE WOULD HEAR SOMETHING OF TOBIAS, WHICH WOULD GIVE HIM A CLUE WHERE TO SEARCH FOR HIM.
HE MADE HIS APPEARANCE ABRUPTLY BEFORE MRS. RAGG.
WHERE DID YOUR SON TOBIAS GO AFTER HE LEFT YOU TO-NIGHT?
LOR! MR. TODD, IS IT YOU?
CLANK
YOU ARE AS GOOD AS A CONJURER, SIR, FOR HE WAS HERE; BUT BLESS YOU, SIR, I KNOW NO MORE WHERE HE IS GONE TO THAN THE MAN IN THE MOON.
HE SAID HE WAS GOING TO SEA, BUT I AM SURE I SHOULD NOT HAVE THOUGHT IT, THAT I SHOULD NOT.

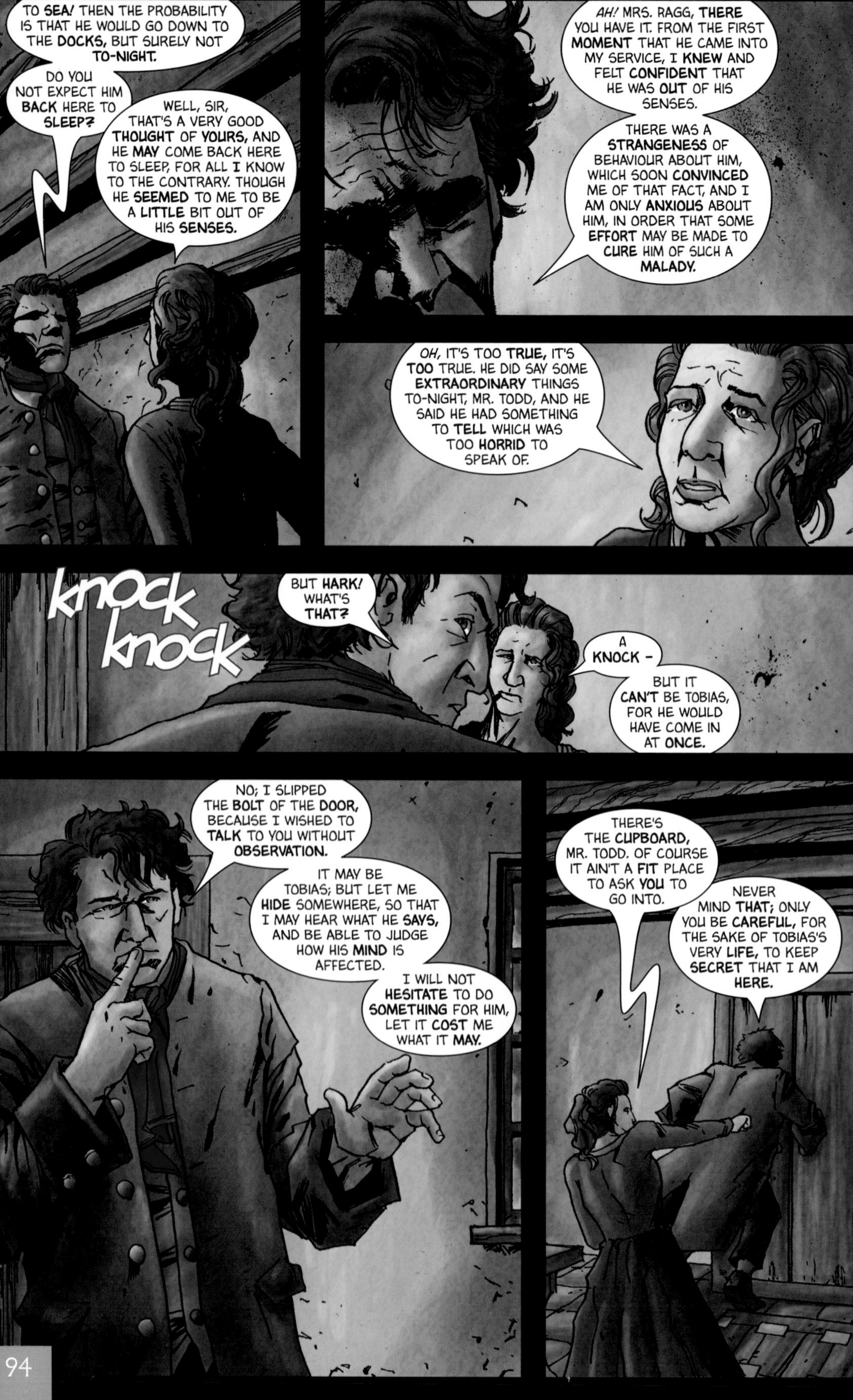
TO SEA! THEN THE PROBABILITY IS THAT HE WOULD GO DOWN TO THE DOCKS, BUT SURELY NOT TO-NIGHT.
DO YOU NOT EXPECT HIM BACK HERE TO SLEEP?
WELL, SIR, THAT'S A VERY GOOD THOUGHT OF YOURS, AND HE MAY COME BACK HERE TO SLEEP, FOR ALL I KNOW TO THE CONTRARY. THOUGH HE SEEMED TO ME TO BE A LITTLE BIT OUT OF HIS SENSES.
AH! MRS. RAGG, THERE YOU HAVE IT. FROM THE FIRST MOMENT THAT HE CAME INTO MY SERVICE, I KNEW AND FELT CONFIDENT THAT HE WAS OUT OF HIS SENSES.
THERE WAS A STRANGENESS OF BEHAVIOUR ABOUT HIM, WHICH SOON CONVINCED ME OF THAT FACT, AND I AM ONLY ANXIOUS ABOUT HIM, IN ORDER THAT SOME EFFORT MAY BE MADE TO CURE HIM OF SUCH A MALADY.
OH, IT'S TOO TRUE, IT'S TOO TRUE. HE DID SAY SOME EXTRAORDINARY THINGS TO-NIGHT, MR. TODD, AND HE SAID HE HAD SOMETHING TO TELL WHICH WAS TOO HORRID TO SPEAK OF.
knock knock
BUT HARK! WHAT'S THAT?
A KNOCK -
BUT IT CAN'T BE TOBIAS, FOR HE WOULD HAVE COME IN AT ONCE.
NO; I SLIPPED THE BOLT OF THE DOOR, BECAUSE I WISHED TO TALK TO YOU WITHOUT OBSERVATION.
IT MAY BE TOBIAS; BUT LET ME HIDE SOMEWHERE, SO THAT I MAY HEAR WHAT HE SAYS, AND BE ABLE TO JUDGE HOW HIS MIND IS AFFECTED.
I WILL NOT HESITATE TO DO SOMETHING FOR HIM, LET IT COST ME WHAT IT MAY.
THERE'S THE CUPBOARD, MR. TODD. OF COURSE IT AIN'T A FIT PLACE TO ASK YOU TO GO INTO.
NEVER MIND THAT; ONLY YOU BE CAREFUL, FOR THE SAKE OF TOBIAS'S VERY LIFE, TO KEEP SECRET THAT I AM HERE.

MOTHER, I HAVE TAKEN A **NEW** THOUGHT, AND HAVE COME **BACK** TO YOU.

WELL, I THOUGHT YOU **WOULD**, TOBIAS; AND A VERY **GOOD** THING IT IS THAT YOU **HAVE**.

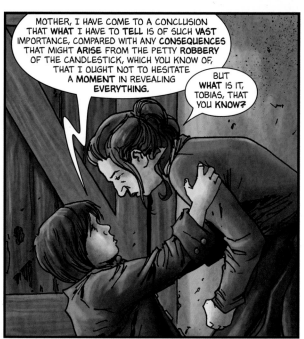

MOTHER, I HAVE COME TO A CONCLUSION THAT **WHAT** I HAVE TO TELL IS OF SUCH **VAST** IMPORTANCE, COMPARED WITH ANY **CONSEQUENCES** THAT MIGHT **ARISE** FROM THE PETTY **ROBBERY** OF THE CANDLESTICK, WHICH YOU KNOW OF, THAT I OUGHT NOT TO HESITATE A **MOMENT** IN REVEALING **EVERYTHING**.

BUT **WHAT** IS IT, TOBIAS, THAT YOU **KNOW?**

SOMETHING TOO **DREADFUL** FOR ME TO UTTER TO YOU **ALONE**.

GO INTO THE **TEMPLE**, MOTHER, TO SOME OF THE GENTLEMEN WHOSE **CHAMBERS** YOU ATTEND TO, AND ASK THEM TO COME TO ME, AND **LISTEN** TO WHAT I HAVE GOT TO SAY; THEY WILL BE AMPLY **REPAID** FOR THEIR **TROUBLE**, FOR THEY WILL HEAR **THAT** WHICH MAY, PERHAPS, SAVE THEIR OWN **LIVES**.

HE IS QUITE **GONE**, AND MR. TODD IS **CORRECT**; POOR **TOBIAS** IS AS **MAD** AS HE CAN BE! PERHAPS, WHILE I AM GONE, MR. TODD CAN **SPEAK** TO HIM!

WELL, MY DEAR, IF IT MUST BE, IT **MUST** BE; AND I WILL **GO**; BUT I HOPE WHILE I HAVE **GONE**, SOMEBODY WILL **SPEAK** TO YOU, AND **CONVINCE** YOU THAT YOU OUGHT TO **TRY** TO **QUIET** YOURSELF.

THE DOOR **CLOSED** AFTER THE **RETREATING** FORM OF MRS. RAGG.

SLAM

95

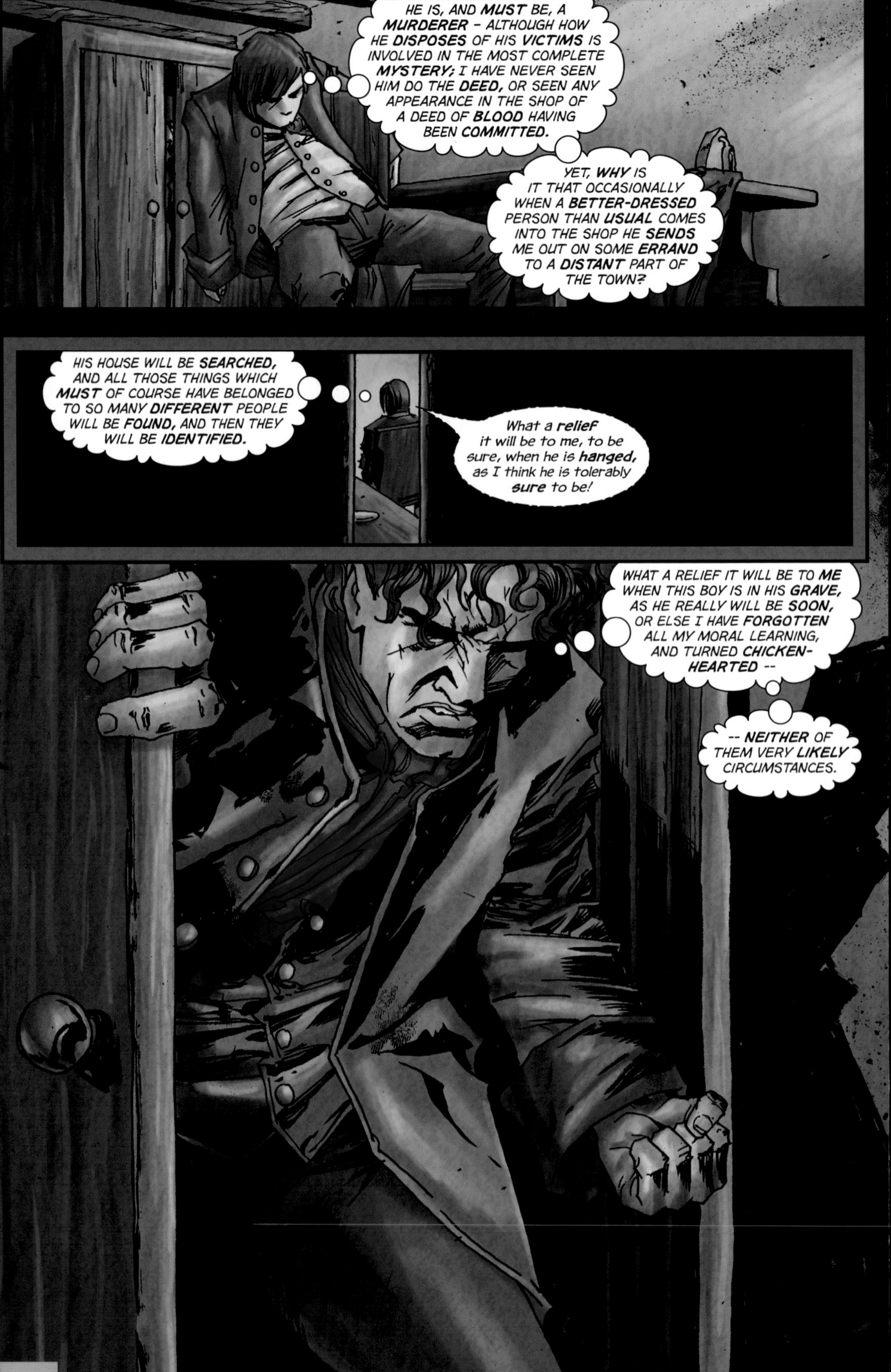
HE IS, AND MUST BE, A MURDERER – ALTHOUGH HOW HE DISPOSES OF HIS VICTIMS IS INVOLVED IN THE MOST COMPLETE MYSTERY; I HAVE NEVER SEEN HIM DO THE DEED, OR SEEN ANY APPEARANCE IN THE SHOP OF A DEED OF BLOOD HAVING BEEN COMMITTED.
YET, WHY IS IT THAT OCCASIONALLY WHEN A BETTER-DRESSED PERSON THAN USUAL COMES INTO THE SHOP HE SENDS ME OUT ON SOME ERRAND TO A DISTANT PART OF THE TOWN?
HIS HOUSE WILL BE SEARCHED, AND ALL THOSE THINGS WHICH MUST OF COURSE HAVE BELONGED TO SO MANY DIFFERENT PEOPLE WILL BE FOUND, AND THEN THEY WILL BE IDENTIFIED.
What a relief it will be to me, to be sure, when he is hanged, as I think he is tolerably sure to be!
WHAT A RELIEF IT WILL BE TO ME WHEN THIS BOY IS IN HIS GRAVE, AS HE REALLY WILL BE SOON, OR ELSE I HAVE FORGOTTEN ALL MY MORAL LEARNING, AND TURNED CHICKEN-HEARTED --
-- NEITHER OF THEM VERY LIKELY CIRCUMSTANCES.

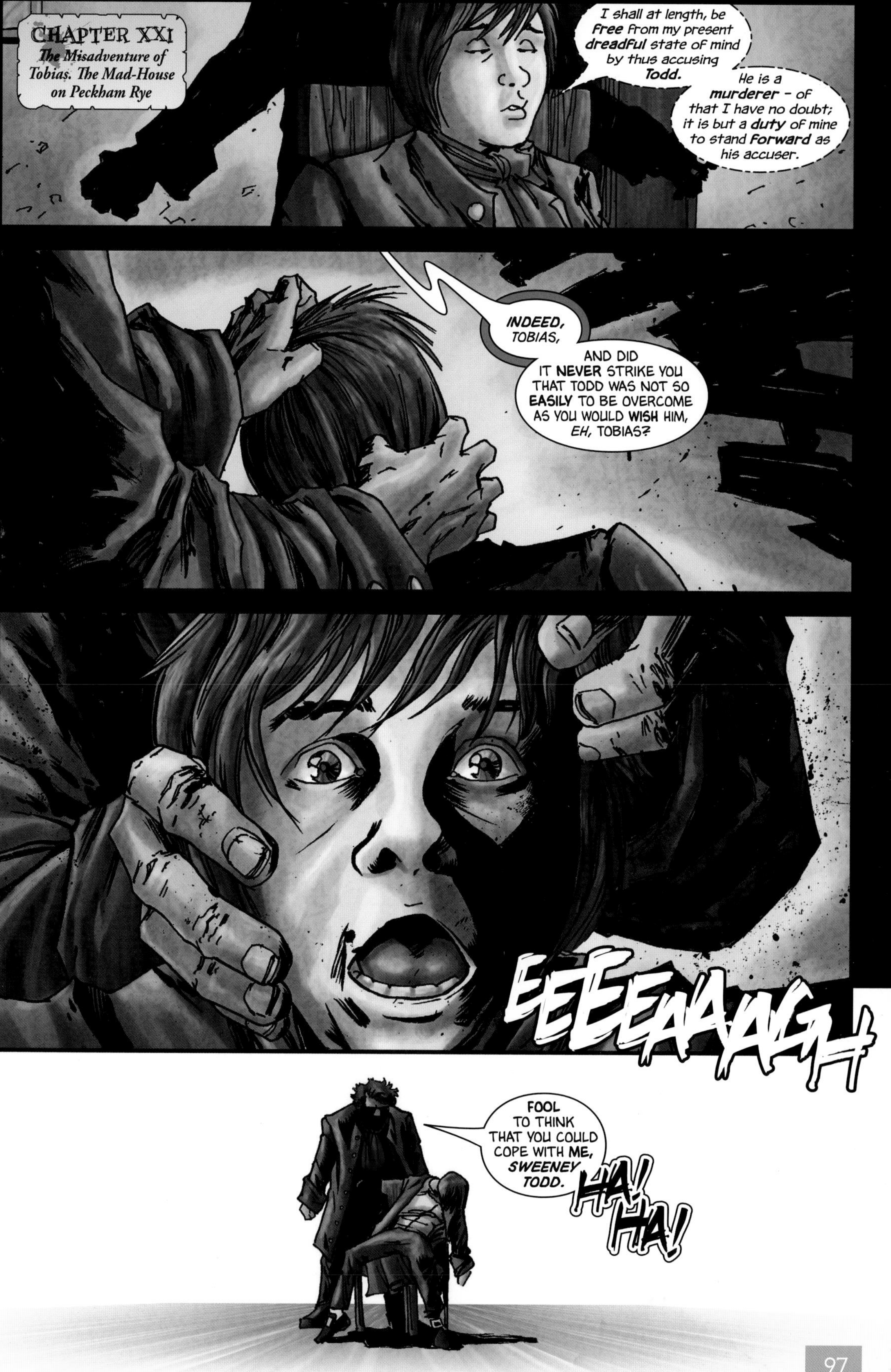
CHAPTER XXI
The Misadventure of Tobias. The Mad-House on Peckham Rye
I shall at length, be free from my present dreadful state of mind by thus accusing Todd.
He is a murderer – of that I have no doubt; it is but a duty of mine to stand forward as his accuser.
INDEED, TOBIAS,
AND DID IT NEVER STRIKE YOU THAT TODD WAS NOT SO EASILY TO BE OVERCOME AS YOU WOULD WISH HIM, EH, TOBIAS?
EEEEAAAAGH
FOOL TO THINK THAT YOU COULD COPE WITH ME, SWEENEY TODD.
HA! HA!

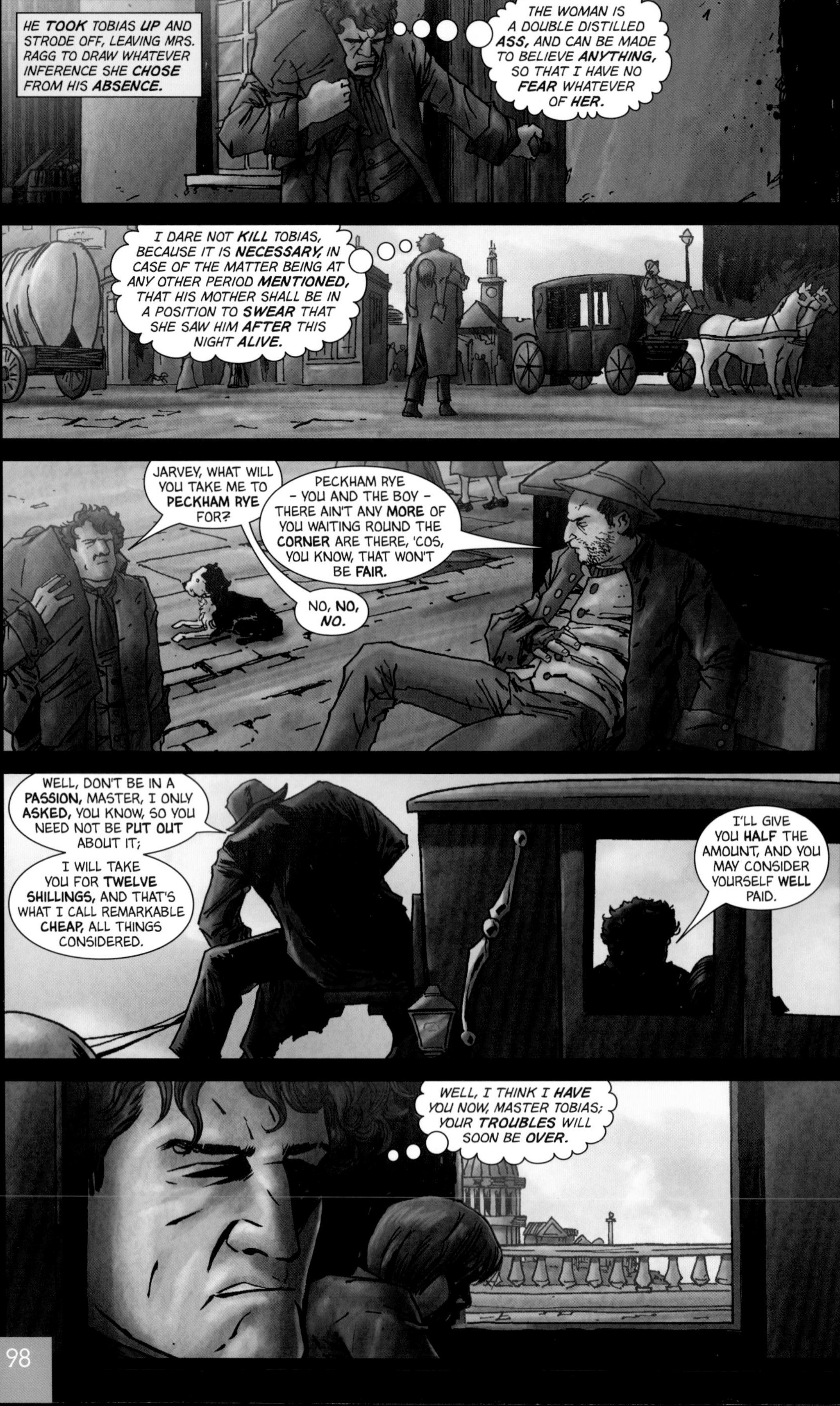
HE TOOK TOBIAS UP AND STRODE OFF, LEAVING MRS. RAGG TO DRAW WHATEVER INFERENCE SHE CHOSE FROM HIS ABSENCE.
THE WOMAN IS A DOUBLE DISTILLED ASS, AND CAN BE MADE TO BELIEVE ANYTHING, SO THAT I HAVE NO FEAR WHATEVER OF HER.
I DARE NOT KILL TOBIAS, BECAUSE IT IS NECESSARY, IN CASE OF THE MATTER BEING AT ANY OTHER PERIOD MENTIONED, THAT HIS MOTHER SHALL BE IN A POSITION TO SWEAR THAT SHE SAW HIM AFTER THIS NIGHT ALIVE.
JARVEY, WHAT WILL YOU TAKE ME TO PECKHAM RYE FOR?
PECKHAM RYE – YOU AND THE BOY – THERE AIN'T ANY MORE OF YOU WAITING ROUND THE CORNER ARE THERE, 'COS, YOU KNOW, THAT WON'T BE FAIR.
NO, NO, NO.
WELL, DON'T BE IN A PASSION, MASTER, I ONLY ASKED, YOU KNOW, SO YOU NEED NOT BE PUT OUT ABOUT IT;
I WILL TAKE YOU FOR TWELVE SHILLINGS, AND THAT'S WHAT I CALL REMARKABLE CHEAP, ALL THINGS CONSIDERED.
I'LL GIVE YOU HALF THE AMOUNT, AND YOU MAY CONSIDER YOURSELF WELL PAID.
WELL, I THINK I HAVE YOU NOW, MASTER TOBIAS; YOUR TROUBLES WILL SOON BE OVER.

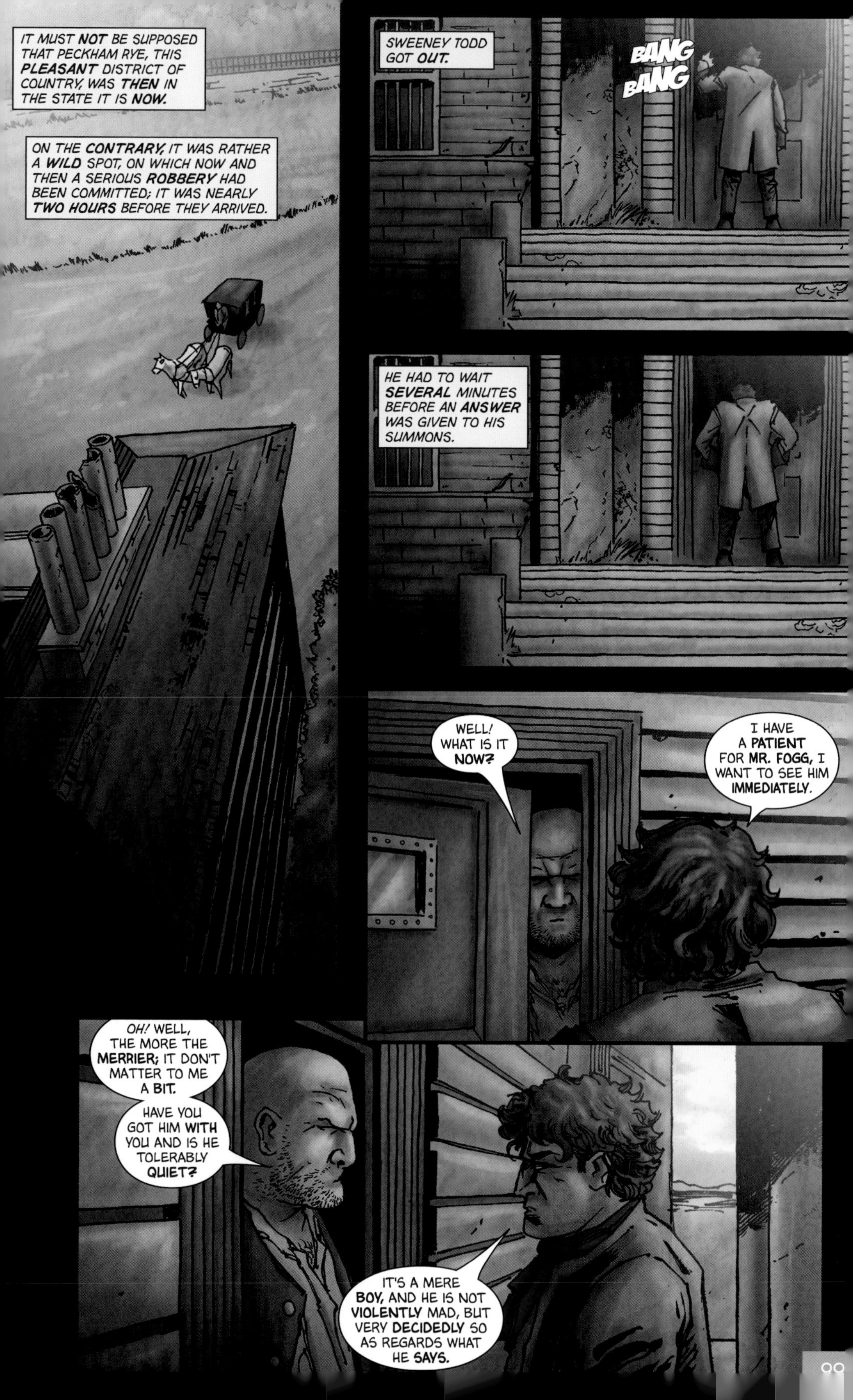
IT MUST NOT BE SUPPOSED THAT PECKHAM RYE, THIS PLEASANT DISTRICT OF COUNTRY, WAS THEN IN THE STATE IT IS NOW.
ON THE CONTRARY, IT WAS RATHER A WILD SPOT, ON WHICH NOW AND THEN A SERIOUS ROBBERY HAD BEEN COMMITTED; IT WAS NEARLY TWO HOURS BEFORE THEY ARRIVED.
SWEENEY TODD GOT OUT.
BANG
BANG
HE HAD TO WAIT SEVERAL MINUTES BEFORE AN ANSWER WAS GIVEN TO HIS SUMMONS.
WELL! WHAT IS IT NOW?
I HAVE A PATIENT FOR MR. FOGG, I WANT TO SEE HIM IMMEDIATELY.
OH! WELL, THE MORE THE MERRIER; IT DON'T MATTER TO ME A BIT.
HAVE YOU GOT HIM WITH YOU AND IS HE TOLERABLY QUIET?
IT'S A MERE BOY, AND HE IS NOT VIOLENTLY MAD, BUT VERY DECIDEDLY SO AS REGARDS WHAT HE SAYS.

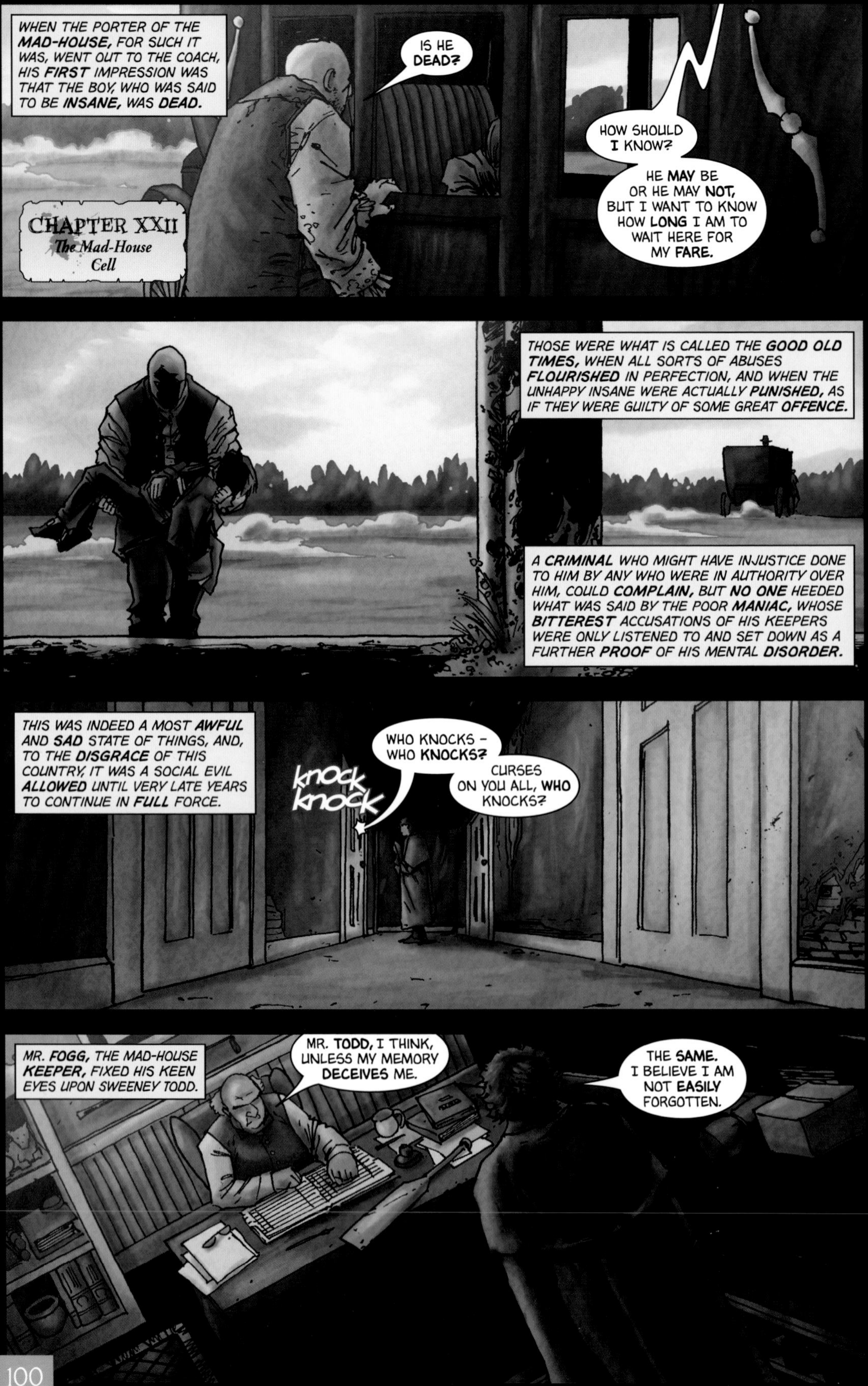
WHEN THE PORTER OF THE MAD-HOUSE, FOR SUCH IT WAS, WENT OUT TO THE COACH, HIS FIRST IMPRESSION WAS THAT THE BOY, WHO WAS SAID TO BE INSANE, WAS DEAD.
IS HE DEAD?
HOW SHOULD I KNOW?
HE MAY BE OR HE MAY NOT, BUT I WANT TO KNOW HOW LONG I AM TO WAIT HERE FOR MY FARE.
CHAPTER XXII
The Mad-House Cell
THOSE WERE WHAT IS CALLED THE GOOD OLD TIMES, WHEN ALL SORTS OF ABUSES FLOURISHED IN PERFECTION, AND WHEN THE UNHAPPY INSANE WERE ACTUALLY PUNISHED, AS IF THEY WERE GUILTY OF SOME GREAT OFFENCE.
A CRIMINAL WHO MIGHT HAVE INJUSTICE DONE TO HIM BY ANY WHO WERE IN AUTHORITY OVER HIM, COULD COMPLAIN, BUT NO ONE HEEDED WHAT WAS SAID BY THE POOR MANIAC, WHOSE BITTEREST ACCUSATIONS OF HIS KEEPERS WERE ONLY LISTENED TO AND SET DOWN AS A FURTHER PROOF OF HIS MENTAL DISORDER.
THIS WAS INDEED A MOST AWFUL AND SAD STATE OF THINGS, AND, TO THE DISGRACE OF THIS COUNTRY, IT WAS A SOCIAL EVIL ALLOWED UNTIL VERY LATE YEARS TO CONTINUE IN FULL FORCE.
knock knock
WHO KNOCKS - WHO KNOCKS?
CURSES ON YOU ALL, WHO KNOCKS?
MR. FOGG, THE MAD-HOUSE KEEPER, FIXED HIS KEEN EYES UPON SWEENEY TODD.
MR. TODD, I THINK, UNLESS MY MEMORY DECEIVES ME.
THE SAME. I BELIEVE I AM NOT EASILY FORGOTTEN.

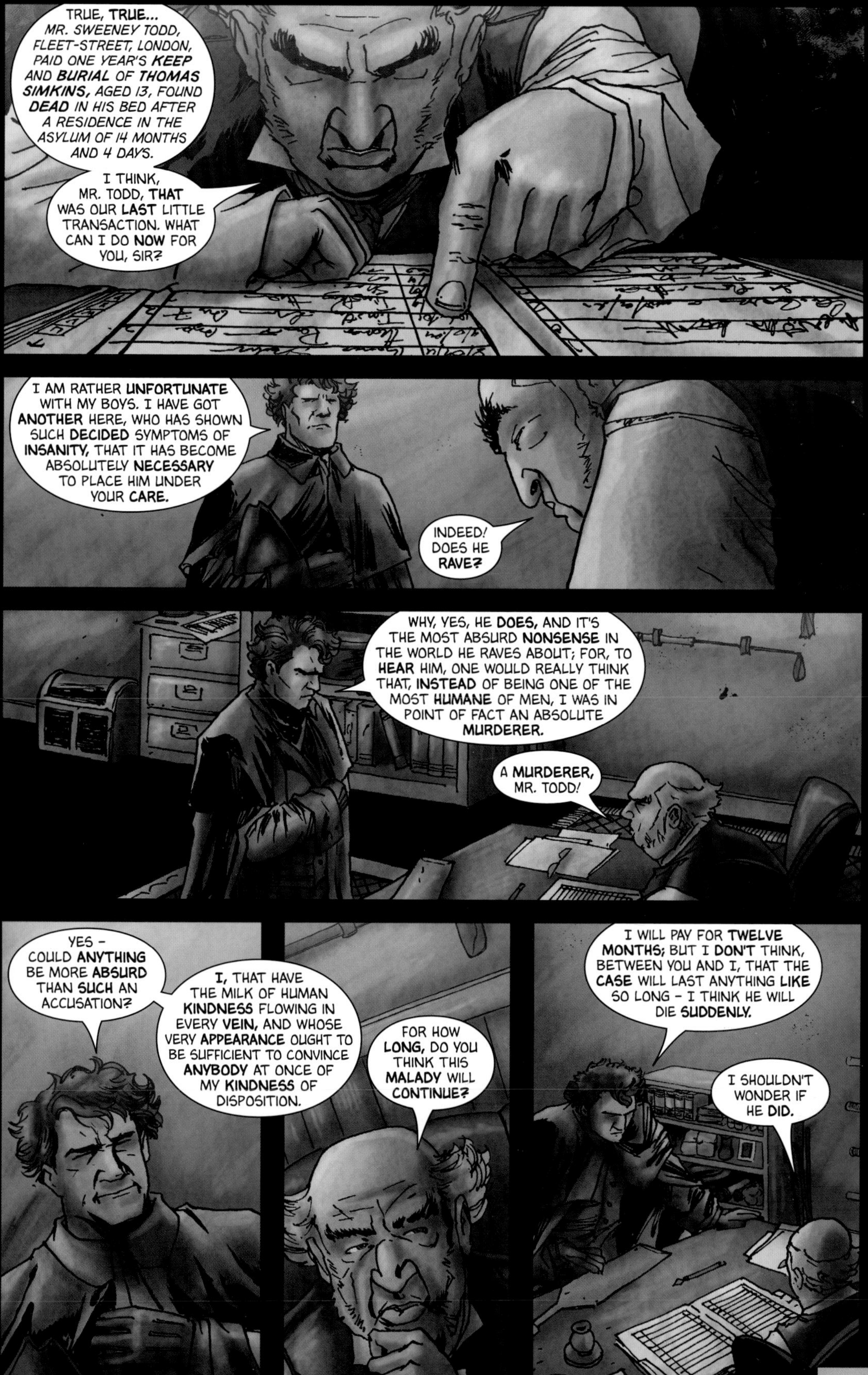
TRUE, TRUE... MR. SWEENEY TODD, FLEET-STREET, LONDON, PAID ONE YEAR'S KEEP AND BURIAL OF THOMAS SIMKINS, AGED 13, FOUND DEAD IN HIS BED AFTER A RESIDENCE IN THE ASYLUM OF 14 MONTHS AND 4 DAYS.
I THINK, MR. TODD, THAT WAS OUR LAST LITTLE TRANSACTION. WHAT CAN I DO NOW FOR YOU, SIR?
I AM RATHER UNFORTUNATE WITH MY BOYS. I HAVE GOT ANOTHER HERE, WHO HAS SHOWN SUCH DECIDED SYMPTOMS OF INSANITY, THAT IT HAS BECOME ABSOLUTELY NECESSARY TO PLACE HIM UNDER YOUR CARE.
INDEED! DOES HE RAVE?
WHY, YES, HE DOES, AND IT'S THE MOST ABSURD NONSENSE IN THE WORLD HE RAVES ABOUT; FOR, TO HEAR HIM, ONE WOULD REALLY THINK THAT, INSTEAD OF BEING ONE OF THE MOST HUMANE OF MEN, I WAS IN POINT OF FACT AN ABSOLUTE MURDERER.
A MURDERER, MR. TODD!
YES - COULD ANYTHING BE MORE ABSURD THAN SUCH AN ACCUSATION?
I, THAT HAVE THE MILK OF HUMAN KINDNESS FLOWING IN EVERY VEIN, AND WHOSE VERY APPEARANCE OUGHT TO BE SUFFICIENT TO CONVINCE ANYBODY AT ONCE OF MY KINDNESS OF DISPOSITION.
FOR HOW LONG, DO YOU THINK THIS MALADY WILL CONTINUE?
I WILL PAY FOR TWELVE MONTHS; BUT I DON'T THINK, BETWEEN YOU AND I, THAT THE CASE WILL LAST ANYTHING LIKE SO LONG - I THINK HE WILL DIE SUDDENLY.
I SHOULDN'T WONDER IF HE DID.

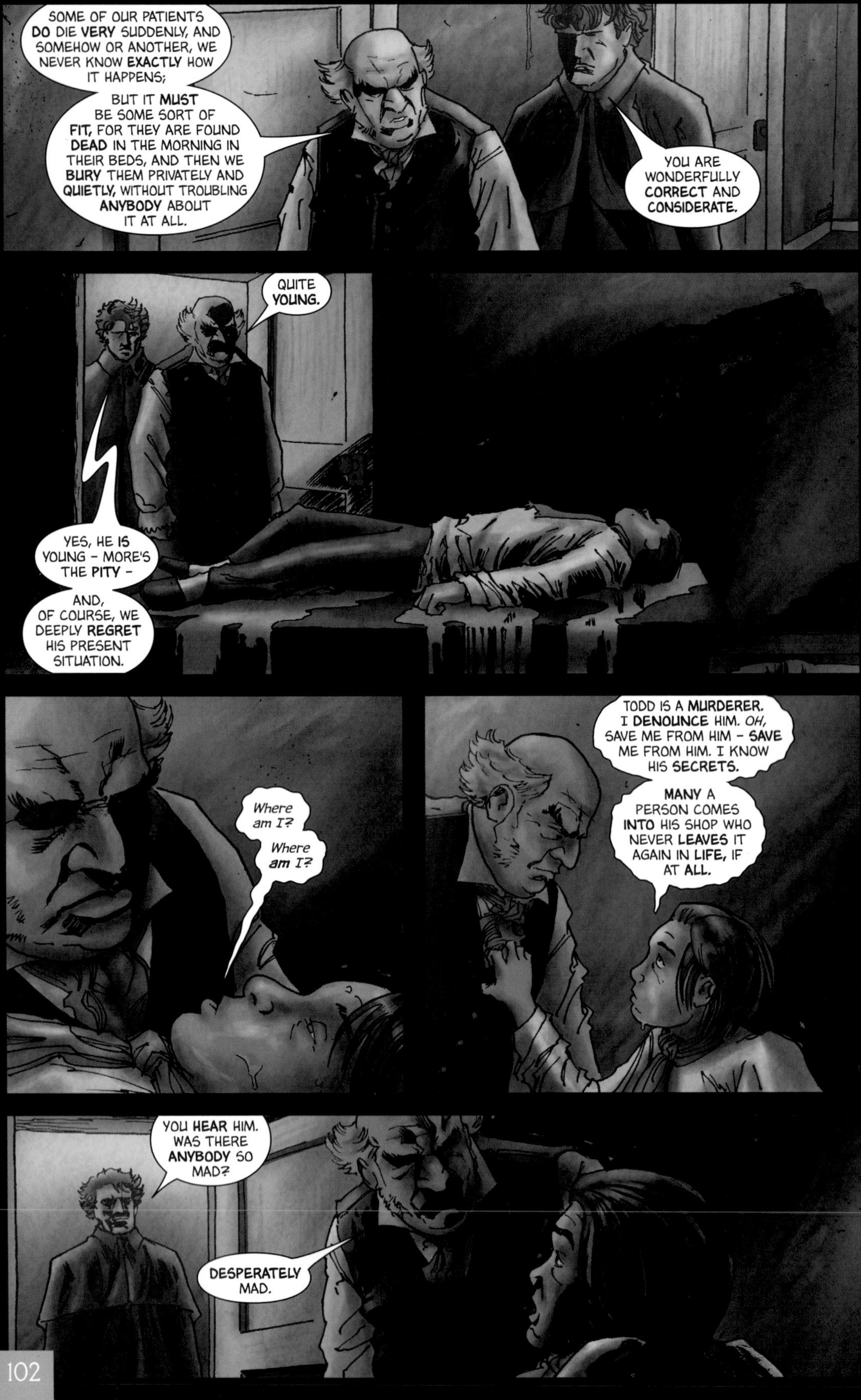
SOME OF OUR PATIENTS DO DIE VERY SUDDENLY, AND SOMEHOW OR ANOTHER, WE NEVER KNOW EXACTLY HOW IT HAPPENS;
BUT IT MUST BE SOME SORT OF FIT, FOR THEY ARE FOUND DEAD IN THE MORNING IN THEIR BEDS, AND THEN WE BURY THEM PRIVATELY AND QUIETLY, WITHOUT TROUBLING ANYBODY ABOUT IT AT ALL.
YOU ARE WONDERFULLY CORRECT AND CONSIDERATE.
QUITE YOUNG.
YES, HE IS YOUNG - MORE'S THE PITY -
AND, OF COURSE, WE DEEPLY REGRET HIS PRESENT SITUATION.
Where am I?
Where am I?
TODD IS A MURDERER. I DENOUNCE HIM. OH, SAVE ME FROM HIM - SAVE ME FROM HIM. I KNOW HIS SECRETS.
MANY A PERSON COMES INTO HIS SHOP WHO NEVER LEAVES IT AGAIN IN LIFE, IF AT ALL.
YOU HEAR HIM. WAS THERE ANYBODY SO MAD?
DESPERATELY MAD.

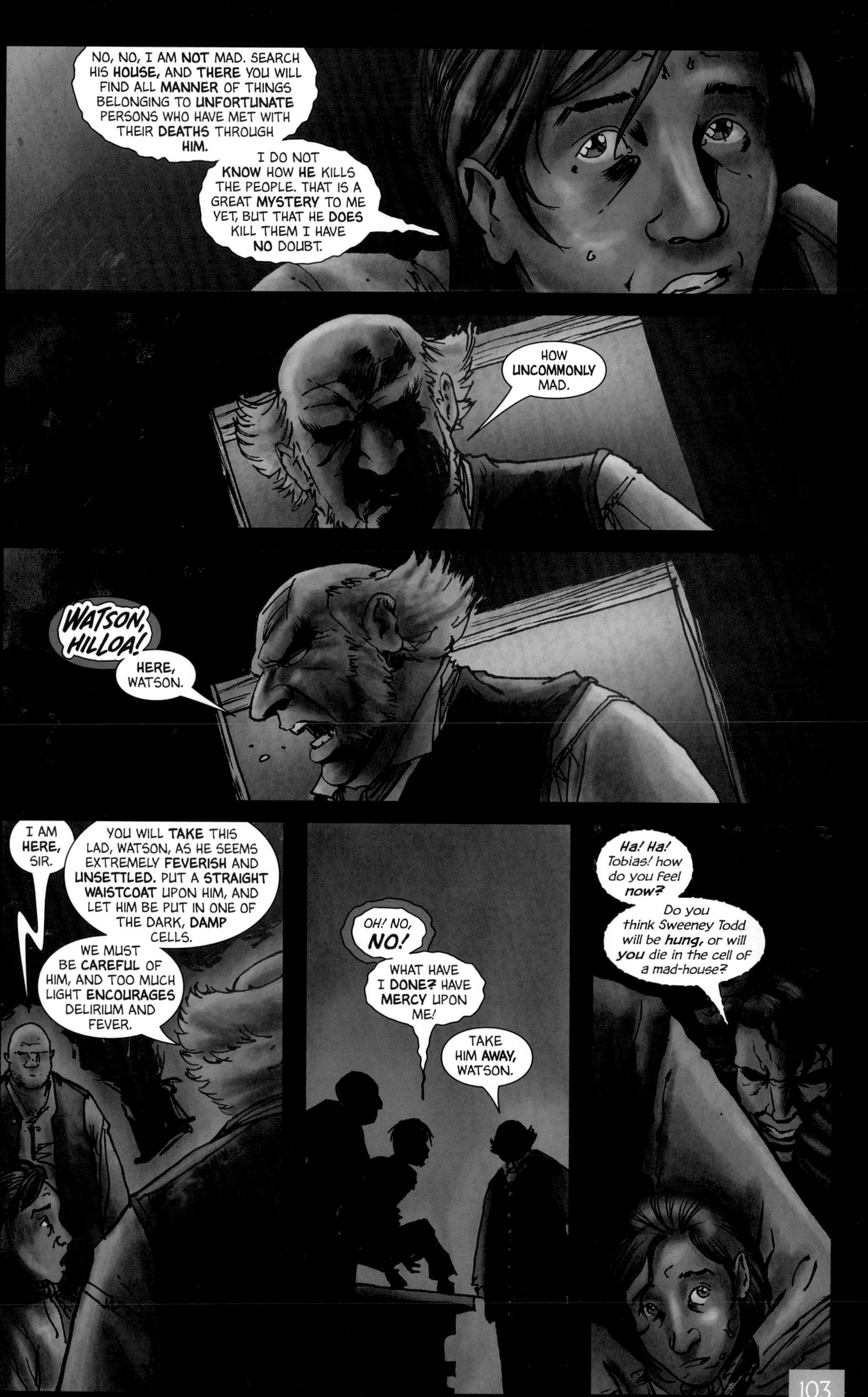
NO, NO, I AM NOT MAD. SEARCH HIS HOUSE, AND THERE YOU WILL FIND ALL MANNER OF THINGS BELONGING TO UNFORTUNATE PERSONS WHO HAVE MET WITH THEIR DEATHS THROUGH HIM.
I DO NOT KNOW HOW HE KILLS THE PEOPLE. THAT IS A GREAT MYSTERY TO ME YET, BUT THAT HE DOES KILL THEM I HAVE NO DOUBT.
HOW UNCOMMONLY MAD.
WATSON, HILLOA!
HERE, WATSON.
I AM HERE, SIR.
YOU WILL TAKE THIS LAD, WATSON, AS HE SEEMS EXTREMELY FEVERISH AND UNSETTLED. PUT A STRAIGHT WAISTCOAT UPON HIM, AND LET HIM BE PUT IN ONE OF THE DARK, DAMP CELLS.
WE MUST BE CAREFUL OF HIM, AND TOO MUCH LIGHT ENCOURAGES DELIRIUM AND FEVER.
OH! NO, NO!
WHAT HAVE I DONE? HAVE MERCY UPON ME!
TAKE HIM AWAY, WATSON.
Ha! Ha! Tobias! how do you feel now?
Do you think Sweeney Todd will be hung, or will you die in the cell of a mad-house?

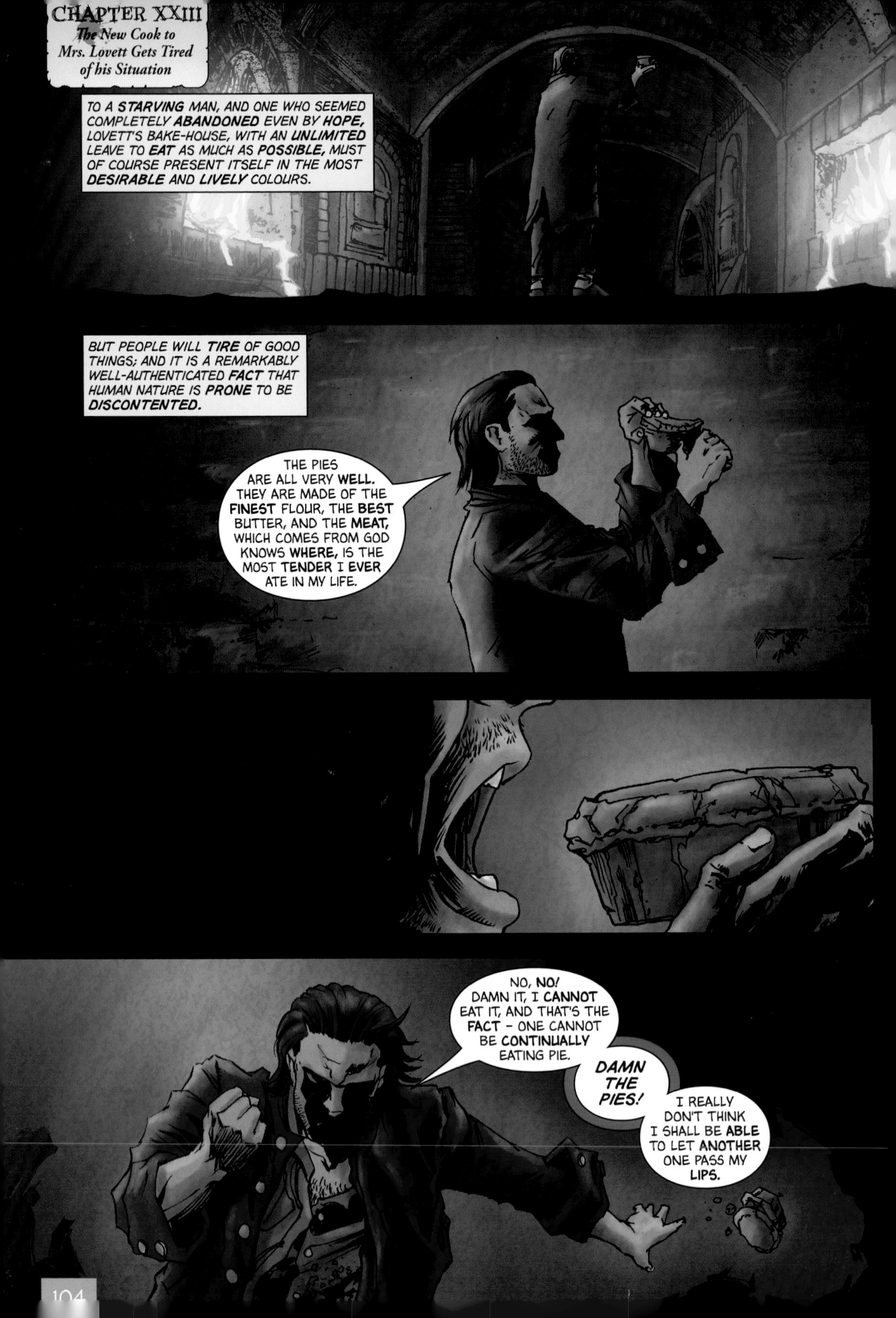

CHAPTER XXIII
The New Cook to Mrs. Lovett Gets Tired of his Situation
TO A STARVING MAN, AND ONE WHO SEEMED COMPLETELY ABANDONED EVEN BY HOPE, LOVETT'S BAKE-HOUSE, WITH AN UNLIMITED LEAVE TO EAT AS MUCH AS POSSIBLE, MUST OF COURSE PRESENT ITSELF IN THE MOST DESIRABLE AND LIVELY COLOURS.
BUT PEOPLE WILL TIRE OF GOOD THINGS; AND IT IS A REMARKABLY WELL-AUTHENTICATED FACT THAT HUMAN NATURE IS PRONE TO BE DISCONTENTED.
THE PIES ARE ALL VERY WELL. THEY ARE MADE OF THE FINEST FLOUR, THE BEST BUTTER, AND THE MEAT, WHICH COMES FROM GOD KNOWS WHERE, IS THE MOST TENDER I EVER ATE IN MY LIFE.
NO, NO! DAMN IT, I CANNOT EAT IT, AND THAT'S THE FACT - ONE CANNOT BE CONTINUALLY EATING PIE.
DAMN THE PIES!
I REALLY DON'T THINK I SHALL BE ABLE TO LET ANOTHER ONE PASS MY LIPS.

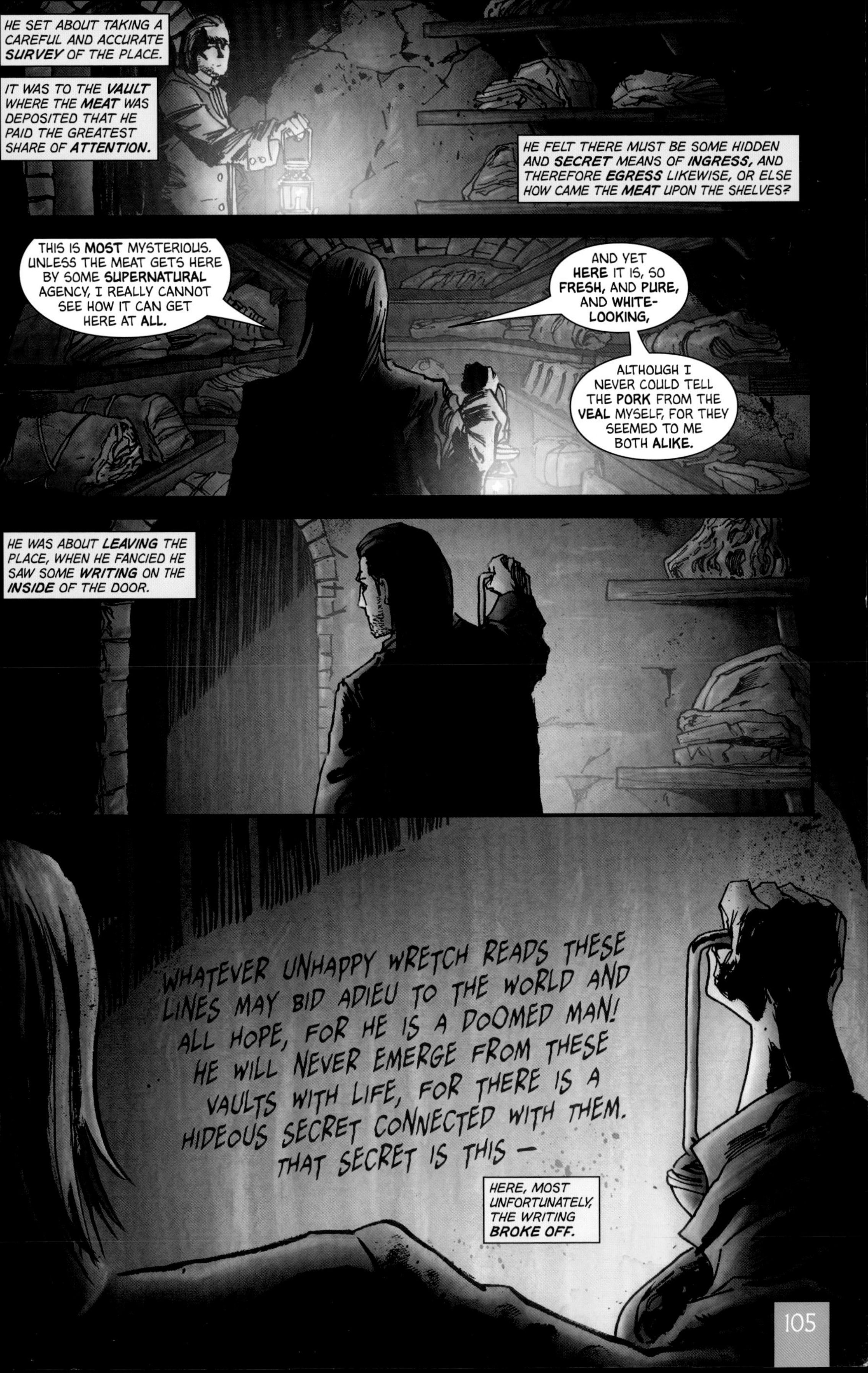
HE SET ABOUT TAKING A CAREFUL AND ACCURATE SURVEY OF THE PLACE.
IT WAS TO THE VAULT WHERE THE MEAT WAS DEPOSITED THAT HE PAID THE GREATEST SHARE OF ATTENTION.
HE FELT THERE MUST BE SOME HIDDEN AND SECRET MEANS OF INGRESS, AND THEREFORE EGRESS LIKEWISE, OR ELSE HOW CAME THE MEAT UPON THE SHELVES?
THIS IS MOST MYSTERIOUS. UNLESS THE MEAT GETS HERE BY SOME SUPERNATURAL AGENCY, I REALLY CANNOT SEE HOW IT CAN GET HERE AT ALL.
AND YET HERE IT IS, SO FRESH, AND PURE, AND WHITE-LOOKING,
ALTHOUGH I NEVER COULD TELL THE PORK FROM THE VEAL MYSELF, FOR THEY SEEMED TO ME BOTH ALIKE.
HE WAS ABOUT LEAVING THE PLACE, WHEN HE FANCIED HE SAW SOME WRITING ON THE INSIDE OF THE DOOR.
WHATEVER UNHAPPY WRETCH READS THESE LINES MAY BID ADIEU TO THE WORLD AND ALL HOPE, FOR HE IS A DOOMED MAN! HE WILL NEVER EMERGE FROM THESE VAULTS WITH LIFE, FOR THERE IS A HIDEOUS SECRET CONNECTED WITH THEM. THAT SECRET IS THIS —
HERE, MOST UNFORTUNATELY, THE WRITING BROKE OFF.

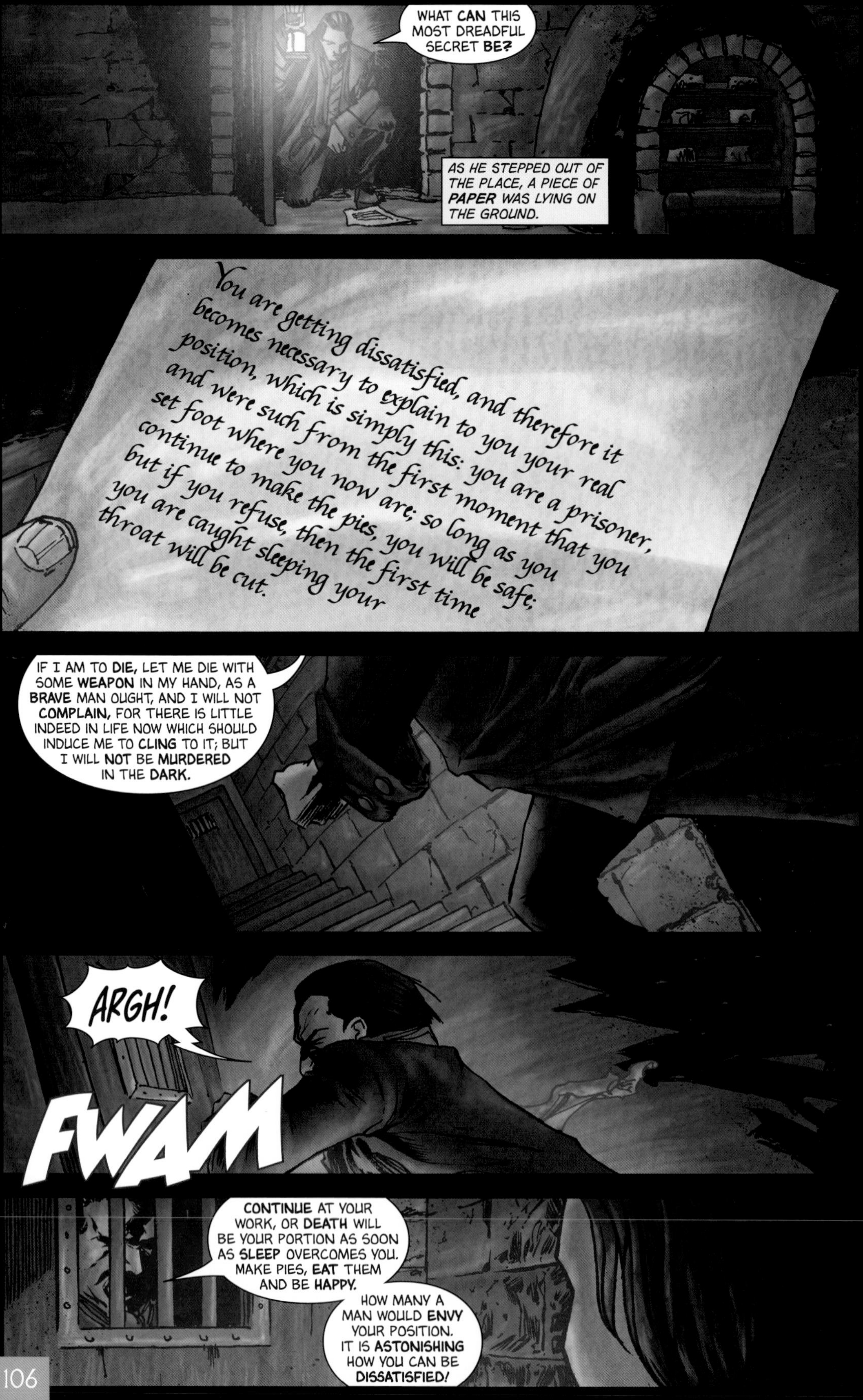
WHAT CAN THIS MOST DREADFUL SECRET BE?
AS HE STEPPED OUT OF THE PLACE, A PIECE OF PAPER WAS LYING ON THE GROUND.
You are getting dissatisfied, and therefore it becomes necessary to explain to you your real position, which is simply this: you are a prisoner, and were such from the first moment that you set foot where you now are; so long as you continue to make the pies, you will be safe; but if you refuse, then the first time you are caught sleeping your throat will be cut.
IF I AM TO DIE, LET ME DIE WITH SOME WEAPON IN MY HAND, AS A BRAVE MAN OUGHT, AND I WILL NOT COMPLAIN, FOR THERE IS LITTLE INDEED IN LIFE NOW WHICH SHOULD INDUCE ME TO CLING TO IT; BUT I WILL NOT BE MURDERED IN THE DARK.
ARGH!
FWAM
CONTINUE AT YOUR WORK, OR DEATH WILL BE YOUR PORTION AS SOON AS SLEEP OVERCOMES YOU. MAKE PIES, EAT THEM AND BE HAPPY.
HOW MANY A MAN WOULD ENVY YOUR POSITION. IT IS ASTONISHING HOW YOU CAN BE DISSATISFIED!

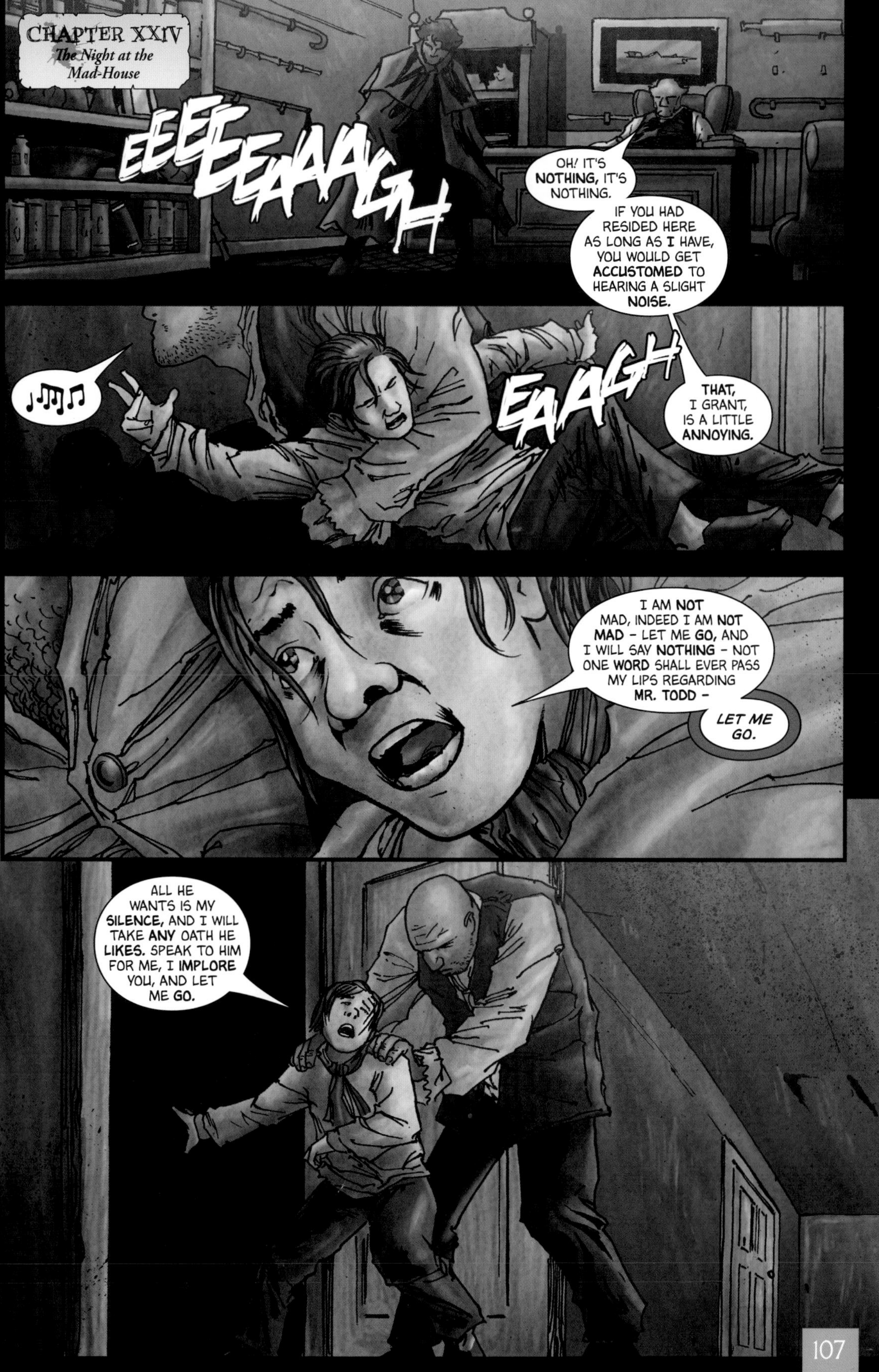

CHAPTER XXIV
The Night at the Mad-House
EEEEEEAAAAGH
OH! IT'S NOTHING, IT'S NOTHING.
IF YOU HAD RESIDED HERE AS LONG AS I HAVE, YOU WOULD GET ACCUSTOMED TO HEARING A SLIGHT NOISE.
EAAGH
THAT, I GRANT, IS A LITTLE ANNOYING.
I AM NOT MAD, INDEED I AM NOT MAD - LET ME GO, AND I WILL SAY NOTHING - NOT ONE WORD SHALL EVER PASS MY LIPS REGARDING MR. TODD -
LET ME GO.
ALL HE WANTS IS MY SILENCE, AND I WILL TAKE ANY OATH HE LIKES. SPEAK TO HIM FOR ME, I IMPLORE YOU, AND LET ME GO.

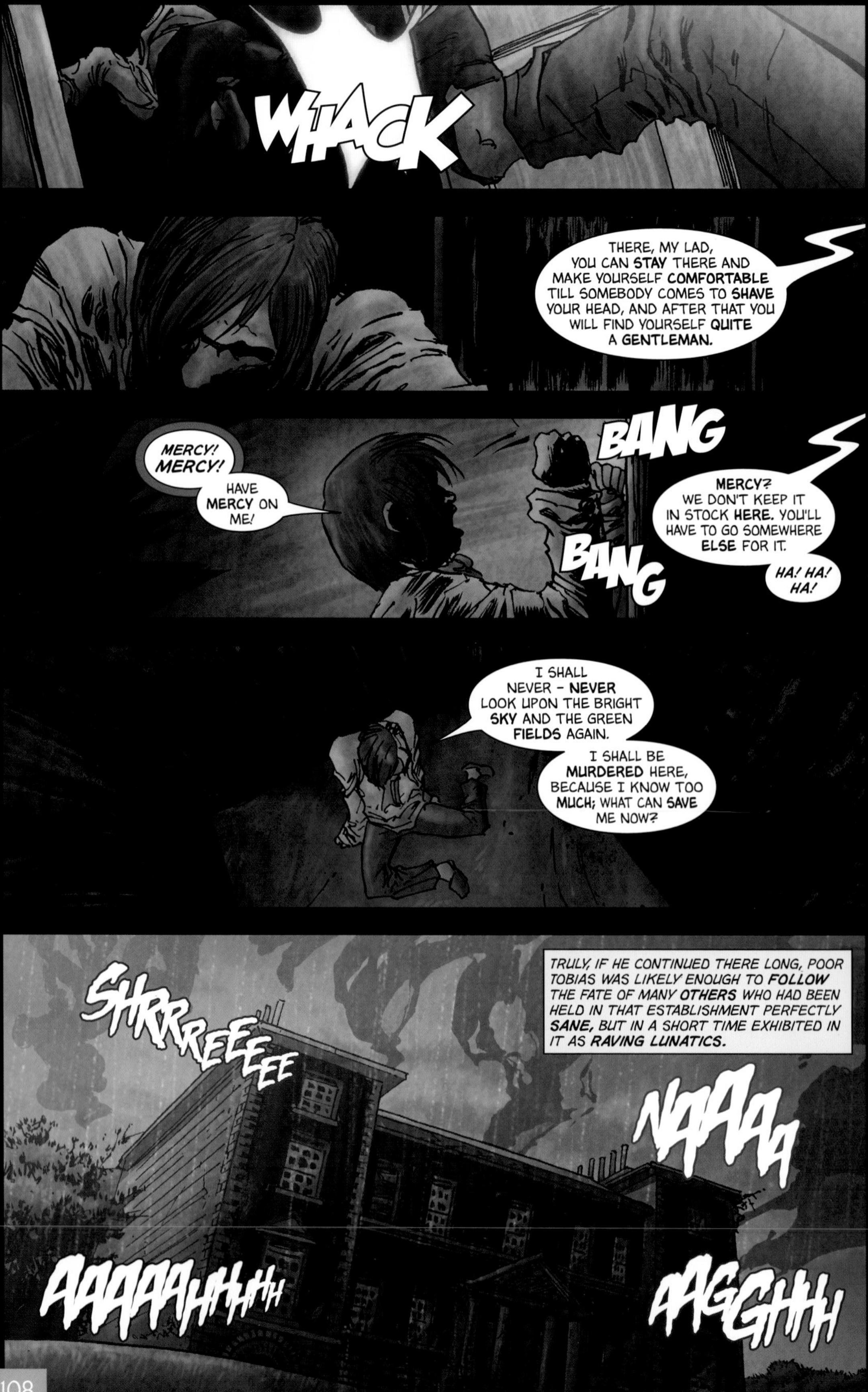
WHACK
THERE, MY LAD, YOU CAN STAY THERE AND MAKE YOURSELF COMFORTABLE TILL SOMEBODY COMES TO SHAVE YOUR HEAD, AND AFTER THAT YOU WILL FIND YOURSELF QUITE A GENTLEMAN.
MERCY! MERCY!
HAVE MERCY ON ME!
BANG
BANG
MERCY? WE DON'T KEEP IT IN STOCK HERE. YOU'LL HAVE TO GO SOMEWHERE ELSE FOR IT.
HA! HA! HA!
I SHALL NEVER - NEVER LOOK UPON THE BRIGHT SKY AND THE GREEN FIELDS AGAIN.
I SHALL BE MURDERED HERE, BECAUSE I KNOW TOO MUCH; WHAT CAN SAVE ME NOW?
TRULY, IF HE CONTINUED THERE LONG, POOR TOBIAS WAS LIKELY ENOUGH TO FOLLOW THE FATE OF MANY OTHERS WHO HAD BEEN HELD IN THAT ESTABLISHMENT PERFECTLY SANE, BUT IN A SHORT TIME EXHIBITED IN IT AS RAVING LUNATICS.
SHRRREEEEEE
NAAAAA
AAAAAHHHHH
AAGGHHH

CHAPTER XXV
*Mr. Fogg's Story at
the Mad-House to
Sweeney Todd*

I HAVE A **TALE** TO TELL. **NONE** OF THE PARTIES ARE NOW **LIVING**, OR, AT LEAST, THEY ARE NOT IN **THIS** COUNTRY, WHICH IS JUST THE **SAME THING**, SO FAR AS I AM CONCERNED.

IT WAS ONE NIGHT – A **DARK** AND **WET** NIGHT TOO, WHEN A **KNOCK** CAME AT THE STREET DOOR – A SHARP **DOUBLE** KNOCK IT WAS.

"I WENT TO THE DOOR AND SAW A TALL **GENTLEMANLY** MAN;

WELL, WHAT IS YOUR **PLEASURE?**

IS YOUR NAME **FOGG?**

YES, IT IS.

I WISH TO HAVE A LITTLE **PRIVATE** CONVERSATION WITH YOU.

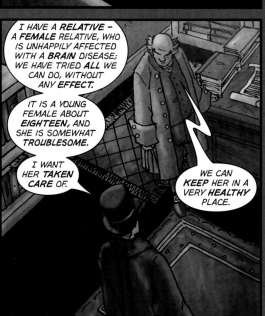

I HAVE A **RELATIVE** – A **FEMALE** RELATIVE, WHO IS UNHAPPILY AFFECTED WITH A **BRAIN** DISEASE; WE HAVE TRIED **ALL** WE CAN DO, WITHOUT ANY **EFFECT.**

IT IS A YOUNG **FEMALE** ABOUT **EIGHTEEN,** AND SHE IS SOMEWHAT **TROUBLESOME.**

I WANT HER **TAKEN CARE** OF.

WE CAN **KEEP** HER IN A VERY **HEALTHY** PLACE.

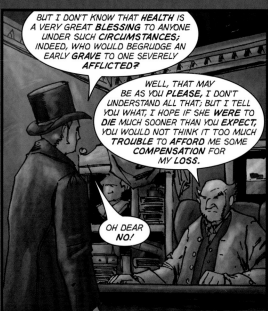

BUT I DON'T KNOW THAT **HEALTH** IS A VERY GREAT **BLESSING** TO ANYONE UNDER SUCH **CIRCUMSTANCES**; INDEED, WHO WOULD BEGRUDGE AN EARLY **GRAVE** TO ONE SEVERELY **AFFLICTED?**

WELL, THAT MAY BE AS YOU **PLEASE,** I DON'T UNDERSTAND ALL THAT; BUT I TELL YOU WHAT, I HOPE IF SHE **WERE** TO **DIE** MUCH SOONER THAN YOU **EXPECT,** YOU WOULD NOT THINK IT TOO MUCH **TROUBLE** TO **AFFORD** ME SOME **COMPENSATION** FOR MY **LOSS.**

OH DEAR **NO!**

AND TO SHOW YOU THAT I SHALL ENTERTAIN **NO** SUCH ILLIBERAL FEELING, I WILL GIVE YOU **TWO HUNDRED POUNDS,** WHEN THE CERTIFICATE OF HER **BURIAL** CAN BE PRODUCED. YOU **UNDERSTAND** ME?

CERTAINLY.

CAN YOU BE AT THE **CORNER** OF GROSVENOR-STREET, NEAR PARK-LANE? WITH A **COACH,** TOO?

YES, I WILL.

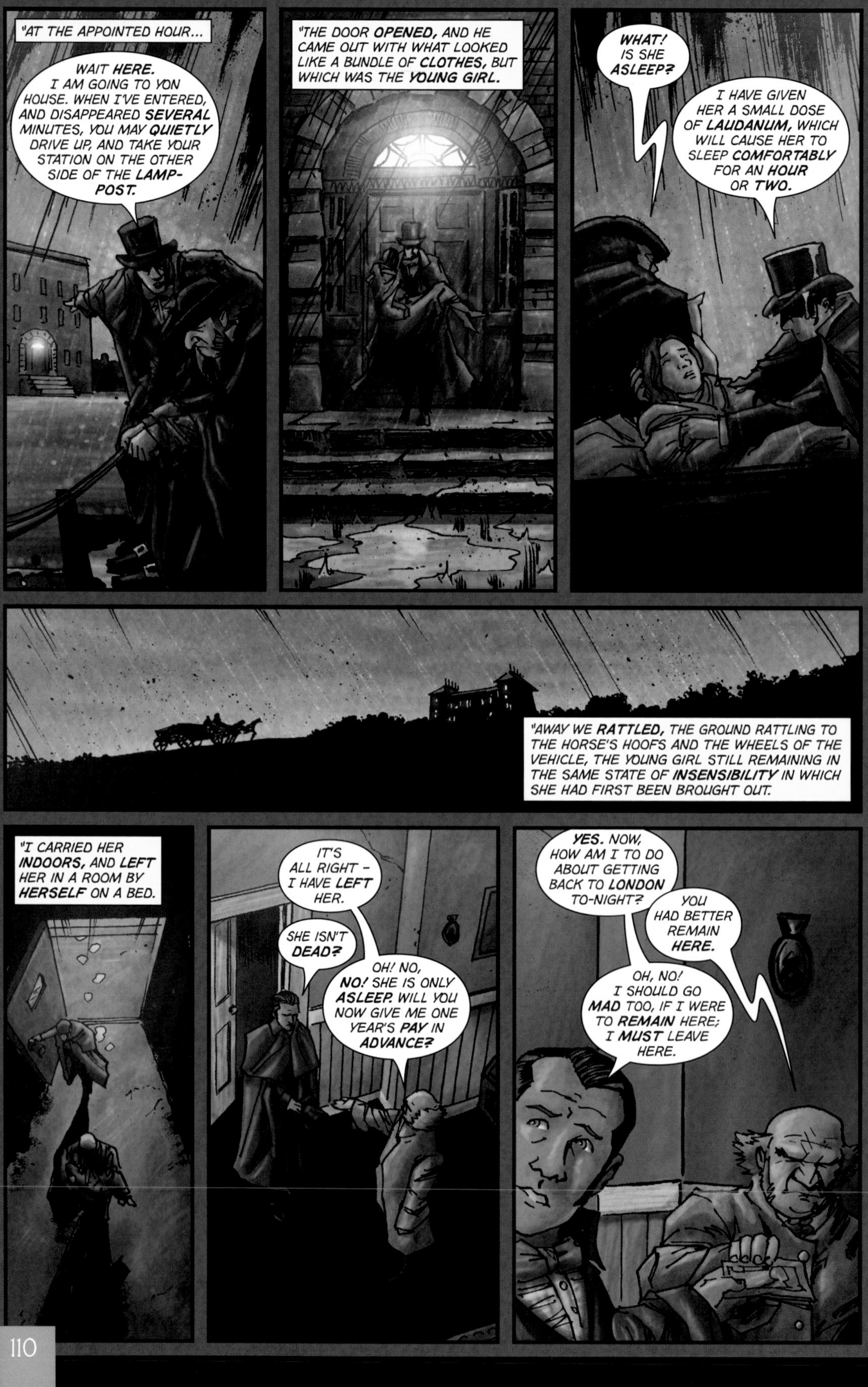
"AT THE APPOINTED HOUR...
WAIT HERE. I AM GOING TO YON HOUSE. WHEN I'VE ENTERED, AND DISAPPEARED SEVERAL MINUTES, YOU MAY QUIETLY DRIVE UP, AND TAKE YOUR STATION ON THE OTHER SIDE OF THE LAMP-POST.
"THE DOOR OPENED, AND HE CAME OUT WITH WHAT LOOKED LIKE A BUNDLE OF CLOTHES, BUT WHICH WAS THE YOUNG GIRL.
WHAT! IS SHE ASLEEP?
I HAVE GIVEN HER A SMALL DOSE OF LAUDANUM, WHICH WILL CAUSE HER TO SLEEP COMFORTABLY FOR AN HOUR OR TWO.
"AWAY WE RATTLED, THE GROUND RATTLING TO THE HORSE'S HOOFS AND THE WHEELS OF THE VEHICLE, THE YOUNG GIRL STILL REMAINING IN THE SAME STATE OF INSENSIBILITY IN WHICH SHE HAD FIRST BEEN BROUGHT OUT.
"I CARRIED HER INDOORS, AND LEFT HER IN A ROOM BY HERSELF ON A BED.
IT'S ALL RIGHT - I HAVE LEFT HER.
SHE ISN'T DEAD?
OH! NO, NO! SHE IS ONLY ASLEEP. WILL YOU NOW GIVE ME ONE YEAR'S PAY IN ADVANCE?
YES. NOW, HOW AM I TO DO ABOUT GETTING BACK TO LONDON TO-NIGHT?
YOU HAD BETTER REMAIN HERE.
OH, NO! I SHOULD GO MAD TOO, IF I WERE TO REMAIN HERE; I MUST LEAVE HERE.

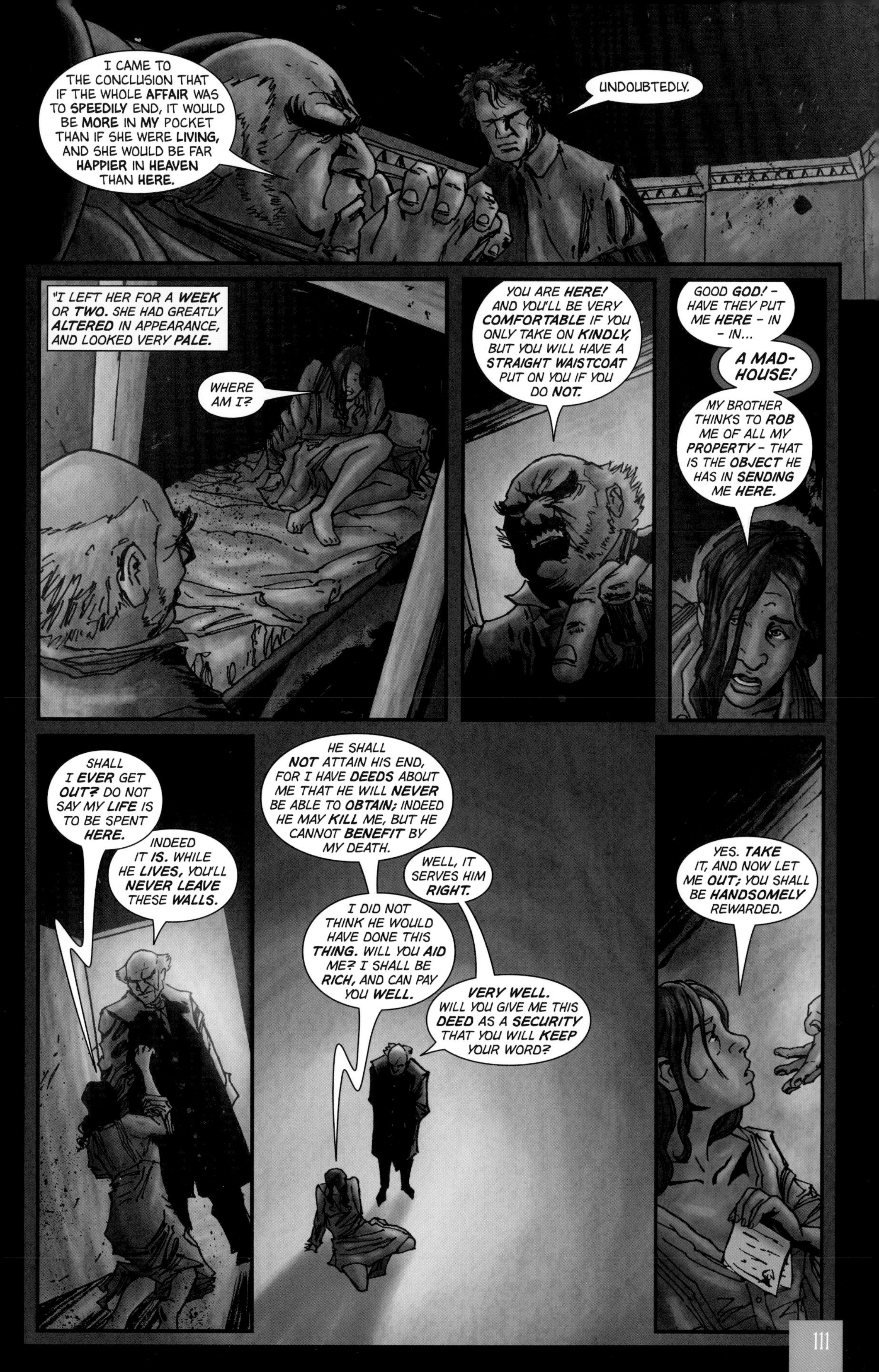
I CAME TO THE CONCLUSION THAT IF THE WHOLE AFFAIR WAS TO SPEEDILY END, IT WOULD BE MORE IN MY POCKET THAN IF SHE WERE LIVING, AND SHE WOULD BE FAR HAPPIER IN HEAVEN THAN HERE.
UNDOUBTEDLY.
"I LEFT HER FOR A WEEK OR TWO. SHE HAD GREATLY ALTERED IN APPEARANCE, AND LOOKED VERY PALE.
WHERE AM I?
YOU ARE HERE! AND YOU'LL BE VERY COMFORTABLE IF YOU ONLY TAKE ON KINDLY, BUT YOU WILL HAVE A STRAIGHT WAISTCOAT PUT ON YOU IF YOU DO NOT.
GOOD GOD! - HAVE THEY PUT ME HERE - IN - IN...
A MAD-HOUSE!
MY BROTHER THINKS TO ROB ME OF ALL MY PROPERTY - THAT IS THE OBJECT HE HAS IN SENDING ME HERE.
SHALL I EVER GET OUT? DO NOT SAY MY LIFE IS TO BE SPENT HERE.
INDEED IT IS. WHILE HE LIVES, YOU'LL NEVER LEAVE THESE WALLS.
HE SHALL NOT ATTAIN HIS END, FOR I HAVE DEEDS ABOUT ME THAT HE WILL NEVER BE ABLE TO OBTAIN; INDEED HE MAY KILL ME, BUT HE CANNOT BENEFIT BY MY DEATH.
WELL, IT SERVES HIM RIGHT.
I DID NOT THINK HE WOULD HAVE DONE THIS THING. WILL YOU AID ME? I SHALL BE RICH, AND CAN PAY YOU WELL.
VERY WELL. WILL YOU GIVE ME THIS DEED AS A SECURITY THAT YOU WILL KEEP YOUR WORD?
YES. TAKE IT, AND NOW LET ME OUT; YOU SHALL BE HANDSOMELY REWARDED.

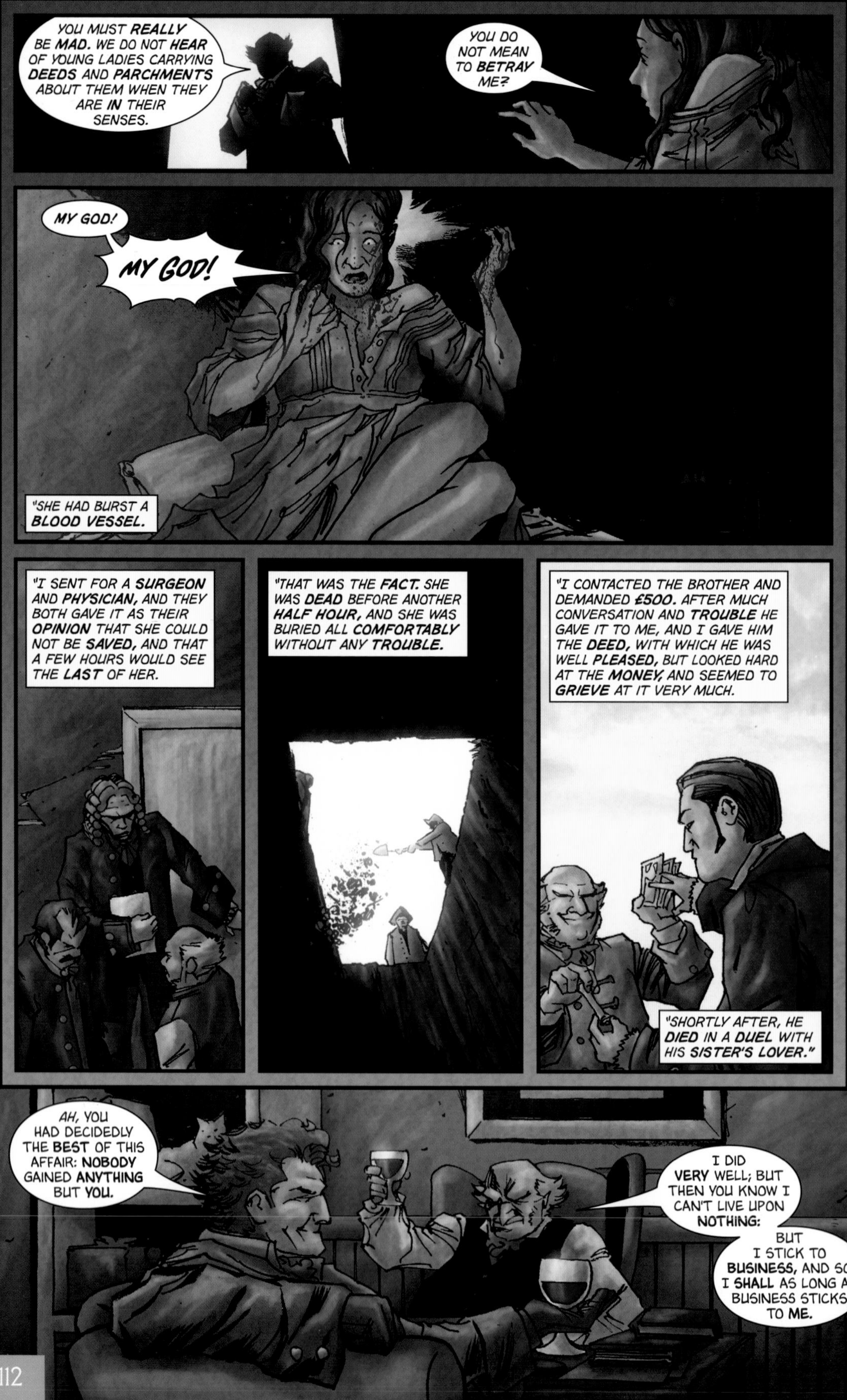
YOU MUST REALLY BE MAD. WE DO NOT HEAR OF YOUNG LADIES CARRYING DEEDS AND PARCHMENTS ABOUT THEM WHEN THEY ARE IN THEIR SENSES.
YOU DO NOT MEAN TO BETRAY ME?
MY GOD!
MY GOD!
"SHE HAD BURST A BLOOD VESSEL.
"I SENT FOR A SURGEON AND PHYSICIAN, AND THEY BOTH GAVE IT AS THEIR OPINION THAT SHE COULD NOT BE SAVED, AND THAT A FEW HOURS WOULD SEE THE LAST OF HER.
"THAT WAS THE FACT. SHE WAS DEAD BEFORE ANOTHER HALF HOUR, AND SHE WAS BURIED ALL COMFORTABLY WITHOUT ANY TROUBLE.
"I CONTACTED THE BROTHER AND DEMANDED £500. AFTER MUCH CONVERSATION AND TROUBLE HE GAVE IT TO ME, AND I GAVE HIM THE DEED, WITH WHICH HE WAS WELL PLEASED, BUT LOOKED HARD AT THE MONEY, AND SEEMED TO GRIEVE AT IT VERY MUCH.
"SHORTLY AFTER, HE DIED IN A DUEL WITH HIS SISTER'S LOVER."
AH, YOU HAD DECIDEDLY THE BEST OF THIS AFFAIR: NOBODY GAINED ANYTHING BUT YOU.
I DID VERY WELL; BUT THEN YOU KNOW I CAN'T LIVE UPON NOTHING:
BUT I STICK TO BUSINESS, AND SO I SHALL AS LONG AS BUSINESS STICKS TO ME.

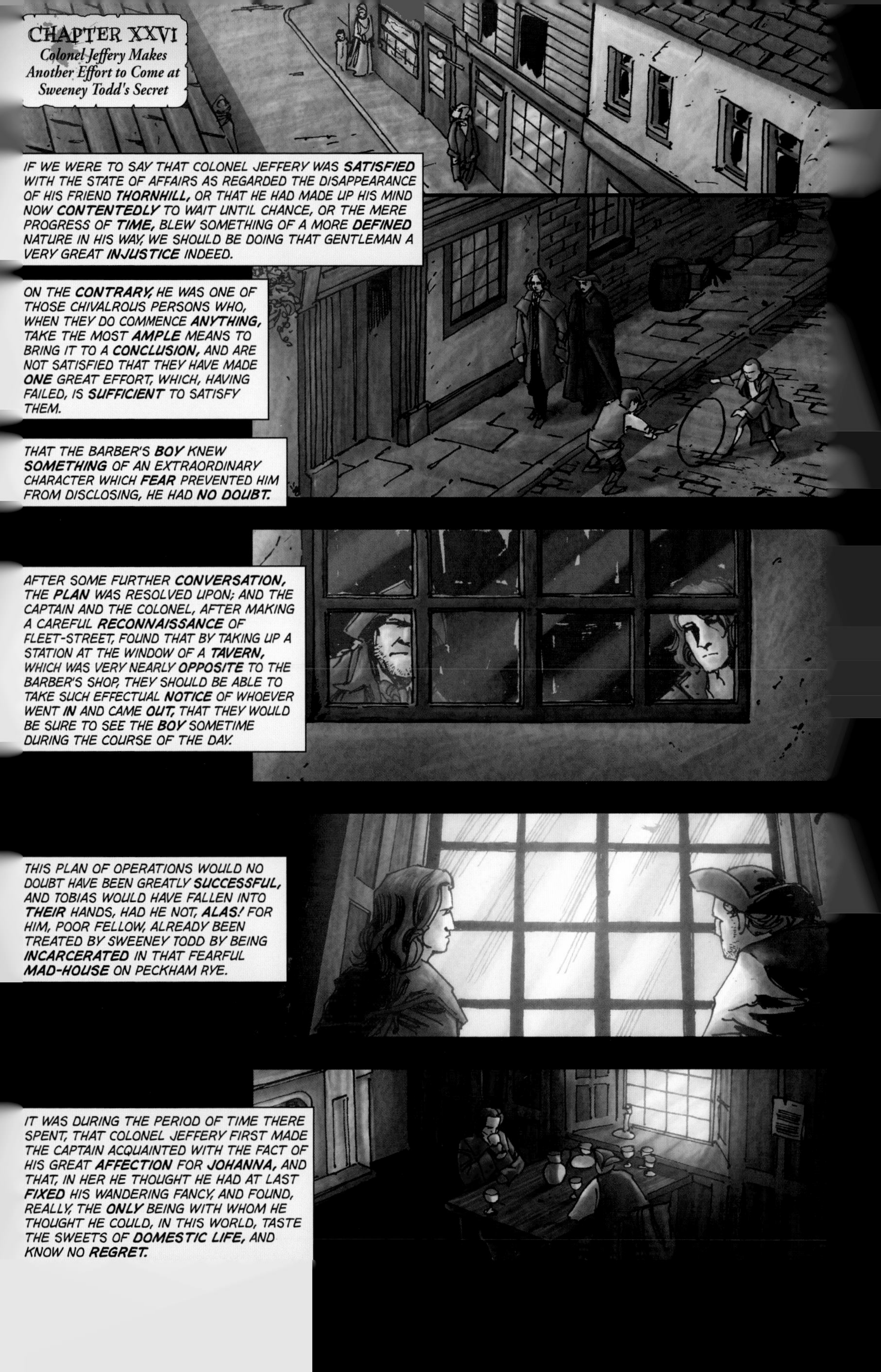
CHAPTER XXVI
Colonel Jeffery Makes Another Effort to Come at Sweeney Todd's Secret
IF WE WERE TO SAY THAT COLONEL JEFFERY WAS SATISFIED WITH THE STATE OF AFFAIRS AS REGARDED THE DISAPPEARANCE OF HIS FRIEND THORNHILL, OR THAT HE HAD MADE UP HIS MIND NOW CONTENTEDLY TO WAIT UNTIL CHANCE, OR THE MERE PROGRESS OF TIME, BLEW SOMETHING OF A MORE DEFINED NATURE IN HIS WAY, WE SHOULD BE DOING THAT GENTLEMAN A VERY GREAT INJUSTICE INDEED.
ON THE CONTRARY, HE WAS ONE OF THOSE CHIVALROUS PERSONS WHO, WHEN THEY DO COMMENCE ANYTHING, TAKE THE MOST AMPLE MEANS TO BRING IT TO A CONCLUSION, AND ARE NOT SATISFIED THAT THEY HAVE MADE ONE GREAT EFFORT, WHICH, HAVING FAILED, IS SUFFICIENT TO SATISFY THEM.
THAT THE BARBER'S BOY KNEW SOMETHING OF AN EXTRAORDINARY CHARACTER WHICH FEAR PREVENTED HIM FROM DISCLOSING, HE HAD NO DOUBT.
AFTER SOME FURTHER CONVERSATION, THE PLAN WAS RESOLVED UPON; AND THE CAPTAIN AND THE COLONEL, AFTER MAKING A CAREFUL RECONNAISSANCE OF FLEET-STREET, FOUND THAT BY TAKING UP A STATION AT THE WINDOW OF A TAVERN, WHICH WAS VERY NEARLY OPPOSITE TO THE BARBER'S SHOP, THEY SHOULD BE ABLE TO TAKE SUCH EFFECTUAL NOTICE OF WHOEVER WENT IN AND CAME OUT, THAT THEY WOULD BE SURE TO SEE THE BOY SOMETIME DURING THE COURSE OF THE DAY.
THIS PLAN OF OPERATIONS WOULD NO DOUBT HAVE BEEN GREATLY SUCCESSFUL, AND TOBIAS WOULD HAVE FALLEN INTO THEIR HANDS, HAD HE NOT, ALAS! FOR HIM, POOR FELLOW, ALREADY BEEN TREATED BY SWEENEY TODD BY BEING INCARCERATED IN THAT FEARFUL MAD-HOUSE ON PECKHAM RYE.
IT WAS DURING THE PERIOD OF TIME THERE SPENT, THAT COLONEL JEFFERY FIRST MADE THE CAPTAIN ACQUAINTED WITH THE FACT OF HIS GREAT AFFECTION FOR JOHANNA, AND THAT, IN HER HE THOUGHT HE HAD AT LAST FIXED HIS WANDERING FANCY, AND FOUND, REALLY, THE ONLY BEING WITH WHOM HE THOUGHT HE COULD, IN THIS WORLD, TASTE THE SWEETS OF DOMESTIC LIFE, AND KNOW NO REGRET.

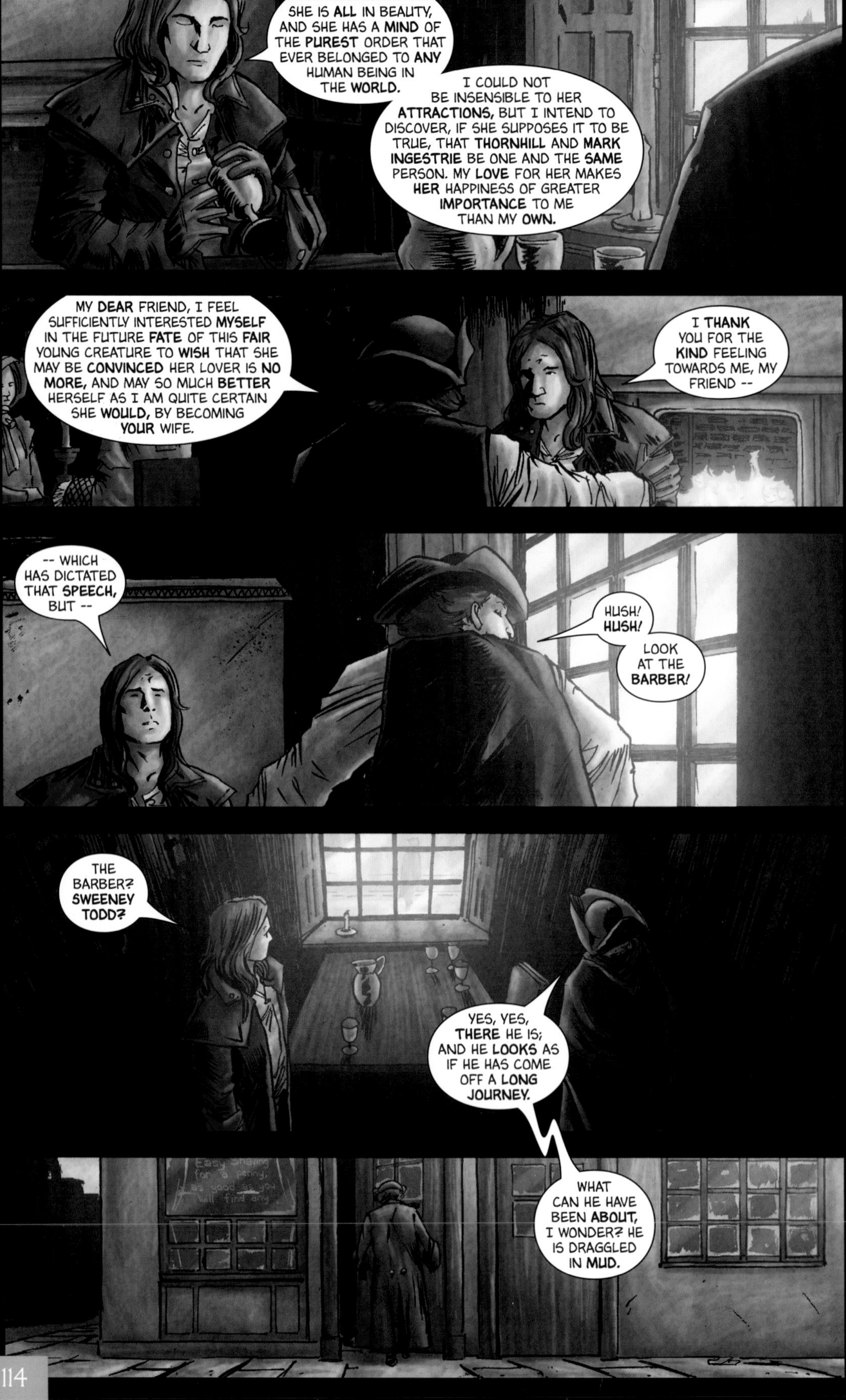

SHE IS ALL IN BEAUTY, AND SHE HAS A MIND OF THE PUREST ORDER THAT EVER BELONGED TO ANY HUMAN BEING IN THE WORLD.
I COULD NOT BE INSENSIBLE TO HER ATTRACTIONS, BUT I INTEND TO DISCOVER, IF SHE SUPPOSES IT TO BE TRUE, THAT THORNHILL AND MARK INGESTRIE BE ONE AND THE SAME PERSON. MY LOVE FOR HER MAKES HER HAPPINESS OF GREATER IMPORTANCE TO ME THAN MY OWN.
MY DEAR FRIEND, I FEEL SUFFICIENTLY INTERESTED MYSELF IN THE FUTURE FATE OF THIS FAIR YOUNG CREATURE TO WISH THAT SHE MAY BE CONVINCED HER LOVER IS NO MORE, AND MAY SO MUCH BETTER HERSELF AS I AM QUITE CERTAIN SHE WOULD, BY BECOMING YOUR WIFE.
I THANK YOU FOR THE KIND FEELING TOWARDS ME, MY FRIEND --
-- WHICH HAS DICTATED THAT SPEECH, BUT --
HUSH! HUSH!
LOOK AT THE BARBER!
THE BARBER? SWEENEY TODD?
YES, YES, THERE HE IS; AND HE LOOKS AS IF HE HAS COME OFF A LONG JOURNEY.
WHAT CAN HE HAVE BEEN ABOUT, I WONDER? HE IS DRAGGLED IN MUD.

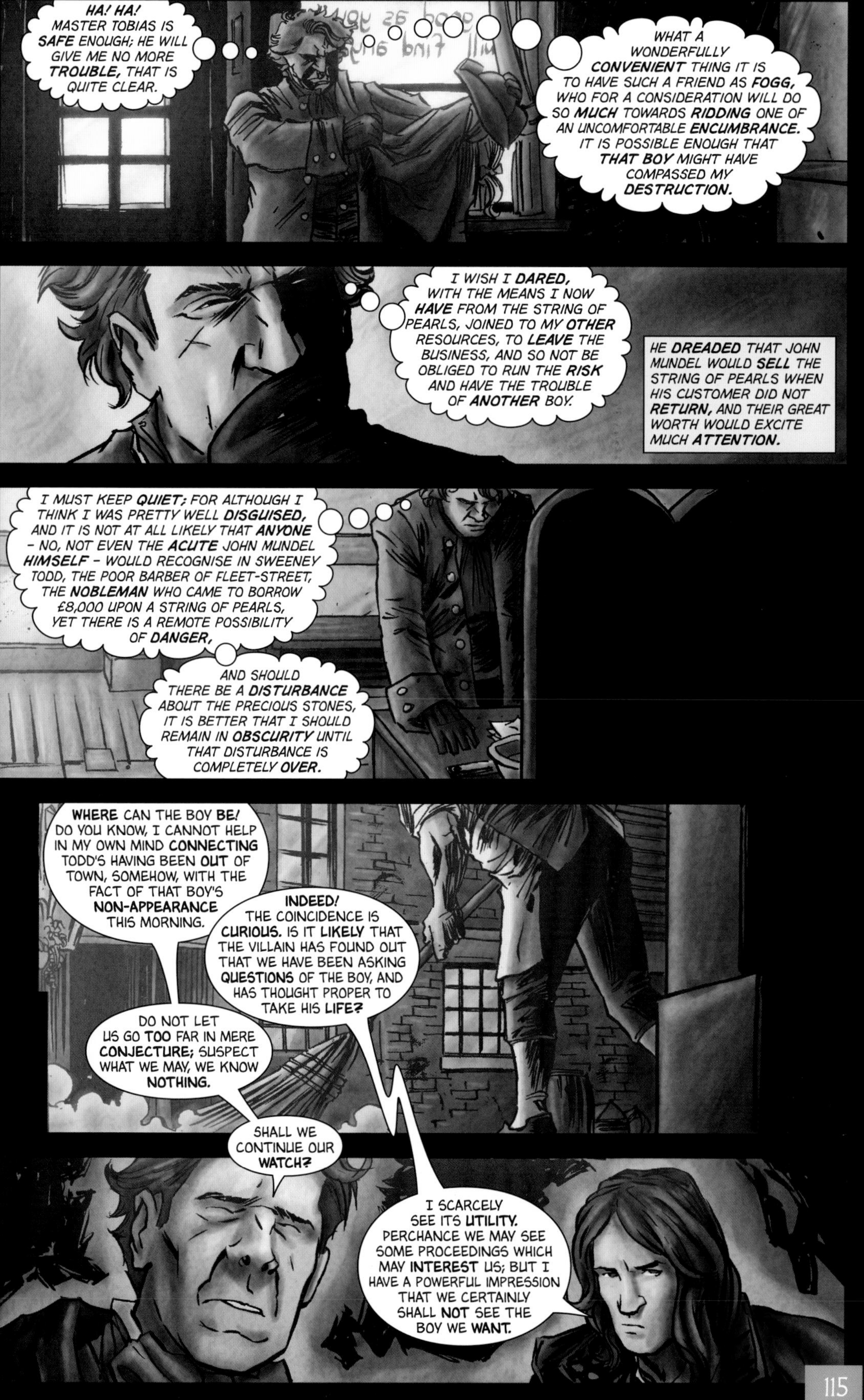
HA! HA! MASTER TOBIAS IS SAFE ENOUGH; HE WILL GIVE ME NO MORE TROUBLE, THAT IS QUITE CLEAR.
WHAT A WONDERFULLY CONVENIENT THING IT IS TO HAVE SUCH A FRIEND AS FOGG, WHO FOR A CONSIDERATION WILL DO SO MUCH TOWARDS RIDDING ONE OF AN UNCOMFORTABLE ENCUMBRANCE. IT IS POSSIBLE ENOUGH THAT THAT BOY MIGHT HAVE COMPASSED MY DESTRUCTION.
I WISH I DARED, WITH THE MEANS I NOW HAVE FROM THE STRING OF PEARLS, JOINED TO MY OTHER RESOURCES, TO LEAVE THE BUSINESS, AND SO NOT BE OBLIGED TO RUN THE RISK AND HAVE THE TROUBLE OF ANOTHER BOY.
HE DREADED THAT JOHN MUNDEL WOULD SELL THE STRING OF PEARLS WHEN HIS CUSTOMER DID NOT RETURN, AND THEIR GREAT WORTH WOULD EXCITE MUCH ATTENTION.
I MUST KEEP QUIET; FOR ALTHOUGH I THINK I WAS PRETTY WELL DISGUISED, AND IT IS NOT AT ALL LIKELY THAT ANYONE – NO, NOT EVEN THE ACUTE JOHN MUNDEL HIMSELF – WOULD RECOGNISE IN SWEENEY TODD, THE POOR BARBER OF FLEET-STREET, THE NOBLEMAN WHO CAME TO BORROW £8,000 UPON A STRING OF PEARLS, YET THERE IS A REMOTE POSSIBILITY OF DANGER,
AND SHOULD THERE BE A DISTURBANCE ABOUT THE PRECIOUS STONES, IT IS BETTER THAT I SHOULD REMAIN IN OBSCURITY UNTIL THAT DISTURBANCE IS COMPLETELY OVER.
WHERE CAN THE BOY BE! DO YOU KNOW, I CANNOT HELP IN MY OWN MIND CONNECTING TODD'S HAVING BEEN OUT OF TOWN, SOMEHOW, WITH THE FACT OF THAT BOY'S NON-APPEARANCE THIS MORNING.
INDEED! THE COINCIDENCE IS CURIOUS. IS IT LIKELY THAT THE VILLAIN HAS FOUND OUT THAT WE HAVE BEEN ASKING QUESTIONS OF THE BOY, AND HAS THOUGHT PROPER TO TAKE HIS LIFE?
DO NOT LET US GO TOO FAR IN MERE CONJECTURE; SUSPECT WHAT WE MAY, WE KNOW NOTHING.
SHALL WE CONTINUE OUR WATCH?
I SCARCELY SEE ITS UTILITY. PERCHANCE WE MAY SEE SOME PROCEEDINGS WHICH MAY INTEREST US; BUT I HAVE A POWERFUL IMPRESSION THAT WE CERTAINLY SHALL NOT SEE THE BOY WE WANT.

BUT, AT ALL EVENTS, THE BARBER, YOU PERCEIVE HAS A **CUSTOMER** ALREADY.

HE WALKED INTO TODD'S SHOP, BEING MOST UNQUESTIONABLY THE **FIRST** CUSTOMER WHICH HE HAD HAD THAT MORNING.

THEY FELT NO GREAT DEGREE OF **INTEREST** IN THIS MAN, WHO WAS A **COMMONPLACE** PERSONAGE ENOUGH, WHO HAD ENTERED SWEENEY TODD'S SHOP...

... BUT WHEN AN **UNREASONABLE** TIME HAD ELAPSED...

...AND HE DID NOT COME **OUT**, THEY DID BEGIN TO FEEL **UNEASY.**

AND WHEN **ANOTHER** MAN WENT IN...

...AND WAS ONLY ABOUT **FIVE** MINUTES BEFORE HE EMERGED **SHAVED**, AND YET THE FIRST MAN DID **NOT** COME, THEY KNEW NOT **WHAT** TO MAKE OF IT.

MY FRIEND, HAVE WE WAITED HERE FOR NOTHING **NOW?** WHAT CAN HAVE **BECOME** OF THAT MAN WHOM WE SAW GO **INTO** THE BARBER'S SHOP; BUT WHO NEVER CAME **OUT?**

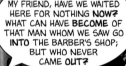

WHAT CONCLUSION **CAN** WE COME TO?

NONE, BUT THAT HE HAS MET HIS **DEATH** THERE; AND THAT, LET HIS FATE BE WHAT IT **MAY**, IS THE SAME WHICH POOR **THORNHILL** HAS SUFFERED.

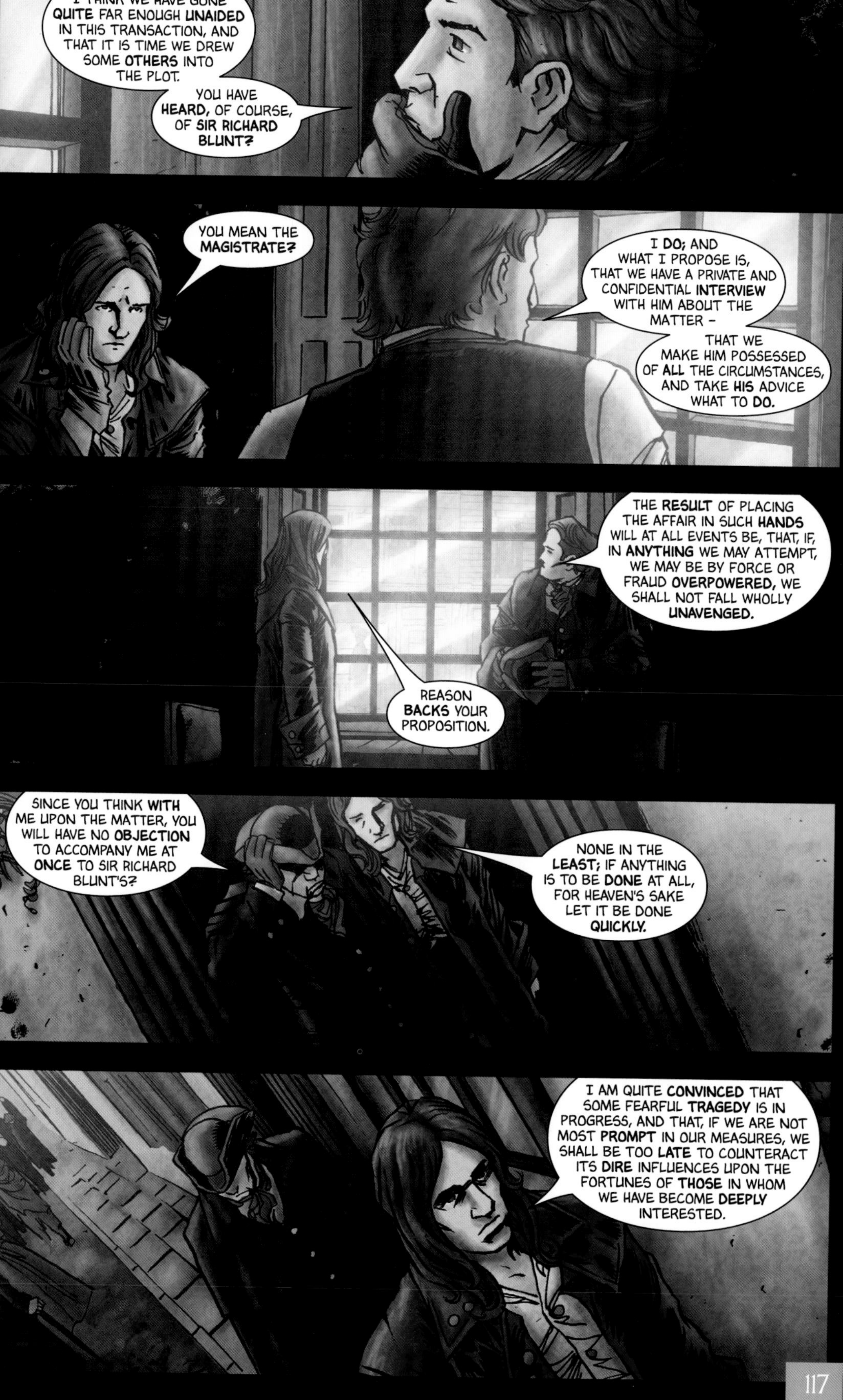
I THINK WE HAVE GONE QUITE FAR ENOUGH UNAIDED IN THIS TRANSACTION, AND THAT IT IS TIME WE DREW SOME OTHERS INTO THE PLOT.
YOU HAVE HEARD, OF COURSE, OF SIR RICHARD BLUNT?
YOU MEAN THE MAGISTRATE?
I DO; AND WHAT I PROPOSE IS, THAT WE HAVE A PRIVATE AND CONFIDENTIAL INTERVIEW WITH HIM ABOUT THE MATTER –
THAT WE MAKE HIM POSSESSED OF ALL THE CIRCUMSTANCES, AND TAKE HIS ADVICE WHAT TO DO.
THE RESULT OF PLACING THE AFFAIR IN SUCH HANDS WILL AT ALL EVENTS BE, THAT, IF, IN ANYTHING WE MAY ATTEMPT, WE MAY BE BY FORCE OR FRAUD OVERPOWERED, WE SHALL NOT FALL WHOLLY UNAVENGED.
REASON BACKS YOUR PROPOSITION.
SINCE YOU THINK WITH ME UPON THE MATTER, YOU WILL HAVE NO OBJECTION TO ACCOMPANY ME AT ONCE TO SIR RICHARD BLUNT'S?
NONE IN THE LEAST; IF ANYTHING IS TO BE DONE AT ALL, FOR HEAVEN'S SAKE LET IT BE DONE QUICKLY.
I AM QUITE CONVINCED THAT SOME FEARFUL TRAGEDY IS IN PROGRESS, AND THAT, IF WE ARE NOT MOST PROMPT IN OUR MEASURES, WE SHALL BE TOO LATE TO COUNTERACT ITS DIRE INFLUENCES UPON THE FORTUNES OF THOSE IN WHOM WE HAVE BECOME DEEPLY INTERESTED.

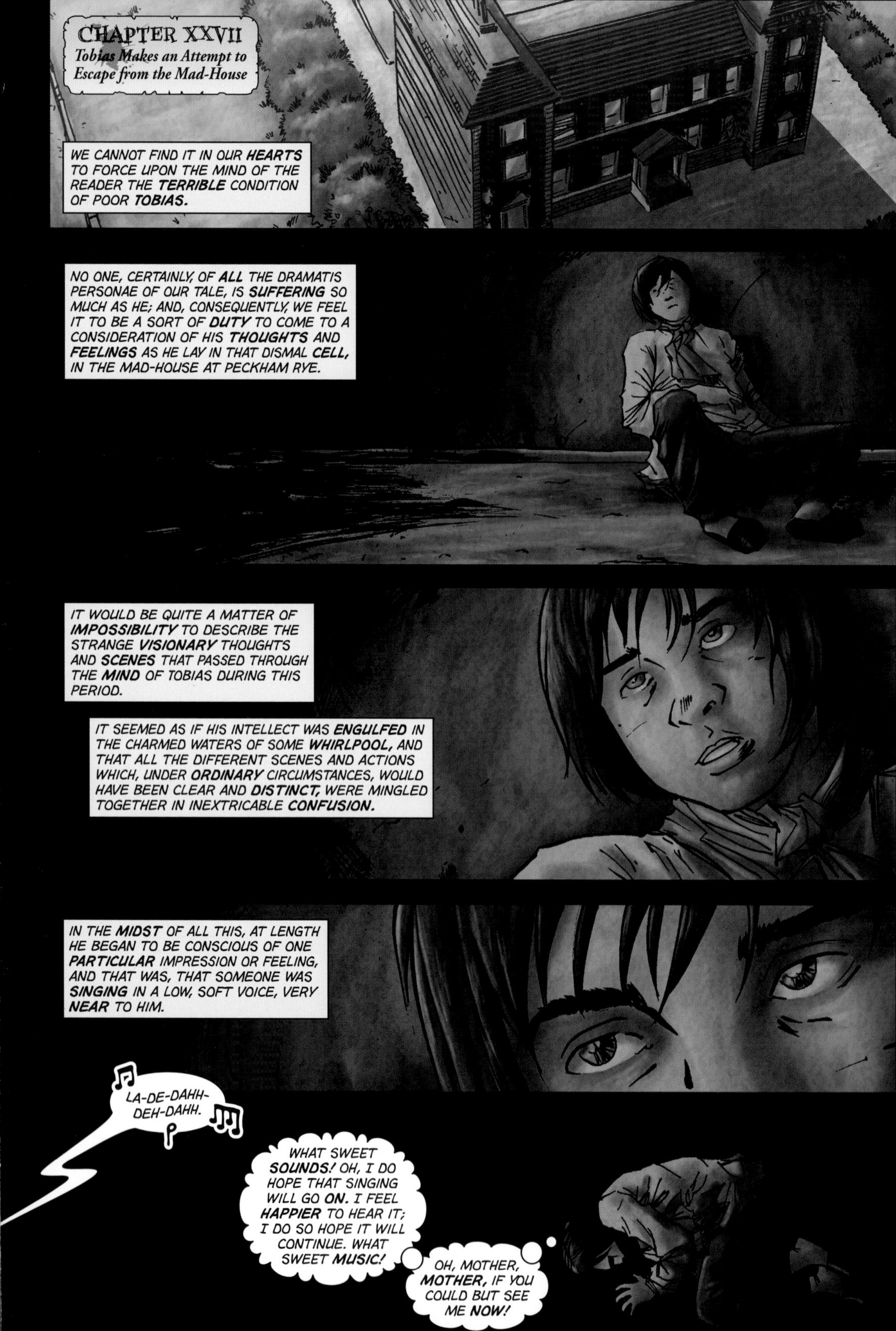
CHAPTER XXVII
Tobias Makes an Attempt to Escape from the Mad-House
WE CANNOT FIND IT IN OUR HEARTS TO FORCE UPON THE MIND OF THE READER THE TERRIBLE CONDITION OF POOR TOBIAS.
NO ONE, CERTAINLY, OF ALL THE DRAMATIS PERSONAE OF OUR TALE, IS SUFFERING SO MUCH AS HE; AND, CONSEQUENTLY, WE FEEL IT TO BE A SORT OF DUTY TO COME TO A CONSIDERATION OF HIS THOUGHTS AND FEELINGS AS HE LAY IN THAT DISMAL CELL, IN THE MAD-HOUSE AT PECKHAM RYE.
IT WOULD BE QUITE A MATTER OF IMPOSSIBILITY TO DESCRIBE THE STRANGE VISIONARY THOUGHTS AND SCENES THAT PASSED THROUGH THE MIND OF TOBIAS DURING THIS PERIOD.
IT SEEMED AS IF HIS INTELLECT WAS ENGULFED IN THE CHARMED WATERS OF SOME WHIRLPOOL, AND THAT ALL THE DIFFERENT SCENES AND ACTIONS WHICH, UNDER ORDINARY CIRCUMSTANCES, WOULD HAVE BEEN CLEAR AND DISTINCT, WERE MINGLED TOGETHER IN INEXTRICABLE CONFUSION.
IN THE MIDST OF ALL THIS, AT LENGTH HE BEGAN TO BE CONSCIOUS OF ONE PARTICULAR IMPRESSION OR FEELING, AND THAT WAS, THAT SOMEONE WAS SINGING IN A LOW, SOFT VOICE, VERY NEAR TO HIM.
LA-DE-DAHH-DEH-DAHH.
WHAT SWEET SOUNDS! OH, I DO HOPE THAT SINGING WILL GO ON. I FEEL HAPPIER TO HEAR IT; I DO SO HOPE IT WILL CONTINUE. WHAT SWEET MUSIC!
OH, MOTHER, MOTHER, IF YOU COULD BUT SEE ME NOW!

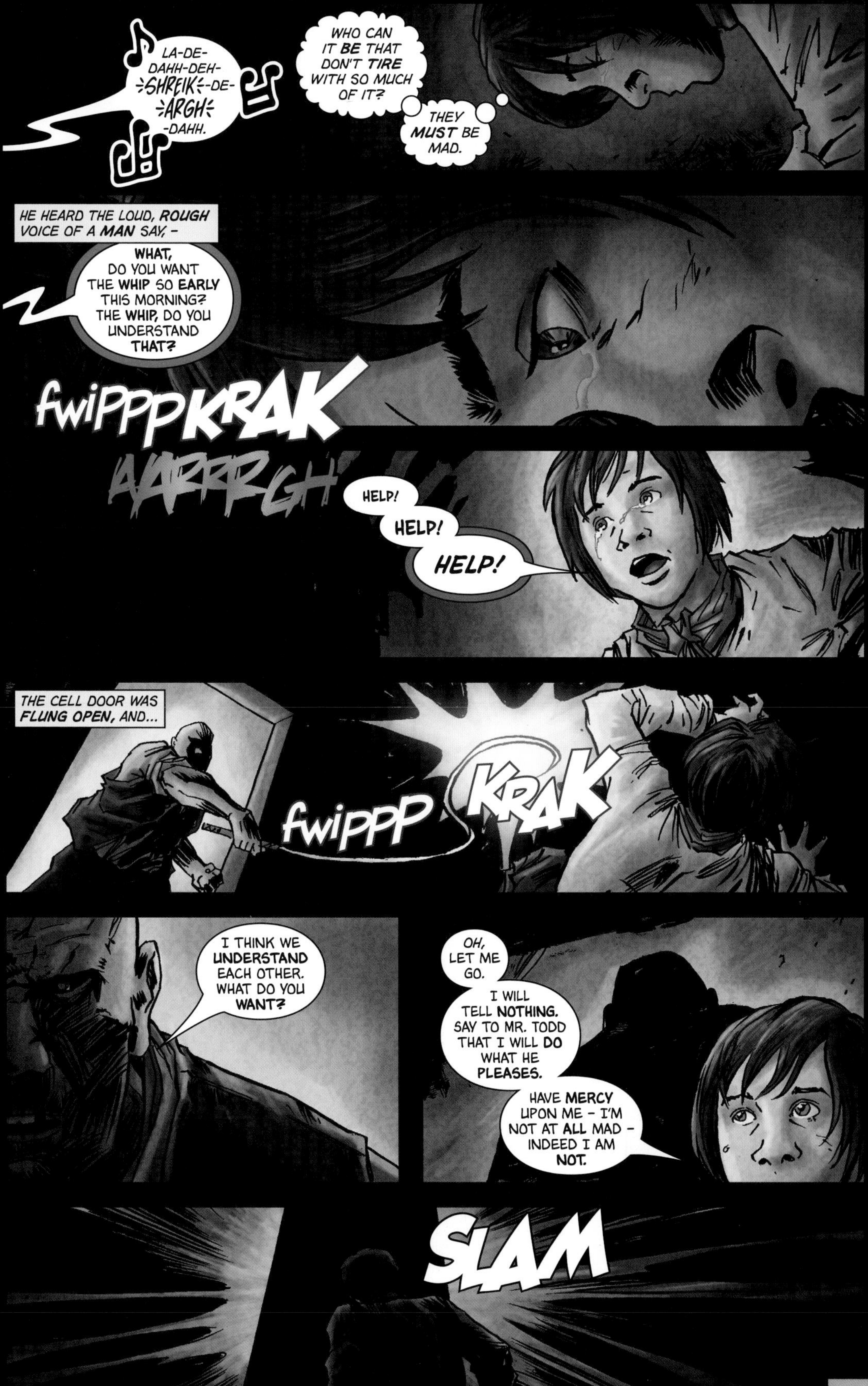
LA-DE-DAHH-DEH-SHREIK-DE-ARGH-DAHH.
WHO CAN IT BE THAT DON'T TIRE WITH SO MUCH OF IT?
THEY MUST BE MAD.
HE HEARD THE LOUD, ROUGH VOICE OF A MAN SAY, –
WHAT, DO YOU WANT THE WHIP SO EARLY THIS MORNING? THE WHIP, DO YOU UNDERSTAND THAT?
fwiPPP KRAK
AARRRGH
HELP!
HELP!
HELP!
THE CELL DOOR WAS FLUNG OPEN, AND...
fwiPPP KRAK
I THINK WE UNDERSTAND EACH OTHER. WHAT DO YOU WANT?
OH, LET ME GO.
I WILL TELL NOTHING. SAY TO MR. TODD THAT I WILL DO WHAT HE PLEASES.
HAVE MERCY UPON ME – I'M NOT AT ALL MAD – INDEED I AM NOT.
SLAM

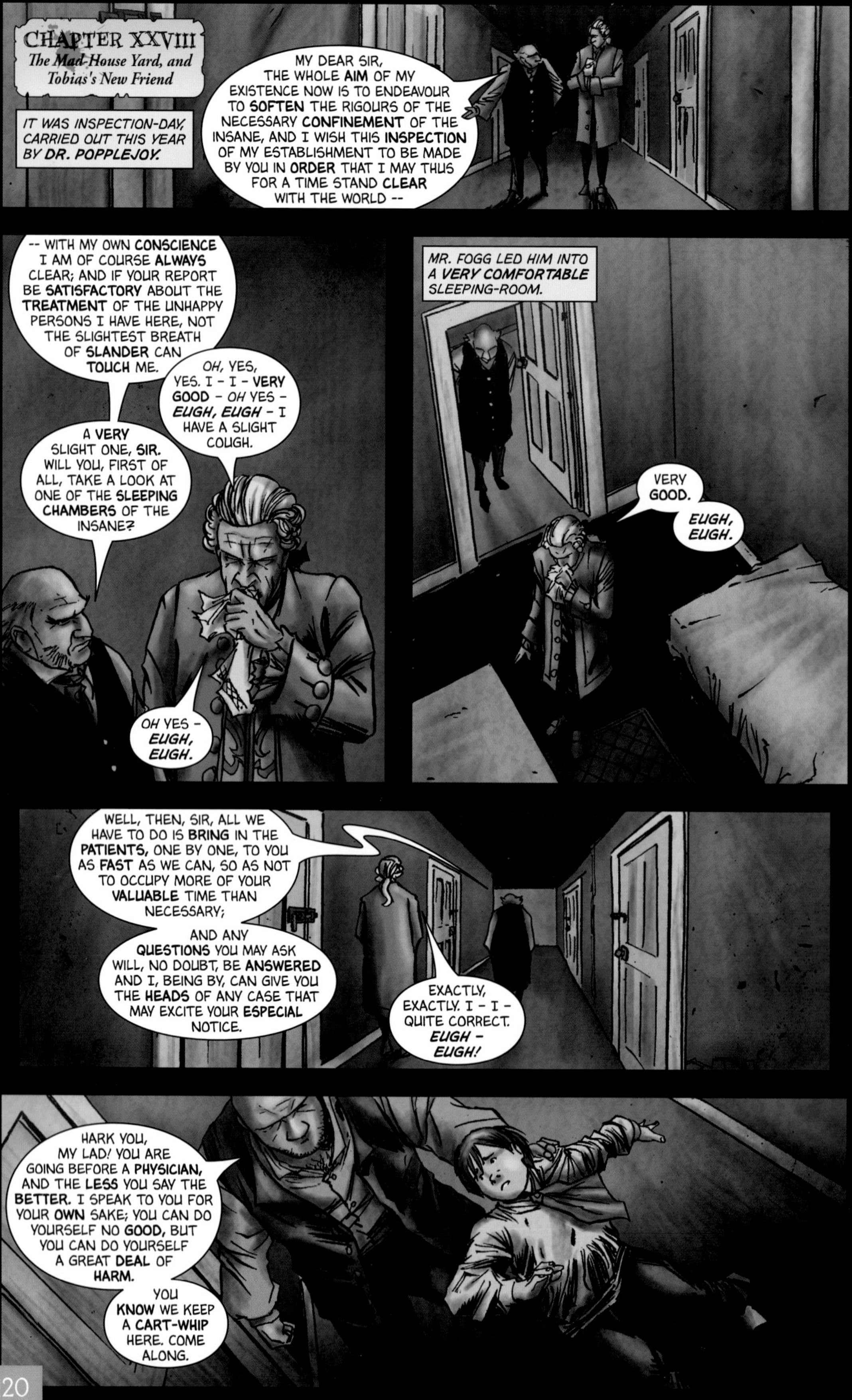
CHAPTER XXVIII
The Mad-House Yard, and Tobias's New Friend
IT WAS INSPECTION-DAY, CARRIED OUT THIS YEAR BY DR. POPPLEJOY.
MY DEAR SIR, THE WHOLE AIM OF MY EXISTENCE NOW IS TO ENDEAVOUR TO SOFTEN THE RIGOURS OF THE NECESSARY CONFINEMENT OF THE INSANE, AND I WISH THIS INSPECTION OF MY ESTABLISHMENT TO BE MADE BY YOU IN ORDER THAT I MAY THUS FOR A TIME STAND CLEAR WITH THE WORLD --
-- WITH MY OWN CONSCIENCE I AM OF COURSE ALWAYS CLEAR; AND IF YOUR REPORT BE SATISFACTORY ABOUT THE TREATMENT OF THE UNHAPPY PERSONS I HAVE HERE, NOT THE SLIGHTEST BREATH OF SLANDER CAN TOUCH ME.
OH, YES, YES. I - I - VERY GOOD - OH YES - EUGH, EUGH - I HAVE A SLIGHT COUGH.
A VERY SLIGHT ONE, SIR. WILL YOU, FIRST OF ALL, TAKE A LOOK AT ONE OF THE SLEEPING CHAMBERS OF THE INSANE?
OH YES - EUGH, EUGH.
MR. FOGG LED HIM INTO A VERY COMFORTABLE SLEEPING-ROOM.
VERY GOOD. EUGH, EUGH.
WELL, THEN, SIR, ALL WE HAVE TO DO IS BRING IN THE PATIENTS, ONE BY ONE, TO YOU AS FAST AS WE CAN, SO AS NOT TO OCCUPY MORE OF YOUR VALUABLE TIME THAN NECESSARY;
AND ANY QUESTIONS YOU MAY ASK WILL, NO DOUBT, BE ANSWERED AND I, BEING BY, CAN GIVE YOU THE HEADS OF ANY CASE THAT MAY EXCITE YOUR ESPECIAL NOTICE.
EXACTLY, EXACTLY. I - I - QUITE CORRECT. EUGH - EUGH!
HARK YOU, MY LAD! YOU ARE GOING BEFORE A PHYSICIAN, AND THE LESS YOU SAY THE BETTER. I SPEAK TO YOU FOR YOUR OWN SAKE; YOU CAN DO YOURSELF NO GOOD, BUT YOU CAN DO YOURSELF A GREAT DEAL OF HARM.
YOU KNOW WE KEEP A CART-WHIP HERE. COME ALONG.

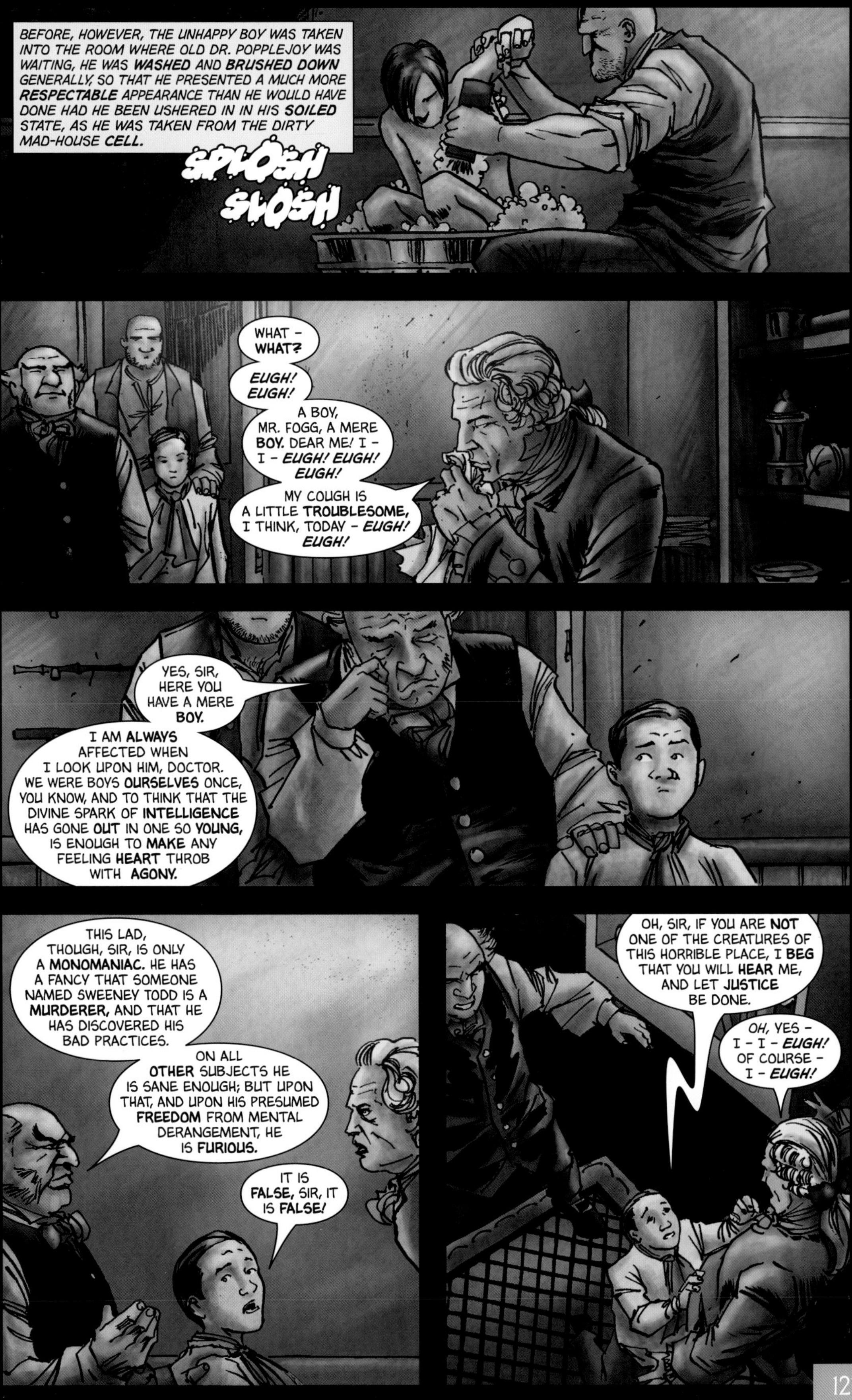
BEFORE, HOWEVER, THE UNHAPPY BOY WAS TAKEN INTO THE ROOM WHERE OLD DR. POPPLEJOY WAS WAITING, HE WAS WASHED AND BRUSHED DOWN GENERALLY, SO THAT HE PRESENTED A MUCH MORE RESPECTABLE APPEARANCE THAN HE WOULD HAVE DONE HAD HE BEEN USHERED IN IN HIS SOILED STATE, AS HE WAS TAKEN FROM THE DIRTY MAD-HOUSE CELL.
SPLOSH
SLOSH
WHAT - WHAT?
EUGH! EUGH!
A BOY, MR. FOGG, A MERE BOY. DEAR ME! I - I - EUGH! EUGH! EUGH!
MY COUGH IS A LITTLE TROUBLESOME, I THINK, TODAY - EUGH! EUGH!
YES, SIR, HERE YOU HAVE A MERE BOY.
I AM ALWAYS AFFECTED WHEN I LOOK UPON HIM, DOCTOR. WE WERE BOYS OURSELVES ONCE, YOU KNOW, AND TO THINK THAT THE DIVINE SPARK OF INTELLIGENCE HAS GONE OUT IN ONE SO YOUNG, IS ENOUGH TO MAKE ANY FEELING HEART THROB WITH AGONY.
THIS LAD, THOUGH, SIR, IS ONLY A MONOMANIAC. HE HAS A FANCY THAT SOMEONE NAMED SWEENEY TODD IS A MURDERER, AND THAT HE HAS DISCOVERED HIS BAD PRACTICES.
ON ALL OTHER SUBJECTS HE IS SANE ENOUGH; BUT UPON THAT, AND UPON HIS PRESUMED FREEDOM FROM MENTAL DERANGEMENT, HE IS FURIOUS.
IT IS FALSE, SIR, IT IS FALSE!
OH, SIR, IF YOU ARE NOT ONE OF THE CREATURES OF THIS HORRIBLE PLACE, I BEG THAT YOU WILL HEAR ME, AND LET JUSTICE BE DONE.
OH, YES - I - I - EUGH! OF COURSE - I - EUGH!

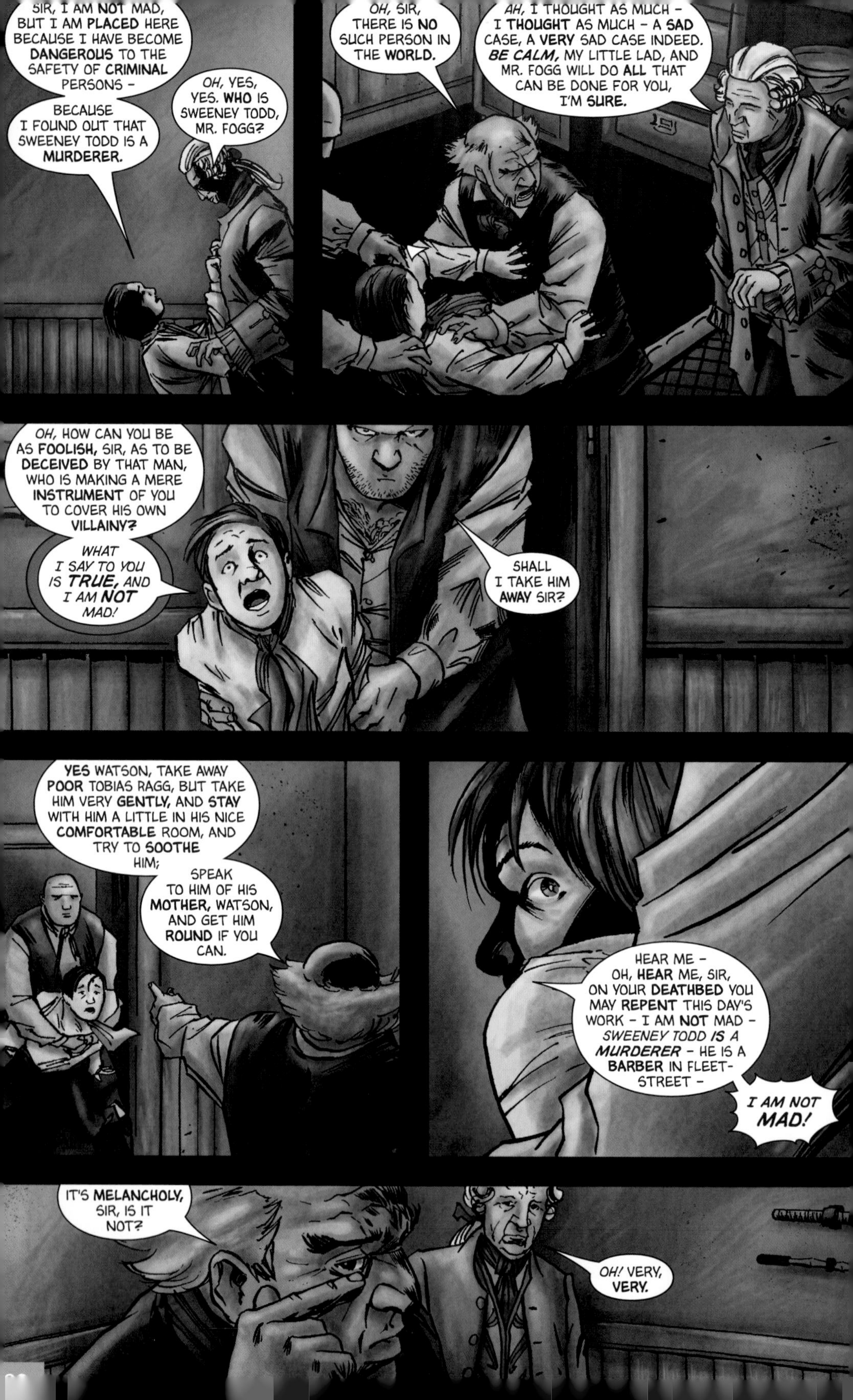
SIR, I AM NOT MAD, BUT I AM PLACED HERE BECAUSE I HAVE BECOME DANGEROUS TO THE SAFETY OF CRIMINAL PERSONS –
BECAUSE I FOUND OUT THAT SWEENEY TODD IS A MURDERER.
OH, YES, YES. WHO IS SWEENEY TODD, MR. FOGG?
OH, SIR, THERE IS NO SUCH PERSON IN THE WORLD.
AH, I THOUGHT AS MUCH – I THOUGHT AS MUCH – A SAD CASE, A VERY SAD CASE INDEED. BE CALM, MY LITTLE LAD, AND MR. FOGG WILL DO ALL THAT CAN BE DONE FOR YOU, I'M SURE.
OH, HOW CAN YOU BE AS FOOLISH, SIR, AS TO BE DECEIVED BY THAT MAN, WHO IS MAKING A MERE INSTRUMENT OF YOU TO COVER HIS OWN VILLAINY?
WHAT I SAY TO YOU IS TRUE, AND I AM NOT MAD!
SHALL I TAKE HIM AWAY SIR?
YES WATSON, TAKE AWAY POOR TOBIAS RAGG, BUT TAKE HIM VERY GENTLY, AND STAY WITH HIM A LITTLE IN HIS NICE COMFORTABLE ROOM, AND TRY TO SOOTHE HIM;
SPEAK TO HIM OF HIS MOTHER, WATSON, AND GET HIM ROUND IF YOU CAN.
HEAR ME – OH, HEAR ME, SIR, ON YOUR DEATHBED YOU MAY REPENT THIS DAY'S WORK – I AM NOT MAD – SWEENEY TODD IS A MURDERER – HE IS A BARBER IN FLEET-STREET –
I AM NOT MAD!
IT'S MELANCHOLY, SIR, IS IT NOT?
OH! VERY, VERY.

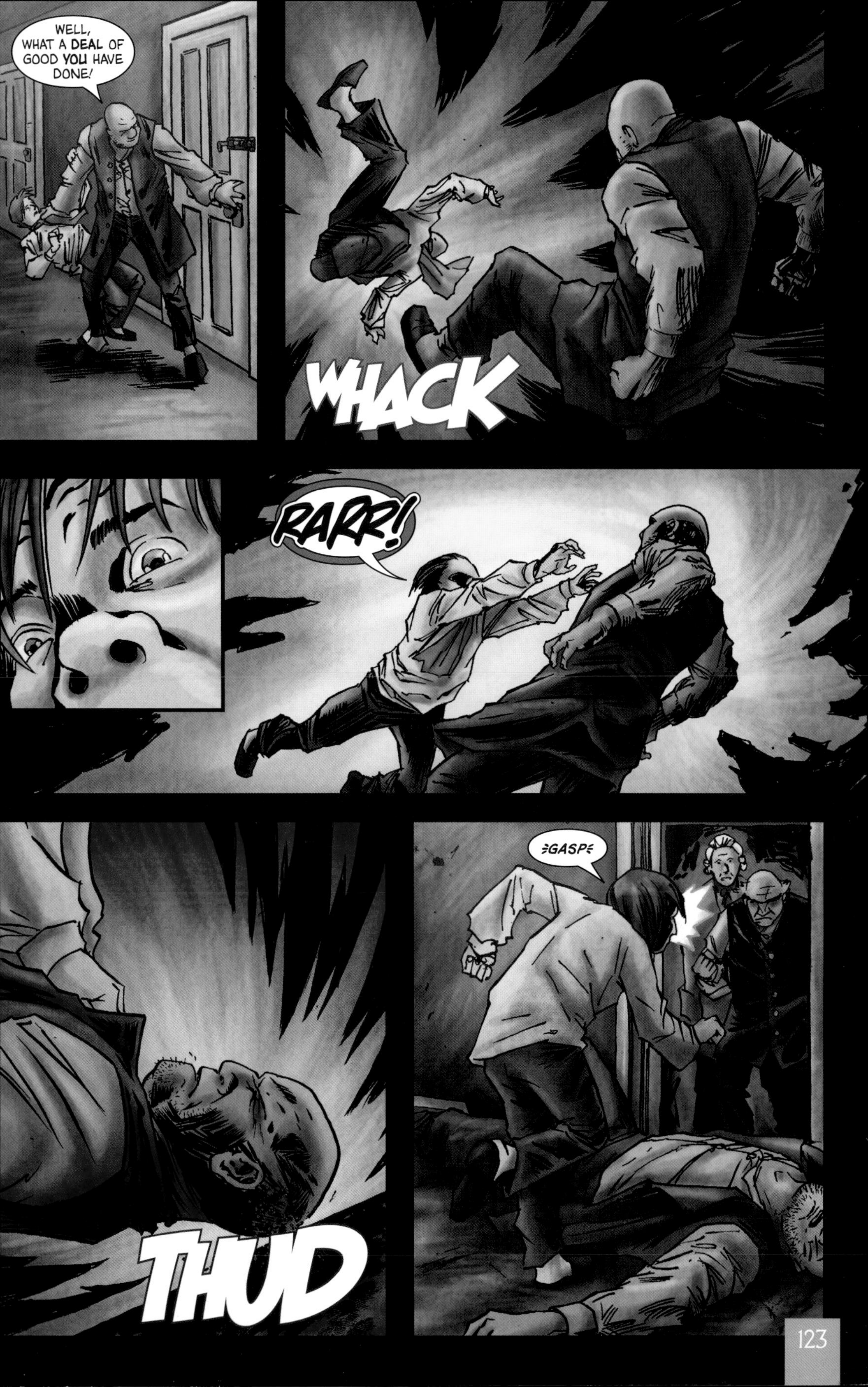
WELL, WHAT A DEAL OF GOOD YOU HAVE DONE!
WHACK
RARR!
THUD
GASP

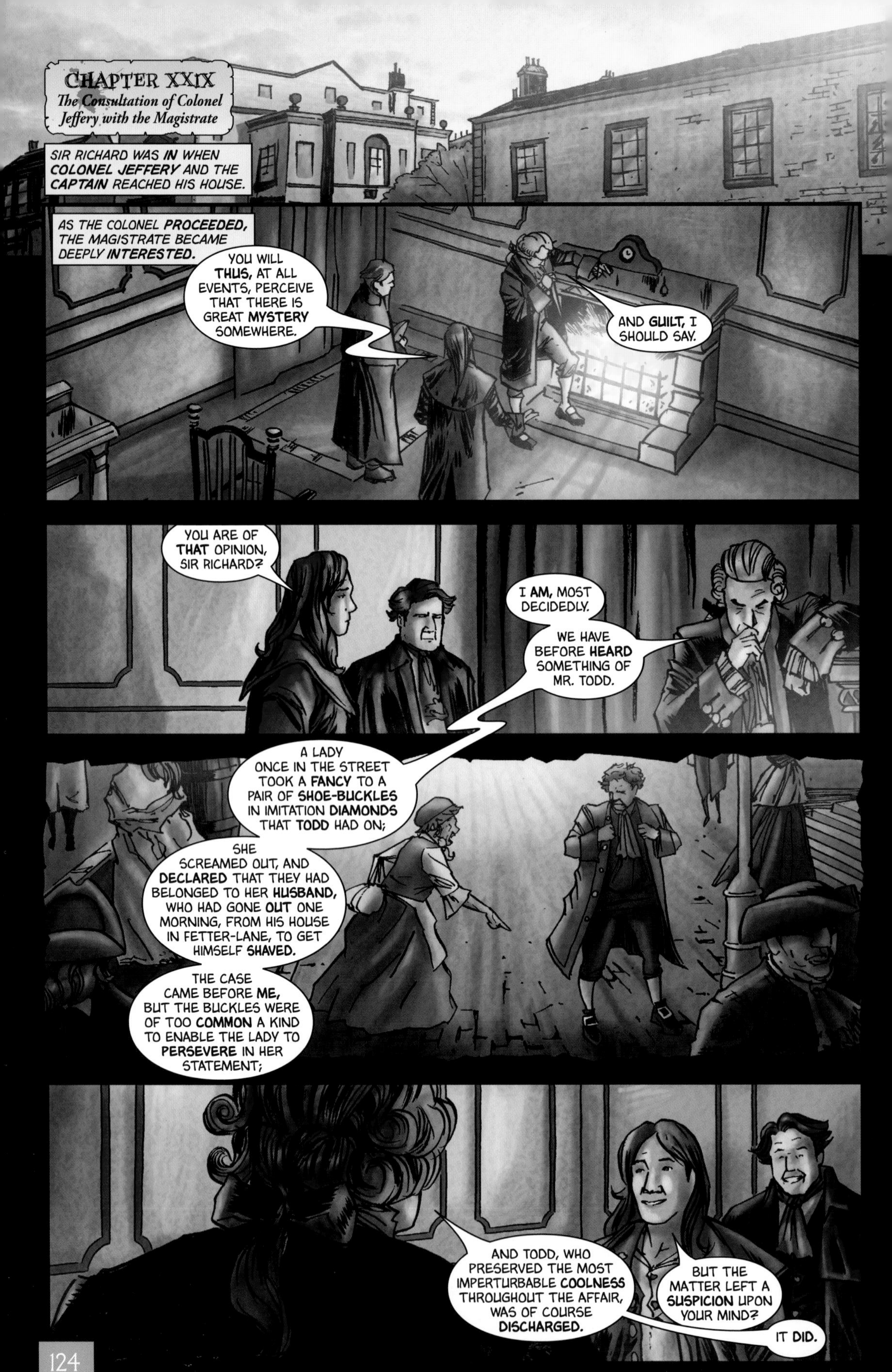
CHAPTER XXIX
The Consultation of Colonel Jeffery with the Magistrate
SIR RICHARD WAS IN WHEN COLONEL JEFFERY AND THE CAPTAIN REACHED HIS HOUSE.
AS THE COLONEL PROCEEDED, THE MAGISTRATE BECAME DEEPLY INTERESTED.
YOU WILL THUS, AT ALL EVENTS, PERCEIVE THAT THERE IS GREAT MYSTERY SOMEWHERE.
AND GUILT, I SHOULD SAY.
YOU ARE OF THAT OPINION, SIR RICHARD?
I AM, MOST DECIDEDLY.
WE HAVE BEFORE HEARD SOMETHING OF MR. TODD.
A LADY ONCE IN THE STREET TOOK A FANCY TO A PAIR OF SHOE-BUCKLES IN IMITATION DIAMONDS THAT TODD HAD ON;
SHE SCREAMED OUT, AND DECLARED THAT THEY HAD BELONGED TO HER HUSBAND, WHO HAD GONE OUT ONE MORNING, FROM HIS HOUSE IN FETTER-LANE, TO GET HIMSELF SHAVED.
THE CASE CAME BEFORE ME, BUT THE BUCKLES WERE OF TOO COMMON A KIND TO ENABLE THE LADY TO PERSEVERE IN HER STATEMENT;
AND TODD, WHO PRESERVED THE MOST IMPERTURBABLE COOLNESS THROUGHOUT THE AFFAIR, WAS OF COURSE DISCHARGED.
BUT THE MATTER LEFT A SUSPICION UPON YOUR MIND?
IT DID.

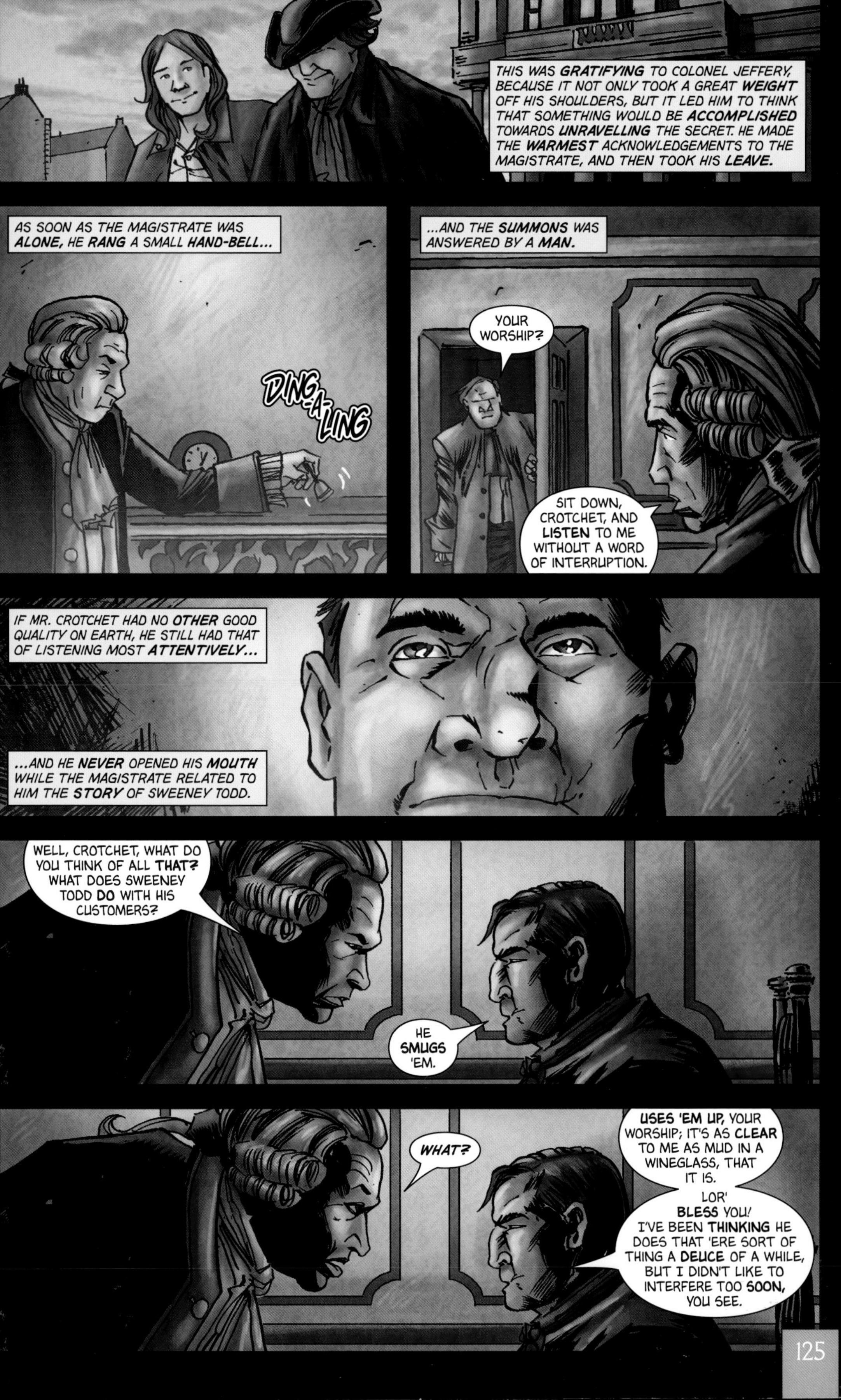

THIS WAS GRATIFYING TO COLONEL JEFFERY, BECAUSE IT NOT ONLY TOOK A GREAT WEIGHT OFF HIS SHOULDERS, BUT IT LED HIM TO THINK THAT SOMETHING WOULD BE ACCOMPLISHED TOWARDS UNRAVELLING THE SECRET. HE MADE THE WARMEST ACKNOWLEDGEMENTS TO THE MAGISTRATE, AND THEN TOOK HIS LEAVE.
AS SOON AS THE MAGISTRATE WAS ALONE, HE RANG A SMALL HAND-BELL...
DING-A-LING
...AND THE SUMMONS WAS ANSWERED BY A MAN.
YOUR WORSHIP?
SIT DOWN, CROTCHET, AND LISTEN TO ME WITHOUT A WORD OF INTERRUPTION.
IF MR. CROTCHET HAD NO OTHER GOOD QUALITY ON EARTH, HE STILL HAD THAT OF LISTENING MOST ATTENTIVELY...
...AND HE NEVER OPENED HIS MOUTH WHILE THE MAGISTRATE RELATED TO HIM THE STORY OF SWEENEY TODD.
WELL, CROTCHET, WHAT DO YOU THINK OF ALL THAT? WHAT DOES SWEENEY TODD DO WITH HIS CUSTOMERS?
HE SMUGS 'EM.
WHAT?
USES 'EM UP, YOUR WORSHIP; IT'S AS CLEAR TO ME AS MUD IN A WINEGLASS, THAT IT IS.
LOR' BLESS YOU! I'VE BEEN THINKING HE DOES THAT 'ERE SORT OF THING A DEUCE OF A WHILE, BUT I DIDN'T LIKE TO INTERFERE TOO SOON, YOU SEE.

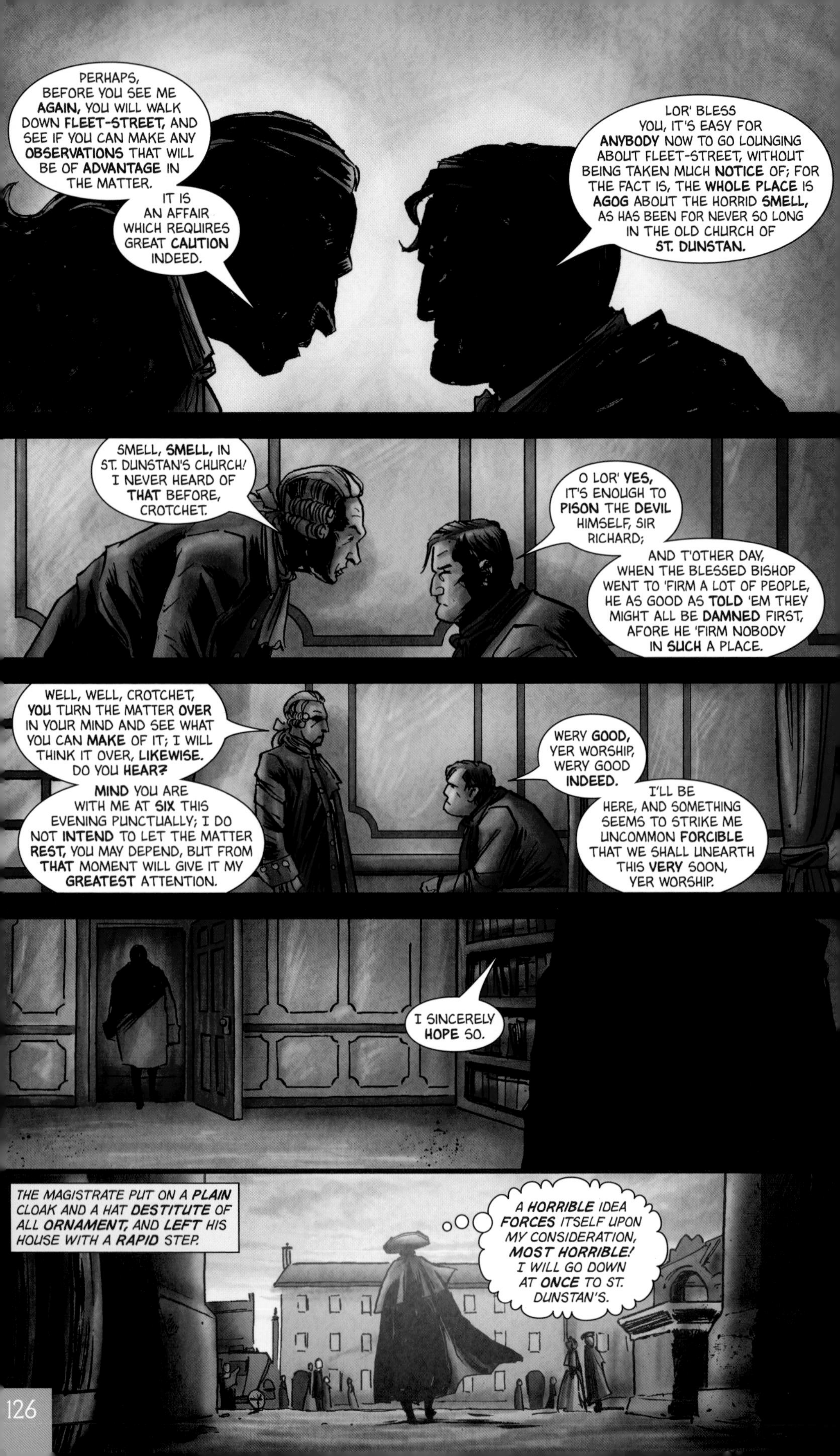
PERHAPS, BEFORE YOU SEE ME AGAIN, YOU WILL WALK DOWN FLEET-STREET, AND SEE IF YOU CAN MAKE ANY OBSERVATIONS THAT WILL BE OF ADVANTAGE IN THE MATTER.
IT IS AN AFFAIR WHICH REQUIRES GREAT CAUTION INDEED.
LOR' BLESS YOU, IT'S EASY FOR ANYBODY NOW TO GO LOUNGING ABOUT FLEET-STREET, WITHOUT BEING TAKEN MUCH NOTICE OF; FOR THE FACT IS, THE WHOLE PLACE IS AGOG ABOUT THE HORRID SMELL, AS HAS BEEN FOR NEVER SO LONG IN THE OLD CHURCH OF ST. DUNSTAN.
SMELL, SMELL, IN ST. DUNSTAN'S CHURCH! I NEVER HEARD OF THAT BEFORE, CROTCHET.
O LOR' YES, IT'S ENOUGH TO PISON THE DEVIL HIMSELF, SIR RICHARD;
AND T'OTHER DAY, WHEN THE BLESSED BISHOP WENT TO 'FIRM A LOT OF PEOPLE, HE AS GOOD AS TOLD 'EM THEY MIGHT ALL BE DAMNED FIRST, AFORE HE 'FIRM NOBODY IN SUCH A PLACE.
WELL, WELL, CROTCHET, YOU TURN THE MATTER OVER IN YOUR MIND AND SEE WHAT YOU CAN MAKE OF IT; I WILL THINK IT OVER, LIKEWISE. DO YOU HEAR?
MIND YOU ARE WITH ME AT SIX THIS EVENING PUNCTUALLY; I DO NOT INTEND TO LET THE MATTER REST, YOU MAY DEPEND, BUT FROM THAT MOMENT WILL GIVE IT MY GREATEST ATTENTION.
WERY GOOD, YER WORSHIP, WERY GOOD INDEED.
I'LL BE HERE, AND SOMETHING SEEMS TO STRIKE ME UNCOMMON FORCIBLE THAT WE SHALL UNEARTH THIS VERY SOON, YER WORSHIP.
I SINCERELY HOPE SO.
THE MAGISTRATE PUT ON A PLAIN CLOAK AND A HAT DESTITUTE OF ALL ORNAMENT, AND LEFT HIS HOUSE WITH A RAPID STEP.
A HORRIBLE IDEA FORCES ITSELF UPON MY CONSIDERATION, MOST HORRIBLE! I WILL GO DOWN AT ONCE TO ST. DUNSTAN'S.

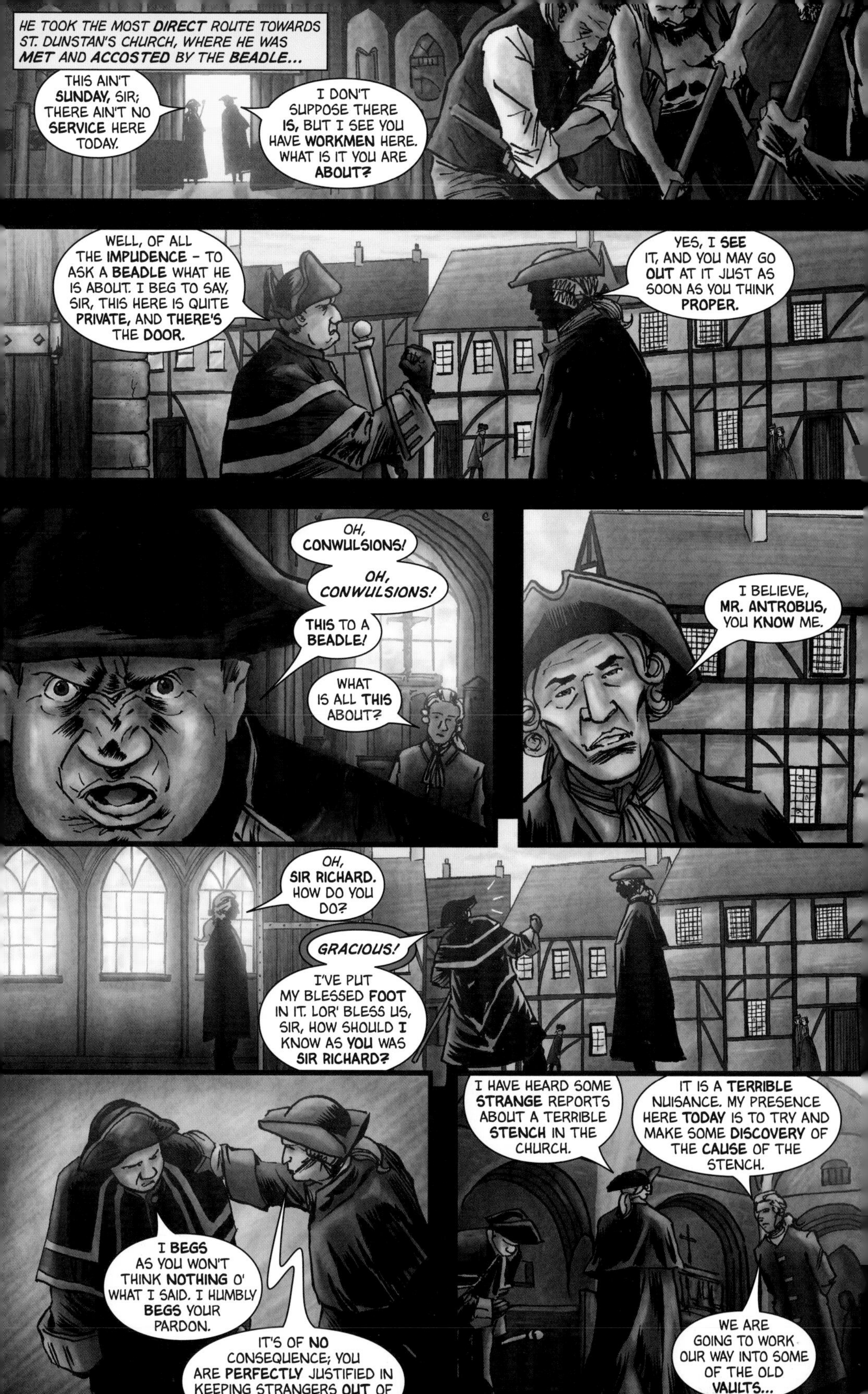
HE TOOK THE MOST DIRECT ROUTE TOWARDS ST. DUNSTAN'S CHURCH, WHERE HE WAS MET AND ACCOSTED BY THE BEADLE...
THIS AIN'T SUNDAY, SIR; THERE AIN'T NO SERVICE HERE TODAY.
I DON'T SUPPOSE THERE IS, BUT I SEE YOU HAVE WORKMEN HERE. WHAT IS IT YOU ARE ABOUT?
WELL, OF ALL THE IMPUDENCE – TO ASK A BEADLE WHAT HE IS ABOUT. I BEG TO SAY, SIR, THIS HERE IS QUITE PRIVATE, AND THERE'S THE DOOR.
YES, I SEE IT, AND YOU MAY GO OUT AT IT JUST AS SOON AS YOU THINK PROPER.
OH, CONWULSIONS!
OH, CONWULSIONS!
THIS TO A BEADLE!
WHAT IS ALL THIS ABOUT?
I BELIEVE, MR. ANTROBUS, YOU KNOW ME.
OH, SIR RICHARD. HOW DO YOU DO?
GRACIOUS!
I'VE PUT MY BLESSED FOOT IN IT. LOR' BLESS US, SIR, HOW SHOULD I KNOW AS YOU WAS SIR RICHARD?
I BEGS AS YOU WON'T THINK NOTHING O' WHAT I SAID. I HUMBLY BEGS YOUR PARDON.
IT'S OF NO CONSEQUENCE; YOU ARE PERFECTLY JUSTIFIED IN KEEPING STRANGERS OUT OF THE CHURCH, MY FRIEND.
I HAVE HEARD SOME STRANGE REPORTS ABOUT A TERRIBLE STENCH IN THE CHURCH.
IT IS A TERRIBLE NUISANCE. MY PRESENCE HERE TODAY IS TO TRY AND MAKE SOME DISCOVERY OF THE CAUSE OF THE STENCH.
WE ARE GOING TO WORK OUR WAY INTO SOME OF THE OLD VAULTS...

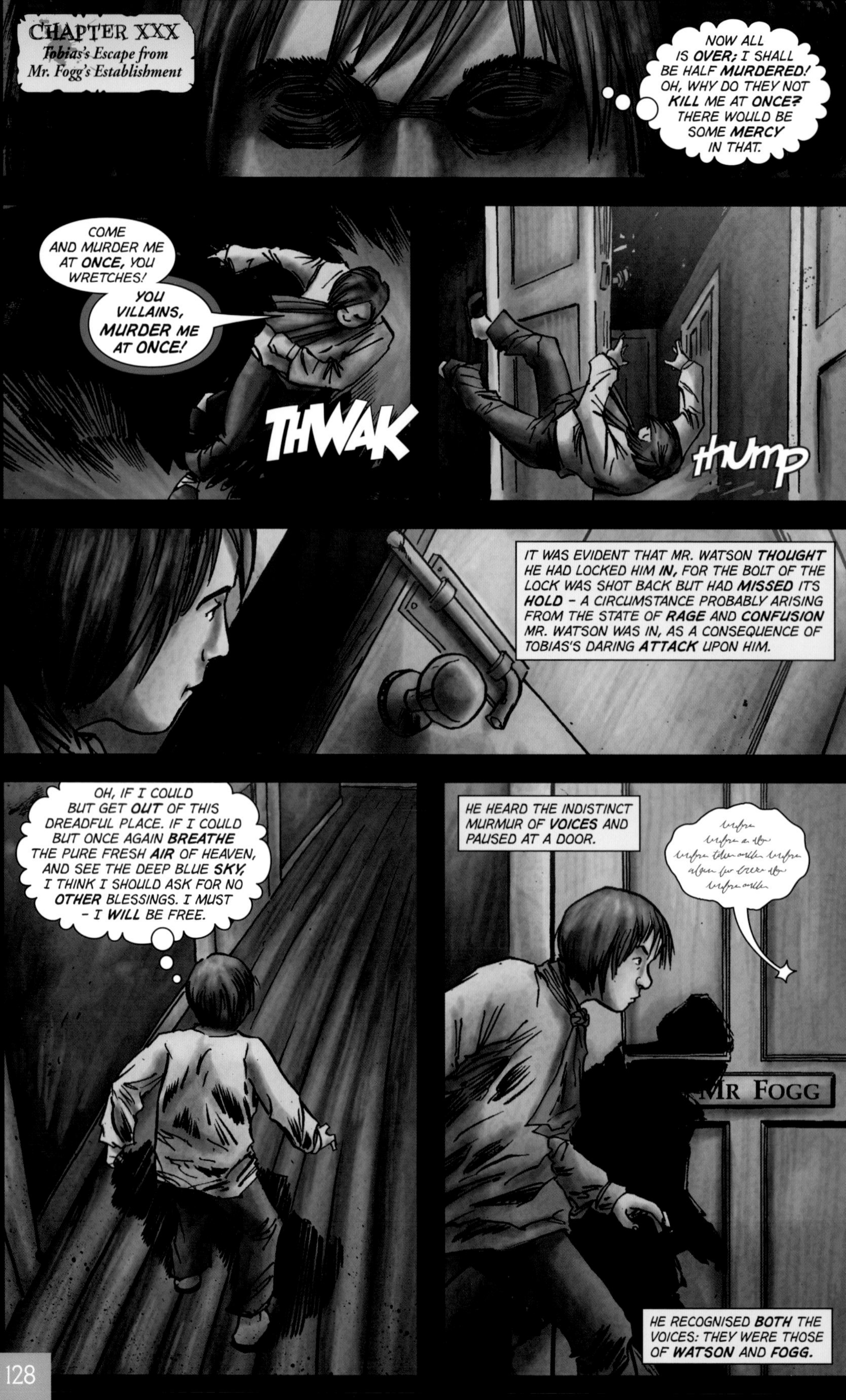
CHAPTER XXX
Tobias's Escape from Mr. Fogg's Establishment
NOW ALL IS OVER; I SHALL BE HALF MURDERED! OH, WHY DO THEY NOT KILL ME AT ONCE? THERE WOULD BE SOME MERCY IN THAT.
COME AND MURDER ME AT ONCE, YOU WRETCHES!
YOU VILLAINS, MURDER ME AT ONCE!
THWAK
thUmp
IT WAS EVIDENT THAT MR. WATSON THOUGHT HE HAD LOCKED HIM IN, FOR THE BOLT OF THE LOCK WAS SHOT BACK BUT HAD MISSED ITS HOLD – A CIRCUMSTANCE PROBABLY ARISING FROM THE STATE OF RAGE AND CONFUSION MR. WATSON WAS IN, AS A CONSEQUENCE OF TOBIAS'S DARING ATTACK UPON HIM.
OH, IF I COULD BUT GET OUT OF THIS DREADFUL PLACE. IF I COULD BUT ONCE AGAIN BREATHE THE PURE FRESH AIR OF HEAVEN, AND SEE THE DEEP BLUE SKY, I THINK I SHOULD ASK FOR NO OTHER BLESSINGS. I MUST – I WILL BE FREE.
HE HEARD THE INDISTINCT MURMUR OF VOICES AND PAUSED AT A DOOR.
MR FOGG
HE RECOGNISED BOTH THE VOICES: THEY WERE THOSE OF WATSON AND FOGG.

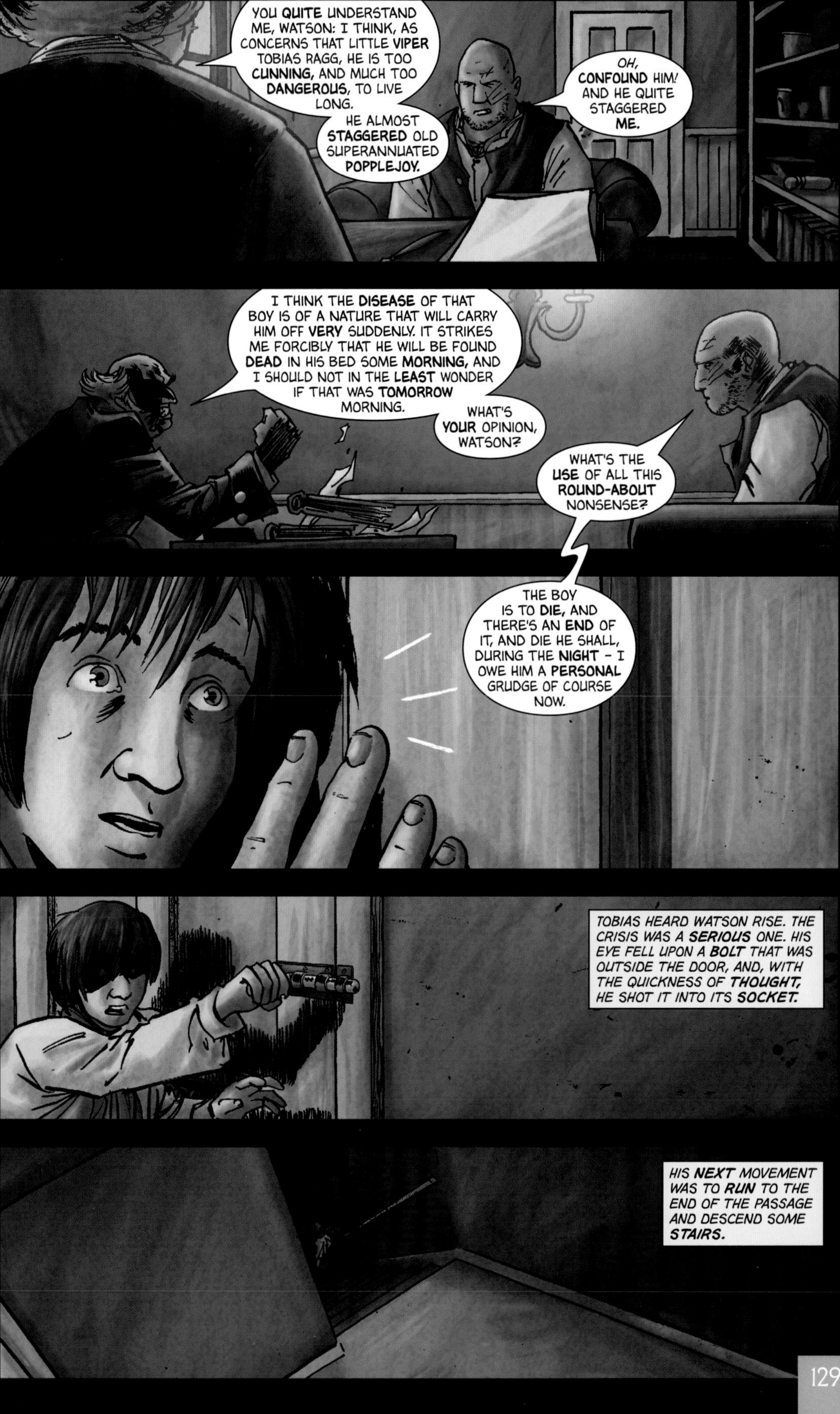

YOU QUITE UNDERSTAND ME, WATSON: I THINK, AS CONCERNS THAT LITTLE VIPER TOBIAS RAGG, HE IS TOO CUNNING, AND MUCH TOO DANGEROUS, TO LIVE LONG.
HE ALMOST STAGGERED OLD SUPERANNUATED POPPLEJOY.
OH, CONFOUND HIM! AND HE QUITE STAGGERED ME.
I THINK THE DISEASE OF THAT BOY IS OF A NATURE THAT WILL CARRY HIM OFF VERY SUDDENLY. IT STRIKES ME FORCIBLY THAT HE WILL BE FOUND DEAD IN HIS BED SOME MORNING, AND I SHOULD NOT IN THE LEAST WONDER IF THAT WAS TOMORROW MORNING.
WHAT'S YOUR OPINION, WATSON?
WHAT'S THE USE OF ALL THIS ROUND-ABOUT NONSENSE?
THE BOY IS TO DIE, AND THERE'S AN END OF IT, AND DIE HE SHALL, DURING THE NIGHT - I OWE HIM A PERSONAL GRUDGE OF COURSE NOW.
TOBIAS HEARD WATSON RISE. THE CRISIS WAS A SERIOUS ONE. HIS EYE FELL UPON A BOLT THAT WAS OUTSIDE THE DOOR, AND, WITH THE QUICKNESS OF THOUGHT, HE SHOT IT INTO ITS SOCKET.
HIS NEXT MOVEMENT WAS TO RUN TO THE END OF THE PASSAGE AND DESCEND SOME STAIRS.

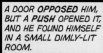
A DOOR *OPPOSED* HIM, BUT A *PUSH* OPENED IT, AND HE FOUND HIMSELF IN A SMALL DIMLY-LIT ROOM.

OH! NO, *NO*, NOT THE LASH! NOT THE LASH!

I AM QUIET. GOD, HOW *QUIET* I AM, ALTHOUGH THE HEART WITHIN IS *BREAKING*. HAVE *MERCY* UPON ME!

HAVE MERCY UPON *ME*, AND *HIDE* ME IF YOU *CAN*.

HIDE YOU! *HIDE* YOU! GOD OF HEAVENS, WHO *ARE* YOU?

A POOR *VICTIM*, WHO HAS *ESCAPED* FROM ONE OF THE *CELLS*, AND I --

HUSH!

SHE MADE TOBIAS *SHRINK DOWN*, COVERING HIM UP WITH *STRAW*.

THE *PRECAUTION* WAS NOT TAKEN A *MOMENT* TOO *SOON*...

HOW THE *DEVIL* CAME THAT DOOR *SHUT*, I WONDER?

Hush! *Hush!* He will only look in. You are *safe*.

I have been only *waiting* for someone who could *assist* me, in order to attempt an *escape*. You must remain *here* until night, and then I will show you how it may be *done*.

WATSON LOOKED INTO THE CELL.

OH, YOU HAVE ENOUGH *BREAD* AND *WATER* TILL TOMORROW *MORNING*, I SHOULD SAY; SO YOU NEED NOT EXPECT TO SEE ME AGAIN TILL *THEN*.

SLAM

OH! WE ARE *SAVED*! WE SHALL *ESCAPE*.

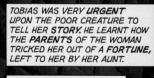
TOBIAS WAS VERY *URGENT* UPON THE POOR CREATURE TO TELL HER *STORY*. HE LEARNT HOW THE *PARENTS* OF THE WOMAN TRICKED HER OUT OF A *FORTUNE*, LEFT TO HER BY HER AUNT.

THEY HAD HER *SEIZED*, GAGGED AND *THRUST* INTO A COACH, AND BROUGHT TO THE MAD-HOUSE...

...WHERE SHE HAD *REMAINED* EVER SINCE.

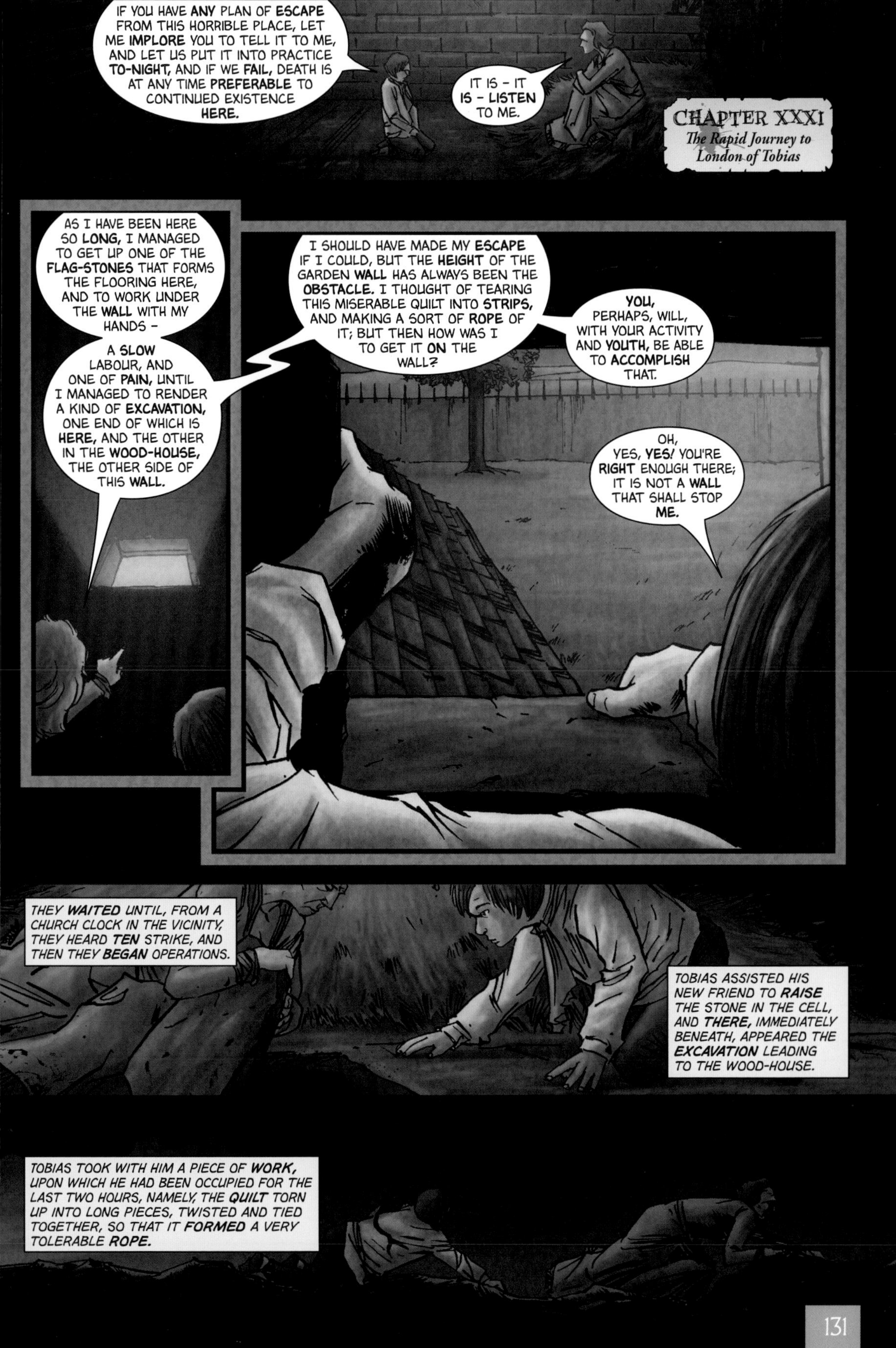
IF YOU HAVE ANY PLAN OF ESCAPE FROM THIS HORRIBLE PLACE, LET ME IMPLORE YOU TO TELL IT TO ME, AND LET US PUT IT INTO PRACTICE TO-NIGHT, AND IF WE FAIL, DEATH IS AT ANY TIME PREFERABLE TO CONTINUED EXISTENCE HERE.
IT IS – IT IS – LISTEN TO ME.
CHAPTER XXXI
The Rapid Journey to London of Tobias
AS I HAVE BEEN HERE SO LONG, I MANAGED TO GET UP ONE OF THE FLAG-STONES THAT FORMS THE FLOORING HERE, AND TO WORK UNDER THE WALL WITH MY HANDS –
A SLOW LABOUR, AND ONE OF PAIN, UNTIL I MANAGED TO RENDER A KIND OF EXCAVATION, ONE END OF WHICH IS HERE, AND THE OTHER IN THE WOOD-HOUSE, THE OTHER SIDE OF THIS WALL.
I SHOULD HAVE MADE MY ESCAPE IF I COULD, BUT THE HEIGHT OF THE GARDEN WALL HAS ALWAYS BEEN THE OBSTACLE. I THOUGHT OF TEARING THIS MISERABLE QUILT INTO STRIPS, AND MAKING A SORT OF ROPE OF IT; BUT THEN HOW WAS I TO GET IT ON THE WALL?
YOU, PERHAPS, WILL, WITH YOUR ACTIVITY AND YOUTH, BE ABLE TO ACCOMPLISH THAT.
OH, YES, YES! YOU'RE RIGHT ENOUGH THERE; IT IS NOT A WALL THAT SHALL STOP ME.
THEY WAITED UNTIL, FROM A CHURCH CLOCK IN THE VICINITY, THEY HEARD TEN STRIKE, AND THEN THEY BEGAN OPERATIONS.
TOBIAS ASSISTED HIS NEW FRIEND TO RAISE THE STONE IN THE CELL, AND THERE, IMMEDIATELY BENEATH, APPEARED THE EXCAVATION LEADING TO THE WOOD-HOUSE.
TOBIAS TOOK WITH HIM A PIECE OF WORK, UPON WHICH HE HAD BEEN OCCUPIED FOR THE LAST TWO HOURS, NAMELY, THE QUILT TORN UP INTO LONG PIECES, TWISTED AND TIED TOGETHER, SO THAT IT FORMED A VERY TOLERABLE ROPE.

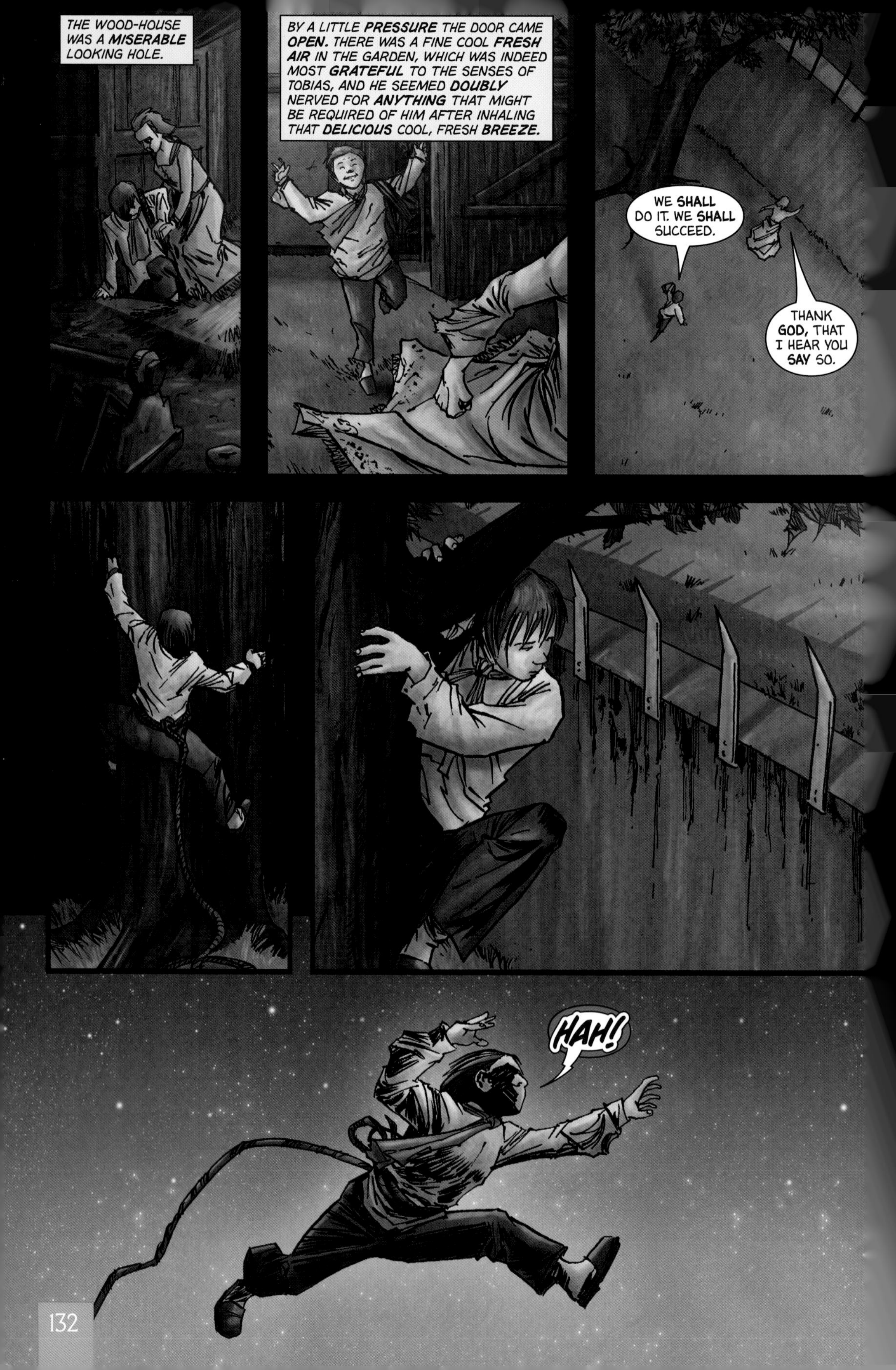
THE WOOD-HOUSE WAS A MISERABLE LOOKING HOLE.
BY A LITTLE PRESSURE THE DOOR CAME OPEN. THERE WAS A FINE COOL FRESH AIR IN THE GARDEN, WHICH WAS INDEED MOST GRATEFUL TO THE SENSES OF TOBIAS, AND HE SEEMED DOUBLY NERVED FOR ANYTHING THAT MIGHT BE REQUIRED OF HIM AFTER INHALING THAT DELICIOUS COOL, FRESH BREEZE.
WE SHALL DO IT. WE SHALL SUCCEED.
THANK GOD, THAT I HEAR YOU SAY SO.
HAH!

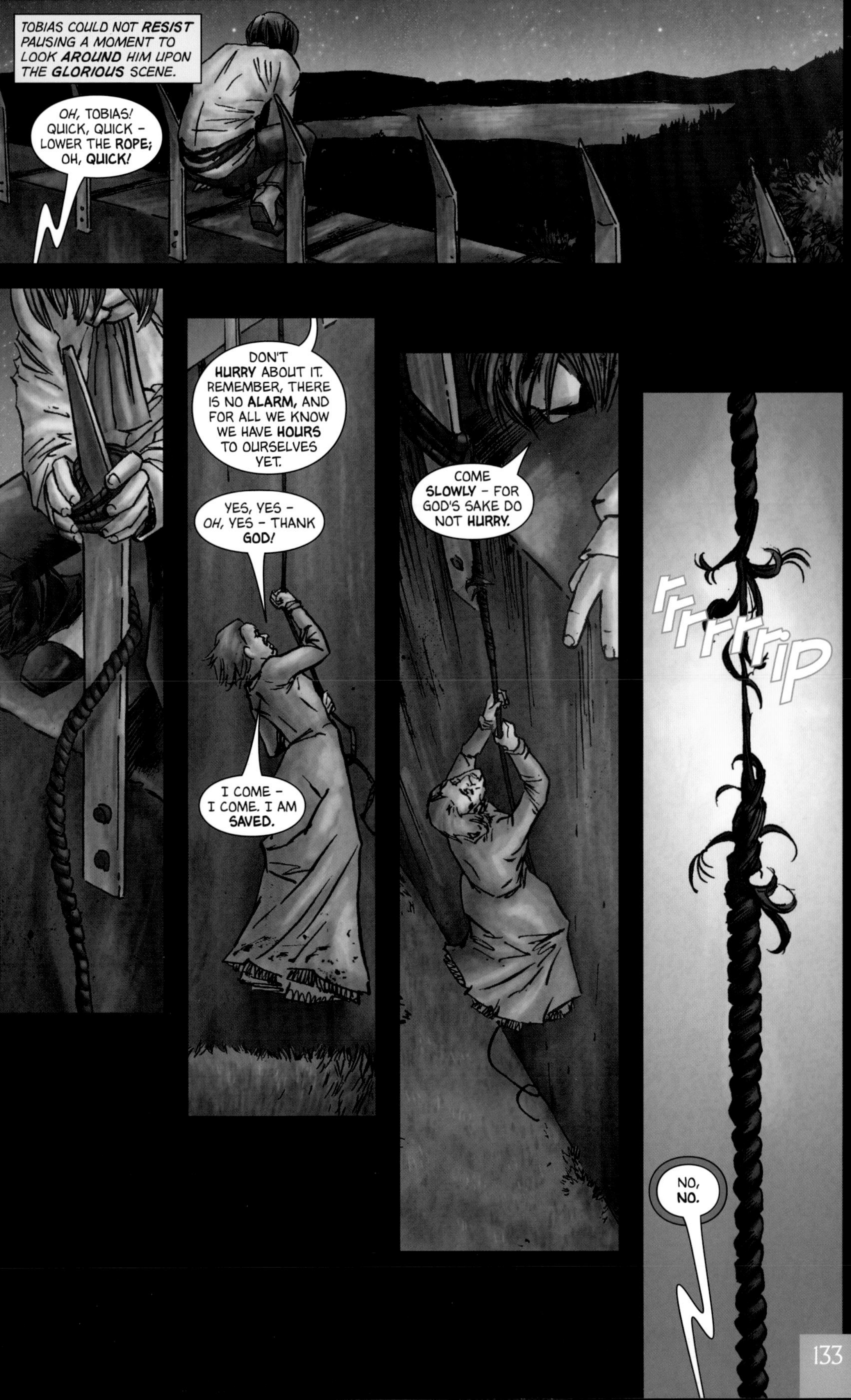
TOBIAS COULD NOT RESIST PAUSING A MOMENT TO LOOK AROUND HIM UPON THE GLORIOUS SCENE.
OH, TOBIAS! QUICK, QUICK – LOWER THE ROPE; OH, QUICK!
DON'T HURRY ABOUT IT. REMEMBER, THERE IS NO ALARM, AND FOR ALL WE KNOW WE HAVE HOURS TO OURSELVES YET.
YES, YES – OH, YES – THANK GOD!
I COME – I COME. I AM SAVED.
COME SLOWLY – FOR GOD'S SAKE DO NOT HURRY.
rrrrrrrip
NO, NO.

THUD

LIGHTS, TOO, AT THAT UNLUCKY MOMENT, FLASHED FROM THE HOUSE...

...AND IT WAS NOW EVIDENT AN ALARM HAD BEEN GIVEN.

IF TWO COULD NOT BE SAVED, ONE COULD BE SAVED.

THDUM

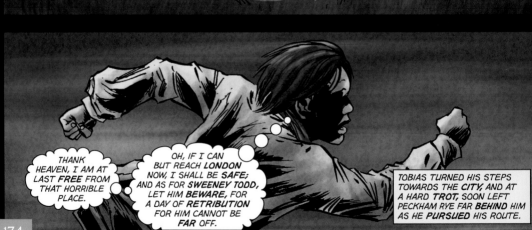

THANK HEAVEN, I AM AT LAST FREE FROM THAT HORRIBLE PLACE.

OH, IF I CAN BUT REACH LONDON NOW, I SHALL BE SAFE; AND AS FOR SWEENEY TODD, LET HIM BEWARE, FOR A DAY OF RETRIBUTION FOR HIM CANNOT BE FAR OFF.

TOBIAS TURNED HIS STEPS TOWARDS THE CITY, AND AT A HARD TROT, SOON LEFT PECKHAM RYE FAR BEHIND HIM AS HE PURSUED HIS ROUTE.

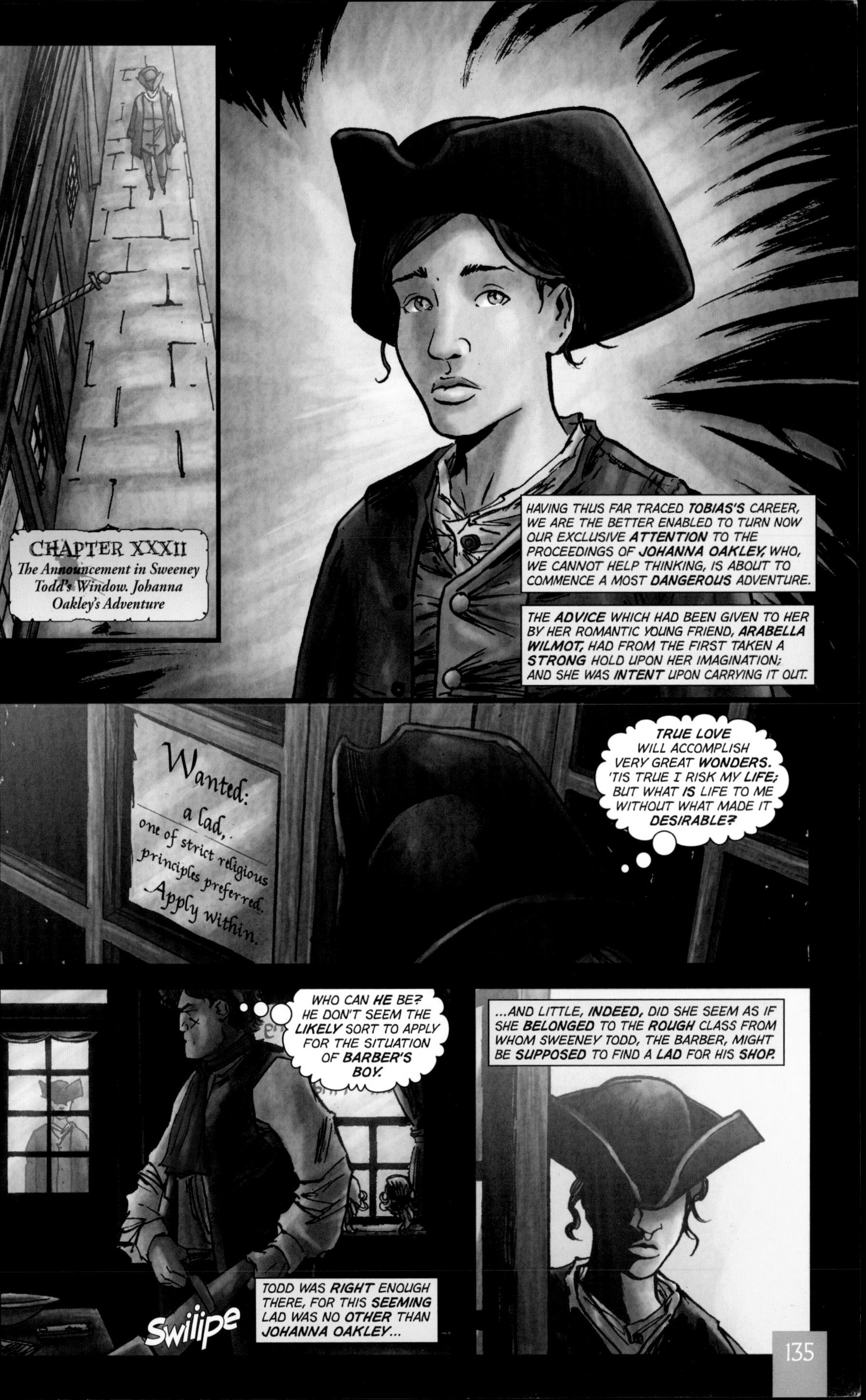

CHAPTER XXXII
The Announcement in Sweeney Todd's Window. Johanna Oakley's Adventure
HAVING THUS FAR TRACED TOBIAS'S CAREER, WE ARE THE BETTER ENABLED TO TURN NOW OUR EXCLUSIVE ATTENTION TO THE PROCEEDINGS OF JOHANNA OAKLEY, WHO, WE CANNOT HELP THINKING, IS ABOUT TO COMMENCE A MOST DANGEROUS ADVENTURE.
THE ADVICE WHICH HAD BEEN GIVEN TO HER BY HER ROMANTIC YOUNG FRIEND, ARABELLA WILMOT, HAD FROM THE FIRST TAKEN A STRONG HOLD UPON HER IMAGINATION; AND SHE WAS INTENT UPON CARRYING IT OUT.
Wanted: a lad, one of strict religious principles preferred. Apply within.
TRUE LOVE WILL ACCOMPLISH VERY GREAT WONDERS. 'TIS TRUE I RISK MY LIFE; BUT WHAT IS LIFE TO ME WITHOUT WHAT MADE IT DESIRABLE?
WHO CAN HE BE? HE DON'T SEEM THE LIKELY SORT TO APPLY FOR THE SITUATION OF BARBER'S BOY.
TODD WAS RIGHT ENOUGH THERE, FOR THIS SEEMING LAD WAS NO OTHER THAN JOHANNA OAKLEY...
Swiiipe
...AND LITTLE, INDEED, DID SHE SEEM AS IF SHE BELONGED TO THE ROUGH CLASS FROM WHOM SWEENEY TODD, THE BARBER, MIGHT BE SUPPOSED TO FIND A LAD FOR HIS SHOP.

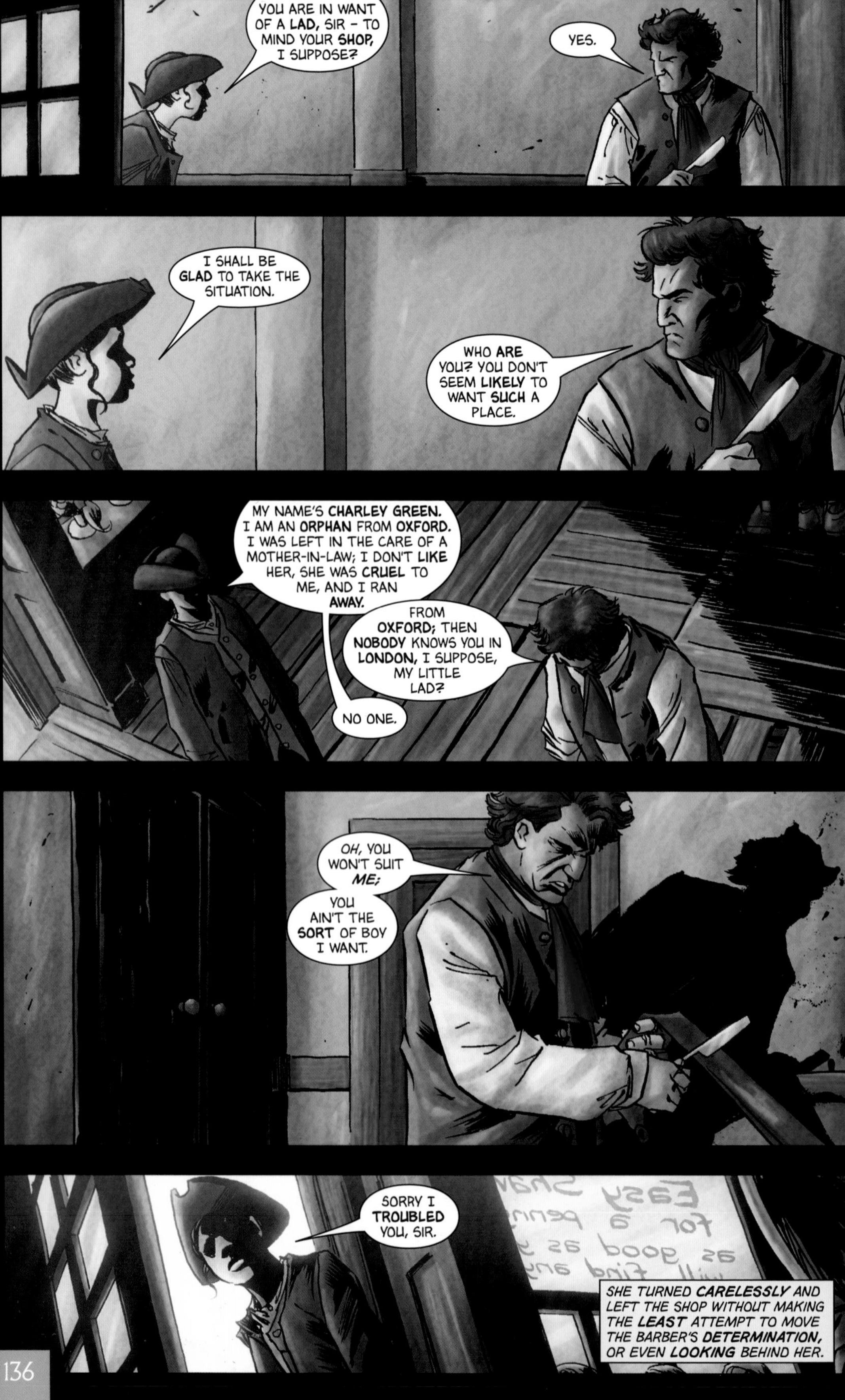

YOU ARE IN WANT OF A **LAD**, SIR – TO MIND YOUR **SHOP**, I SUPPOSE?
YES.
I SHALL BE **GLAD** TO TAKE THE SITUATION.
WHO **ARE** YOU? YOU DON'T SEEM **LIKELY** TO WANT **SUCH** A PLACE.
MY NAME'S **CHARLEY GREEN.** I AM AN **ORPHAN** FROM **OXFORD.** I WAS LEFT IN THE CARE OF A MOTHER-IN-LAW; I DON'T **LIKE** HER, SHE WAS **CRUEL** TO ME, AND I RAN **AWAY.**
FROM **OXFORD;** THEN **NOBODY** KNOWS YOU IN **LONDON,** I SUPPOSE, MY LITTLE LAD?
NO ONE.
OH, YOU WON'T SUIT ***ME;***
YOU AIN'T THE **SORT** OF BOY I WANT.
SORRY I **TROUBLED** YOU, SIR.
SHE TURNED ***CARELESSLY*** *AND LEFT THE SHOP WITHOUT MAKING THE* ***LEAST*** *ATTEMPT TO MOVE THE BARBER'S* ***DETERMINATION,*** *OR EVEN* ***LOOKING*** *BEHIND HER.*

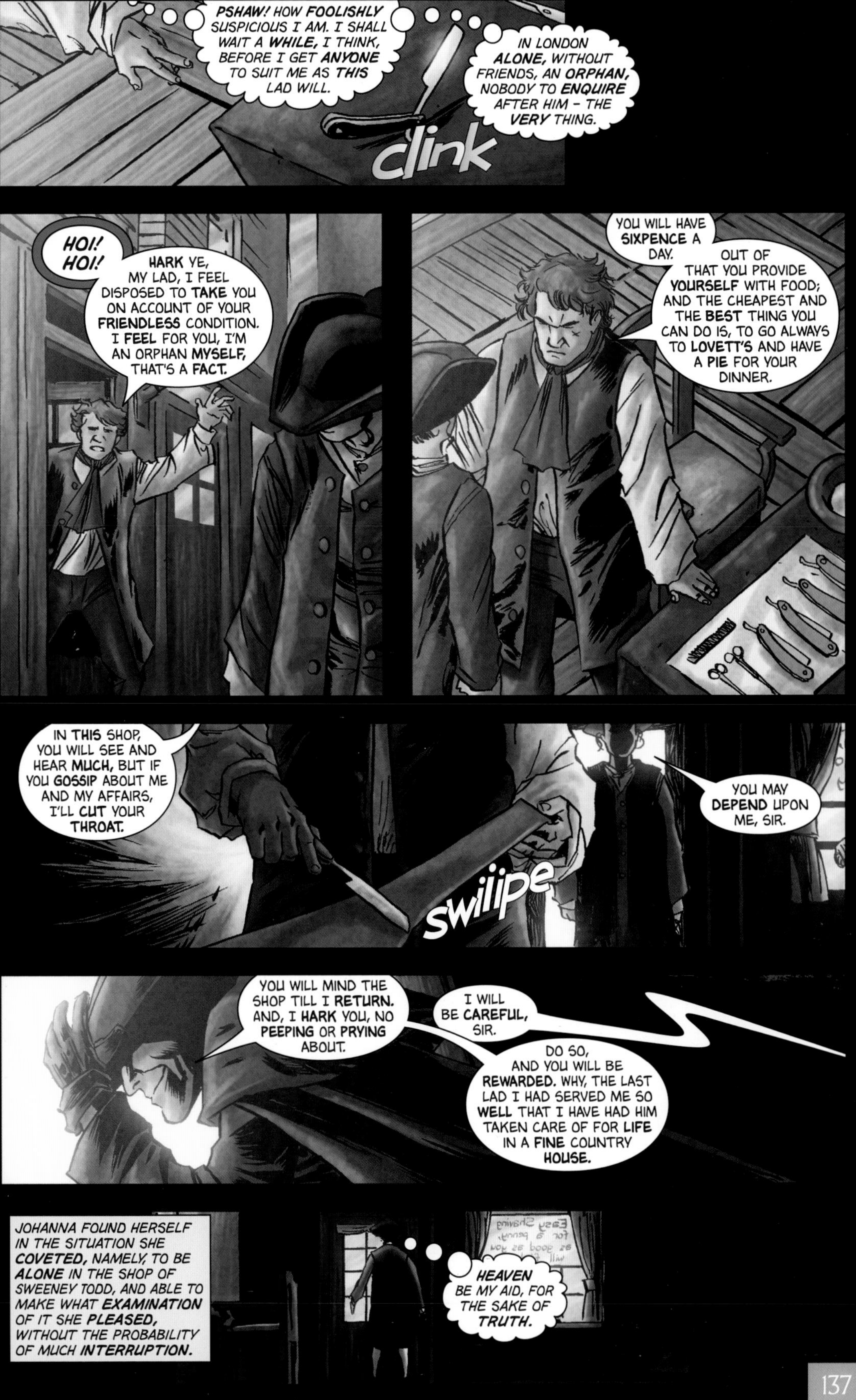
PSHAW! HOW FOOLISHLY SUSPICIOUS I AM. I SHALL WAIT A WHILE, I THINK, BEFORE I GET ANYONE TO SUIT ME AS THIS LAD WILL.
IN LONDON ALONE, WITHOUT FRIENDS, AN ORPHAN, NOBODY TO ENQUIRE AFTER HIM – THE VERY THING.
clink
HOI! HOI!
HARK YE, MY LAD, I FEEL DISPOSED TO TAKE YOU ON ACCOUNT OF YOUR FRIENDLESS CONDITION. I FEEL FOR YOU, I'M AN ORPHAN MYSELF, THAT'S A FACT.
YOU WILL HAVE SIXPENCE A DAY.
OUT OF THAT YOU PROVIDE YOURSELF WITH FOOD; AND THE CHEAPEST AND THE BEST THING YOU CAN DO IS, TO GO ALWAYS TO LOVETT'S AND HAVE A PIE FOR YOUR DINNER.
IN THIS SHOP, YOU WILL SEE AND HEAR MUCH, BUT IF YOU GOSSIP ABOUT ME AND MY AFFAIRS, I'LL CUT YOUR THROAT.
YOU MAY DEPEND UPON ME, SIR.
swiiipe
YOU WILL MIND THE SHOP TILL I RETURN. AND, I HARK YOU, NO PEEPING OR PRYING ABOUT.
I WILL BE CAREFUL, SIR.
DO SO, AND YOU WILL BE REWARDED. WHY, THE LAST LAD I HAD SERVED ME SO WELL THAT I HAVE HAD HIM TAKEN CARE OF FOR LIFE IN A FINE COUNTRY HOUSE.
JOHANNA FOUND HERSELF IN THE SITUATION SHE COVETED, NAMELY, TO BE ALONE IN THE SHOP OF SWEENEY TODD, AND ABLE TO MAKE WHAT EXAMINATION OF IT SHE PLEASED, WITHOUT THE PROBABILITY OF MUCH INTERRUPTION.
HEAVEN BE MY AID, FOR THE SAKE OF TRUTH.

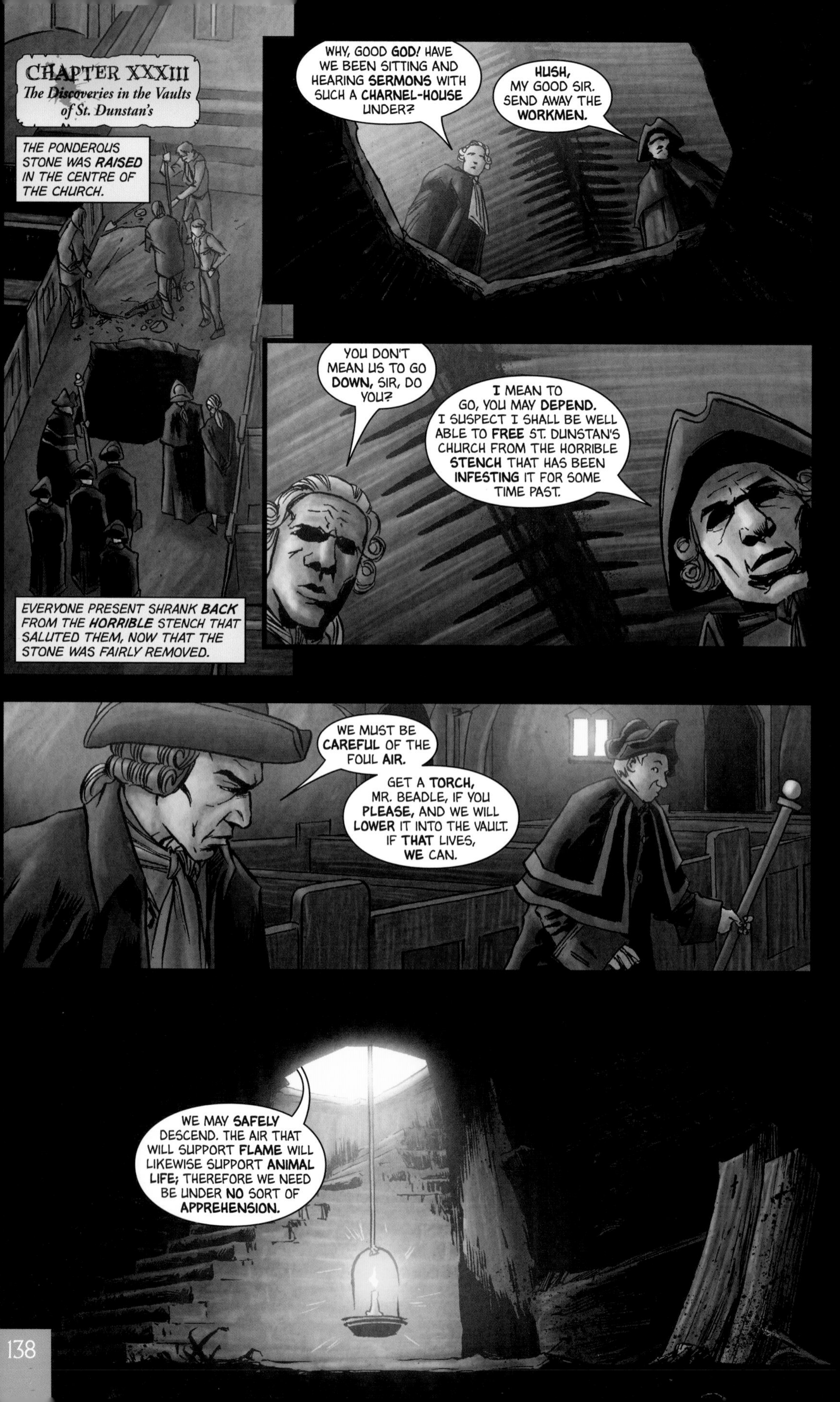
CHAPTER XXXIII
The Discoveries in the Vaults of St. Dunstan's
THE PONDEROUS STONE WAS RAISED IN THE CENTRE OF THE CHURCH.
EVERYONE PRESENT SHRANK BACK FROM THE HORRIBLE STENCH THAT SALUTED THEM, NOW THAT THE STONE WAS FAIRLY REMOVED.
WHY, GOOD GOD! HAVE WE BEEN SITTING AND HEARING SERMONS WITH SUCH A CHARNEL-HOUSE UNDER?
HUSH, MY GOOD SIR. SEND AWAY THE WORKMEN.
YOU DON'T MEAN US TO GO DOWN, SIR, DO YOU?
I MEAN TO GO, YOU MAY DEPEND. I SUSPECT I SHALL BE WELL ABLE TO FREE ST. DUNSTAN'S CHURCH FROM THE HORRIBLE STENCH THAT HAS BEEN INFESTING IT FOR SOME TIME PAST.
WE MUST BE CAREFUL OF THE FOUL AIR.
GET A TORCH, MR. BEADLE, IF YOU PLEASE, AND WE WILL LOWER IT INTO THE VAULT. IF THAT LIVES, WE CAN.
WE MAY SAFELY DESCEND. THE AIR THAT WILL SUPPORT FLAME WILL LIKEWISE SUPPORT ANIMAL LIFE; THEREFORE WE NEED BE UNDER NO SORT OF APPREHENSION.

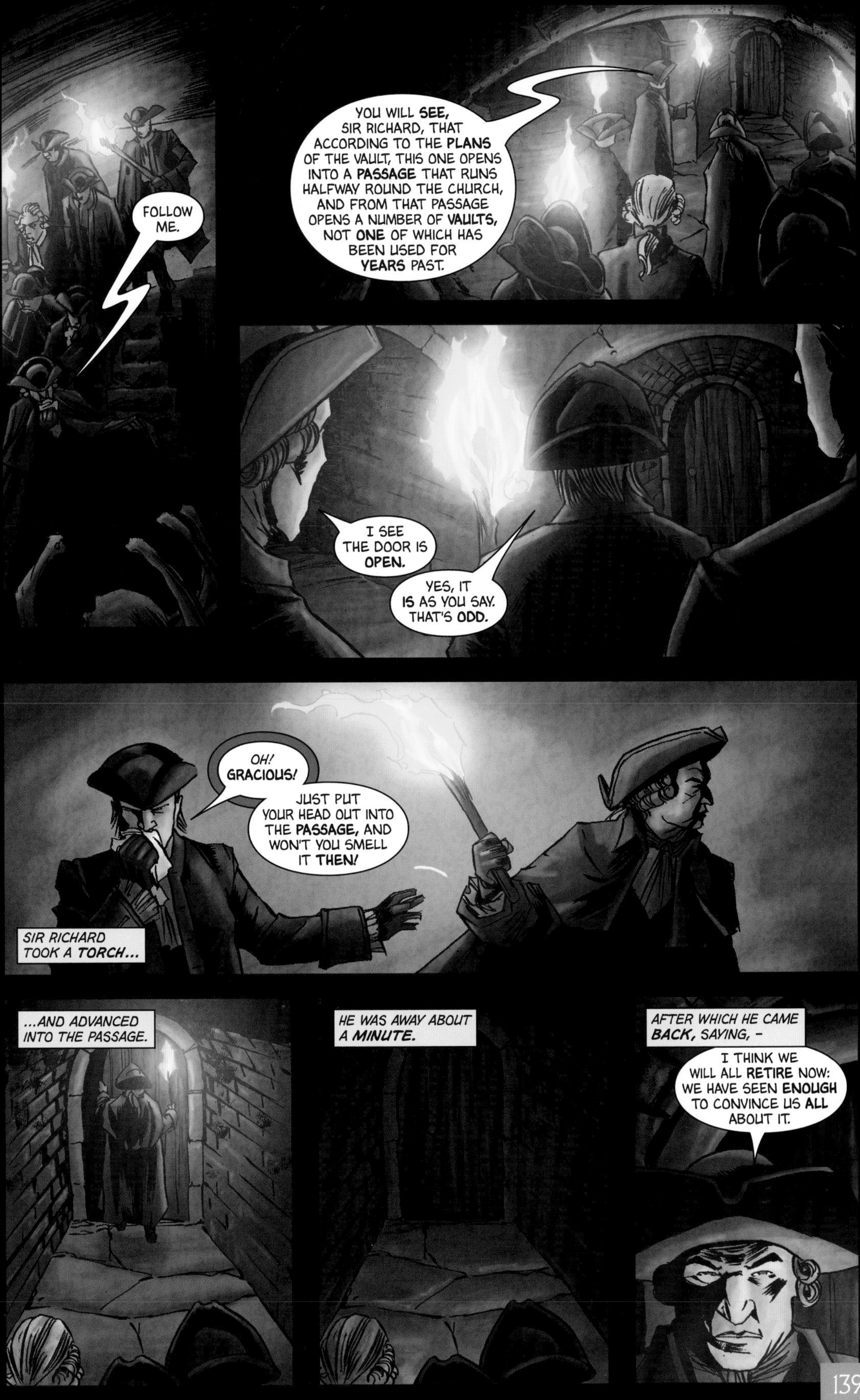
FOLLOW ME.
YOU WILL SEE, SIR RICHARD, THAT ACCORDING TO THE PLANS OF THE VAULT, THIS ONE OPENS INTO A PASSAGE THAT RUNS HALFWAY ROUND THE CHURCH, AND FROM THAT PASSAGE OPENS A NUMBER OF VAULTS, NOT ONE OF WHICH HAS BEEN USED FOR YEARS PAST.
I SEE THE DOOR IS OPEN.
YES, IT IS AS YOU SAY. THAT'S ODD.
SIR RICHARD TOOK A TORCH...
OH! GRACIOUS!
JUST PUT YOUR HEAD OUT INTO THE PASSAGE, AND WON'T YOU SMELL IT THEN!
...AND ADVANCED INTO THE PASSAGE.
HE WAS AWAY ABOUT A MINUTE.
AFTER WHICH HE CAME BACK, SAYING, –
I THINK WE WILL ALL RETIRE NOW: WE HAVE SEEN ENOUGH TO CONVINCE US ALL ABOUT IT.

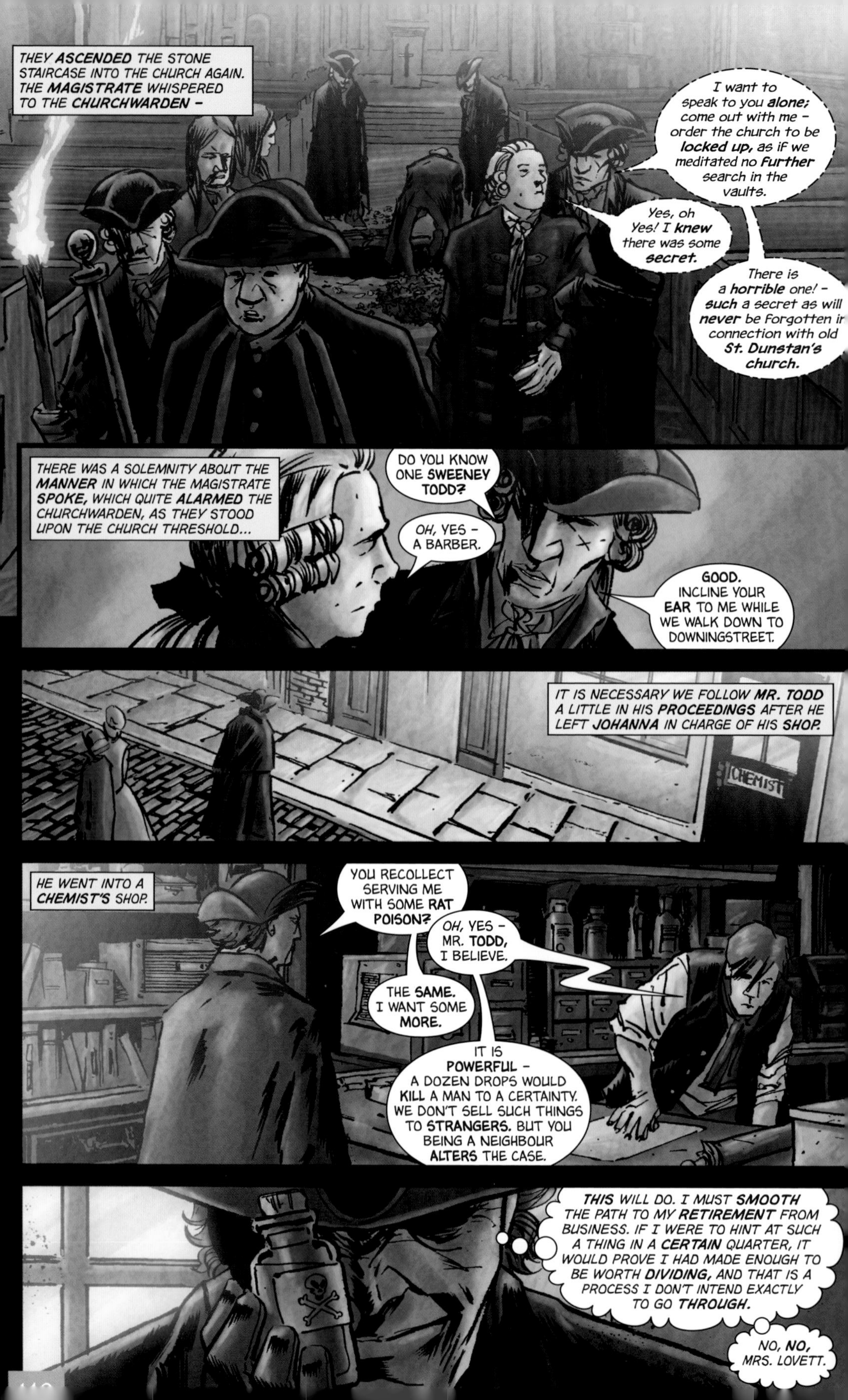
THEY ASCENDED THE STONE STAIRCASE INTO THE CHURCH AGAIN. THE MAGISTRATE WHISPERED TO THE CHURCHWARDEN –
I want to speak to you alone; come out with me – order the church to be locked up, as if we meditated no further search in the vaults.
Yes, oh Yes! I knew there was some secret.
There is a horrible one! – such a secret as will never be forgotten in connection with old St. Dunstan's church.
THERE WAS A SOLEMNITY ABOUT THE MANNER IN WHICH THE MAGISTRATE SPOKE, WHICH QUITE ALARMED THE CHURCHWARDEN, AS THEY STOOD UPON THE CHURCH THRESHOLD...
DO YOU KNOW ONE SWEENEY TODD?
OH, YES – A BARBER.
GOOD. INCLINE YOUR EAR TO ME WHILE WE WALK DOWN TO DOWNINGSTREET.
IT IS NECESSARY WE FOLLOW MR. TODD A LITTLE IN HIS PROCEEDINGS AFTER HE LEFT JOHANNA IN CHARGE OF HIS SHOP.
CHEMIST
HE WENT INTO A CHEMIST'S SHOP.
YOU RECOLLECT SERVING ME WITH SOME RAT POISON?
OH, YES – MR. TODD, I BELIEVE.
THE SAME. I WANT SOME MORE.
IT IS POWERFUL – A DOZEN DROPS WOULD KILL A MAN TO A CERTAINTY. WE DON'T SELL SUCH THINGS TO STRANGERS. BUT YOU BEING A NEIGHBOUR ALTERS THE CASE.
THIS WILL DO. I MUST SMOOTH THE PATH TO MY RETIREMENT FROM BUSINESS. IF I WERE TO HINT AT SUCH A THING IN A CERTAIN QUARTER, IT WOULD PROVE I HAD MADE ENOUGH TO BE WORTH DIVIDING, AND THAT IS A PROCESS I DON'T INTEND EXACTLY TO GO THROUGH.
NO, NO, MRS. LOVETT.

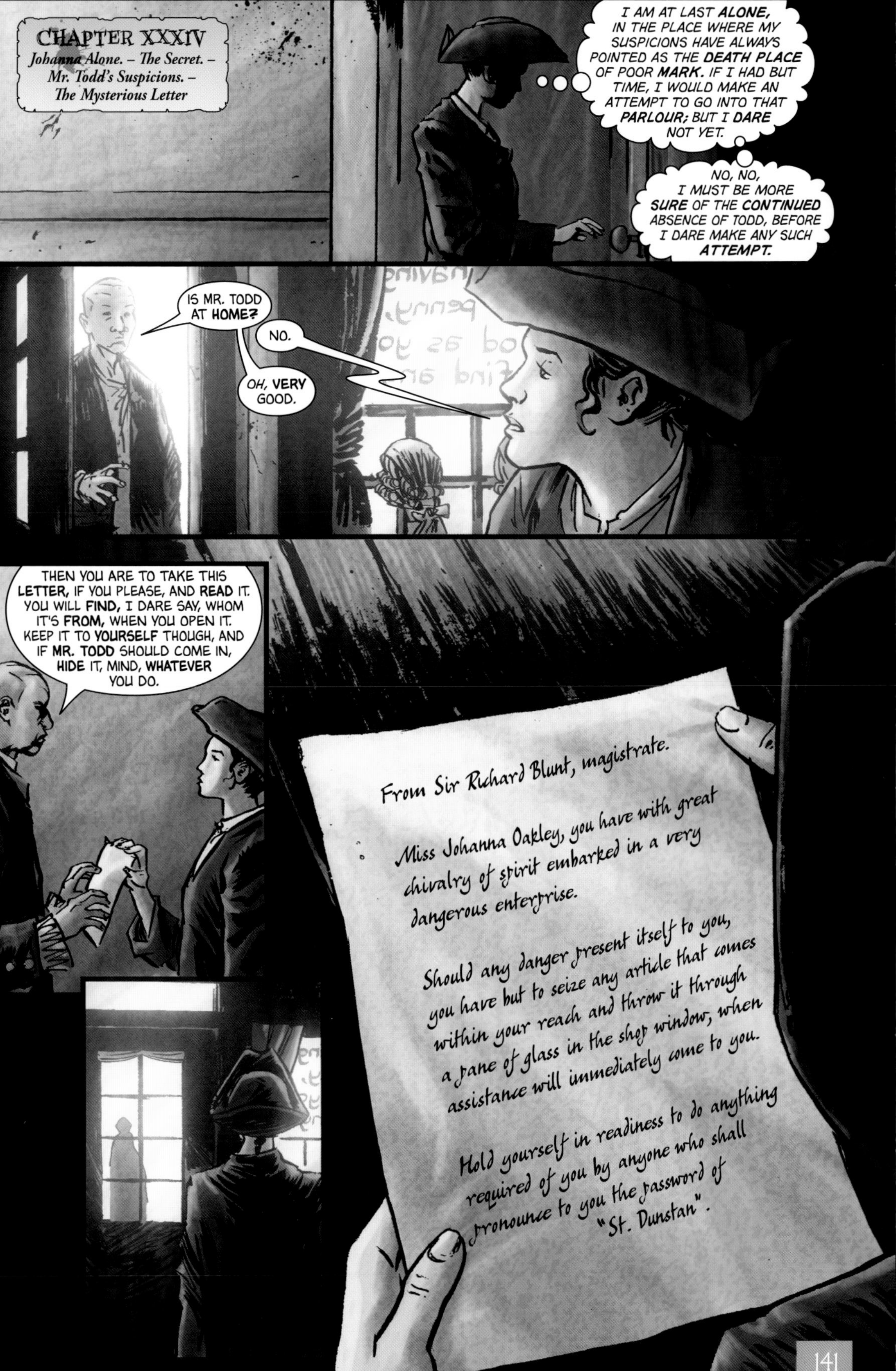
CHAPTER XXXIV
Johanna Alone. – The Secret. – Mr. Todd's Suspicions. – The Mysterious Letter
I AM AT LAST ALONE, IN THE PLACE WHERE MY SUSPICIONS HAVE ALWAYS POINTED AS THE DEATH PLACE OF POOR MARK. IF I HAD BUT TIME, I WOULD MAKE AN ATTEMPT TO GO INTO THAT PARLOUR; BUT I DARE NOT YET.
NO, NO, I MUST BE MORE SURE OF THE CONTINUED ABSENCE OF TODD, BEFORE I DARE MAKE ANY SUCH ATTEMPT.
IS MR. TODD AT HOME?
NO.
OH, VERY GOOD.
THEN YOU ARE TO TAKE THIS LETTER, IF YOU PLEASE, AND READ IT. YOU WILL FIND, I DARE SAY, WHOM IT'S FROM, WHEN YOU OPEN IT. KEEP IT TO YOURSELF THOUGH, AND IF MR. TODD SHOULD COME IN, HIDE IT, MIND, WHATEVER YOU DO.
From Sir Richard Blunt, magistrate.
Miss Johanna Oakley, you have with great chivalry of spirit embarked in a very dangerous enterprise.
Should any danger present itself to you, you have but to seize any article that comes within your reach and throw it through a pane of glass in the shop window, when assistance will immediately come to you.
Hold yourself in readiness to do anything required of you by anyone who shall pronounce to you the password of "St. Dunstan".

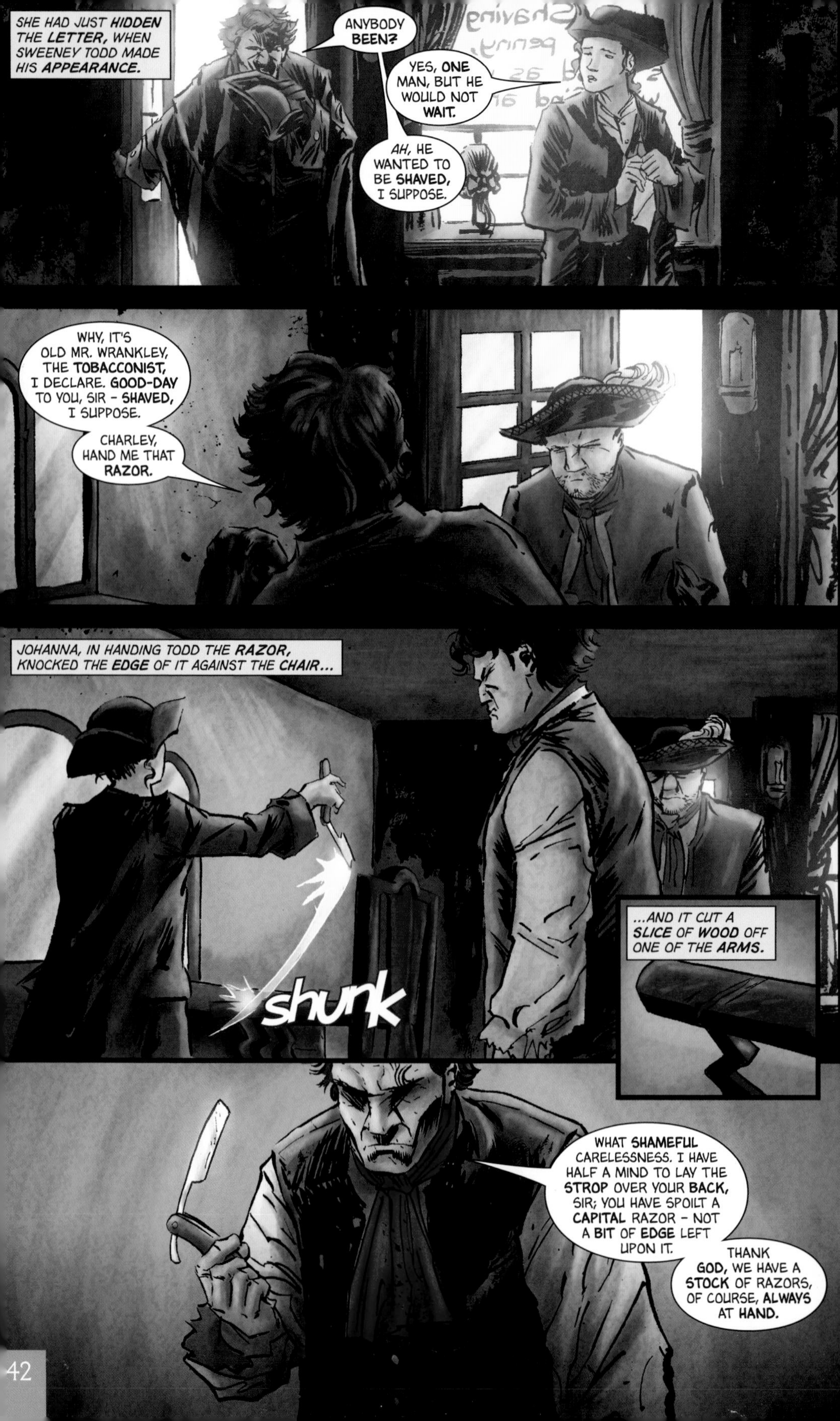
SHE HAD JUST HIDDEN THE LETTER, WHEN SWEENEY TODD MADE HIS APPEARANCE.
ANYBODY BEEN?
YES, ONE MAN, BUT HE WOULD NOT WAIT.
AH, HE WANTED TO BE SHAVED, I SUPPOSE.
WHY, IT'S OLD MR. WRANKLEY, THE TOBACCONIST, I DECLARE. GOOD-DAY TO YOU, SIR - SHAVED, I SUPPOSE.
CHARLEY, HAND ME THAT RAZOR.
JOHANNA, IN HANDING TODD THE RAZOR, KNOCKED THE EDGE OF IT AGAINST THE CHAIR...
shunk
...AND IT CUT A SLICE OF WOOD OFF ONE OF THE ARMS.
WHAT SHAMEFUL CARELESSNESS. I HAVE HALF A MIND TO LAY THE STROP OVER YOUR BACK, SIR; YOU HAVE SPOILT A CAPITAL RAZOR - NOT A BIT OF EDGE LEFT UPON IT.
THANK GOD, WE HAVE A STOCK OF RAZORS, OF COURSE, ALWAYS AT HAND.

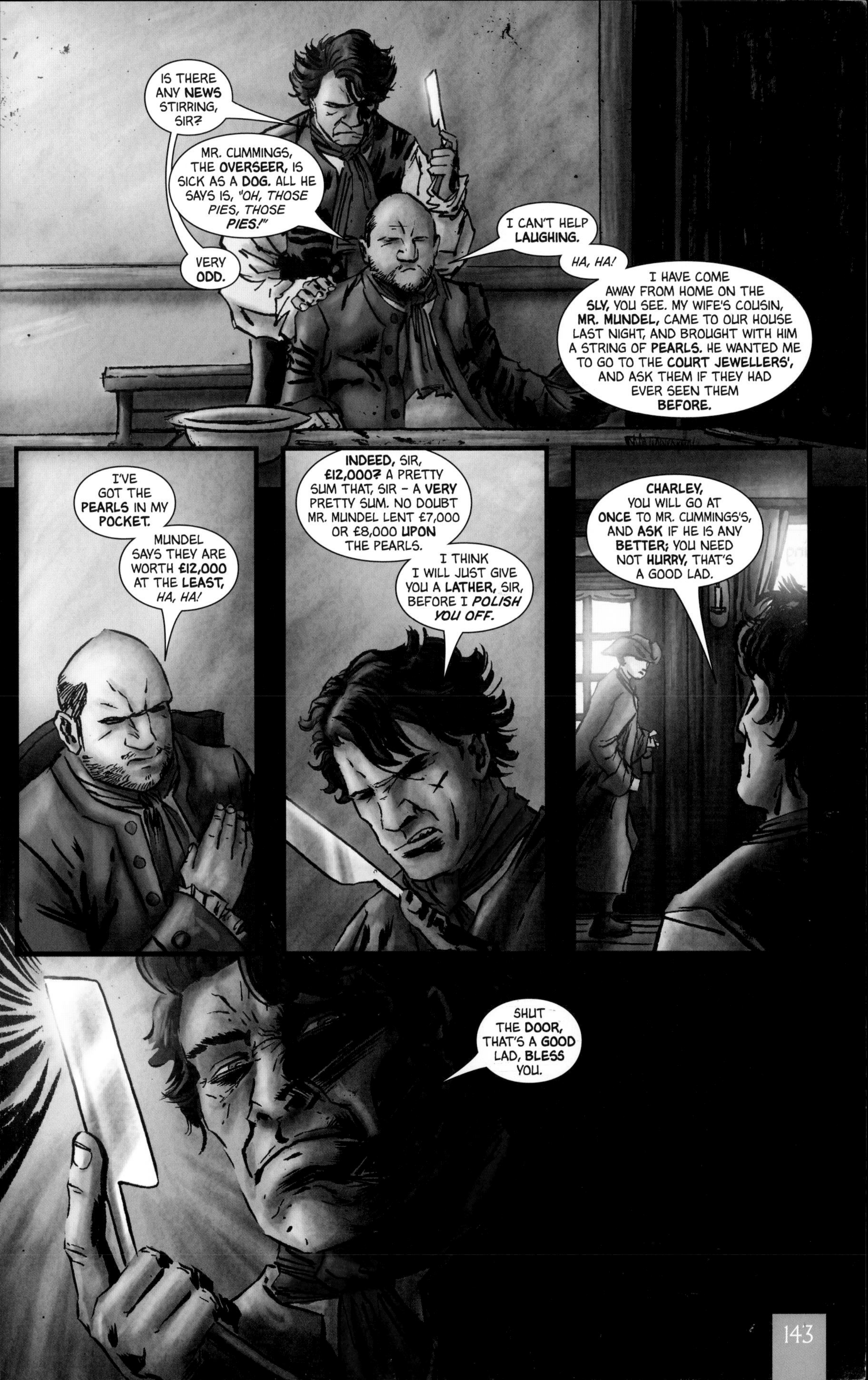
IS THERE ANY NEWS STIRRING, SIR?
MR. CUMMINGS, THE OVERSEER, IS SICK AS A DOG. ALL HE SAYS IS, "OH, THOSE PIES, THOSE PIES!"
VERY ODD.
I CAN'T HELP LAUGHING.
HA, HA!
I HAVE COME AWAY FROM HOME ON THE SLY, YOU SEE. MY WIFE'S COUSIN, MR. MUNDEL, CAME TO OUR HOUSE LAST NIGHT, AND BROUGHT WITH HIM A STRING OF PEARLS. HE WANTED ME TO GO TO THE COURT JEWELLERS', AND ASK THEM IF THEY HAD EVER SEEN THEM BEFORE.
I'VE GOT THE PEARLS IN MY POCKET.
MUNDEL SAYS THEY ARE WORTH £12,000 AT THE LEAST, HA, HA!
INDEED, SIR, £12,000? A PRETTY SUM THAT, SIR – A VERY PRETTY SUM. NO DOUBT MR. MUNDEL LENT £7,000 OR £8,000 UPON THE PEARLS.
I THINK I WILL JUST GIVE YOU A LATHER, SIR, BEFORE I POLISH YOU OFF.
CHARLEY, YOU WILL GO AT ONCE TO MR. CUMMINGS'S, AND ASK IF HE IS ANY BETTER; YOU NEED NOT HURRY, THAT'S A GOOD LAD.
SHUT THE DOOR, THAT'S A GOOD LAD, BLESS YOU.

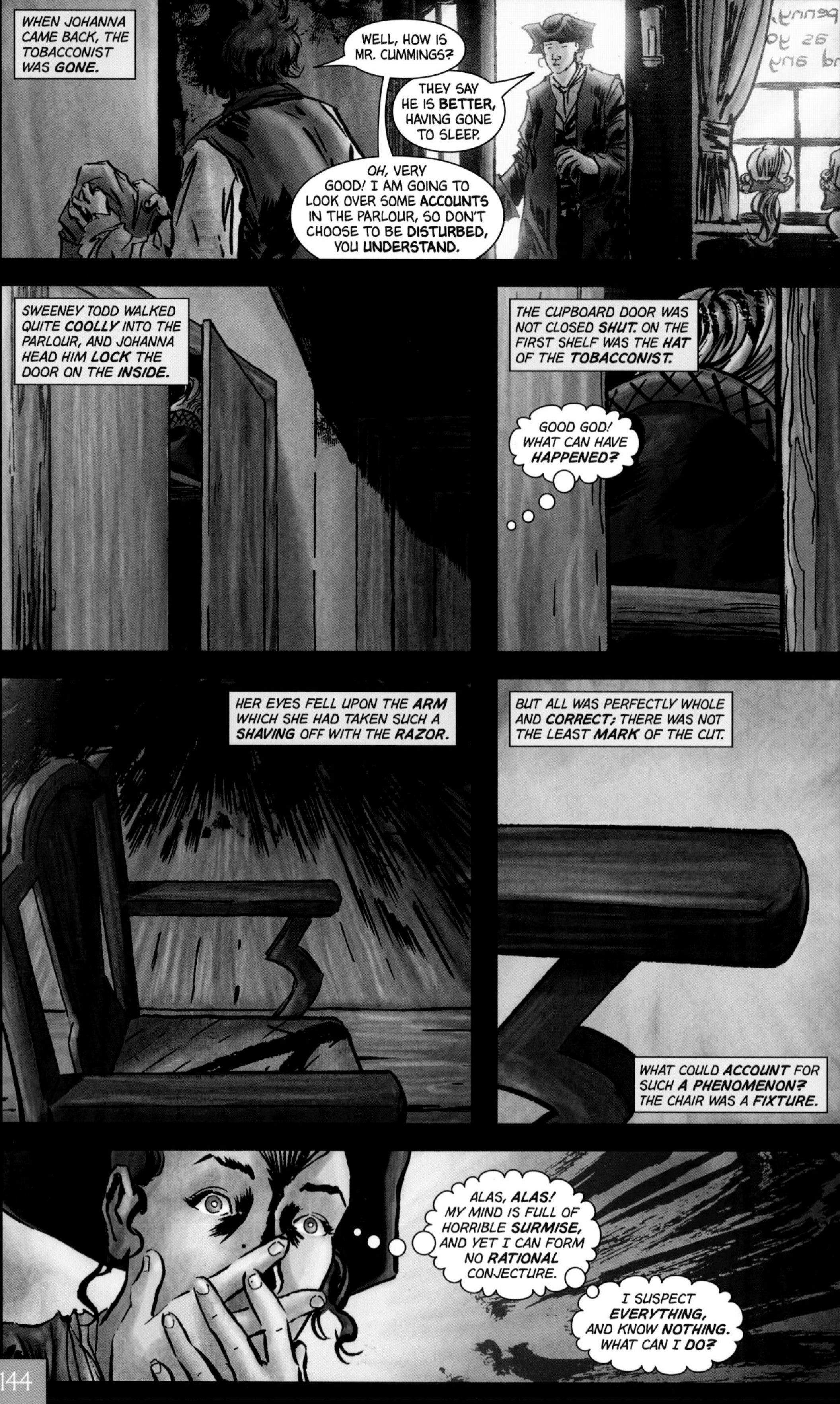
WHEN JOHANNA CAME BACK, THE TOBACCONIST WAS GONE.
WELL, HOW IS MR. CUMMINGS?
THEY SAY HE IS BETTER, HAVING GONE TO SLEEP.
OH, VERY GOOD! I AM GOING TO LOOK OVER SOME ACCOUNTS IN THE PARLOUR, SO DON'T CHOOSE TO BE DISTURBED, YOU UNDERSTAND.
SWEENEY TODD WALKED QUITE COOLLY INTO THE PARLOUR, AND JOHANNA HEAD HIM LOCK THE DOOR ON THE INSIDE.
THE CUPBOARD DOOR WAS NOT CLOSED SHUT. ON THE FIRST SHELF WAS THE HAT OF THE TOBACCONIST.
GOOD GOD! WHAT CAN HAVE HAPPENED?
HER EYES FELL UPON THE ARM WHICH SHE HAD TAKEN SUCH A SHAVING OFF WITH THE RAZOR.
BUT ALL WAS PERFECTLY WHOLE AND CORRECT; THERE WAS NOT THE LEAST MARK OF THE CUT.
WHAT COULD ACCOUNT FOR SUCH A PHENOMENON? THE CHAIR WAS A FIXTURE.
ALAS, ALAS! MY MIND IS FULL OF HORRIBLE SURMISE, AND YET I CAN FORM NO RATIONAL CONJECTURE.
I SUSPECT EVERYTHING, AND KNOW NOTHING. WHAT CAN I DO?

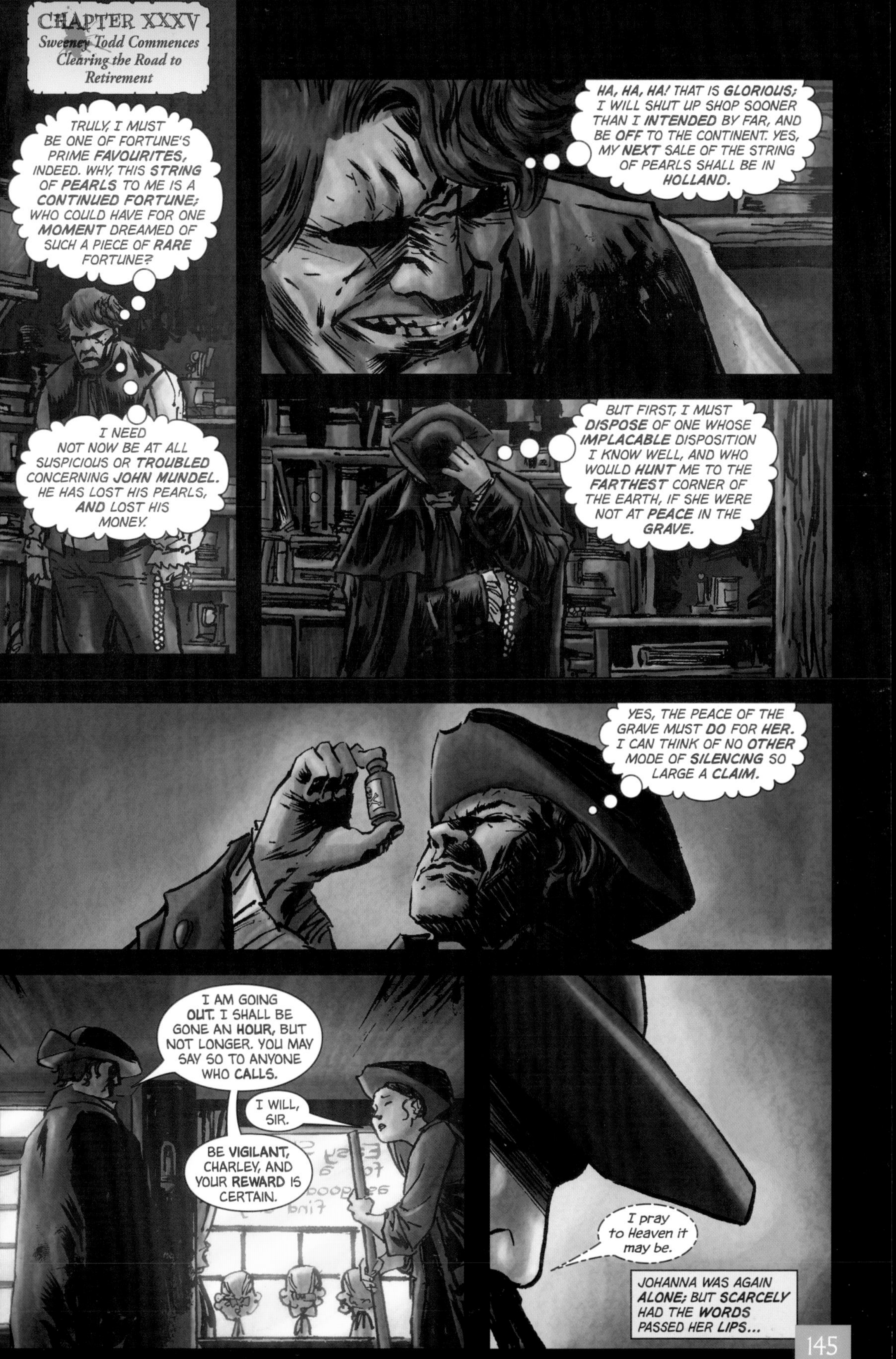
CHAPTER XXXV
Sweeney Todd Commences Clearing the Road to Retirement
TRULY, I MUST BE ONE OF FORTUNE'S PRIME FAVOURITES, INDEED. WHY, THIS STRING OF PEARLS TO ME IS A CONTINUED FORTUNE; WHO COULD HAVE FOR ONE MOMENT DREAMED OF SUCH A PIECE OF RARE FORTUNE?
HA, HA, HA! THAT IS GLORIOUS; I WILL SHUT UP SHOP SOONER THAN I INTENDED BY FAR, AND BE OFF TO THE CONTINENT. YES, MY NEXT SALE OF THE STRING OF PEARLS SHALL BE IN HOLLAND.
I NEED NOT NOW BE AT ALL SUSPICIOUS OR TROUBLED CONCERNING JOHN MUNDEL. HE HAS LOST HIS PEARLS, AND LOST HIS MONEY.
BUT FIRST, I MUST DISPOSE OF ONE WHOSE IMPLACABLE DISPOSITION I KNOW WELL, AND WHO WOULD HUNT ME TO THE FARTHEST CORNER OF THE EARTH, IF SHE WERE NOT AT PEACE IN THE GRAVE.
YES, THE PEACE OF THE GRAVE MUST DO FOR HER. I CAN THINK OF NO OTHER MODE OF SILENCING SO LARGE A CLAIM.
I AM GOING OUT. I SHALL BE GONE AN HOUR, BUT NOT LONGER. YOU MAY SAY SO TO ANYONE WHO CALLS.
I WILL, SIR.
BE VIGILANT, CHARLEY, AND YOUR REWARD IS CERTAIN.
I pray to Heaven it may be.
JOHANNA WAS AGAIN ALONE; BUT SCARCELY HAD THE WORDS PASSED HER LIPS...

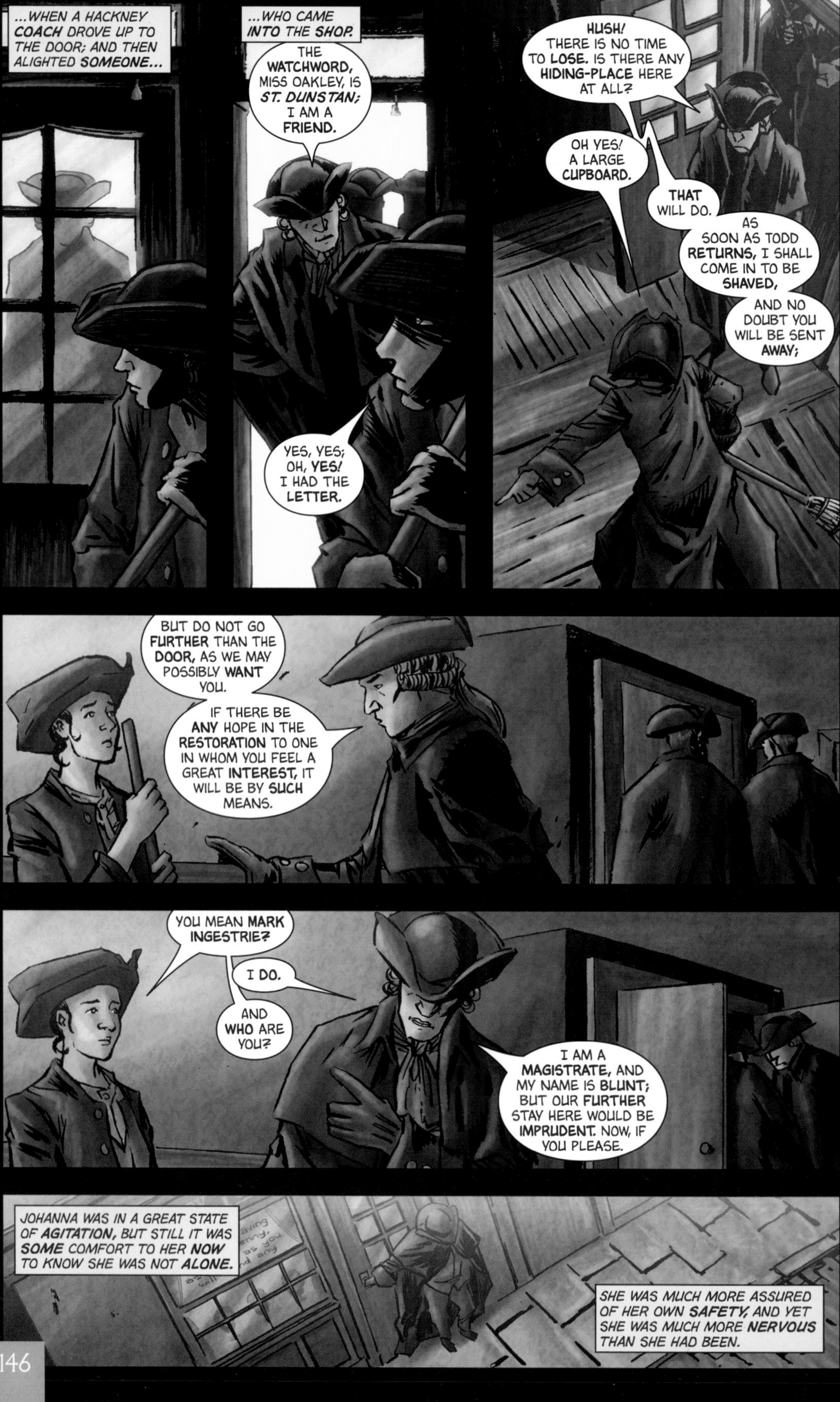
...WHEN A HACKNEY COACH DROVE UP TO THE DOOR; AND THEN ALIGHTED SOMEONE...
...WHO CAME INTO THE SHOP.
THE WATCHWORD, MISS OAKLEY, IS ST. DUNSTAN; I AM A FRIEND.
YES, YES; OH, YES! I HAD THE LETTER.
HUSH! THERE IS NO TIME TO LOSE. IS THERE ANY HIDING-PLACE HERE AT ALL?
OH YES! A LARGE CUPBOARD.
THAT WILL DO.
AS SOON AS TODD RETURNS, I SHALL COME IN TO BE SHAVED,
AND NO DOUBT YOU WILL BE SENT AWAY;
BUT DO NOT GO FURTHER THAN THE DOOR, AS WE MAY POSSIBLY WANT YOU.
IF THERE BE ANY HOPE IN THE RESTORATION TO ONE IN WHOM YOU FEEL A GREAT INTEREST, IT WILL BE BY SUCH MEANS.
YOU MEAN MARK INGESTRIE?
I DO.
AND WHO ARE YOU?
I AM A MAGISTRATE, AND MY NAME IS BLUNT; BUT OUR FURTHER STAY HERE WOULD BE IMPRUDENT. NOW, IF YOU PLEASE.
JOHANNA WAS IN A GREAT STATE OF AGITATION, BUT STILL IT WAS SOME COMFORT TO HER NOW TO KNOW SHE WAS NOT ALONE.
SHE WAS MUCH MORE ASSURED OF HER OWN SAFETY, AND YET SHE WAS MUCH MORE NERVOUS THAN SHE HAD BEEN.

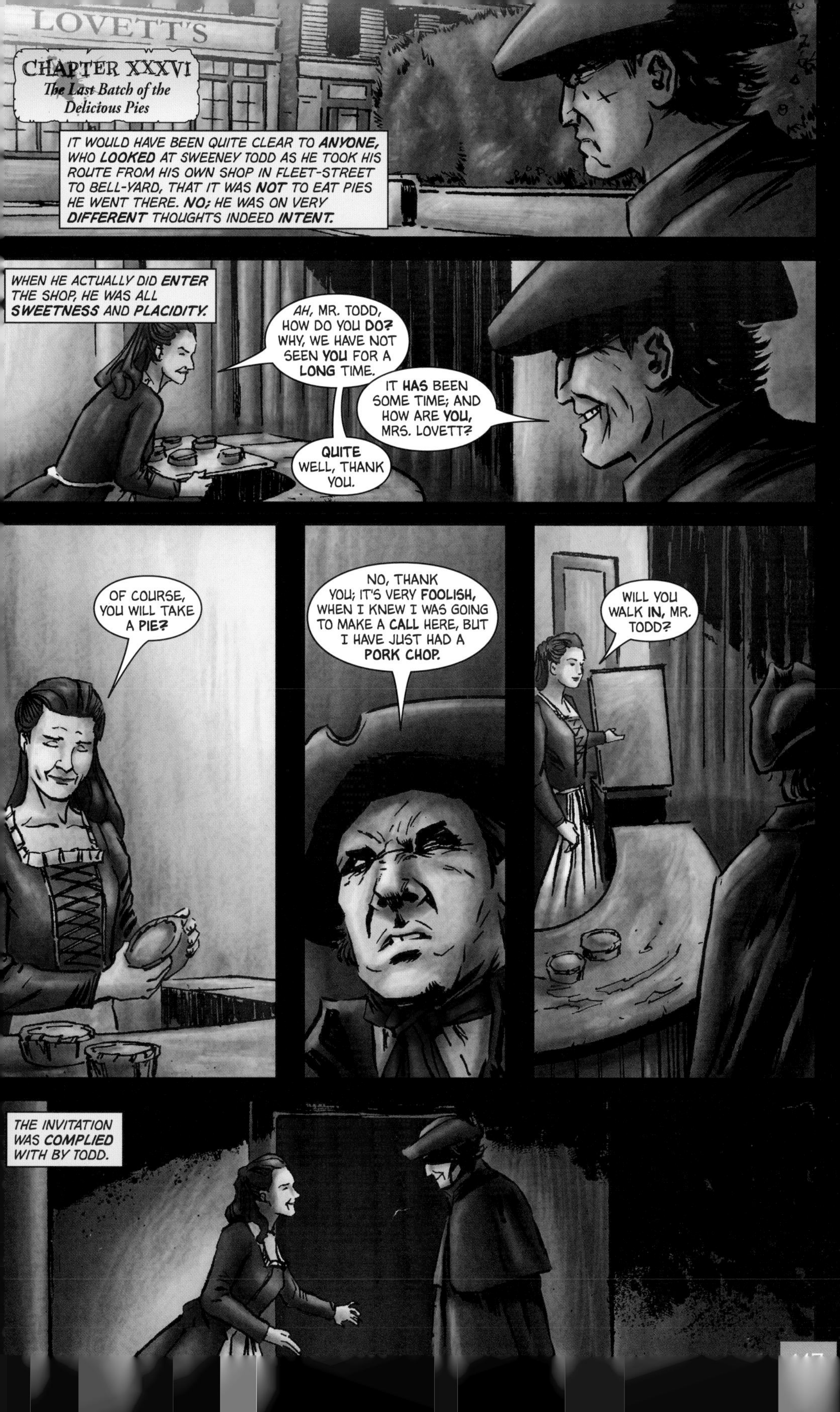
LOVETT'S
CHAPTER XXXVI
The Last Batch of the Delicious Pies
IT WOULD HAVE BEEN QUITE CLEAR TO ANYONE, WHO LOOKED AT SWEENEY TODD AS HE TOOK HIS ROUTE FROM HIS OWN SHOP IN FLEET-STREET TO BELL-YARD, THAT IT WAS NOT TO EAT PIES HE WENT THERE. NO; HE WAS ON VERY DIFFERENT THOUGHTS INDEED INTENT.
WHEN HE ACTUALLY DID ENTER THE SHOP, HE WAS ALL SWEETNESS AND PLACIDITY.
AH, MR. TODD, HOW DO YOU DO? WHY, WE HAVE NOT SEEN YOU FOR A LONG TIME.
IT HAS BEEN SOME TIME; AND HOW ARE YOU, MRS. LOVETT?
QUITE WELL, THANK YOU.
OF COURSE, YOU WILL TAKE A PIE?
NO, THANK YOU; IT'S VERY FOOLISH, WHEN I KNEW I WAS GOING TO MAKE A CALL HERE, BUT I HAVE JUST HAD A PORK CHOP.
WILL YOU WALK IN, MR. TODD?
THE INVITATION WAS COMPLIED WITH BY TODD.

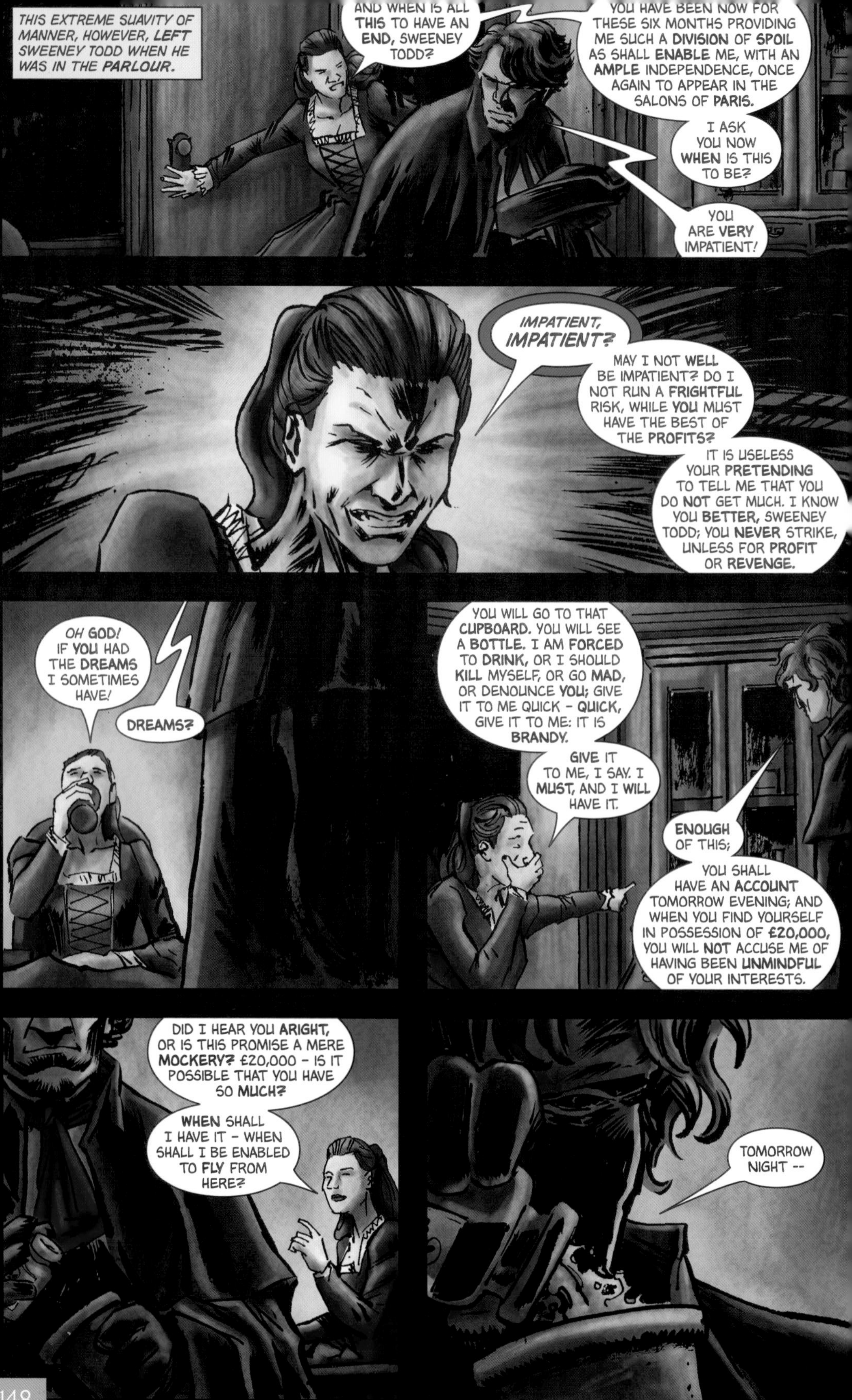
THIS EXTREME SUAVITY OF MANNER, HOWEVER, LEFT SWEENEY TODD WHEN HE WAS IN THE PARLOUR.
AND WHEN IS ALL THIS TO HAVE AN END, SWEENEY TODD?
YOU HAVE BEEN NOW FOR THESE SIX MONTHS PROVIDING ME SUCH A DIVISION OF SPOIL AS SHALL ENABLE ME, WITH AN AMPLE INDEPENDENCE, ONCE AGAIN TO APPEAR IN THE SALONS OF PARIS.
I ASK YOU NOW WHEN IS THIS TO BE?
YOU ARE VERY IMPATIENT!
IMPATIENT, IMPATIENT?
MAY I NOT WELL BE IMPATIENT? DO I NOT RUN A FRIGHTFUL RISK, WHILE YOU MUST HAVE THE BEST OF THE PROFITS?
IT IS USELESS YOUR PRETENDING TO TELL ME THAT YOU DO NOT GET MUCH. I KNOW YOU BETTER, SWEENEY TODD; YOU NEVER STRIKE, UNLESS FOR PROFIT OR REVENGE.
OH GOD! IF YOU HAD THE DREAMS I SOMETIMES HAVE!
DREAMS?
YOU WILL GO TO THAT CUPBOARD. YOU WILL SEE A BOTTLE. I AM FORCED TO DRINK, OR I SHOULD KILL MYSELF, OR GO MAD, OR DENOUNCE YOU; GIVE IT TO ME QUICK - QUICK, GIVE IT TO ME: IT IS BRANDY.
GIVE IT TO ME, I SAY. I MUST, AND I WILL HAVE IT.
ENOUGH OF THIS;
YOU SHALL HAVE AN ACCOUNT TOMORROW EVENING; AND WHEN YOU FIND YOURSELF IN POSSESSION OF £20,000, YOU WILL NOT ACCUSE ME OF HAVING BEEN UNMINDFUL OF YOUR INTERESTS.
DID I HEAR YOU ARIGHT, OR IS THIS PROMISE A MERE MOCKERY? £20,000 - IS IT POSSIBLE THAT YOU HAVE SO MUCH?
WHEN SHALL I HAVE IT - WHEN SHALL I BE ENABLED TO FLY FROM HERE?
TOMORROW NIGHT --

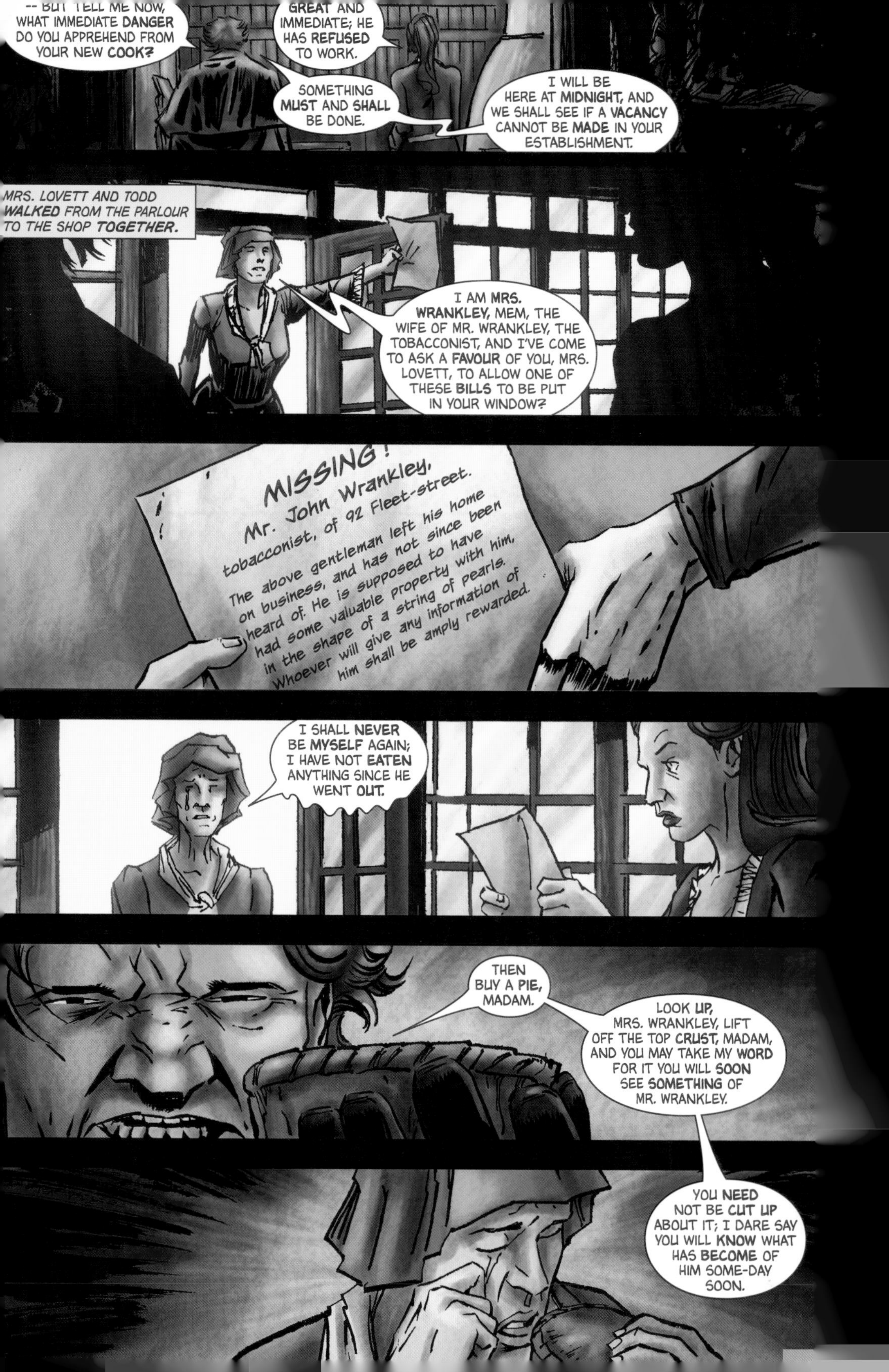
-- BUT TELL ME NOW, WHAT IMMEDIATE DANGER DO YOU APPREHEND FROM YOUR NEW COOK?
GREAT AND IMMEDIATE; HE HAS REFUSED TO WORK.
SOMETHING MUST AND SHALL BE DONE.
I WILL BE HERE AT MIDNIGHT, AND WE SHALL SEE IF A VACANCY CANNOT BE MADE IN YOUR ESTABLISHMENT.
MRS. LOVETT AND TODD WALKED FROM THE PARLOUR TO THE SHOP TOGETHER.
I AM MRS. WRANKLEY, MEM, THE WIFE OF MR. WRANKLEY, THE TOBACCONIST, AND I'VE COME TO ASK A FAVOUR OF YOU, MRS. LOVETT, TO ALLOW ONE OF THESE BILLS TO BE PUT IN YOUR WINDOW?
MISSING!
Mr. John Wrankley, tobacconist, of 92 Fleet-street.
The above gentleman left his home on business, and has not since been heard of. He is supposed to have had some valuable property with him, in the shape of a string of pearls. Whoever will give any information of him shall be amply rewarded.
I SHALL NEVER BE MYSELF AGAIN; I HAVE NOT EATEN ANYTHING SINCE HE WENT OUT.
THEN BUY A PIE, MADAM.
LOOK UP, MRS. WRANKLEY, LIFT OFF THE TOP CRUST, MADAM, AND YOU MAY TAKE MY WORD FOR IT YOU WILL SOON SEE SOMETHING OF MR. WRANKLEY.
YOU NEED NOT BE CUT UP ABOUT IT; I DARE SAY YOU WILL KNOW WHAT HAS BECOME OF HIM SOME-DAY SOON.

CHAPTER XXXVII
The Prisoner's Plan of Escape from the Pies

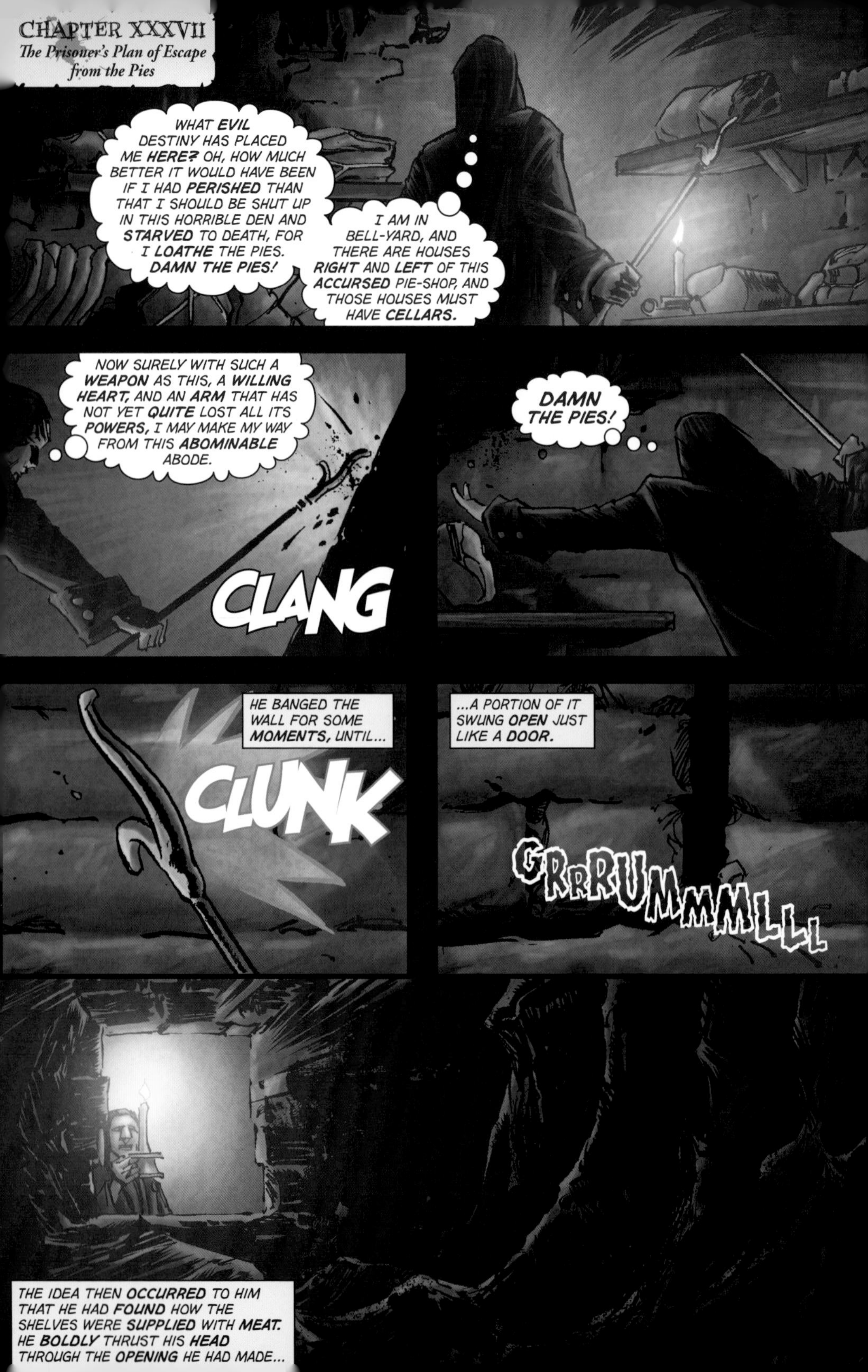
WHAT EVIL DESTINY HAS PLACED ME HERE? OH, HOW MUCH BETTER IT WOULD HAVE BEEN IF I HAD PERISHED THAN THAT I SHOULD BE SHUT UP IN THIS HORRIBLE DEN AND STARVED TO DEATH, FOR I LOATHE THE PIES. DAMN THE PIES!
I AM IN BELL-YARD, AND THERE ARE HOUSES RIGHT AND LEFT OF THIS ACCURSED PIE-SHOP, AND THOSE HOUSES MUST HAVE CELLARS.
NOW SURELY WITH SUCH A WEAPON AS THIS, A WILLING HEART, AND AN ARM THAT HAS NOT YET QUITE LOST ALL ITS POWERS, I MAY MAKE MY WAY FROM THIS ABOMINABLE ABODE.
CLANG
DAMN THE PIES!
HE BANGED THE WALL FOR SOME MOMENTS, UNTIL...
CLUNK
...A PORTION OF IT SWUNG OPEN JUST LIKE A DOOR.
GRRRUMMMLLL
THE IDEA THEN OCCURRED TO HIM THAT HE HAD FOUND HOW THE SHELVES WERE SUPPLIED WITH MEAT. HE BOLDLY THRUST HIS HEAD THROUGH THE OPENING HE HAD MADE...

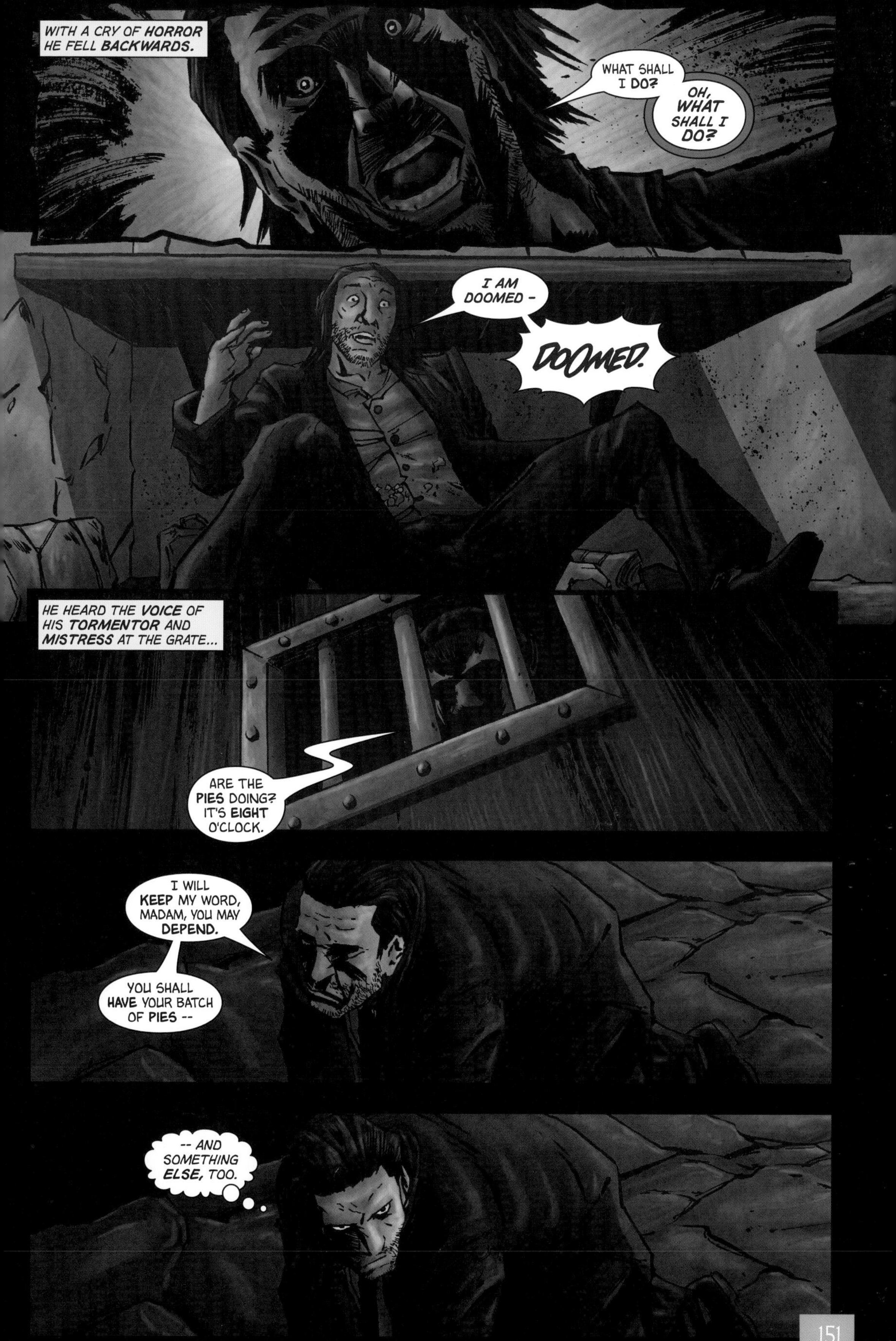
WITH A CRY OF HORROR HE FELL BACKWARDS.
WHAT SHALL I DO?
OH, WHAT SHALL I DO?
I AM DOOMED -
DOOMED.
HE HEARD THE VOICE OF HIS TORMENTOR AND MISTRESS AT THE GRATE...
ARE THE PIES DOING? IT'S EIGHT O'CLOCK.
I WILL KEEP MY WORD, MADAM, YOU MAY DEPEND.
YOU SHALL HAVE YOUR BATCH OF PIES --
-- AND SOMETHING ELSE, TOO.

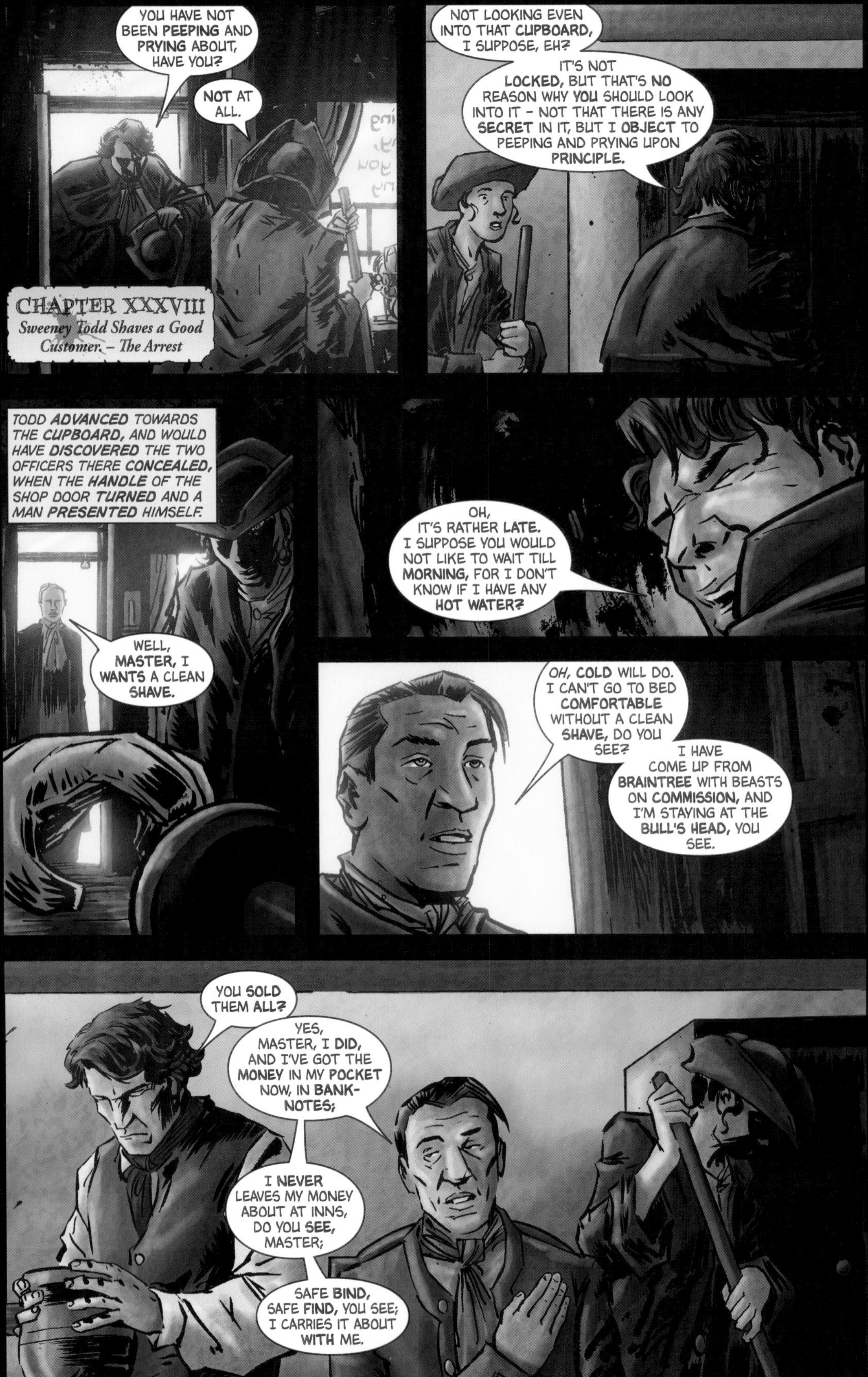
YOU HAVE NOT BEEN PEEPING AND PRYING ABOUT, HAVE YOU?
NOT AT ALL.
CHAPTER XXXVIII
Sweeney Todd Shaves a Good Customer. – The Arrest
NOT LOOKING EVEN INTO THAT CUPBOARD, I SUPPOSE, EH?
IT'S NOT LOCKED, BUT THAT'S NO REASON WHY YOU SHOULD LOOK INTO IT - NOT THAT THERE IS ANY SECRET IN IT, BUT I OBJECT TO PEEPING AND PRYING UPON PRINCIPLE.
TODD ADVANCED TOWARDS THE CUPBOARD, AND WOULD HAVE DISCOVERED THE TWO OFFICERS THERE CONCEALED, WHEN THE HANDLE OF THE SHOP DOOR TURNED AND A MAN PRESENTED HIMSELF.
WELL, MASTER, I WANTS A CLEAN SHAVE.
OH, IT'S RATHER LATE. I SUPPOSE YOU WOULD NOT LIKE TO WAIT TILL MORNING, FOR I DON'T KNOW IF I HAVE ANY HOT WATER?
OH, COLD WILL DO. I CAN'T GO TO BED COMFORTABLE WITHOUT A CLEAN SHAVE, DO YOU SEE?
I HAVE COME UP FROM BRAINTREE WITH BEASTS ON COMMISSION, AND I'M STAYING AT THE BULL'S HEAD, YOU SEE.
YOU SOLD THEM ALL?
YES, MASTER, I DID, AND I'VE GOT THE MONEY IN MY POCKET NOW, IN BANK-NOTES;
I NEVER LEAVES MY MONEY ABOUT AT INNS, DO YOU SEE, MASTER;
SAFE BIND, SAFE FIND, YOU SEE; I CARRIES IT ABOUT WITH ME.

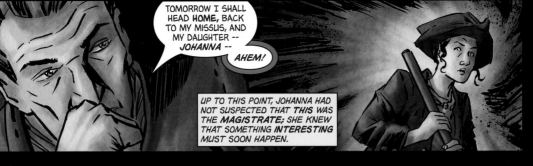

TOMORROW I SHALL HEAD **HOME**, BACK TO MY MISSUS, AND MY DAUGHTER -- *JOHANNA* --

AHEM!

UP TO THIS POINT, JOHANNA HAD NOT SUSPECTED THAT **THIS** WAS THE **MAGISTRATE**; SHE KNEW THAT SOMETHING **INTERESTING** MUST SOON HAPPEN.

CHARLEY, WHILE I AM JUST **FINISHING OFF** THIS GENTLEMAN, YOU MAY AS WELL JUST RUN TO THE **TEMPLE** TO MR. SERJEANT **TOLDRUNIS** AND ASK FOR HIS **WIG**;

WE SHALL HAVE TO DO IT IN THE **MORNING**, AND MAY AS WELL HAVE IT THE FIRST THING IN THE DAY TO **BEGIN** UPON.

YOU NEED NOT **HURRY**, CHARLEY.

I SUPPOSE YOU DIDN'T COME TO LONDON **ALONE**, SIR?

OH, YES, QUITE ALONE; I HAD **NO** COMPANY WITH ME.

I'LL GET ANOTHER **RAZOR** WITH A **KEENER** EDGE.

DON'T **MOVE**, SIR, I SHALL NOT DETAIN YOU A **MOMENT**; I HAVE MY OTHER RAZORS IN THE NEXT ROOM, AND WILL **POLISH YOU OFF** NOW, SIR.

SWEENEY TODD WALKED INTO HIS **BACK-PARLOUR**.

THE MOMENT HIS BACK WAS TURNED, SIR RICHARD **SPRANG** FROM THE SHAVING CHAIR, AS IF HE HAD BEEN **ELECTRIFIED**.

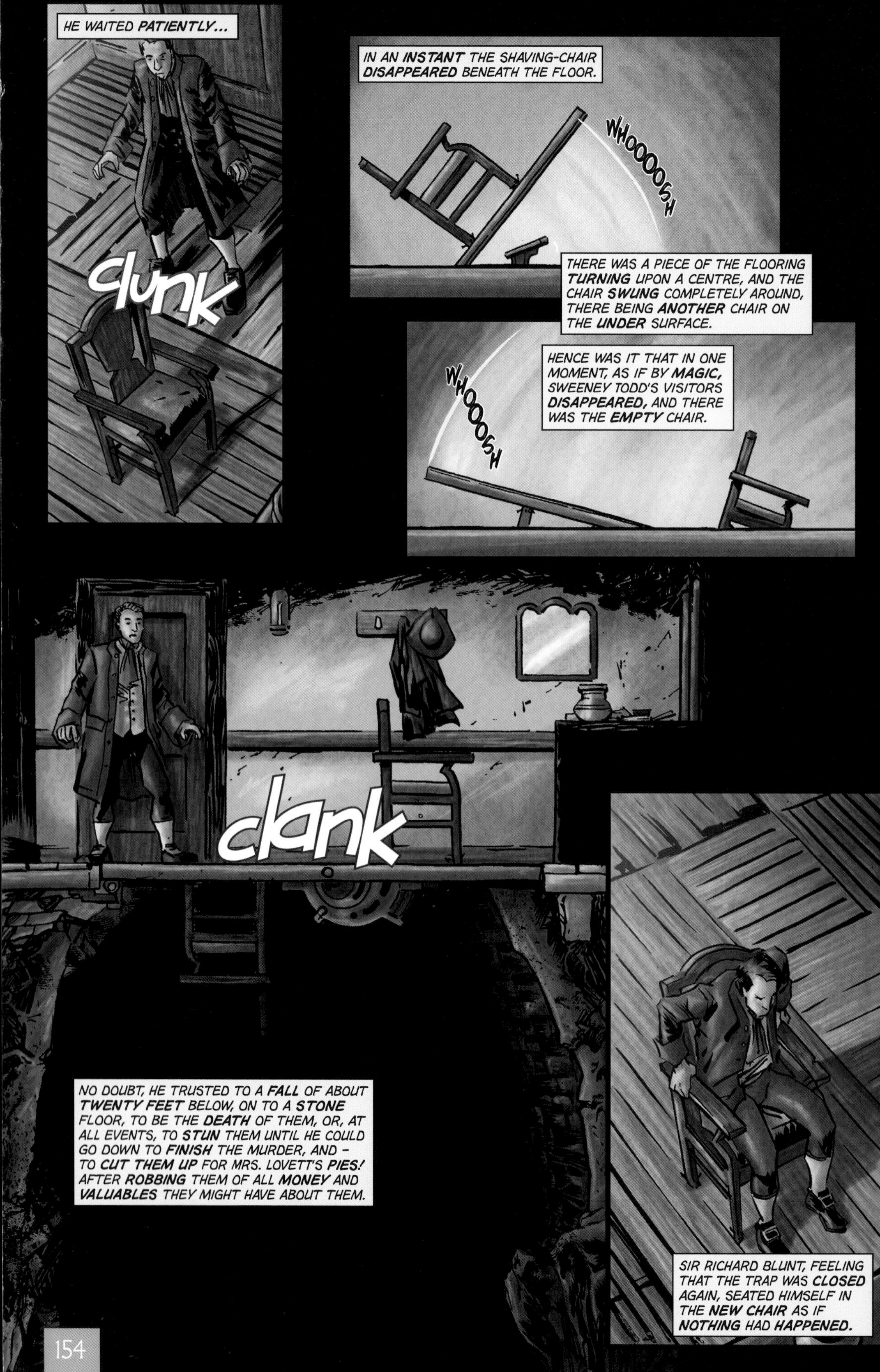
HE WAITED PATIENTLY...
CLUNK
IN AN INSTANT THE SHAVING-CHAIR DISAPPEARED BENEATH THE FLOOR.
WHOOOOOSH
THERE WAS A PIECE OF THE FLOORING TURNING UPON A CENTRE, AND THE CHAIR SWUNG COMPLETELY AROUND, THERE BEING ANOTHER CHAIR ON THE UNDER SURFACE.
HENCE WAS IT THAT IN ONE MOMENT, AS IF BY MAGIC, SWEENEY TODD'S VISITORS DISAPPEARED, AND THERE WAS THE EMPTY CHAIR.
WHOOOOSH
CLANK
NO DOUBT, HE TRUSTED TO A FALL OF ABOUT TWENTY FEET BELOW, ON TO A STONE FLOOR, TO BE THE DEATH OF THEM, OR, AT ALL EVENTS, TO STUN THEM UNTIL HE COULD GO DOWN TO FINISH THE MURDER, AND - TO CUT THEM UP FOR MRS. LOVETT'S PIES! AFTER ROBBING THEM OF ALL MONEY AND VALUABLES THEY MIGHT HAVE ABOUT THEM.
SIR RICHARD BLUNT, FEELING THAT THE TRAP WAS CLOSED AGAIN, SEATED HIMSELF IN THE NEW CHAIR AS IF NOTHING HAD HAPPENED.

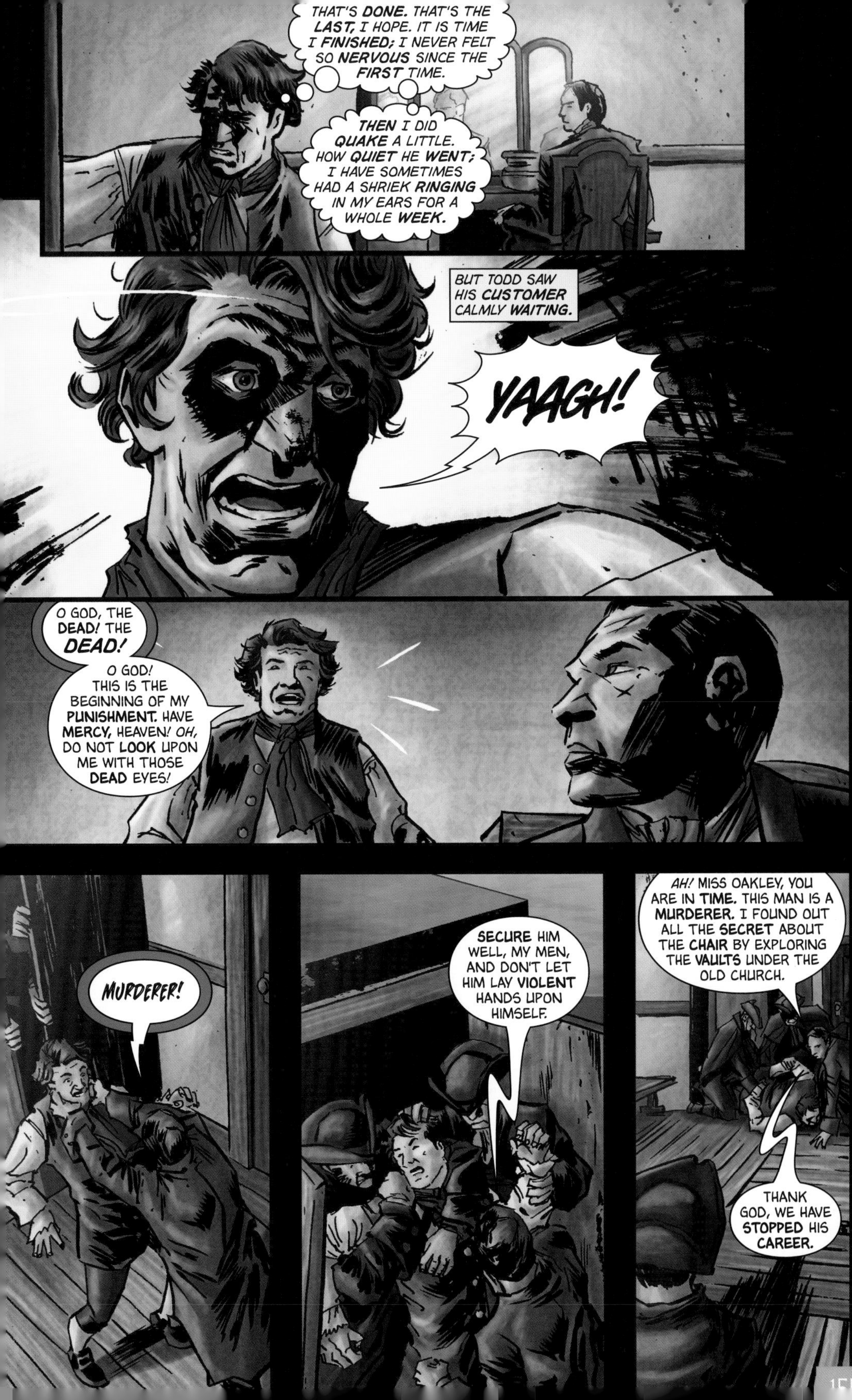
THAT'S DONE. THAT'S THE LAST, I HOPE. IT IS TIME I FINISHED; I NEVER FELT SO NERVOUS SINCE THE FIRST TIME.
THEN I DID QUAKE A LITTLE. HOW QUIET HE WENT; I HAVE SOMETIMES HAD A SHRIEK RINGING IN MY EARS FOR A WHOLE WEEK.
BUT TODD SAW HIS CUSTOMER CALMLY WAITING.
YAAGH!
O GOD, THE DEAD! THE DEAD!
O GOD! THIS IS THE BEGINNING OF MY PUNISHMENT. HAVE MERCY, HEAVEN! OH, DO NOT LOOK UPON ME WITH THOSE DEAD EYES!
MURDERER!
SECURE HIM WELL, MY MEN, AND DON'T LET HIM LAY VIOLENT HANDS UPON HIMSELF.
AH! MISS OAKLEY, YOU ARE IN TIME. THIS MAN IS A MURDERER. I FOUND OUT ALL THE SECRET ABOUT THE CHAIR BY EXPLORING THE VAULTS UNDER THE OLD CHURCH.
THANK GOD, WE HAVE STOPPED HIS CAREER.

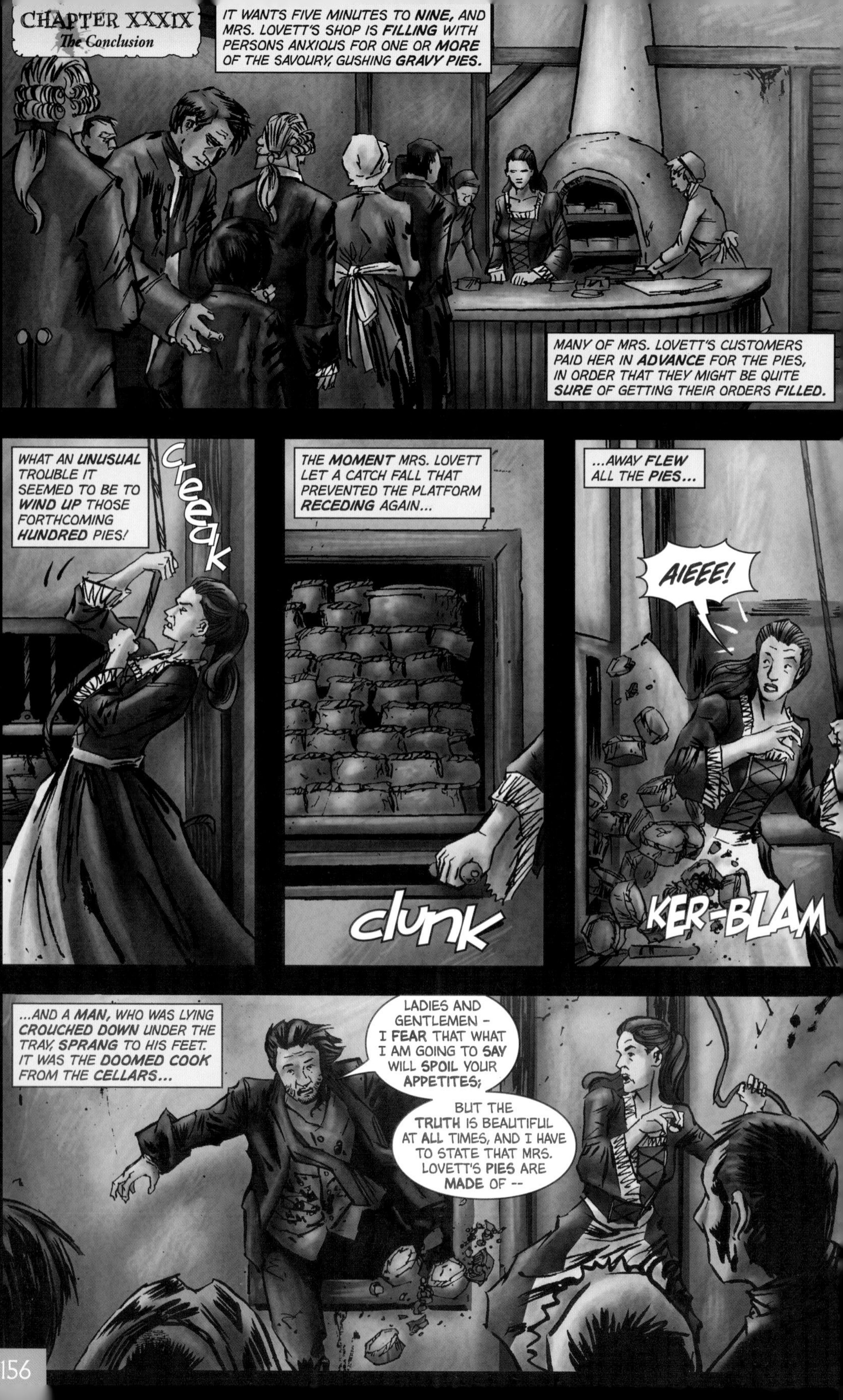
CHAPTER XXXIX
The Conclusion
IT WANTS FIVE MINUTES TO NINE, AND MRS. LOVETT'S SHOP IS FILLING WITH PERSONS ANXIOUS FOR ONE OR MORE OF THE SAVOURY, GUSHING GRAVY PIES.
MANY OF MRS. LOVETT'S CUSTOMERS PAID HER IN ADVANCE FOR THE PIES, IN ORDER THAT THEY MIGHT BE QUITE SURE OF GETTING THEIR ORDERS FILLED.
WHAT AN UNUSUAL TROUBLE IT SEEMED TO BE TO WIND UP THOSE FORTHCOMING HUNDRED PIES!
CREAK
THE MOMENT MRS. LOVETT LET A CATCH FALL THAT PREVENTED THE PLATFORM RECEDING AGAIN...
CLUNK
...AWAY FLEW ALL THE PIES...
AIEEE!
KER-BLAM
...AND A MAN, WHO WAS LYING CROUCHED DOWN UNDER THE TRAY, SPRANG TO HIS FEET. IT WAS THE DOOMED COOK FROM THE CELLARS...
LADIES AND GENTLEMEN – I FEAR THAT WHAT I AM GOING TO SAY WILL SPOIL YOUR APPETITES;
BUT THE TRUTH IS BEAUTIFUL AT ALL TIMES, AND I HAVE TO STATE THAT MRS. LOVETT'S PIES ARE MADE OF --

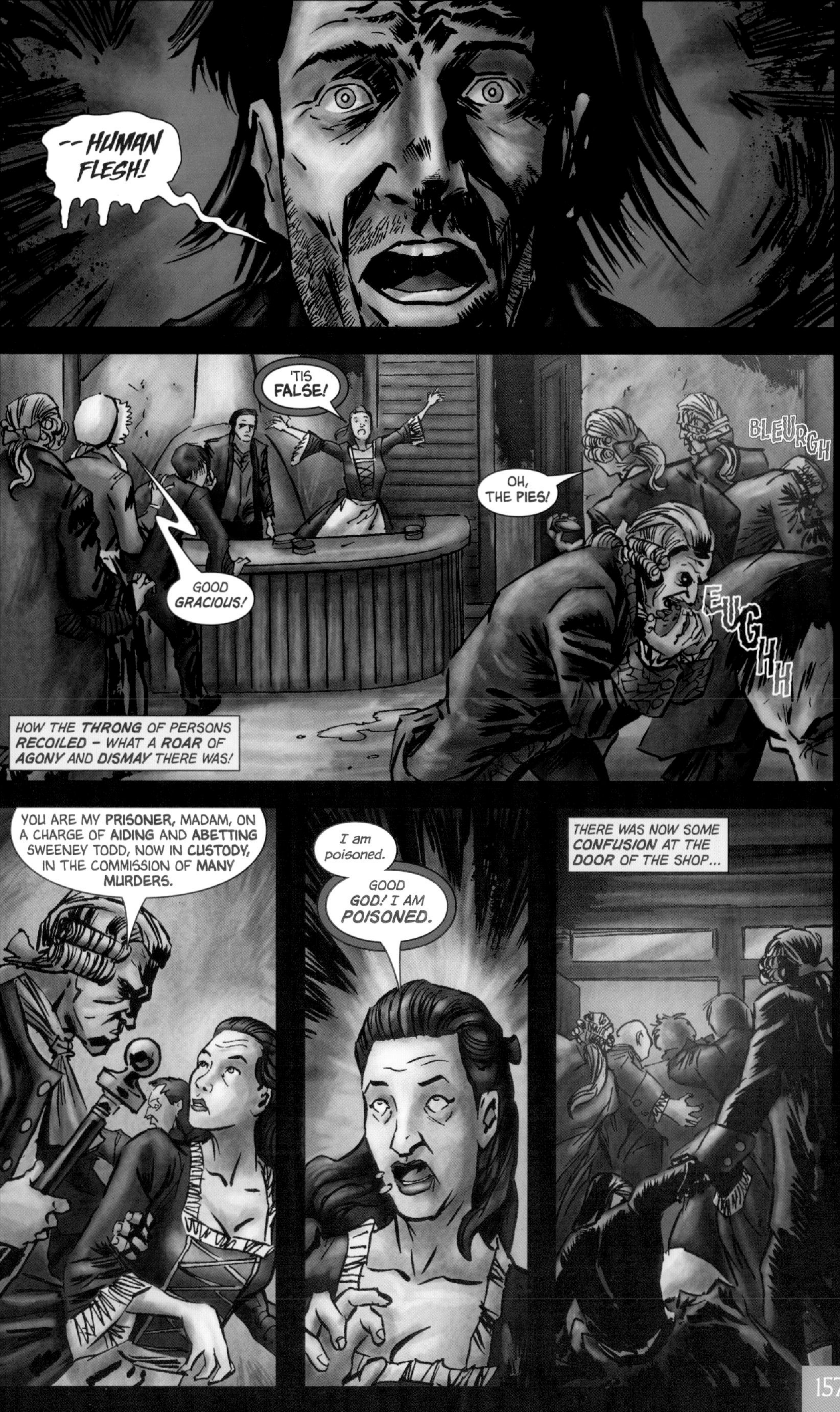

--HUMAN FLESH!
'TIS FALSE!
GOOD GRACIOUS!
OH, THE PIES!
BLEURGH
EUGHH
HOW THE THRONG OF PERSONS RECOILED – WHAT A ROAR OF AGONY AND DISMAY THERE WAS!
YOU ARE MY PRISONER, MADAM, ON A CHARGE OF AIDING AND ABETTING SWEENEY TODD, NOW IN CUSTODY, IN THE COMMISSION OF MANY MURDERS.
I am poisoned.
GOOD GOD! I AM POISONED.
THERE WAS NOW SOME CONFUSION AT THE DOOR OF THE SHOP...

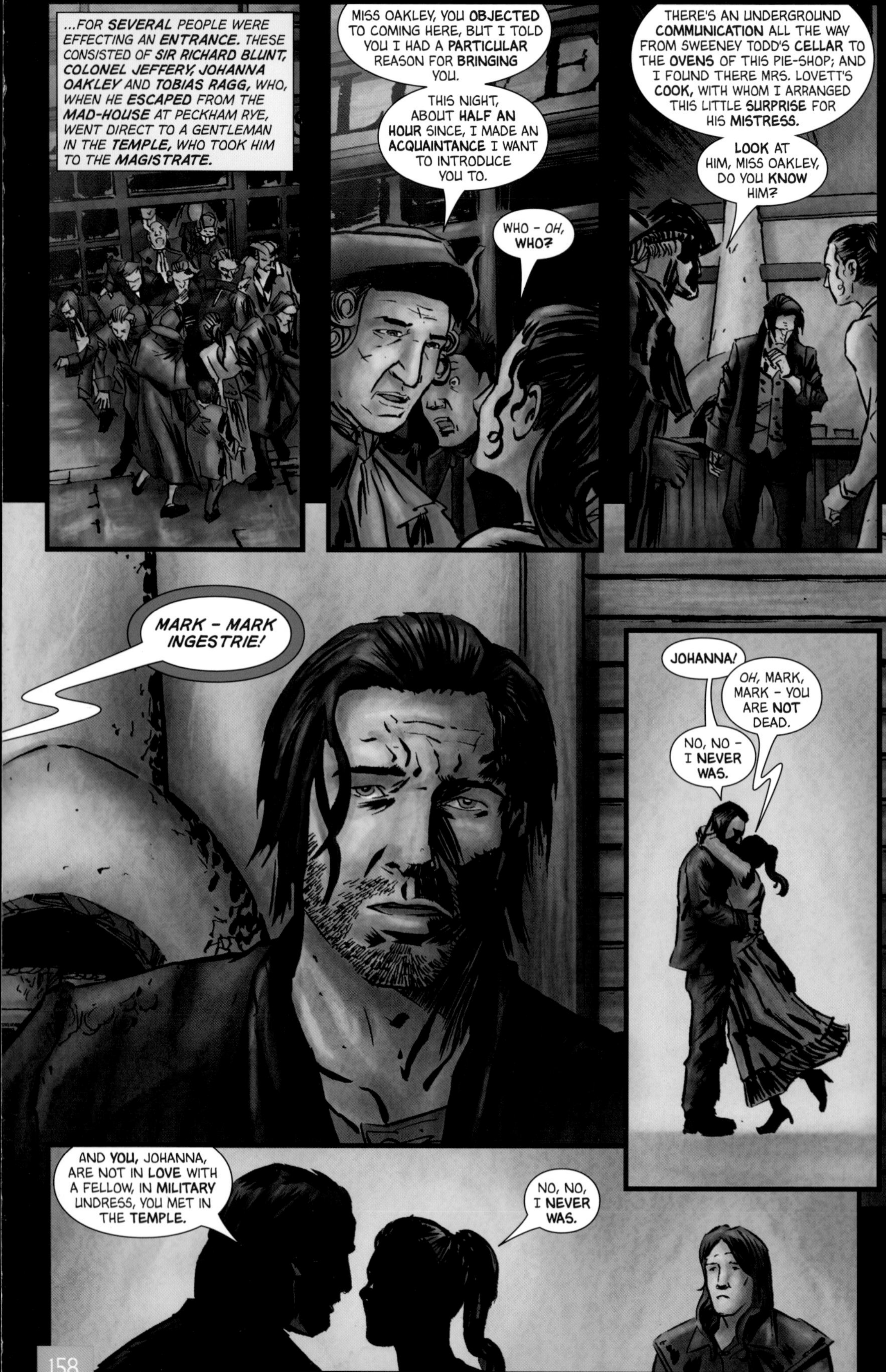
...FOR SEVERAL PEOPLE WERE EFFECTING AN ENTRANCE. THESE CONSISTED OF SIR RICHARD BLUNT, COLONEL JEFFERY, JOHANNA OAKLEY AND TOBIAS RAGG, WHO, WHEN HE ESCAPED FROM THE MAD-HOUSE AT PECKHAM RYE, WENT DIRECT TO A GENTLEMAN IN THE TEMPLE, WHO TOOK HIM TO THE MAGISTRATE.
MISS OAKLEY, YOU OBJECTED TO COMING HERE, BUT I TOLD YOU I HAD A PARTICULAR REASON FOR BRINGING YOU.
THIS NIGHT, ABOUT HALF AN HOUR SINCE, I MADE AN ACQUAINTANCE I WANT TO INTRODUCE YOU TO.
WHO - OH, WHO?
THERE'S AN UNDERGROUND COMMUNICATION ALL THE WAY FROM SWEENEY TODD'S CELLAR TO THE OVENS OF THIS PIE-SHOP; AND I FOUND THERE MRS. LOVETT'S COOK, WITH WHOM I ARRANGED THIS LITTLE SURPRISE FOR HIS MISTRESS.
LOOK AT HIM, MISS OAKLEY, DO YOU KNOW HIM?
MARK - MARK INGESTRIE!
JOHANNA!
OH, MARK, MARK - YOU ARE NOT DEAD.
NO, NO - I NEVER WAS.
AND YOU, JOHANNA, ARE NOT IN LOVE WITH A FELLOW, IN MILITARY UNDRESS, YOU MET IN THE TEMPLE.
NO, NO, I NEVER WAS.

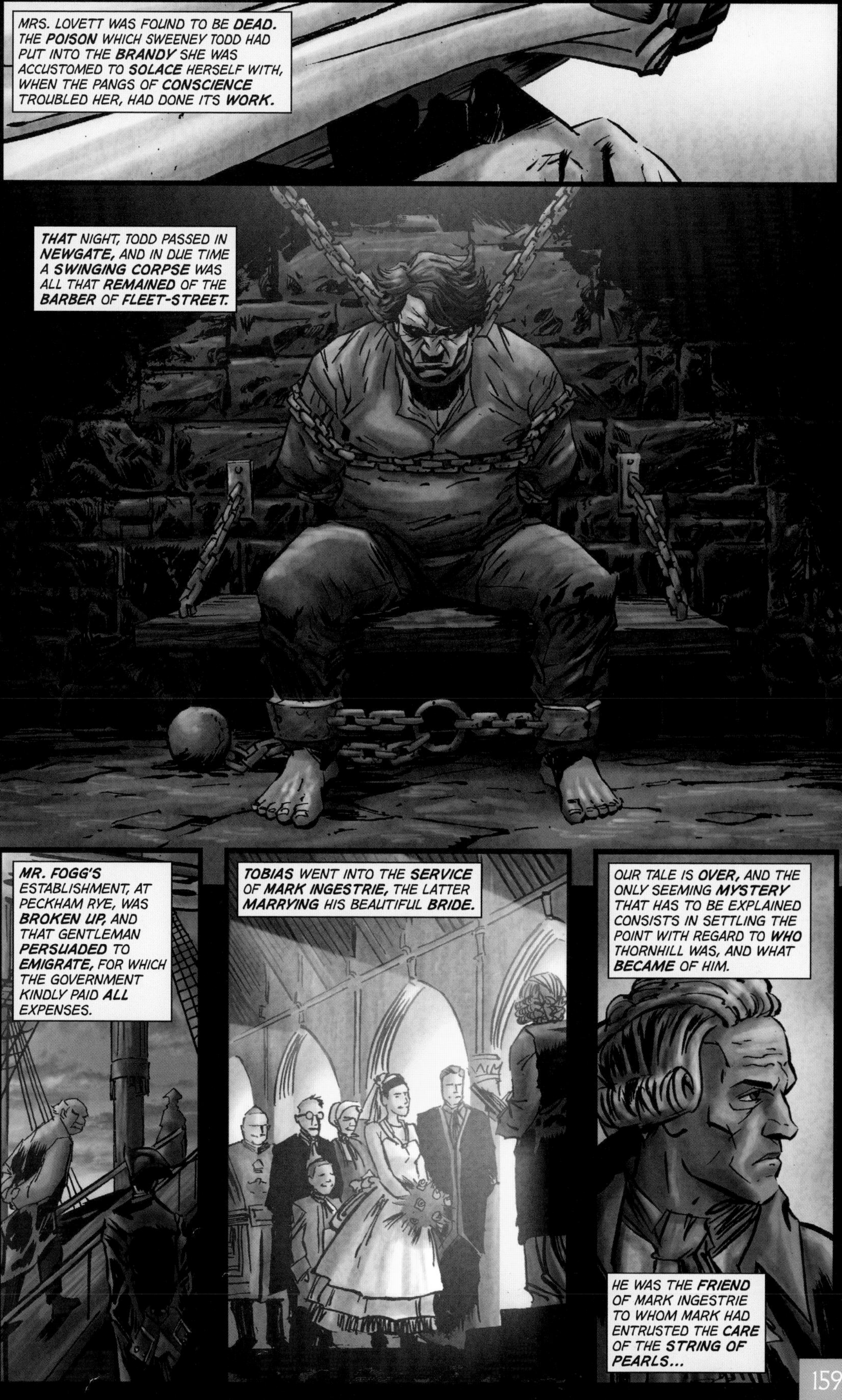
MRS. LOVETT WAS FOUND TO BE DEAD. THE POISON WHICH SWEENEY TODD HAD PUT INTO THE BRANDY SHE WAS ACCUSTOMED TO SOLACE HERSELF WITH, WHEN THE PANGS OF CONSCIENCE TROUBLED HER, HAD DONE ITS WORK.
THAT NIGHT, TODD PASSED IN NEWGATE, AND IN DUE TIME A SWINGING CORPSE WAS ALL THAT REMAINED OF THE BARBER OF FLEET-STREET.
MR. FOGG'S ESTABLISHMENT, AT PECKHAM RYE, WAS BROKEN UP, AND THAT GENTLEMAN PERSUADED TO EMIGRATE, FOR WHICH THE GOVERNMENT KINDLY PAID ALL EXPENSES.
TOBIAS WENT INTO THE SERVICE OF MARK INGESTRIE, THE LATTER MARRYING HIS BEAUTIFUL BRIDE.
OUR TALE IS OVER, AND THE ONLY SEEMING MYSTERY THAT HAS TO BE EXPLAINED CONSISTS IN SETTLING THE POINT WITH REGARD TO WHO THORNHILL WAS, AND WHAT BECAME OF HIM.
HE WAS THE FRIEND OF MARK INGESTRIE TO WHOM MARK HAD ENTRUSTED THE CARE OF THE STRING OF PEARLS...

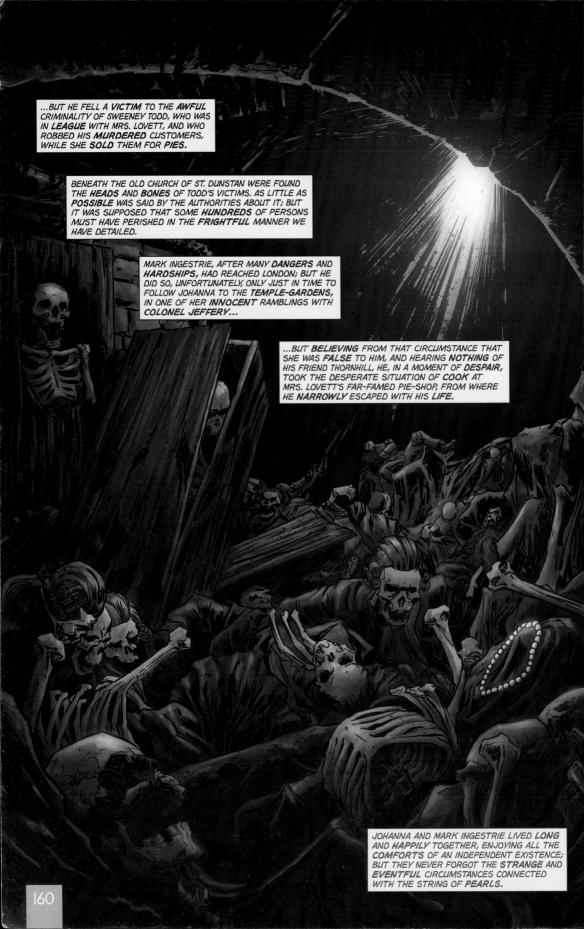

...BUT HE FELL A *VICTIM* TO THE *AWFUL* CRIMINALITY OF SWEENEY TODD, WHO WAS IN *LEAGUE* WITH MRS. LOVETT, AND WHO ROBBED HIS *MURDERED* CUSTOMERS, WHILE SHE *SOLD* THEM FOR *PIES*.

BENEATH THE OLD CHURCH OF ST. DUNSTAN WERE FOUND THE *HEADS* AND *BONES* OF TODD'S VICTIMS. AS LITTLE AS *POSSIBLE* WAS SAID BY THE AUTHORITIES ABOUT IT; BUT IT WAS SUPPOSED THAT SOME *HUNDREDS* OF PERSONS MUST HAVE PERISHED IN THE *FRIGHTFUL* MANNER WE HAVE DETAILED.

MARK INGESTRIE, AFTER MANY *DANGERS* AND *HARDSHIPS*, HAD REACHED LONDON; BUT HE DID SO, UNFORTUNATELY, ONLY JUST IN TIME TO FOLLOW JOHANNA TO THE *TEMPLE-GARDENS*, IN ONE OF HER *INNOCENT* RAMBLINGS WITH *COLONEL JEFFERY*...

...BUT *BELIEVING* FROM THAT CIRCUMSTANCE THAT SHE WAS *FALSE* TO HIM, AND HEARING *NOTHING* OF HIS FRIEND THORNHILL, HE, IN A MOMENT OF *DESPAIR*, TOOK THE DESPERATE SITUATION OF *COOK* AT MRS. LOVETT'S FAR-FAMED PIE-SHOP, FROM WHERE HE *NARROWLY* ESCAPED WITH HIS *LIFE*.

JOHANNA AND MARK INGESTRIE LIVED *LONG* AND *HAPPILY* TOGETHER, ENJOYING ALL THE *COMFORTS* OF AN INDEPENDENT EXISTENCE; BUT THEY NEVER FORGOT THE *STRANGE* AND *EVENTFUL* CIRCUMSTANCES CONNECTED WITH THE STRING OF *PEARLS*.

SWEENEY TODD

THE END

Sweeney Todd – The Legend

No one knows for certain whether Sweeney Todd actually existed. Much like Robin Hood and Sherwood Forest, the tale has become part of London folklore, with some defending it as fact and others denying any truth in it. In 1993, Peter Haining published a remarkable book, ***Sweeney Todd – The Real Story of the Demon Barber of Fleet Street***, in which he argues that Todd was definitely a real person, even giving dates for his birth and execution. Unfortunately, although it is a wonderful read and a very appealing notion, the sources of his information are dubious.

This graphic novel has been adapted from the original story of Sweeney Todd that appeared in weekly installments in ***The People's Periodical and Family Library*** from November 1846 to March 1847. The story carried the title ***The String of Pearls: A Romance*** to make it appeal to the readership of the newspaper. Publications such as ***The People's Periodical*** were the soap operas of the day, designed for quick, mass entertainment. They employed teams of writers to produce the pieces quickly enough to meet the strict printing deadlines. Because of this, although it is believed that much of ***The String of Pearls*** was written by Thomas Peckett Prest, there is no official record of its authorship. However, we do know that the periodical's editor, Edward Lloyd, controlled the publication as the story unfolded. Indeed, it was Lloyd who quickly latched onto the appeal of this villainous barber, producing a much expanded edition of the story that was sold in weekly installments in 1847-8. Those installments were then collected into a single book that was published in 1850. Lloyd realized that if readers believed it was based on fact, the story would become hugely popular, which in turn would lead to higher sales. In the preface to the 1850 edition, he writes,

In answer to the many inquiries that have been, from time to time, made regarding the fact of whether there ever was such a person as Sweeney Todd in existence, we can unhesitatingly say, that there certainly was such a man; and the record of his crimes is still to be found in the chronicles of criminality of this country. The house in Fleet Street, which was the scene of Todd's crimes, is no more. A fire, which destroyed some half–dozen buildings on that side of the way, involved Todd's in destruction; but the secret passage, although no doubt, partially blocked up with the rebuilding of St. Dunstan's Church, connecting the vaults of that edifice with the cellars of what was Todd's house in Fleet Street, still remains.

From Haining's book, we learn that the trial of Sweeney Todd was covered in another periodical, ***The Newgate Calendar.*** This paper was more along the lines of the "Penny Dreadfuls" that were so popular with Victorian readers, featuring gripping stories of crime and violence, raising criminals almost to celebrity status. ***The Newgate Calendar*** did not have a reputation for being factually correct, often containing stories that were either grossly exaggerated or simply made up. According to ***The Newgate Calendar,*** Todd's trial took place at the Old Bailey in 1801, during which all the gruesome details of his murders were revealed, although the trial itself centered around the murder of Mr. Francis Thornhill.

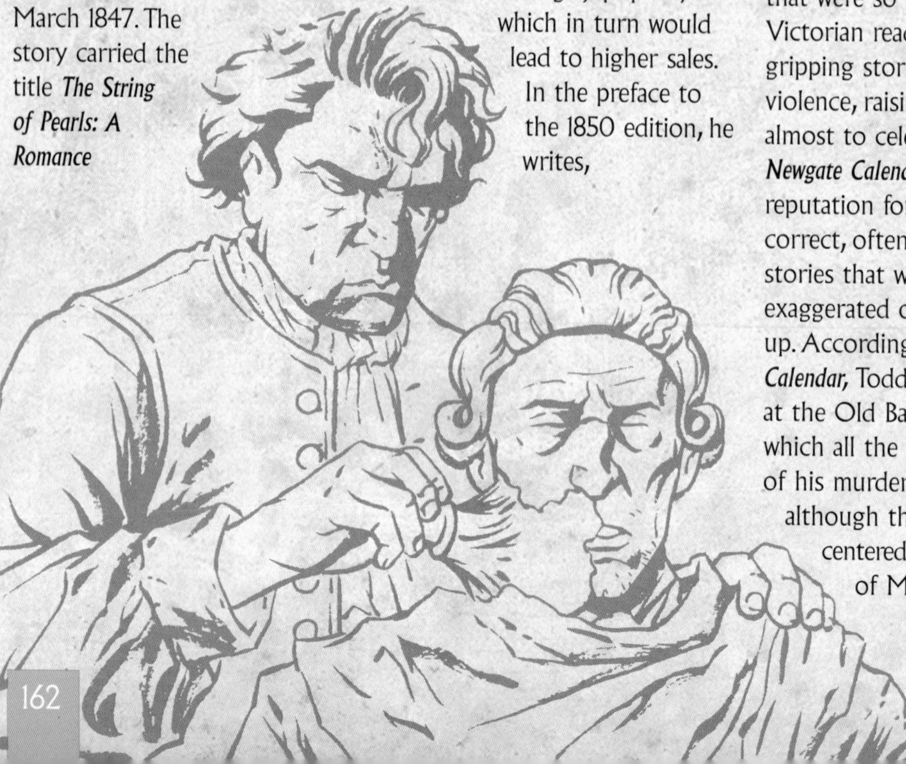

Unfortunately, there is no official evidence that this trial ever took place. With a body count in excess of 160 individuals, this would not have been a small case, yet there are no records of the trial in the Old Bailey archives. It would also have received widespread press coverage, but it only appears in *The Newgate Calendar*. This leads us to believe that the accounts of *The Newgate Calendar* and Edward Lloyd's claims of truth must have been manufactured with the intention of creating a frenzy that would lead to greater sales of their publications.

Todd on Stage and Screen

On March 1, 1847, three weeks before the story had concluded in *The People's Periodical*, the first stage production of the tale of *Sweeney Todd* appeared. The two-act play, entitled *String of Pearls or, The Barber Fiend of Fleet Street*, was written by the prolific playwright George Dibdin Pitt. It is believed that Pitt was aided by Thomas Peckett Prest (a main writer of the serialized story) which would explain how the play could appear before the final installments were printed. Promotional posters for the play drew on the success of the story running in *The People's Periodical* and, interestingly, also carried the words, "FOUNDED ON FACT."

The first screen appearance of *Sweeney Todd* was a short, silent movie in 1926, based on the Dibdin Pitt play, which attempted to turn the story into a slapstick comedy. Although a more serious movie appeared two years later, it is the "talkie" of 1936 that is considered to be the first authentic adaptation, with the role of Sweeney Todd played by the aptly named Tod Slaughter.

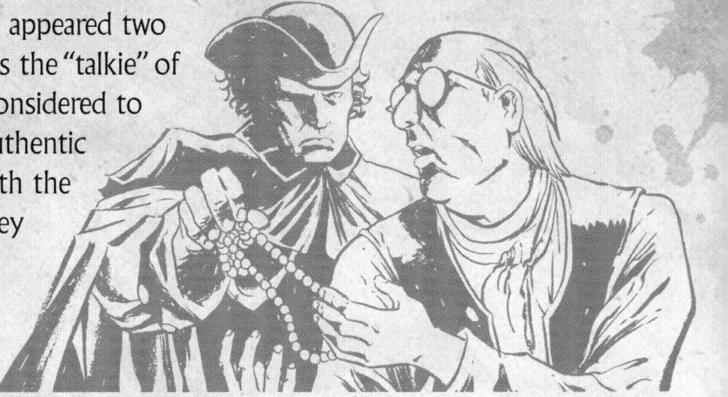

In 1973, Christopher Bond wrote a stage version of the story that introduced a "back story", adding a new dimension to Sweeney Todd's character – that he was not simply motivated by greed, but sought revenge. In Bond's play, a barber called Benjamin Barker is wrongly arrested and deported to Australia by Judge Turpin. Barker changes his name to Sweeney Todd and returns to London, vowing to kill the corrupt Judge Turpin for attacking and murdering Todd's wife. Although that is Todd's reason for returning, he happens to murder a good many other people along the way.

Stephen Sondheim saw Bond's play and liked it so much, he wrote a musical version of it that opened on Broadway in 1979. The stage show was a huge success, and has played to audiences around the world ever since. Sondheim's musical was famously adapted to the big screen in Tim Burton's 2008 movie, starring Johnny Depp as Sweeney Todd, with Helena Bonham Carter as Mrs. Lovett.

Typical of Burton's productions, the film is dark and gruesome, and although it matches the nature of the events, it strays a fair distance from the 1846 story and consequently loses much of the original mystery.

While we cannot be sure if Sweeney Todd was even a real person, or if the events of the story actually took place, the tale of the murderous villain truly captures the imagination. However, one thing is a certainty – that the enduring legend of Sweeney Todd, the Demon Barber of Fleet Street, will live with us forever.

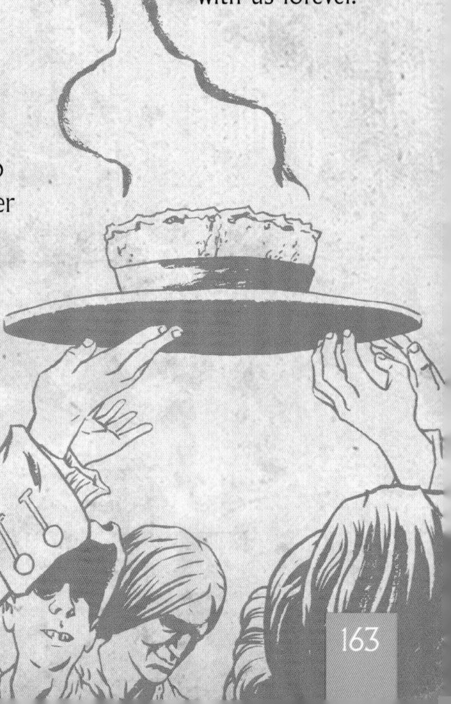

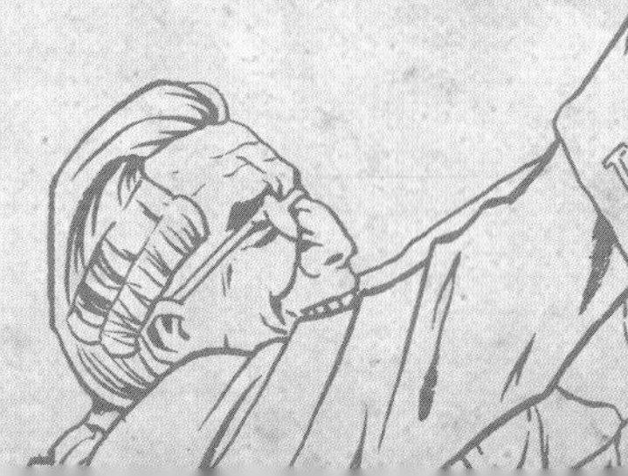

PAGE CREATION

1. Script

The scriptwriter takes the original text and breaks it down into a series of episodes that tell the whole story. Each episode is captured in a series of panels, which are detailed to the artist as descriptive text. The Original Text captions and dialogue are taken from the original book, with the Quick Text adapted from that selection.

PAGE 8

Panel 1: Todd is sitting in his shop looking at his assistant TOBIAS RAGG who sits there silently, clearly nervous in the presence of his strange master. Todd pointing at Tobias, a scary finger.

	ORIGINAL TEXT	QUICK TEXT
TODD	You will remember, Tobias Ragg, that you are now my apprentice, that you have of me had board, washing, and lodging, with the exception that you don't sleep here, that you take your meals at home: as for lodging, you lodge here in the shop all day. Now, are you not a happy dog?	Remember, Tobias Ragg, you work for me now.
TOBIAS	Yes, sir.	Yes, sir.

Panel 2: Todd touching his head in a tapping motion to indicate a weak mind.

TODD	You will acquire a first-rate profession, and quite as good as the law, which your mother tells me she would have put you to, only that a little weakness of the headpiece unqualified you. And now, Tobias, listen to me, and treasure up every word I say.	Here you will learn my trade – so let me make one thing clear.

Panel 3: Tobias responds

TOBIAS	Yes, sir.	Yes, sir.

Panel 4: Todd making a throat cutting gesture.

TODD	I'll cut your throat from ear to ear, if you repeat one word of what passes in this shop, or dare to make any supposition, or draw any conclusion from anything you may see, or hear, or fancy you see or hear. I'll cut your throat from ear to ear – do you understand me?	I will cut your throat if you tell anyone what goes on in this shop. Do you understand?

Panel 5: Tobias looks scared

TOBIAS	Yes, sir, I won't say nothing. I wish, sir, as I may be made into veal pies at Lovett's in Bell Yard if I as much as says a word.	Yes sir. I won't say a word. Let me be made into one of Mrs. Lovett's meat pies if I do.

Panel 6: Sweeney Todd rises from his seat; looking down on Tobias. opens his large mouth as if he is going to really blast him (because of the innocent but accurate mention of people going INTO those pies!). Shown from low angle to feel the menace small Tobias feels.

TODD	Hmmm…very good. I am satisfied, I am quite satisfied; and mark me – the shop, and the shop only, is your place.	Hmmm… very well then – and remember you are not allowed to go into the back rooms.

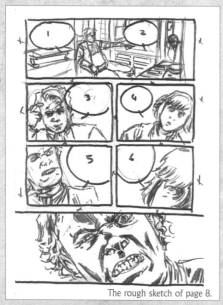

Page 8 from the script of *Sweeney Todd* showing two versions of the text.

2. Rough Sketch

The artist converts the panel descriptions into artwork, and the first stage of this is to lay out how the page will look. This is done as a quick and rough sketch, with a number of ideas often tried out. Because this sketch will determine how the page will end up, the artist must consider numerous elements, including pacing of the action, emphasis of certain elements to tell the story in the best way, the location of the lettering and even lighting of the scene. If any changes need to be made, then it is far easier to make them at this early stage, before the page is drawn.

The rough sketch of page 8.

3. Pencils

Once the artist is happy with the rough sketch, he creates a pencil drawing of the page. Pencil is used so that alterations and refinements can still be made.

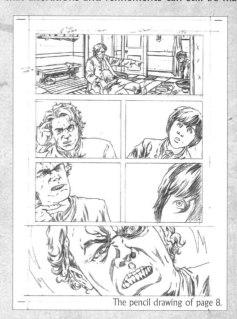

The pencil drawing of page 8.

4. Inking

The inking stage is important because it clarifies the pencil lines and finalizes the linework. However, inking is not simply tracing over the pencil sketch! It is more like a pre-coloring stage, where black ink is used to fill in shaded areas, capture lighting using shadows, and to provide texture.

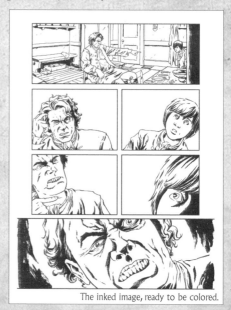

The inked image, ready to be colored.

5. Coloring

Adding color really brings the page and its characters to life.

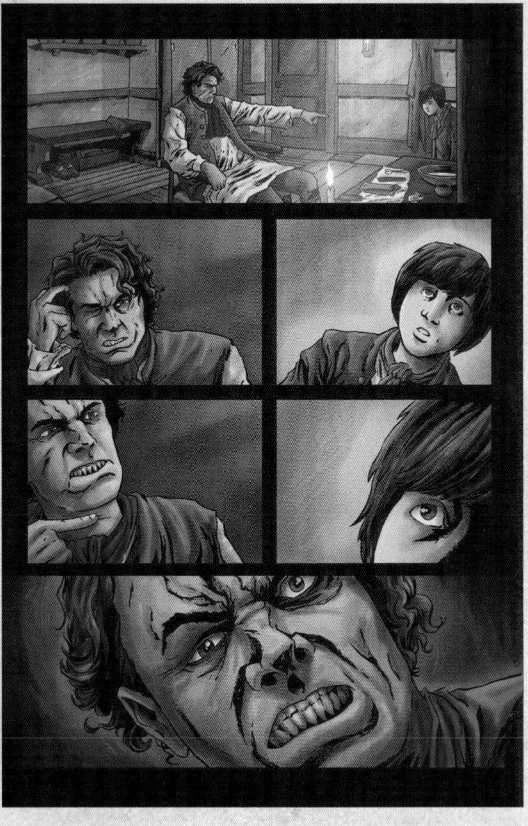

The final colored artwork.

There is far more to the coloring stage than simply replacing the white areas with flat color. Some of the linework itself is shaded, while great emphasis is placed upon texture and light sources to get realistic shadows and highlights. Finally, the whole page is color-balanced to the other pages of that scene and to the overall book.

6. Lettering

The final stage is to add the captions, sound effects, and speech bubbles from the script. These are laid on top of the finished colored pages. Two versions of each page are lettered, one for each of the two versions of the book (Original Text and Quick Text).

These lettered images are then saved as final artwork pages and compiled into the finished book.

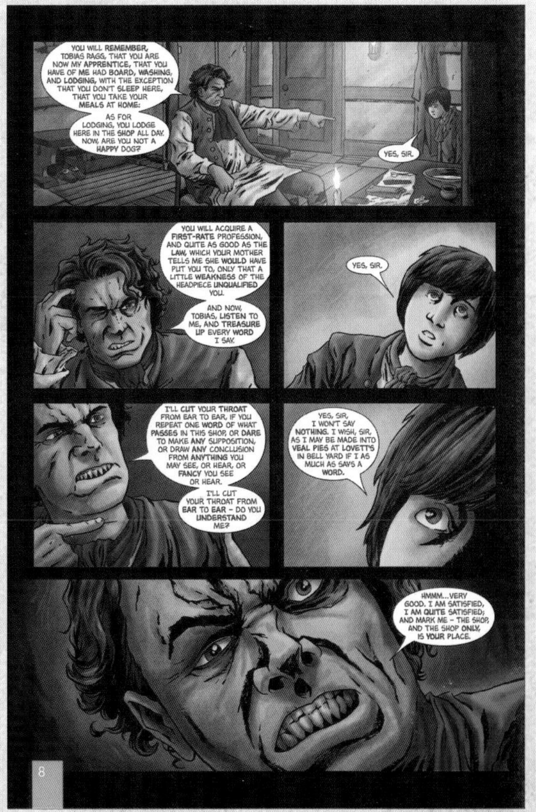
YOU WILL REMEMBER, TOBIAS RAGG, THAT YOU ARE NOW MY APPRENTICE, THAT YOU HAVE OF ME HAD BOARD, WASHING, AND LODGING, WITH THE EXCEPTION THAT YOU DON'T SLEEP HERE, THAT YOU TAKE YOUR MEALS AT HOME:
AS FOR LODGING, YOU LODGE HERE IN THE SHOP ALL DAY. NOW, ARE YOU NOT A HAPPY DOG?
YES, SIR.
YOU WILL ACQUIRE A FIRST-RATE PROFESSION, AND QUITE AS GOOD AS THE LAW, WHICH YOUR MOTHER TELLS ME SHE WOULD HAVE PUT YOU TO, ONLY THAT A LITTLE WEAKNESS OF THE HEADPIECE UNQUALIFIED YOU.
AND NOW, TOBIAS, LISTEN TO ME, AND TREASURE UP EVERY WORD I SAY.
YES, SIR.
I'LL CUT YOUR THROAT FROM EAR TO EAR, IF YOU REPEAT ONE WORD OF WHAT PASSES IN THIS SHOP, OR DARE TO MAKE ANY SUPPOSITION, OR DRAW ANY CONCLUSION FROM ANYTHING YOU MAY SEE, OR HEAR, OR FANCY YOU SEE OR HEAR.
I'LL CUT YOUR THROAT FROM EAR TO EAR - DO YOU UNDERSTAND ME?
YES, SIR, I WON'T SAY NOTHING. I WISH, SIR, AS I MAY BE MADE INTO VEAL PIES AT LOVETT'S IN BELL YARD IF I AS MUCH AS SAYS A WORD.
HMMM...VERY GOOD. I AM SATISFIED, I AM QUITE SATISFIED; AND MARK ME - THE SHOP, AND THE SHOP ONLY, IS YOUR PLACE.
8

The finished page 8 with Original Text lettering.

Original Text

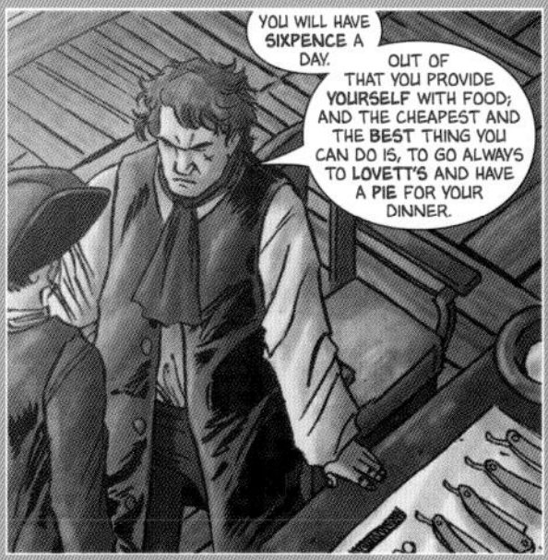
YOU WILL HAVE SIXPENCE A DAY.
OUT OF THAT YOU PROVIDE YOURSELF WITH FOOD; AND THE CHEAPEST AND THE BEST THING YOU CAN DO IS, TO GO ALWAYS TO LOVETT'S AND HAVE A PIE FOR YOUR DINNER.

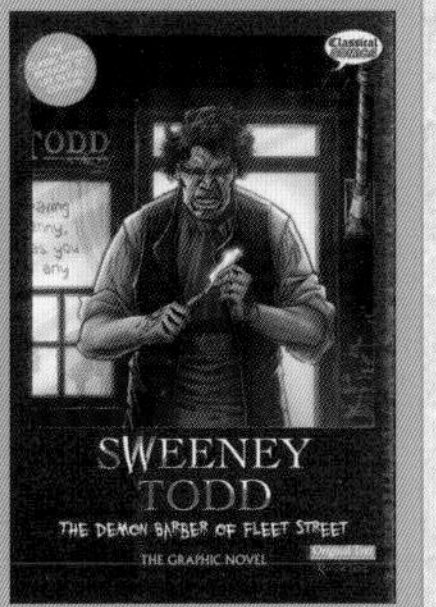
TODD
SWEENEY TODD
THE DEMON BARBER OF FLEET STREET
THE GRAPHIC NOVEL

ISBN: 978-1-907127-09-0

Quick Text

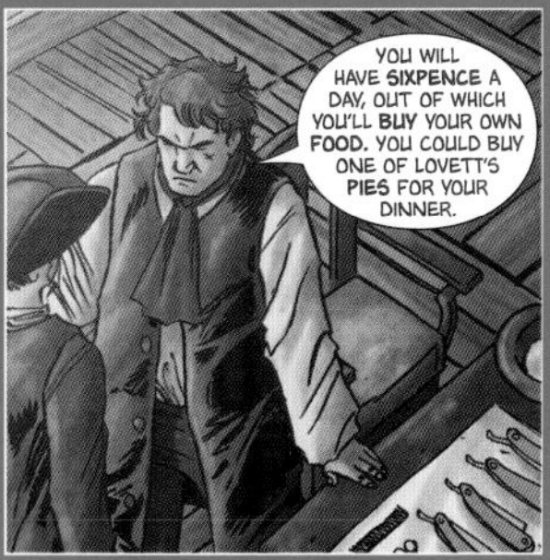
YOU WILL HAVE SIXPENCE A DAY, OUT OF WHICH YOU'LL BUY YOUR OWN FOOD. YOU COULD BUY ONE OF LOVETT'S PIES FOR YOUR DINNER.

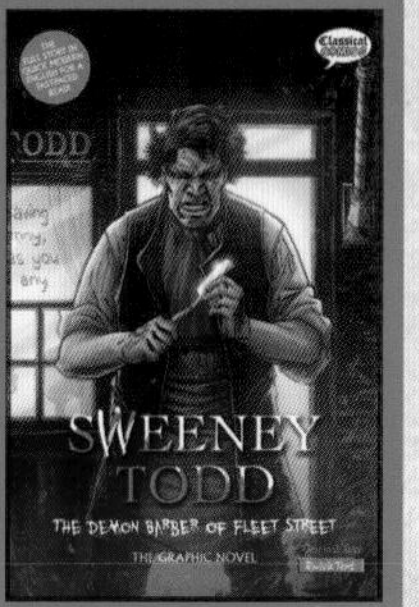
TODD
SWEENEY TODD
THE DEMON BARBER OF FLEET STREET
THE GRAPHIC NOVEL

ISBN: 978-1-907127-10-6

MORE TITLES AVAILABLE FROM

Classic Literature in a choice of 2 text versions. Simply choose the text version to match your reading level.

Original Text THE CLASSIC NOVEL BROUGHT TO LIFE IN FULL COLOR!

Quick Text THE FULL STORY IN QUICK MODERN ENGLISH FOR A FAST-PACED READ!

Jane Eyre: The Graphic Novel (Charlotte Brontë)

• Script Adaptation: Amy Corzine • Artwork: John M. Burns
• Letters: Terry Wiley

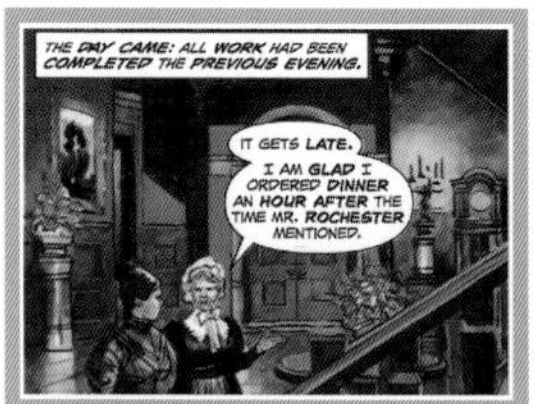
THE DAY CAME: ALL WORK HAD BEEN COMPLETED THE PREVIOUS EVENING.
IT GETS LATE. I AM GLAD I ORDERED DINNER AN HOUR AFTER THE TIME MR. ROCHESTER MENTIONED.

ISBN: 978-1-906332-47-1

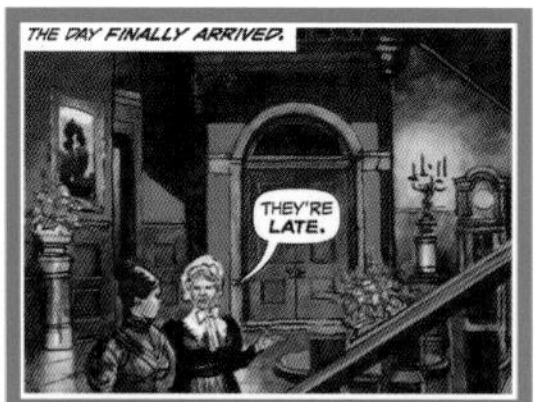
THE DAY FINALLY ARRIVED.
THEY'RE LATE.

ISBN: 978-1-906332-48-8

"I scorn your idea of love and the counterfeit sentiment you offer. And I scorn you when you offer it."

• 144 Pages • $16.95

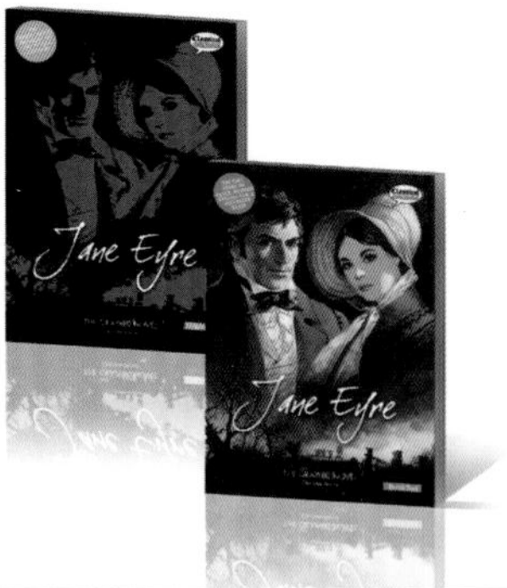
Jane Eyre

Frankenstein: The Graphic Novel (Mary Shelley)

• Script Adaptation: Jason Cobley • Linework: Declan Shalvey • Art Direction: Jon Haward
• Colors: Jason Cardy & Kat Nicholson • Letters: Terry Wiley

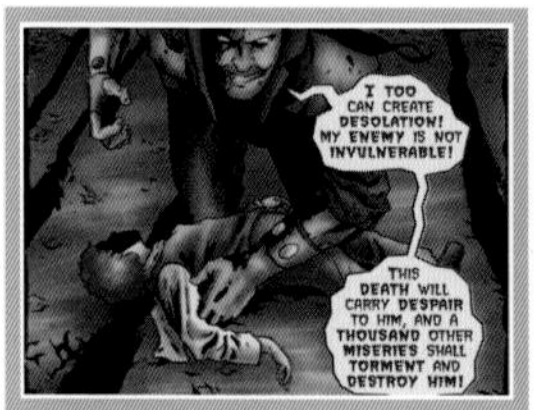
I TOO CAN CREATE DESOLATION! MY ENEMY IS NOT INVULNERABLE!
THIS DEATH WILL CARRY DESPAIR TO HIM, AND A THOUSAND OTHER MISERIES SHALL TORMENT AND DESTROY HIM!

ISBN: 978-1-906332-49-5

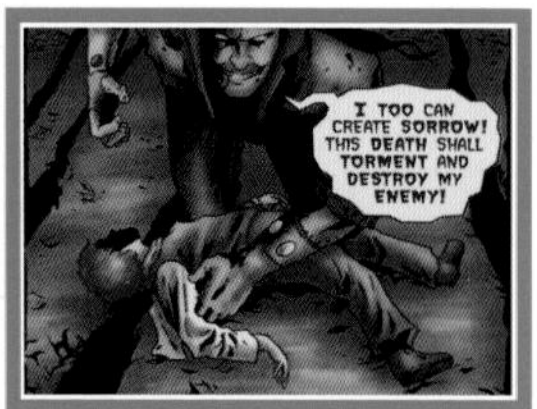
I TOO CAN CREATE SORROW! THIS DEATH SHALL TORMENT AND DESTROY MY ENEMY!

ISBN: 978-1-906332-50-1

"Cursed be the hands that formed you!"

• 144 Pages • $16.95

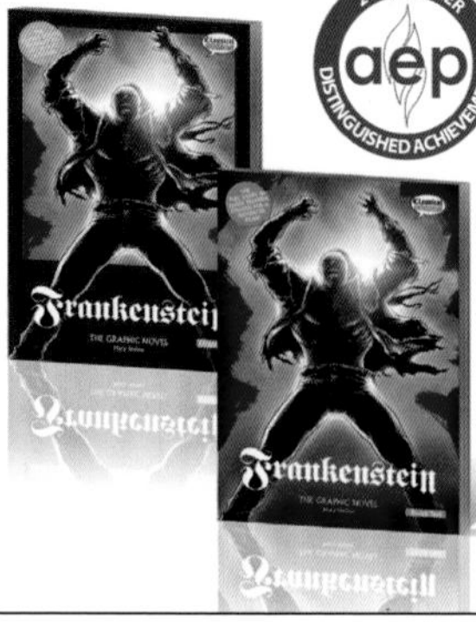
Frankenstein

2009 WINNER aep DISTINGUISHED ACHIEVEMENT

A Christmas Carol: The Graphic Novel (Charles Dickens)

• Script Adaptation: Seán Michael Wilson • Pencils: Mike Collins
• Inks: David Roach • Colors: James Offredi • Letters: Terry Wiley

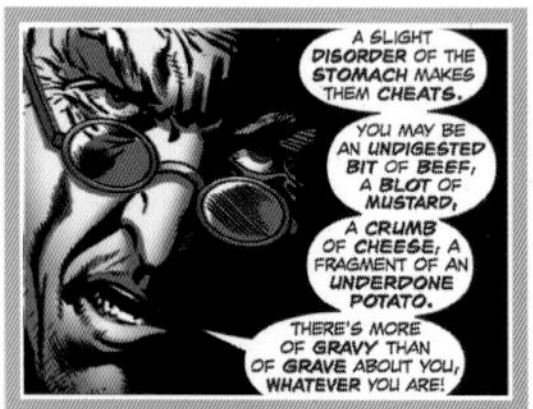
A SLIGHT DISORDER OF THE STOMACH MAKES THEM CHEATS.
YOU MAY BE AN UNDIGESTED BIT OF BEEF, A BLOT OF MUSTARD,
A CRUMB OF CHEESE, A FRAGMENT OF AN UNDERDONE POTATO.
THERE'S MORE OF GRAVY THAN OF GRAVE ABOUT YOU, WHATEVER YOU ARE!

ISBN: 978-1-906332-51-8

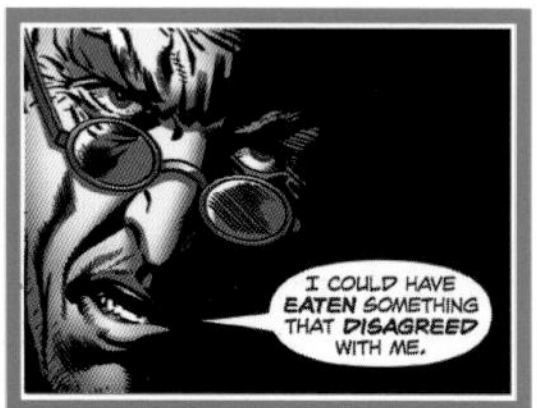
I COULD HAVE EATEN SOMETHING THAT DISAGREED WITH ME.

ISBN: 978-1-906332-52-5

"I will honour Christmas in my heart, and try to keep it all the year. I will live in the Past, the Present, and the Future."

• 160 Pages • $16.95

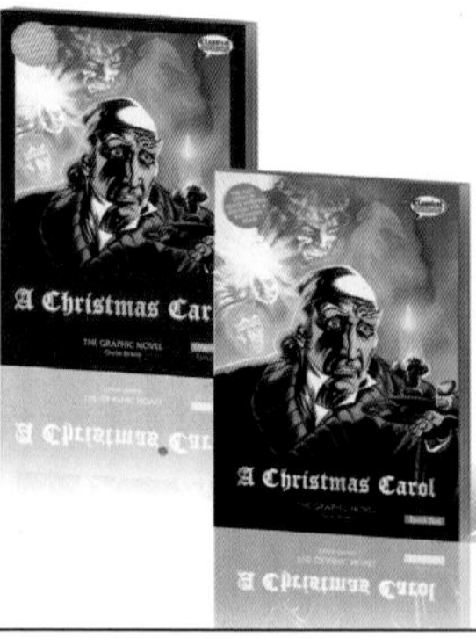
A Christmas Carol

Great Expectations: The Graphic Novel (Charles Dickens)

• Script Adaptation: Jen Green • Linework: John Stokes • Colouring: Digikore Studios Ltd
• Color Finishing: Jason Cardy • Letters: Jim Campbell

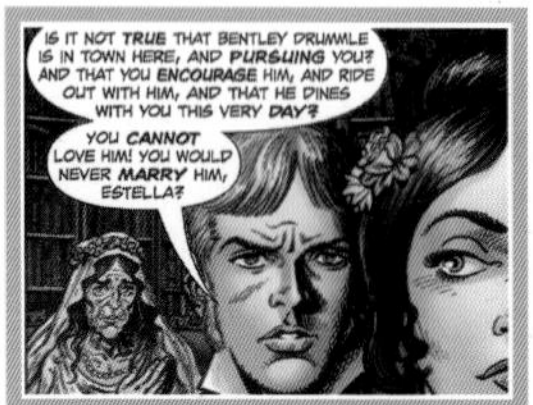
IS IT NOT TRUE THAT BENTLEY DRUMMLE IS IN TOWN HERE, AND PURSUING YOU? AND THAT YOU ENCOURAGE HIM, AND RIDE OUT WITH HIM, AND THAT HE DINES WITH YOU THIS VERY DAY?
YOU CANNOT LOVE HIM! YOU WOULD NEVER MARRY HIM, ESTELLA?

ISBN: 978-1-906332-59-4

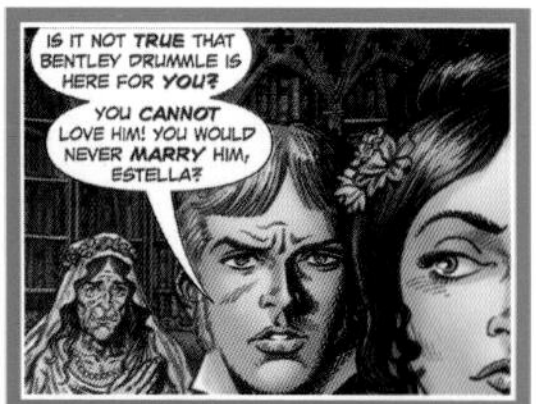
IS IT NOT TRUE THAT BENTLEY DRUMMLE IS HERE FOR YOU?
YOU CANNOT LOVE HIM! YOU WOULD NEVER MARRY HIM, ESTELLA?

ISBN: 978-1-906332-60-0

"I never saw my father or my mother, and never saw any likeness of either of them."

• 160 Pages • $16.95

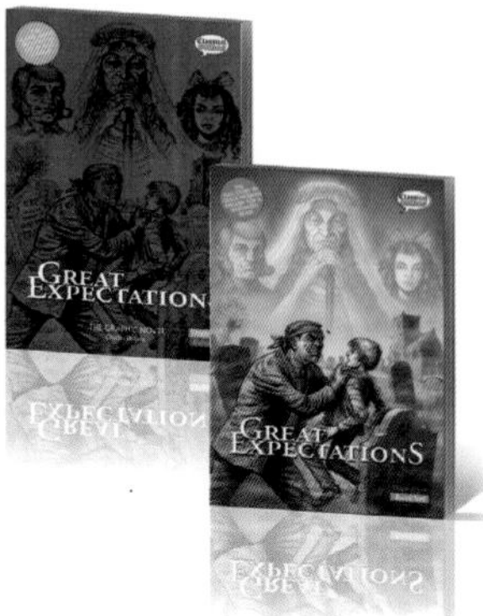
GREAT EXPECTATIONS